"I LOVED Katie!"
—LUCY KNISLEY, *New York Times* bestselling author of *Stepping Stones*

"A pro-girl comic to encourage adventure, entrepreneurship, and excellent, pun-filled pet names."
—*The Bulletin of the Center for Children's Books*

KATIE THE CATSITTER
BEST FRIENDS FOR NEVER

"The new Feline Queen of All-Ages Superhero Comic Books. A . . . universal story about growing up."
—ComicBookResources.com

"Super fun and utterly delightful!"
—GENE LUEN YANG, creator of *American Born Chinese*

"A winner!"
—NICK BRUEL, creator of the Bad Kitty series

"Venable's twisty plot swoops gleefully around Manhattan . . . combining to tell the story of one of the least boring summers ever."
—*BookPage*

"Ideal for readers seeking the whimsy of Dav Pilkey's Dog Man tempered with the reassuring tone of Raina Telgemeier's work."
—*School Library Journal*

"Sight gags, sly humor, pop-culture references, and a dollop of animal-rights activism combine to make Katie's story a fun one."
—*Booklist*

Random House  New York

KATIE THE CATSITTER

BEST FRIENDS FOR NEVER

Colleen
AF Venable

ILLUSTRATED BY
Stephanie Yue

WITH COLORS BY
Braden Lamb

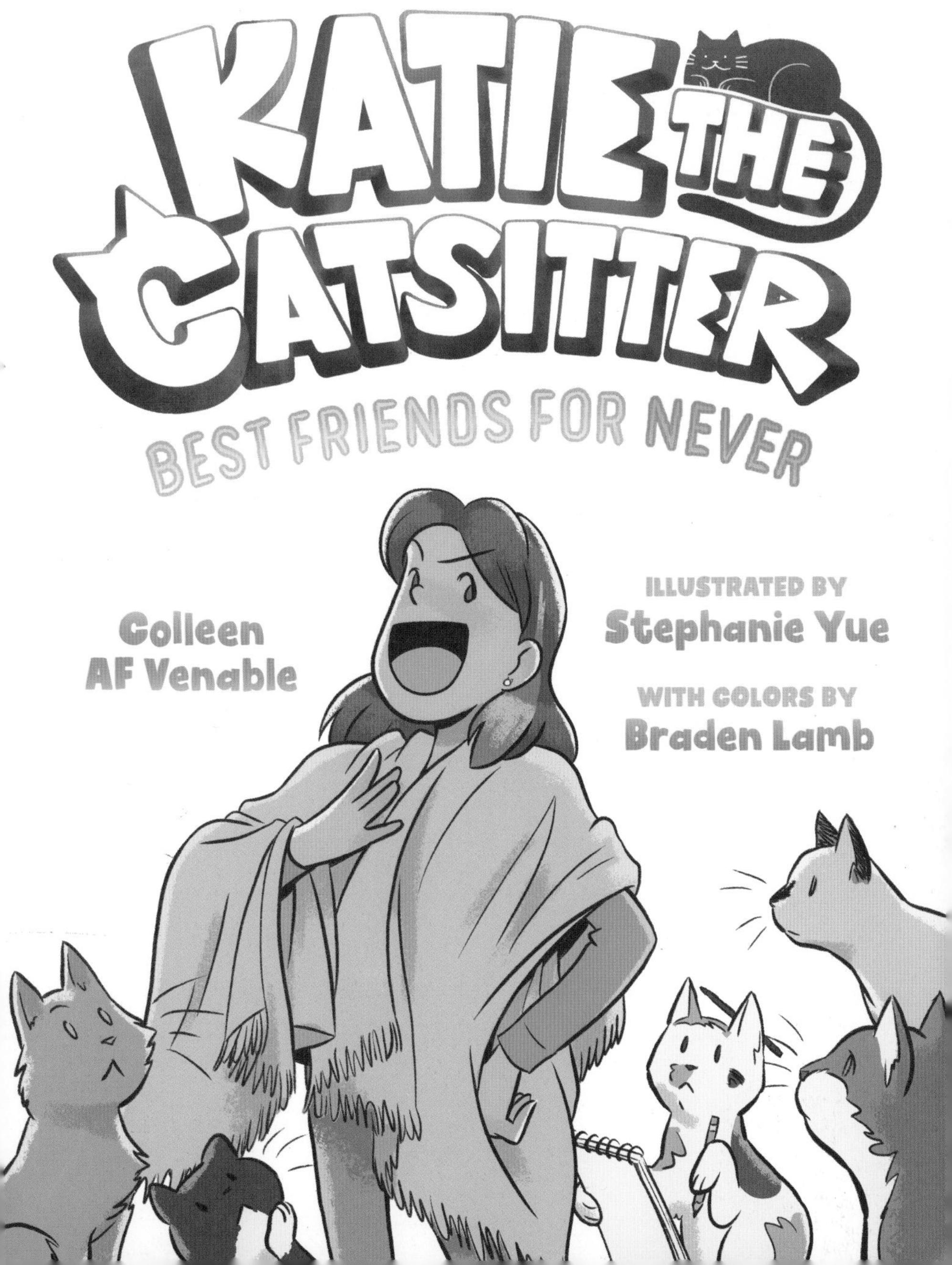

With grateful thanks to Shasta Clinch, Barbara Perez Marquez, and Polo Orozco for their invaluable feedback.

Visit us on the Web! rhcbooks.com

Educators and librarians, for a variety of teaching tools, visit us at RHTeachersLibrarians.com

Library of Congress Cataloging-in-Publication Data
Names: Venable, Colleen A. F., author. | Yue, Stephanie, illustrator.
Title: Best friends for never / Colleen AF Venable; illustrated by Stephanie Yue.
Description: New York: Random House Children's Books, [2022] | Series: Katie the catsitter; 2
Summary: Twelve-year-old Katie now knows her neighbor Madeline is also the Mousetress, the city's most feared villain (or most misunderstood superhero), and she is ready to become the super sidekick she always wanted to be.
Identifiers: LCCN 2021005451 | ISBN 978-0-593-37546-4 (hardcover) | ISBN 978-1-9848-9566-0 (trade pbk.) | ISBN 978-1-9848-9567-7 (lib. bdg.) | ISBN 978-1-9848-9568-4 (ebook)
Subjects: LCSH: Graphic novels. | CYAC: Graphic novels. | Supervillains—Fiction. | Neighbors—Fiction. | Pet sitting—Fiction.
Classification: LCC PZ7.7.V46 Be 2022 | DDC 741.5/973—dc23

Book design by Stephanie Yue, April Ward, and Sylvia Bi

MANUFACTURED IN CHINA
10 9 8 7 6 5 4 3 2 1
First Edition

To my big sis, Kath,
who is stronger than Stainless Steel,
more brilliant than the Mousetress, and
smart enough to own only one cat

—C.A.F.V.

To Mendel, Salem, Olie, Poffie,
Mr. Puddinton, and friends around the
world, both two- and four-legged, who
kept me company from afar

—S.Y.

CHAPTER ONE

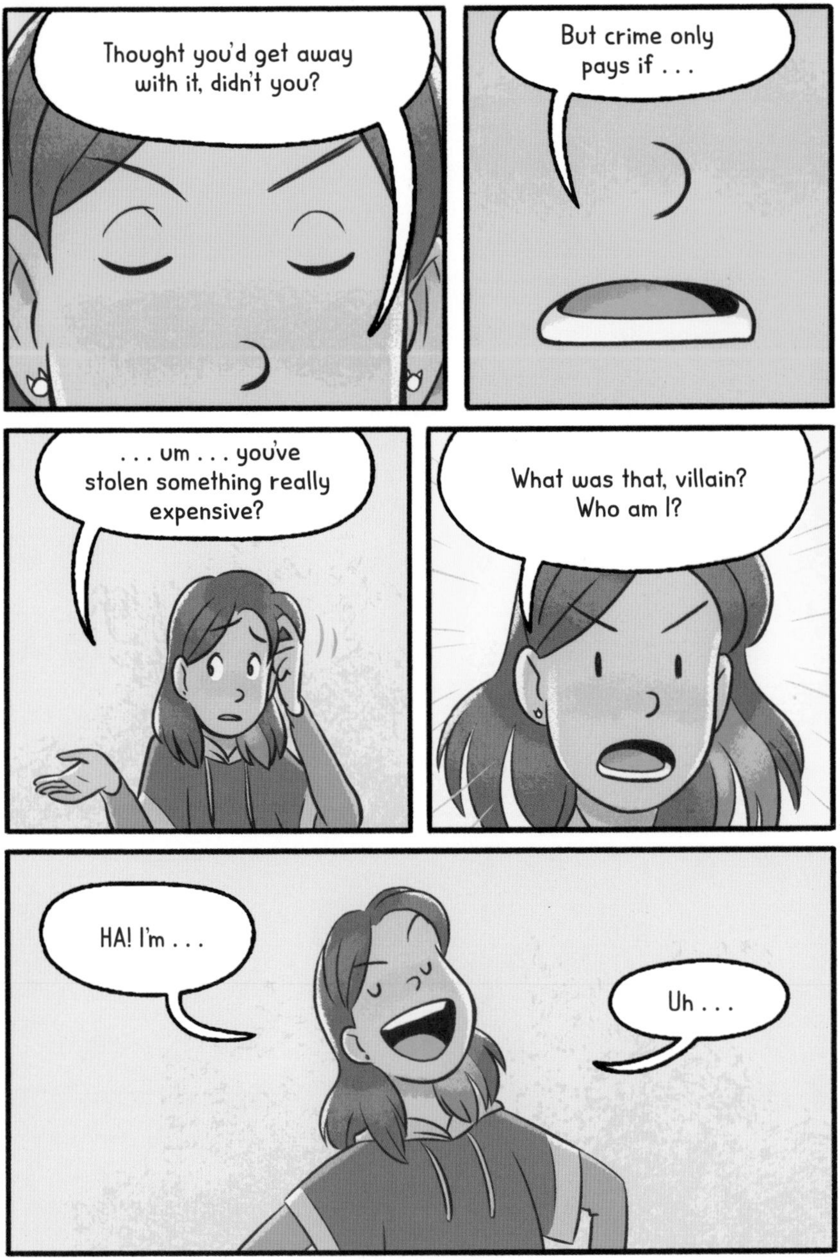
Thought you'd get away with it, didn't you?
But crime only pays if . . .
. . . um . . . you've stolen something really expensive?
What was that, villain? Who am I?
HA! I'm . . .
Uh . . .

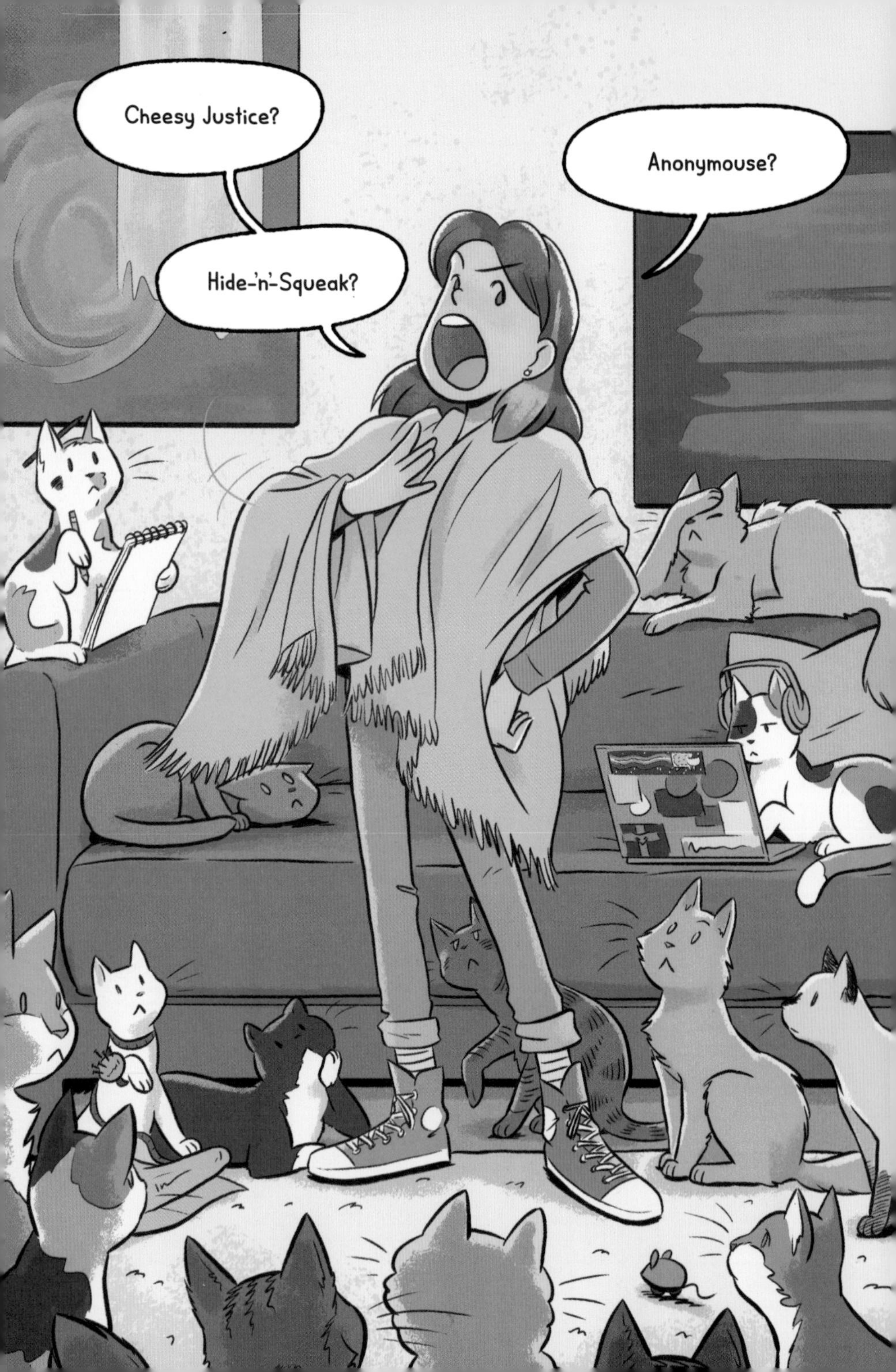
Cheesy Justice?
Hide-'n'-Squeak?
Anonymouse?

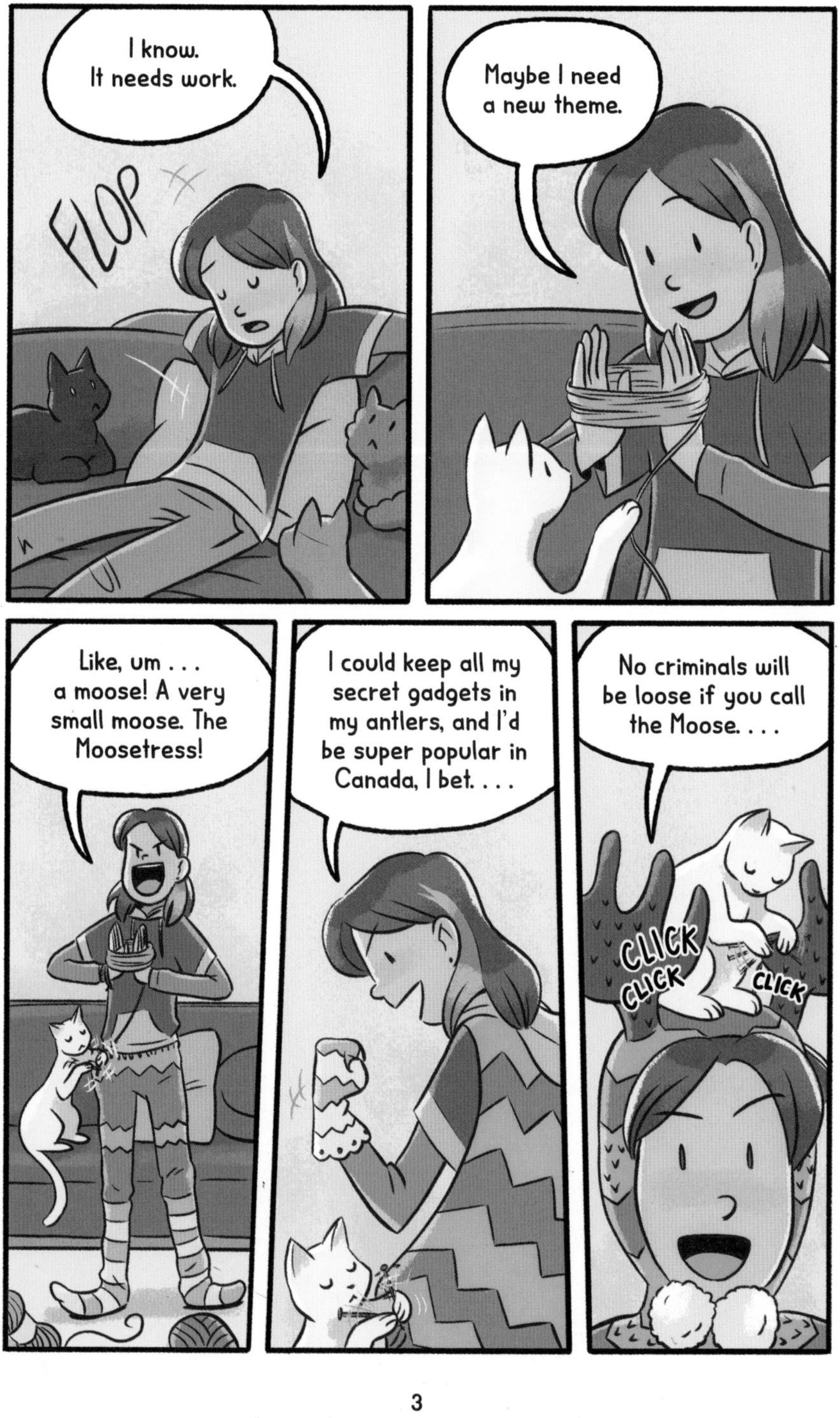
I know.
It needs work.
FLOP
Maybe I need
a new theme.
Like, um . . .
a moose! A very
small moose. The
Moosetress!
I could keep all my
secret gadgets in
my antlers, and I'd
be super popular in
Canada, I bet. . . .
No criminals will
be loose if you call
the Moose. . . .
CLICK
CLICK
CLICK

CREAK

Hi, Madeline! You're back!

Ack!

Spent forever trying to fix your Wikipedia entry. People should know how great you are! Like when you saved the bunnies from the factory and the dogs from the fighting ring, and stopped that lady from hunting endangered animals . . .

But turns out Jolie is, like, SUPER banned from Wikipedia for messing with the Owl Guy entry.

Meow.

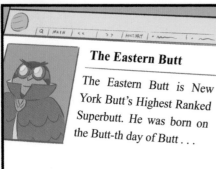

Q MAIN << >> HISTORY

The Eastern Butt

The Eastern Butt is New York Butt's Highest Ranked Superbutt. He was born on the Butt-th day of Butt . . .

We'll figure out a work-around!

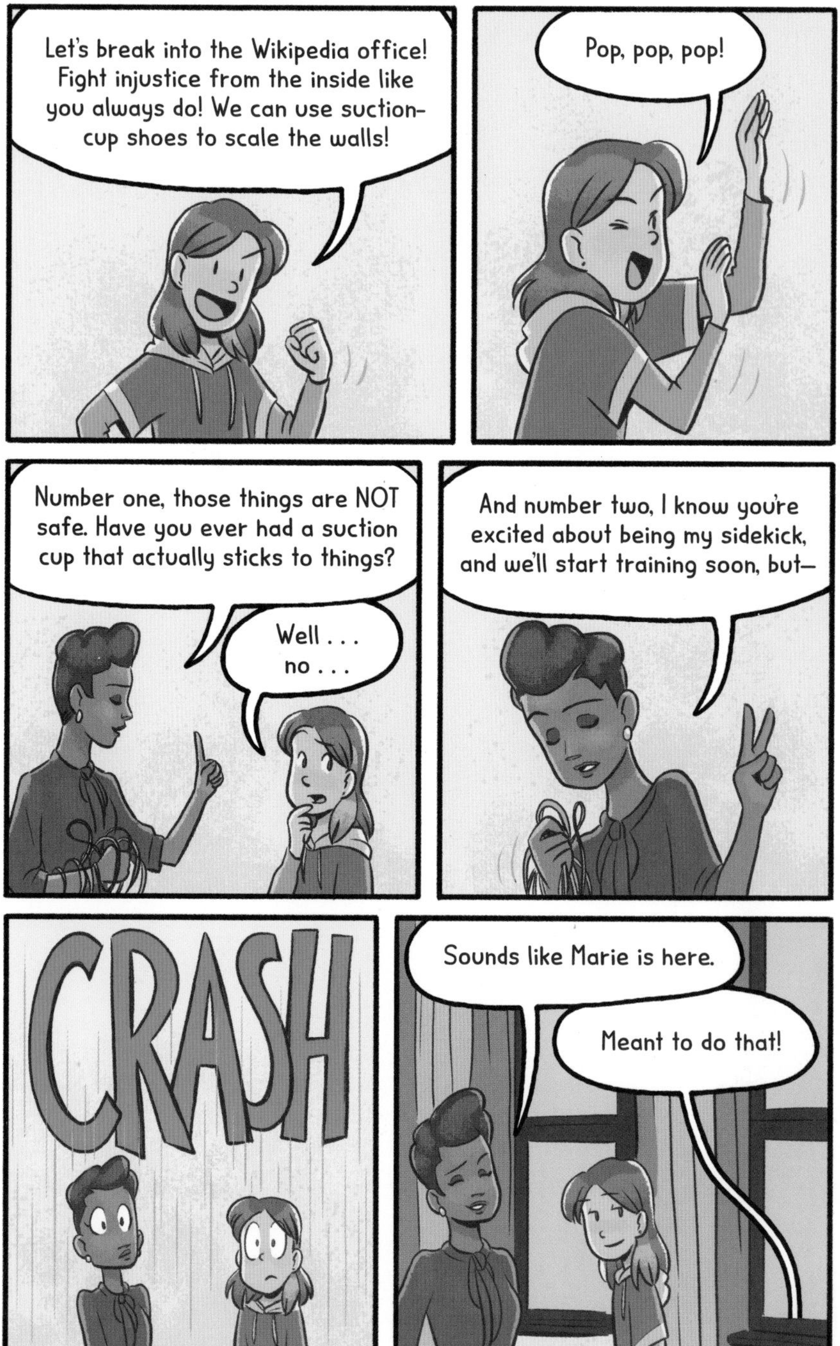

Let's break into the Wikipedia office! Fight injustice from the inside like you always do! We can use suction-cup shoes to scale the walls!
Pop, pop, pop!
Number one, those things are NOT safe. Have you ever had a suction cup that actually sticks to things?
Well . . . no . . .
And number two, I know you're excited about being my sidekick, and we'll start training soon, but—
CRASH
Sounds like Marie is here.
Meant to do that!

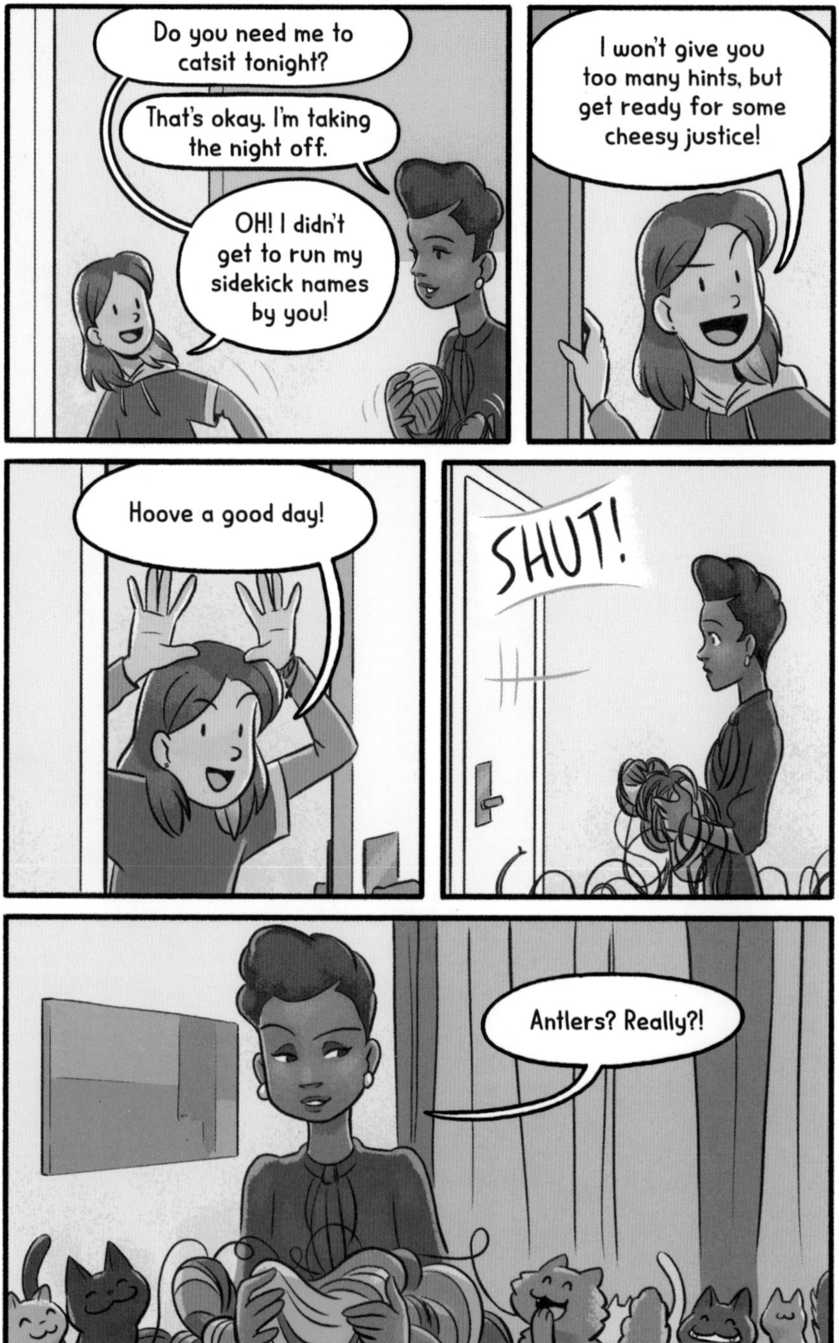
Do you need me to catsit tonight?
That's okay. I'm taking the night off.
OH! I didn't get to run my sidekick names by you!
I won't give you too many hints, but get ready for some cheesy justice!
Hoove a good day!
SHUT!
Antlers? Really?!

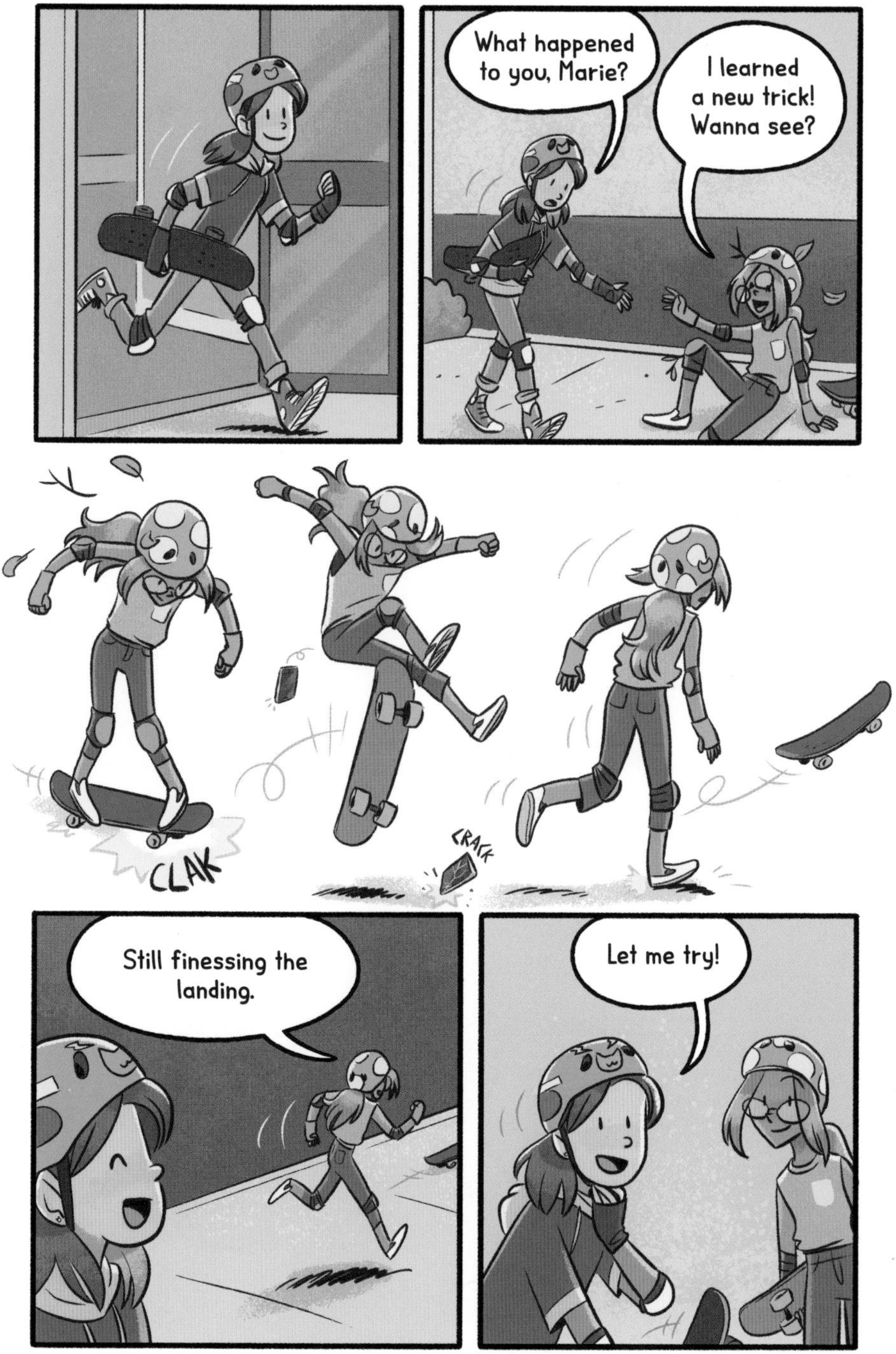
What happened to you, Marie?
I learned a new trick! Wanna see?
CLAK
CRACK
Still finessing the landing.
Let me try!

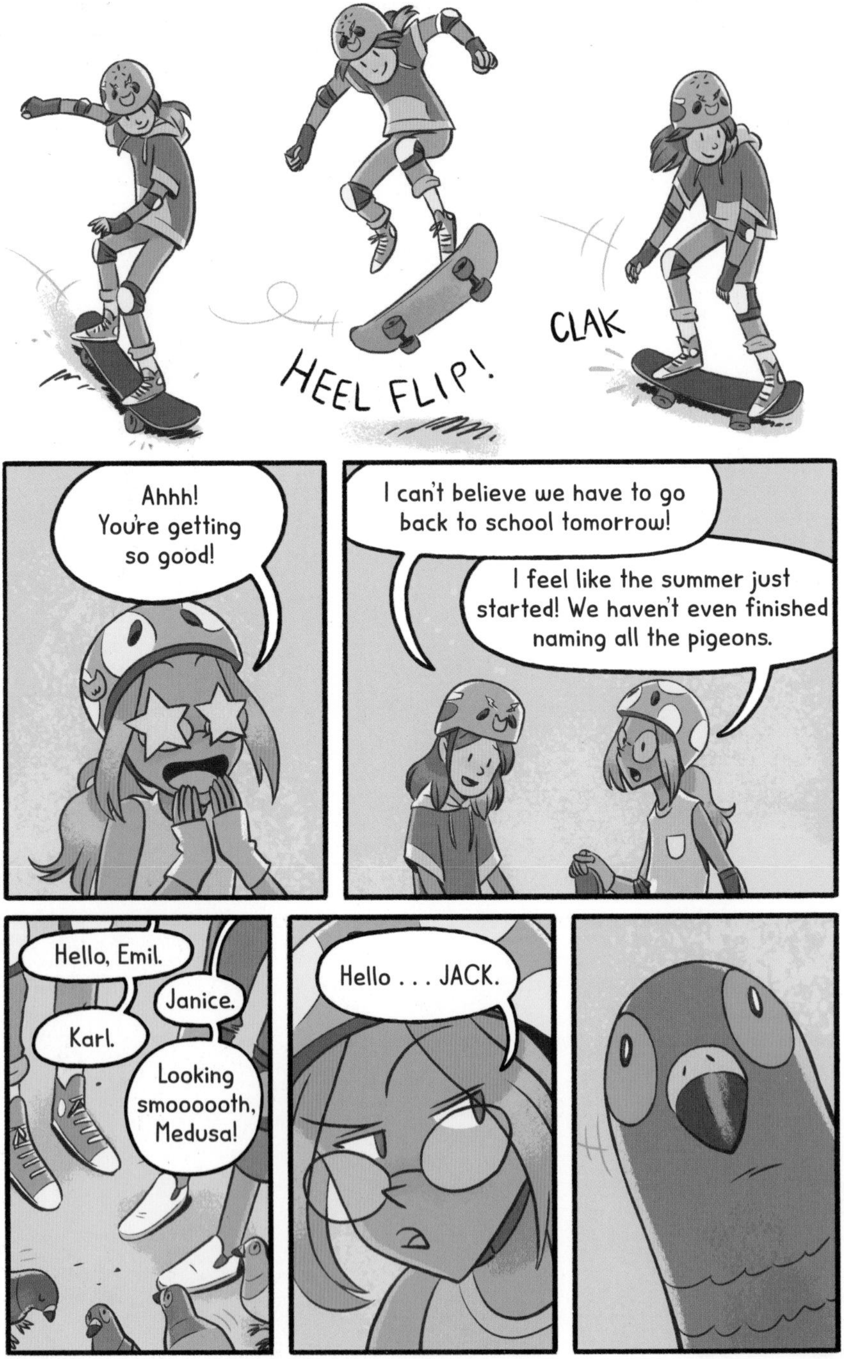
HEEL FLIP!
CLAK
Ahhh! You're getting so good!
I can't believe we have to go back to school tomorrow!
I feel like the summer just started! We haven't even finished naming all the pigeons.
Hello, Emil.
Janice.
Karl.
Looking smoooooth, Medusa!
Hello . . . JACK.

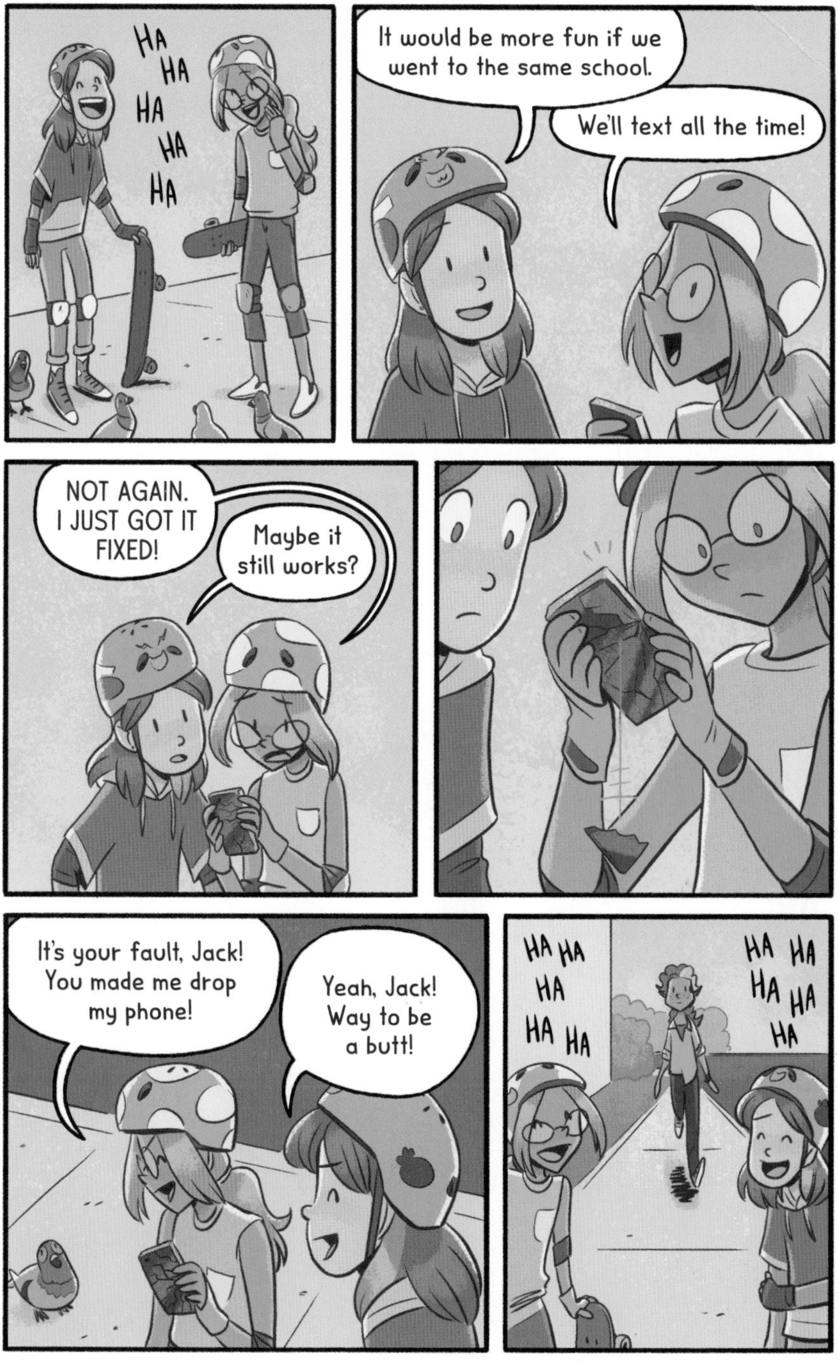
HA
HA
HA
HA
HA
It would be more fun if we went to the same school.
We'll text all the time!
NOT AGAIN. I JUST GOT IT FIXED!
Maybe it still works?
It's your fault, Jack! You made me drop my phone!
Yeah, Jack! Way to be a butt!
HA HA
HA
HA HA
HA HA
HA HA
HA

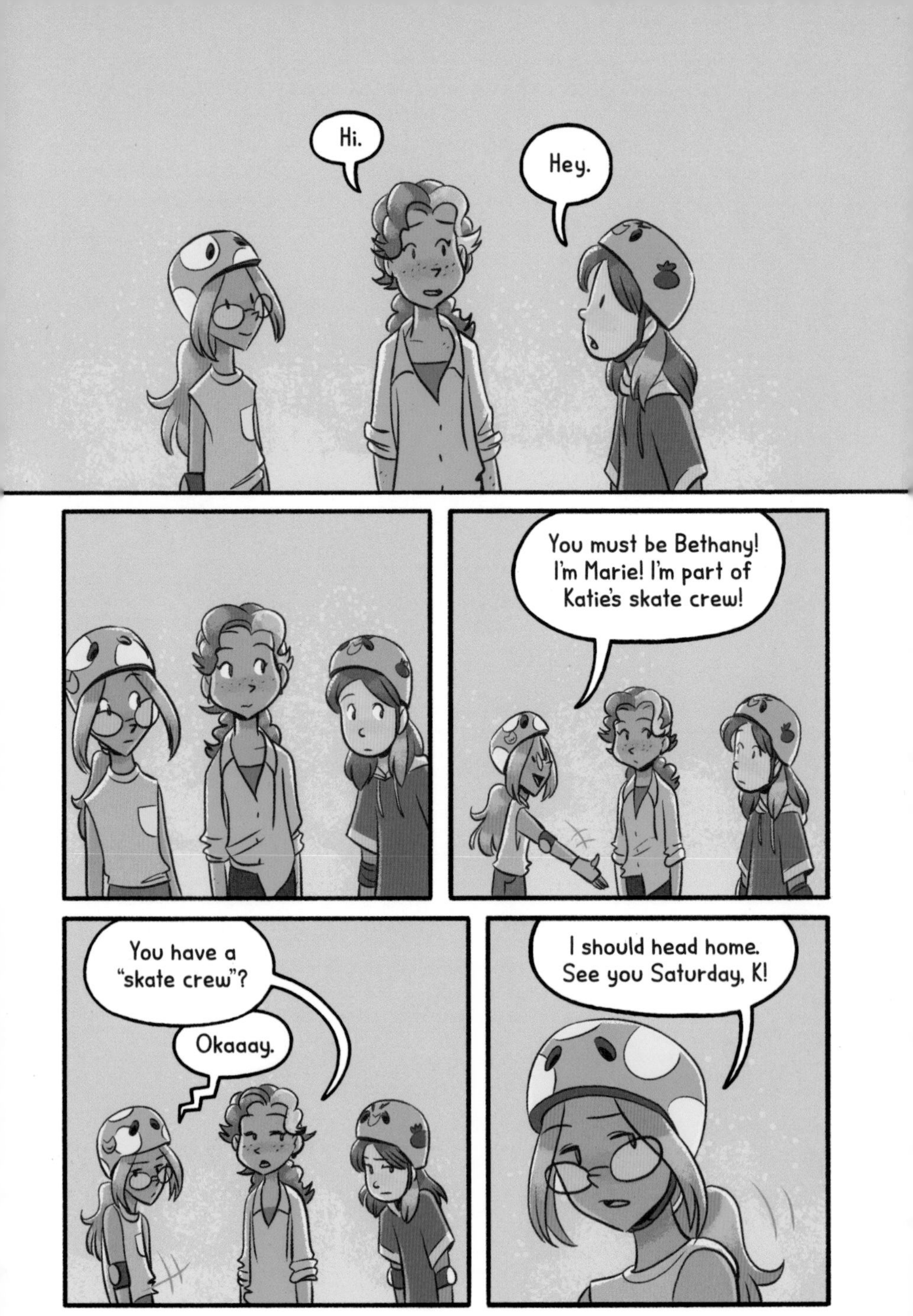
Hi.
Hey.
You must be Bethany! I'm Marie! I'm part of Katie's skate crew!
You have a "skate crew"?
Okaaay.
I should head home. See you Saturday, K!

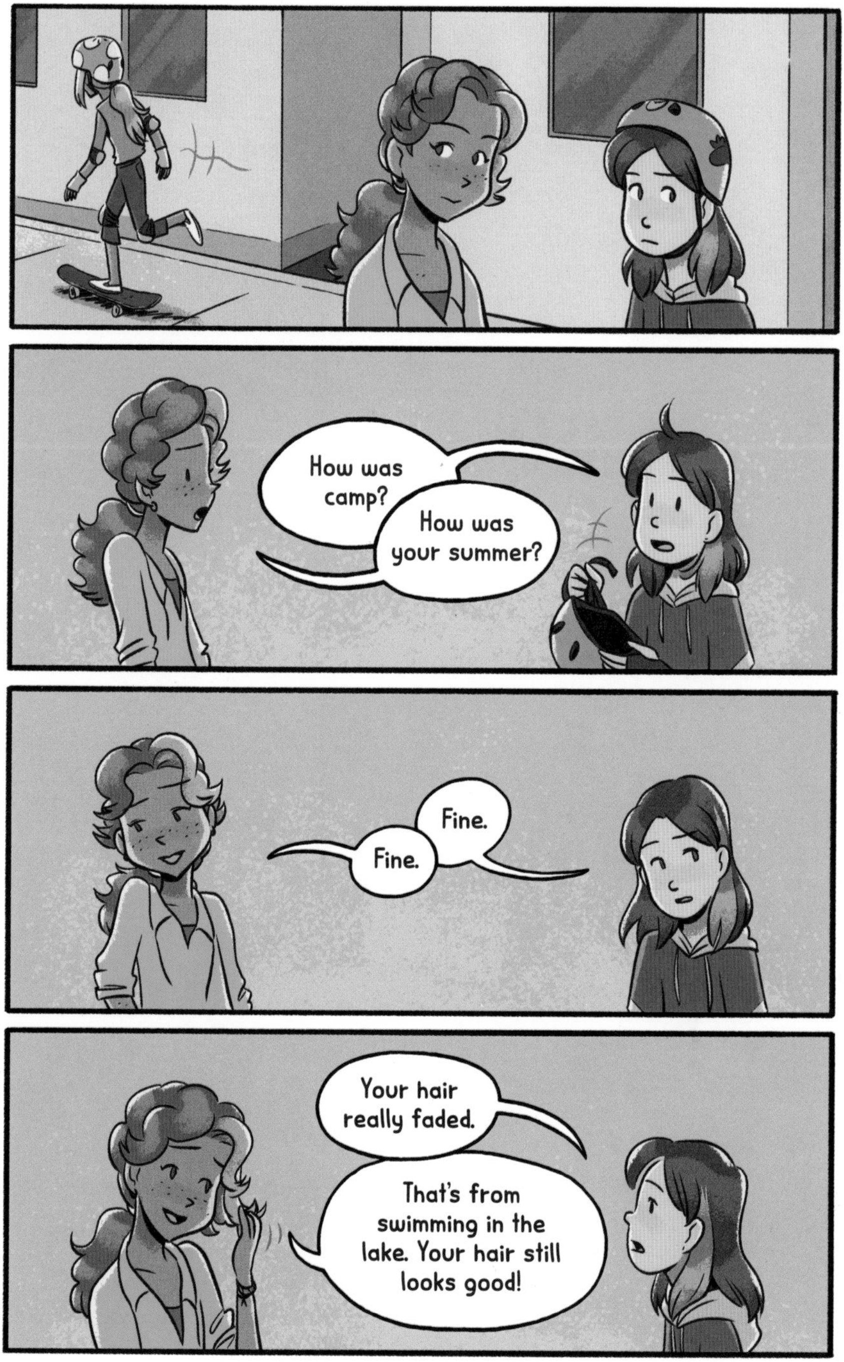
How was camp?
How was your summer?
Fine.
Fine.
Your hair really faded.
That's from swimming in the lake. Your hair still looks good!

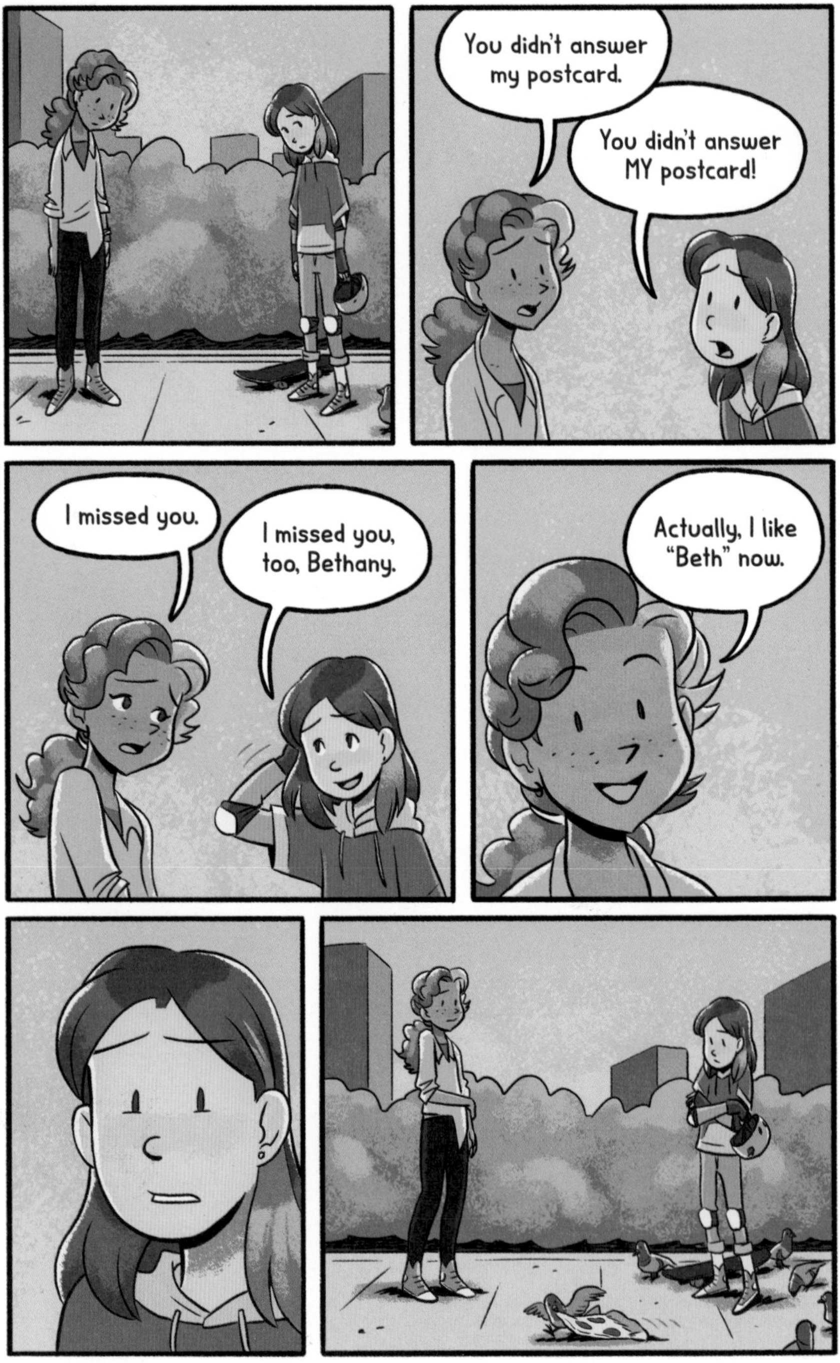
You didn't answer my postcard.
You didn't answer MY postcard!
I missed you.
I missed you, too, Bethany.
Actually, I like "Beth" now.

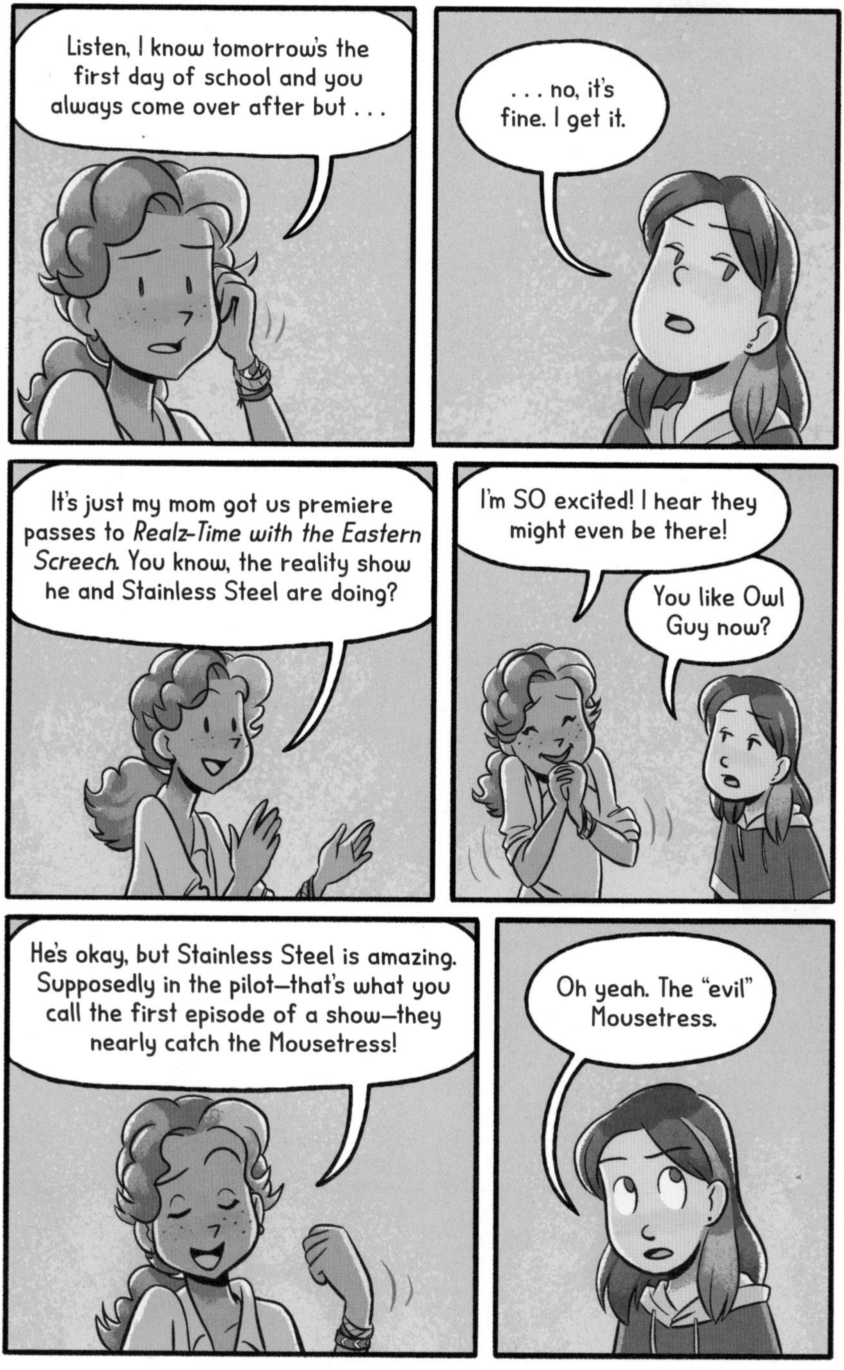
Listen, I know tomorrow's the first day of school and you always come over after but . . .
. . . no, it's fine. I get it.
It's just my mom got us premiere passes to *Realz-Time with the Eastern Screech*. You know, the reality show he and Stainless Steel are doing?
I'm SO excited! I hear they might even be there!
You like Owl Guy now?
He's okay, but Stainless Steel is amazing. Supposedly in the pilot—that's what you call the first episode of a show—they nearly catch the Mousetress!
Oh yeah. The "evil" Mousetress.

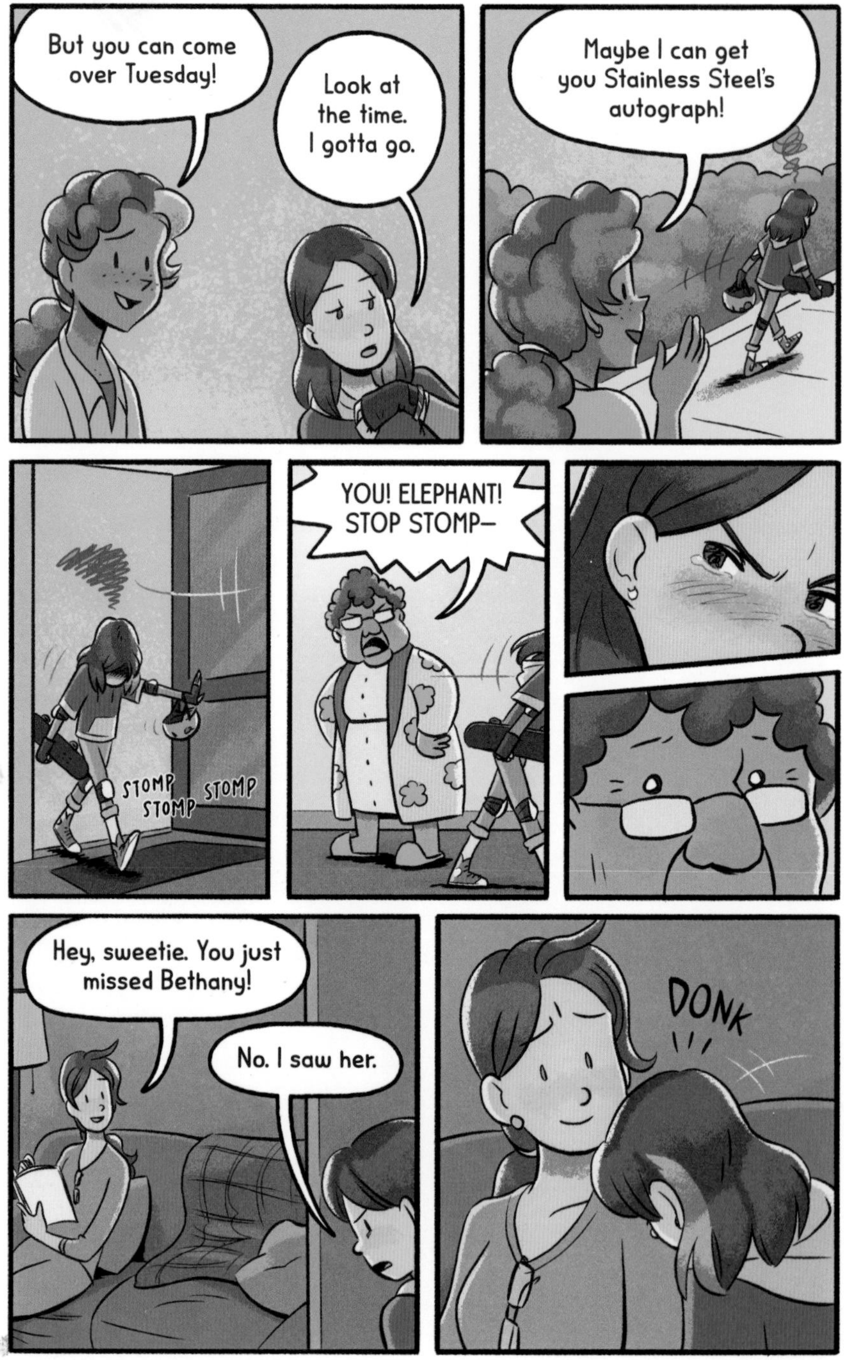
But you can come over Tuesday!
Look at the time. I gotta go.
Maybe I can get you Stainless Steel's autograph!
STOMP STOMP STOMP
YOU! ELEPHANT! STOP STOMP–
Hey, sweetie. You just missed Bethany!
No. I saw her.
DONK

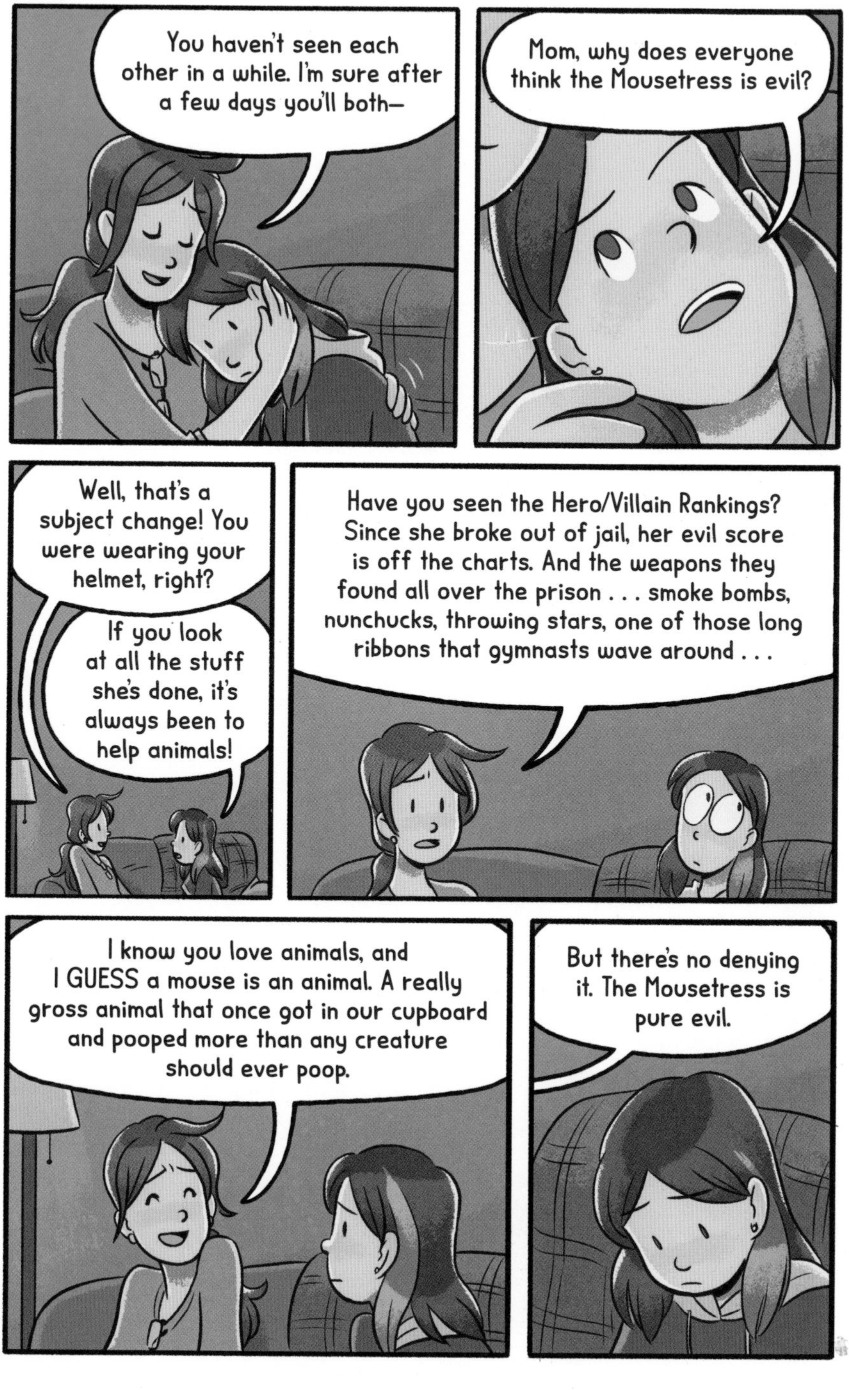
You haven't seen each other in a while. I'm sure after a few days you'll both—
Mom, why does everyone think the Mousetress is evil?
Well, that's a subject change! You were wearing your helmet, right?
If you look at all the stuff she's done, it's always been to help animals!
Have you seen the Hero/Villain Rankings? Since she broke out of jail, her evil score is off the charts. And the weapons they found all over the prison . . . smoke bombs, nunchucks, throwing stars, one of those long ribbons that gymnasts wave around . . .
I know you love animals, and I GUESS a mouse is an animal. A really gross animal that once got in our cupboard and pooped more than any creature should ever poop.
But there's no denying it. The Mousetress is pure evil.

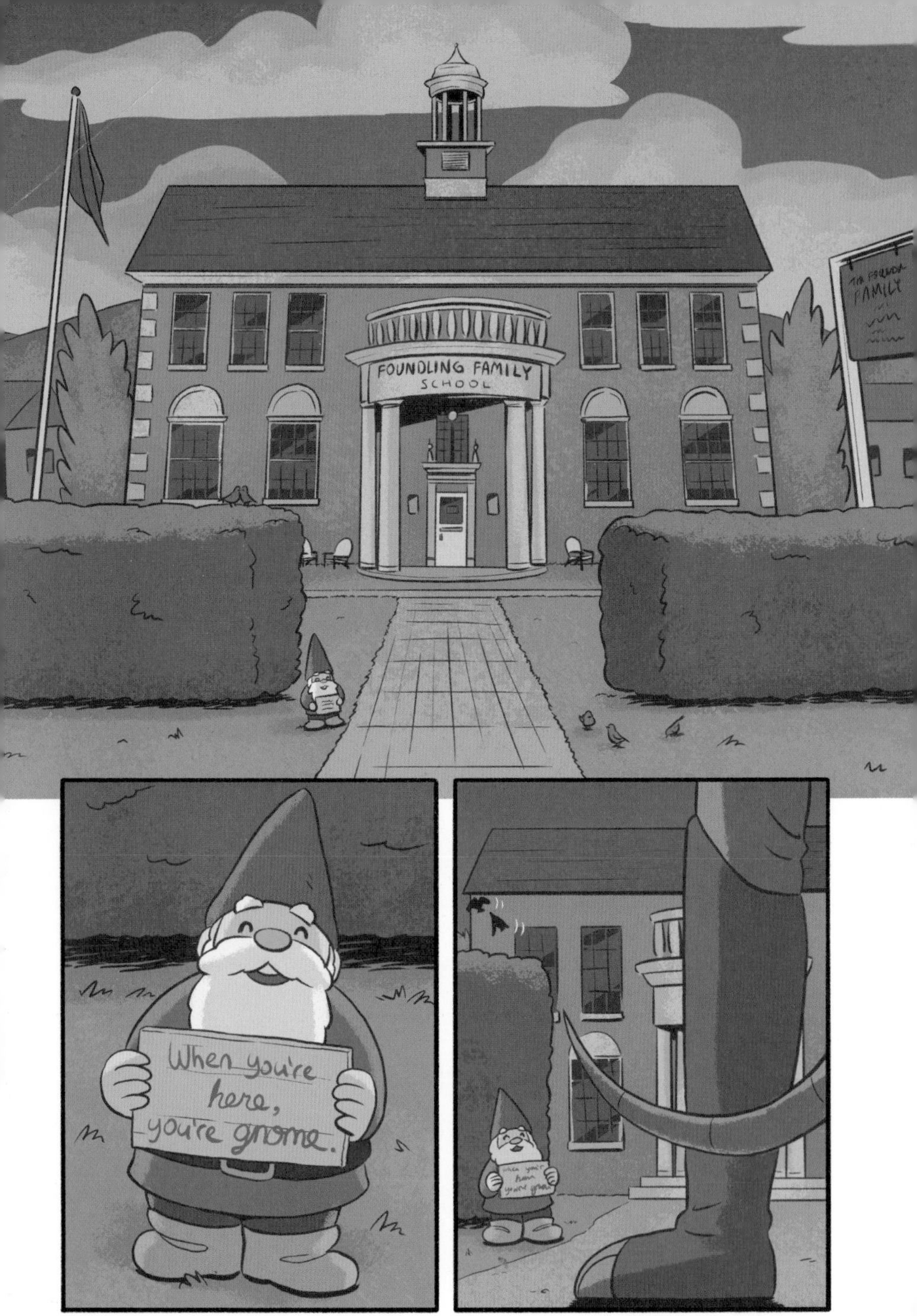
FOUNDLING FAMILY
SCHOOL
When you're here, you're gnome.

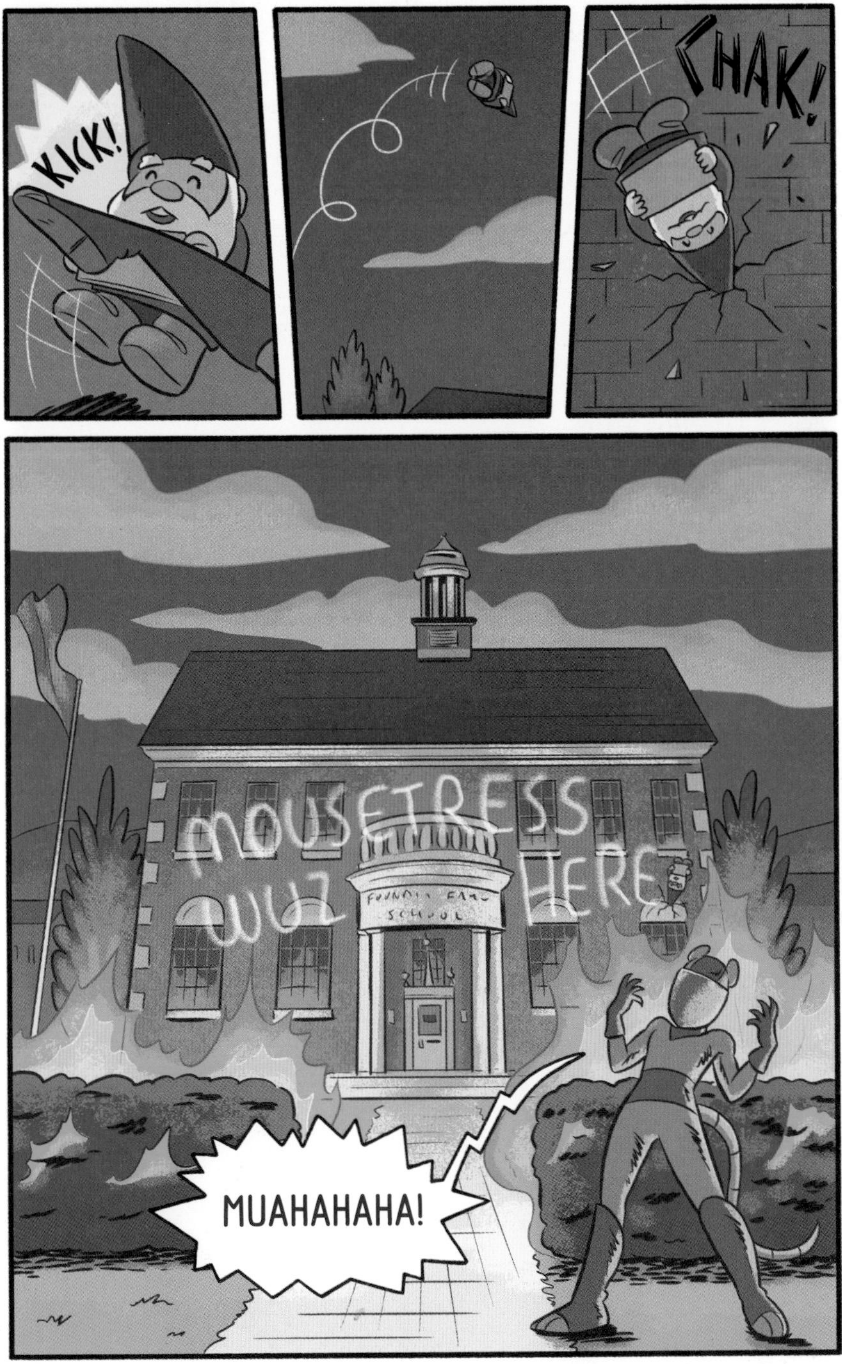
KICK!
CHAK!
MOUSETRESS WUZ HERE
MUAHAHAHA!

CHAPTER TWO

7,300!

That's how many hours you have till camp next year.

You missed out on so much fun this summer! Did Beth show you pictures of her boyfriend, Ben? He's super hot!

Jess!

BRRUINNNG

This year is gonna be the BEST!

Katie, can we talk?

Welcome to a year!

Good morning, class! Please arrange yourselves alphabetically by first name. Katie Spera, over here. Bethany Tinoco, over there.

Welcome to a new year!

DREAM BIG

BEE YOURSELF

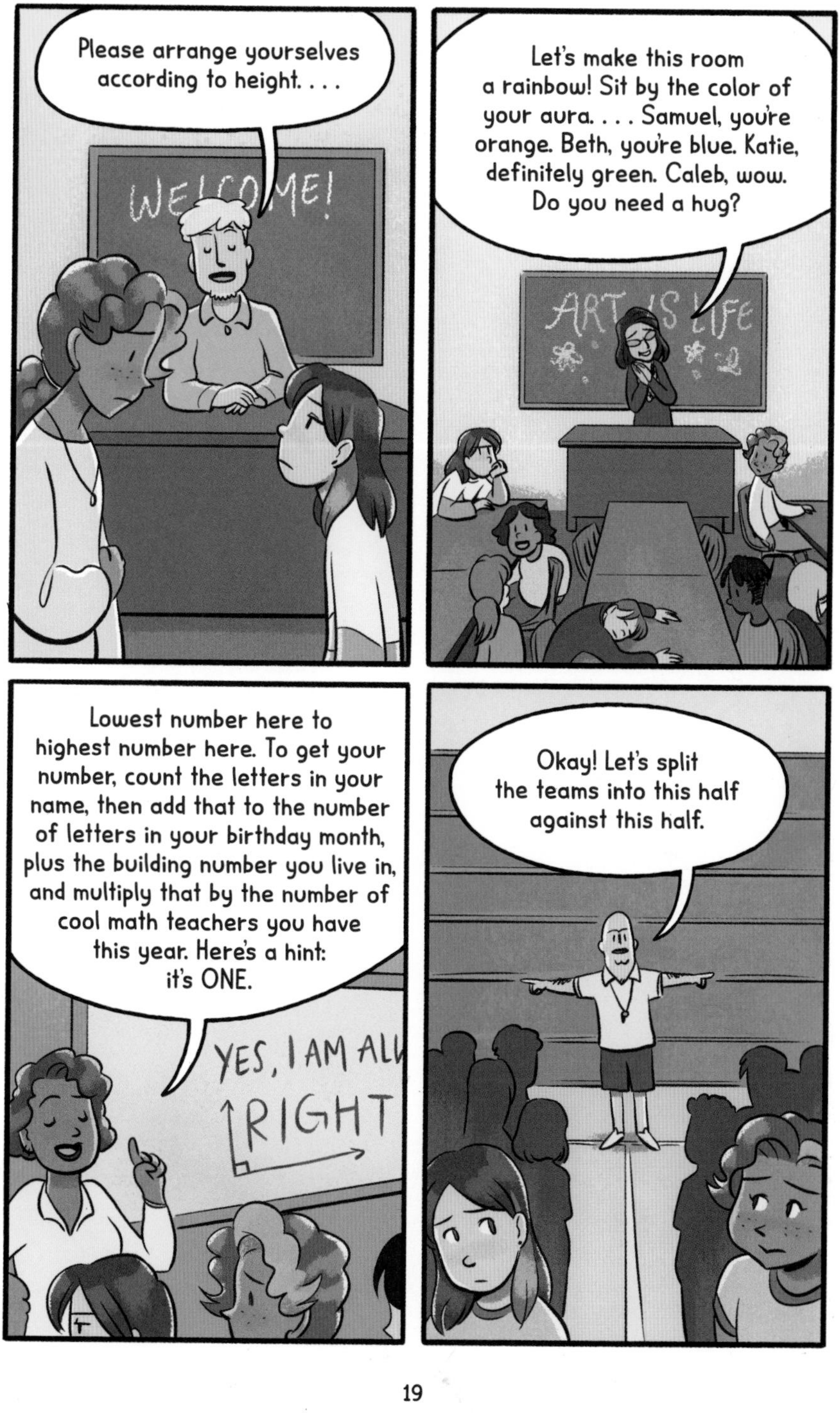
Please arrange yourselves according to height. . . .
WELCOME!
Let's make this room a rainbow! Sit by the color of your aura. . . . Samuel, you're orange. Beth, you're blue. Katie, definitely green. Caleb, wow. Do you need a hug?
ART IS LIFE
Lowest number here to highest number here. To get your number, count the letters in your name, then add that to the number of letters in your birthday month, plus the building number you live in, and multiply that by the number of cool math teachers you have this year. Here's a hint: it's ONE.
YES, I AM ALL
RIGHT
Okay! Let's split the teams into this half against this half.

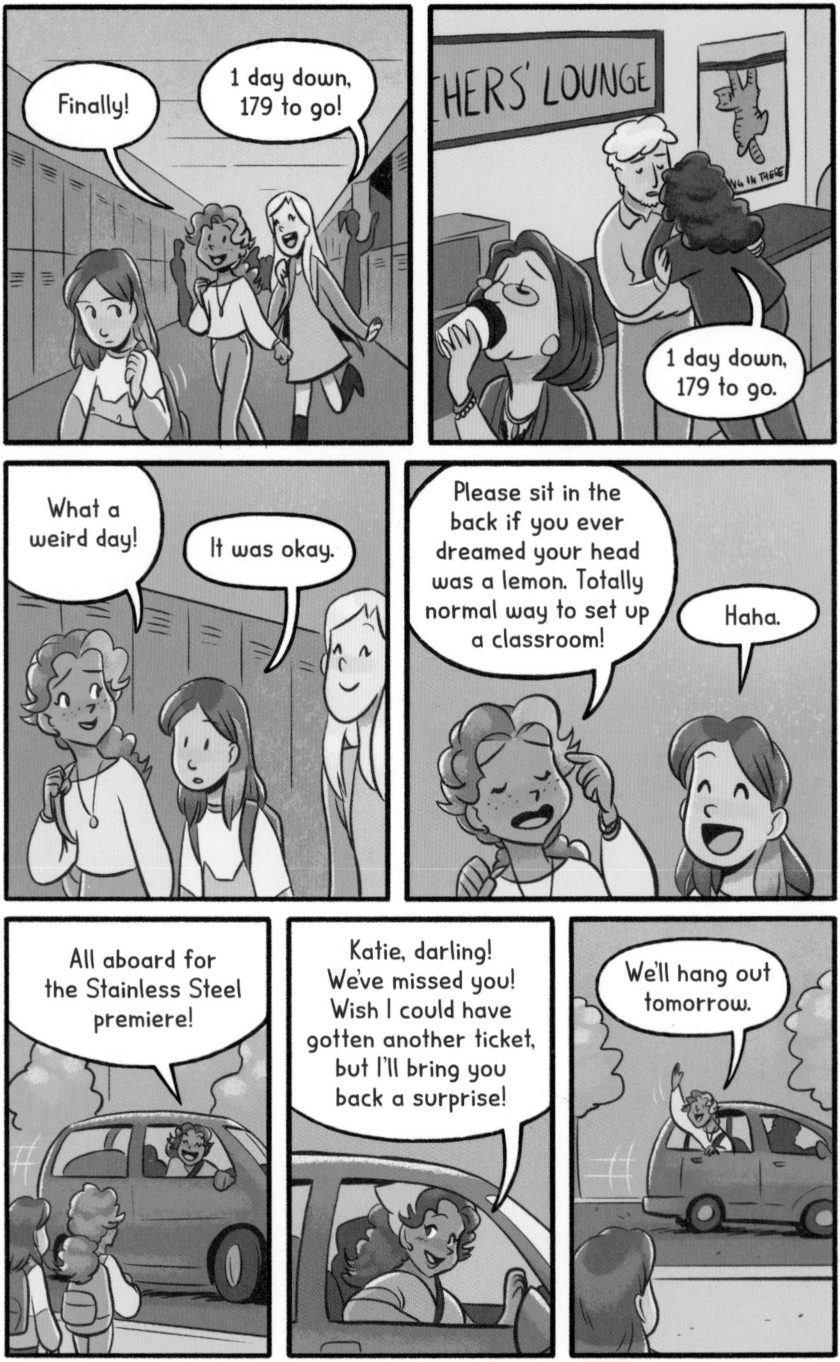
Finally!
1 day down, 179 to go!
HERS' LOUNGE
1 day down, 179 to go.
What a weird day!
It was okay.
Please sit in the back if you ever dreamed your head was a lemon. Totally normal way to set up a classroom!
Haha.
All aboard for the Stainless Steel premiere!
Katie, darling! We've missed you! Wish I could have gotten another ticket, but I'll bring you back a surprise!
We'll hang out tomorrow.

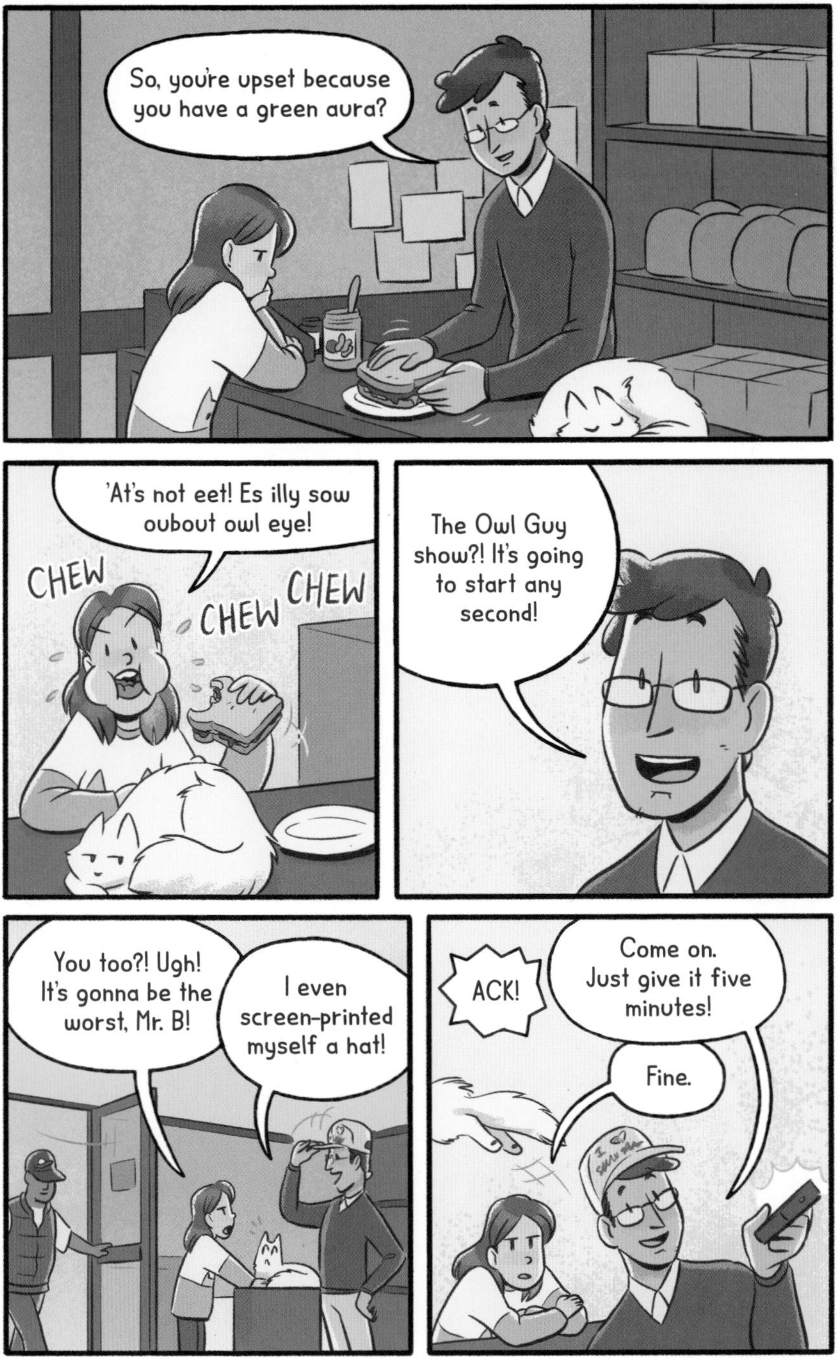
So, you're upset because you have a green aura?
'At's not eet! Es illy sow oubout owl eye!
CHEW
CHEW
CHEW
The Owl Guy show?! It's going to start any second!
You too?! Ugh! It's gonna be the worst, Mr. B!
I even screen-printed myself a hat!
ACK!
Come on. Just give it five minutes!
Fine.

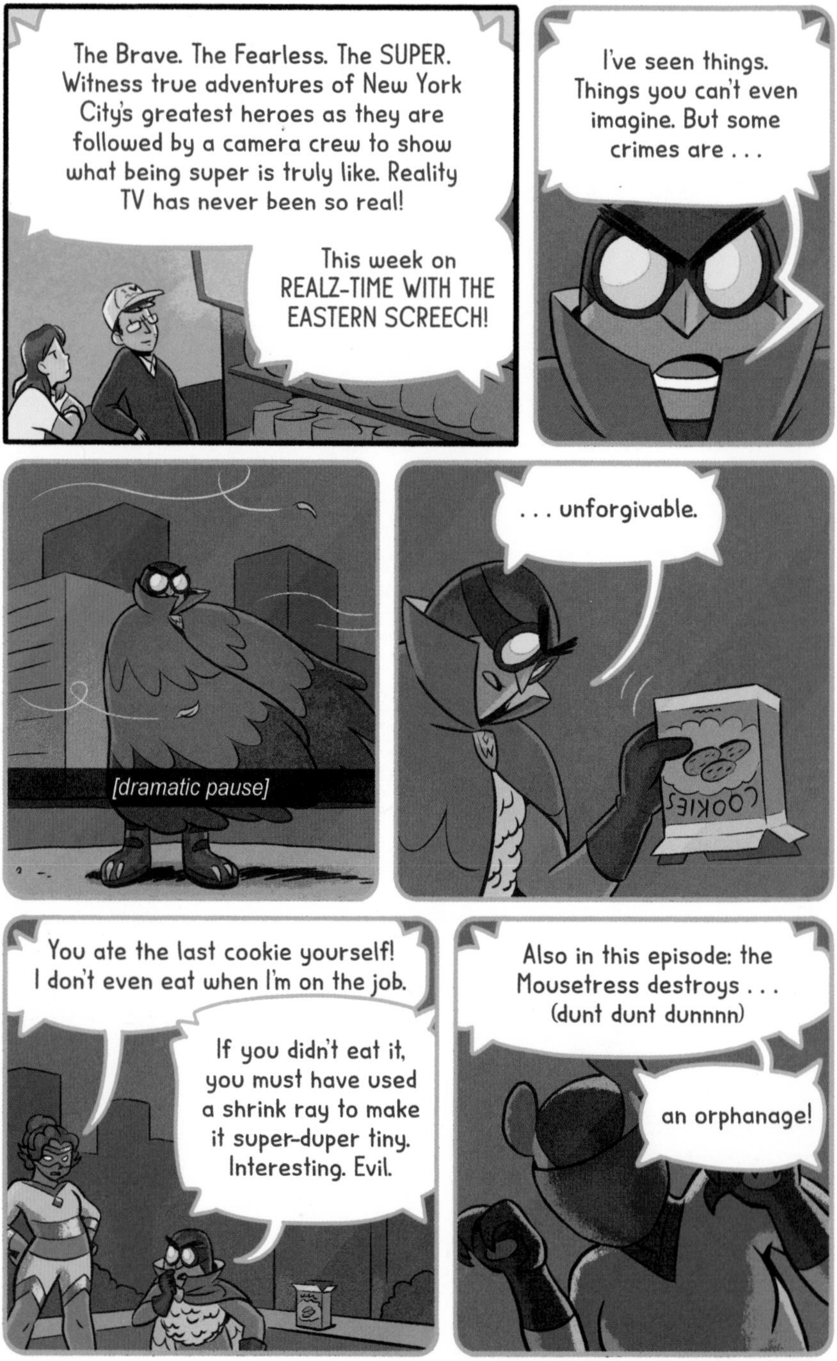
The Brave. The Fearless. The SUPER. Witness true adventures of New York City's greatest heroes as they are followed by a camera crew to show what being super is truly like. Reality TV has never been so real!
This week on REALZ-TIME WITH THE EASTERN SCREECH!
I've seen things. Things you can't even imagine. But some crimes are . . .
[dramatic pause]
. . . unforgivable.
COOKIES
You ate the last cookie yourself! I don't even eat when I'm on the job.
If you didn't eat it, you must have used a shrink ray to make it super-duper tiny. Interesting. Evil.
Also in this episode: the Mousetress destroys . . . (dunt dunt dunnnn)
an orphanage!

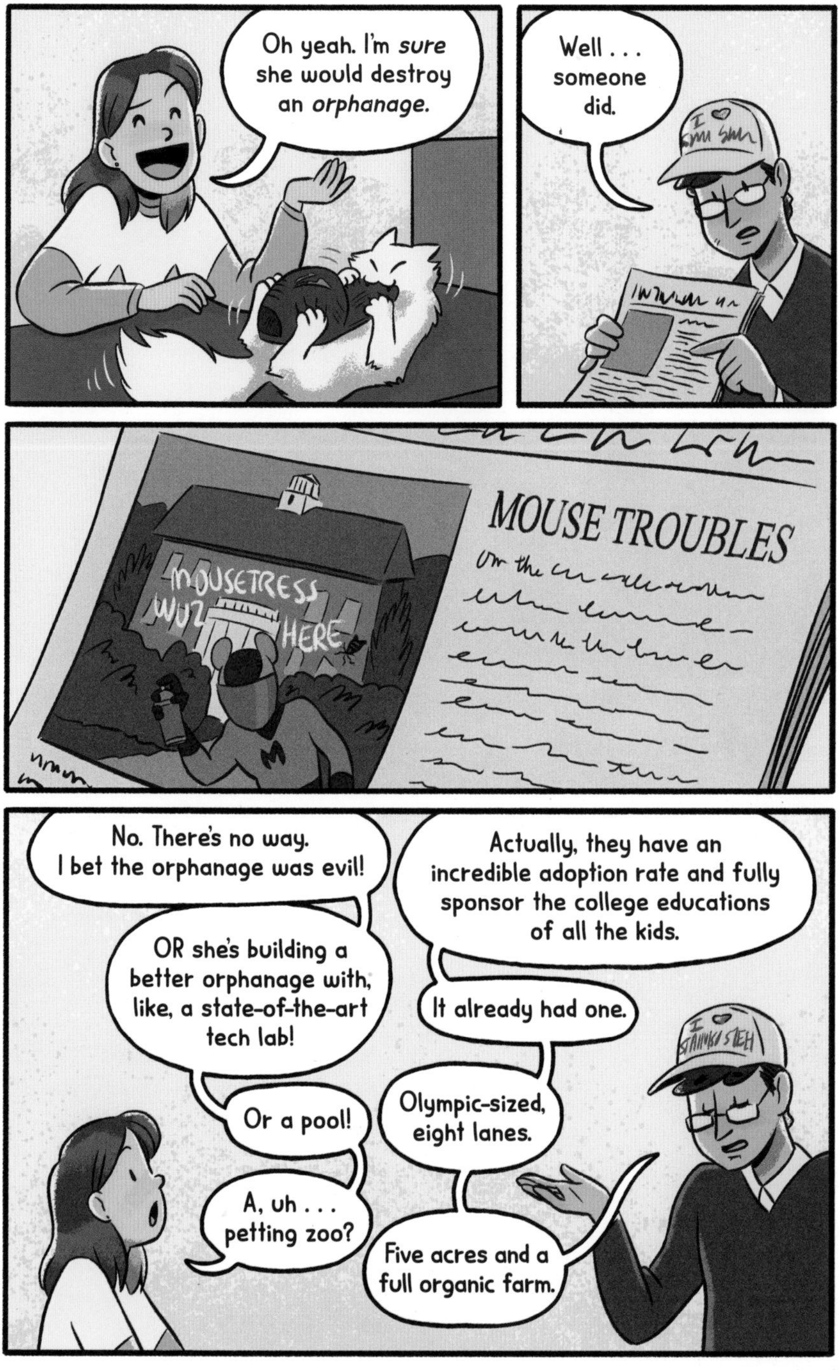
Oh yeah. I'm *sure* she would destroy an *orphanage.*
Well . . . someone did.
MOUSE TROUBLES
MOUSETRESS WUZ HERE
No. There's no way. I bet the orphanage was evil!
OR she's building a better orphanage with, like, a state-of-the-art tech lab!
Actually, they have an incredible adoption rate and fully sponsor the college educations of all the kids.
It already had one.
Or a pool!
Olympic-sized, eight lanes.
A, uh . . . petting zoo?
Five acres and a full organic farm.

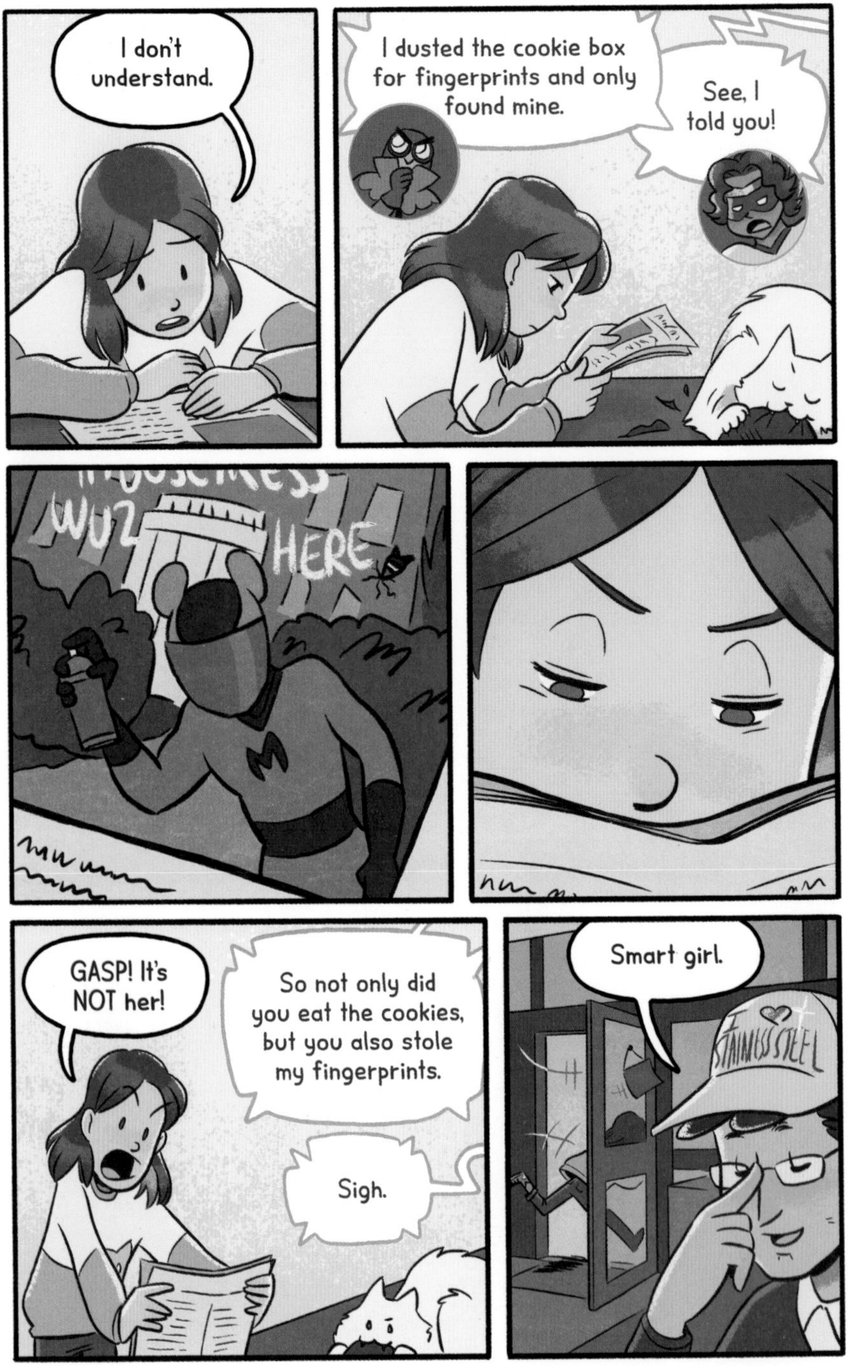
I don't understand.
I dusted the cookie box for fingerprints and only found mine.
See, I told you!
WUZ
HERE
GASP! It's NOT her!
So not only did you eat the cookies, but you also stole my fingerprints.
Sigh.
Smart girl.

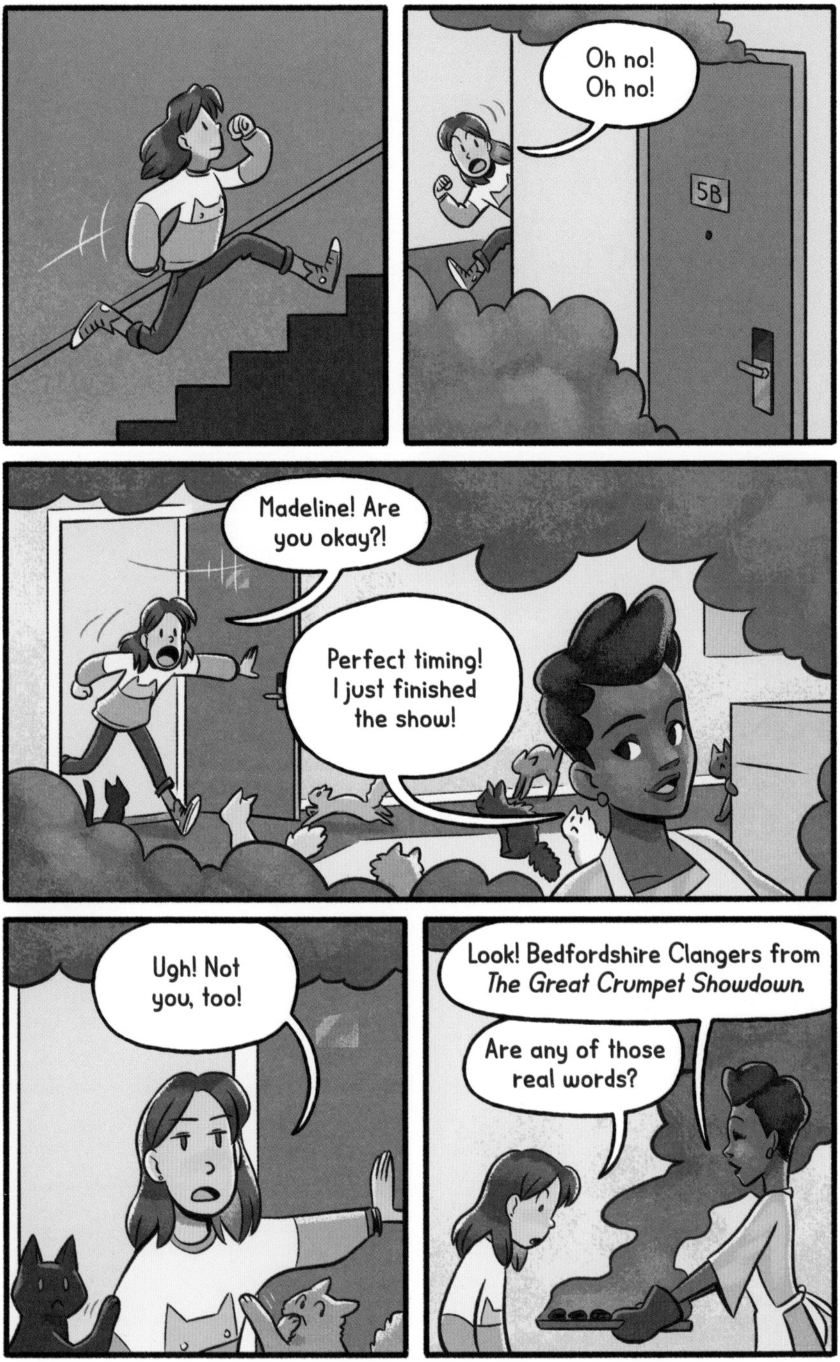
Oh no!
Oh no!
5B
Madeline! Are you okay?!
Perfect timing! I just finished the show!
Ugh! Not you, too!
Look! Bedfordshire Clangers from *The Great Crumpet Showdown.*
Are any of those real words?

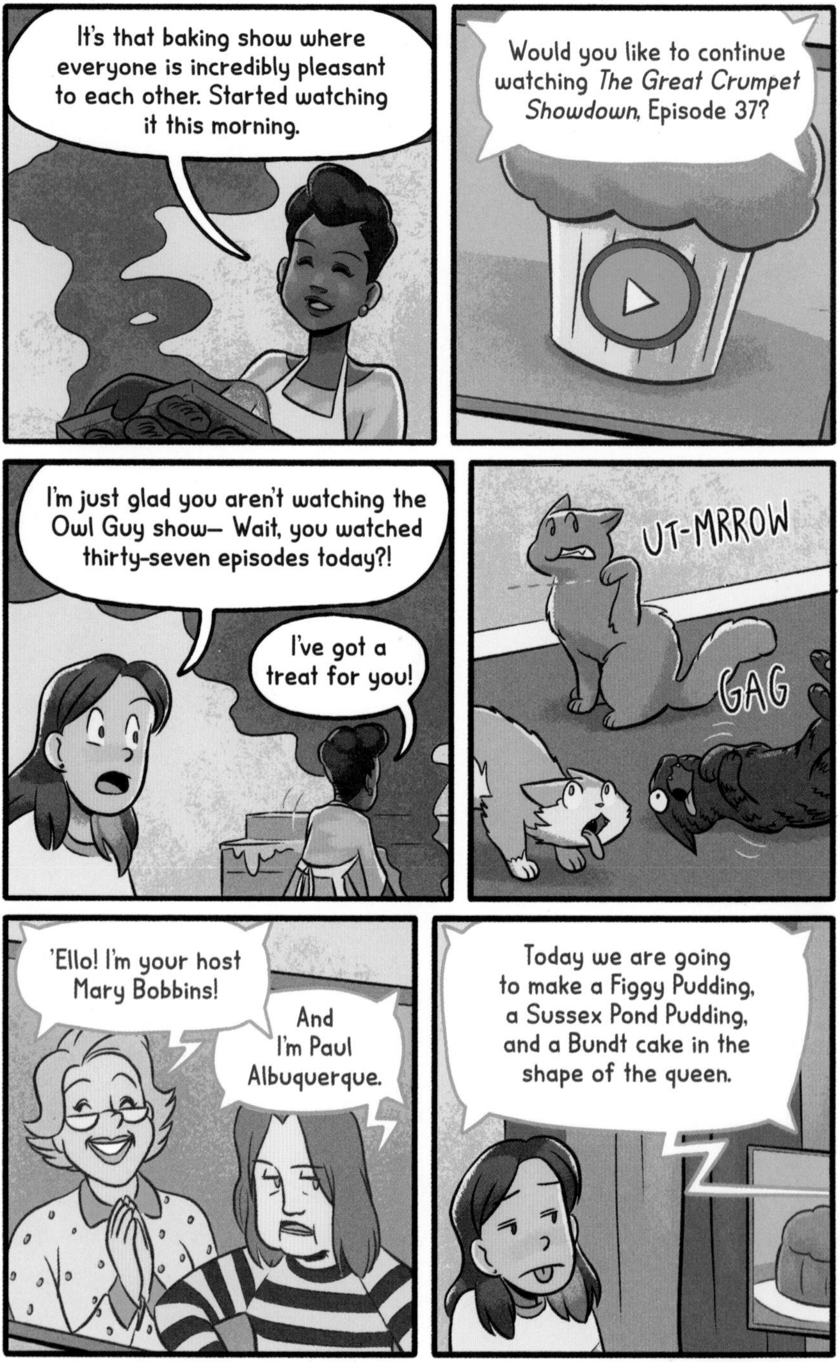
It's that baking show where everyone is incredibly pleasant to each other. Started watching it this morning.
Would you like to continue watching *The Great Crumpet Showdown*, Episode 37?
I'm just glad you aren't watching the Owl Guy show— Wait, you watched thirty-seven episodes today?!
I've got a treat for you!
UT-MRROW
GAG
'Ello! I'm your host Mary Bobbins!
And I'm Paul Albuquerque.
Today we are going to make a Figgy Pudding, a Sussex Pond Pudding, and a Bundt cake in the shape of the queen.

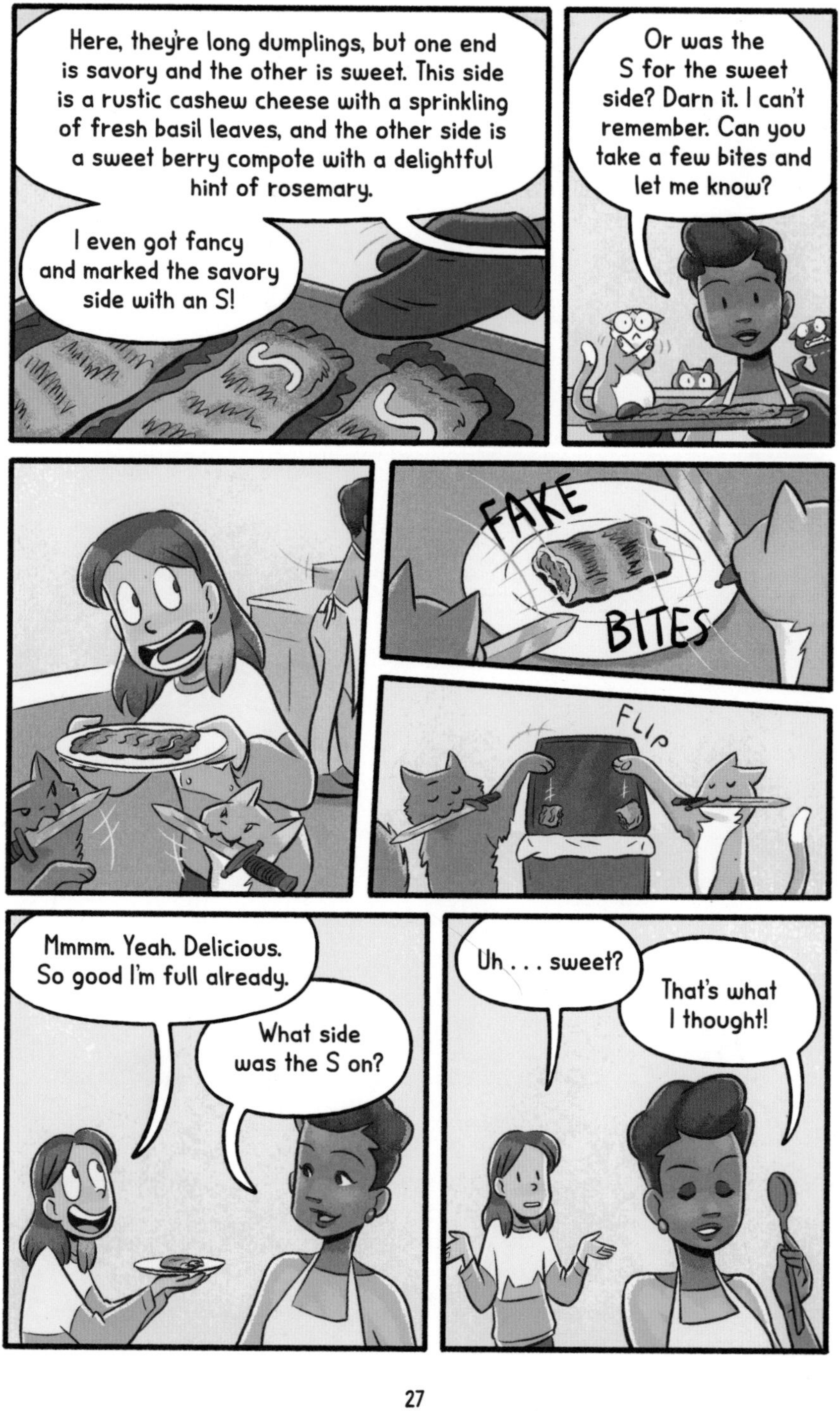
Here, they're long dumplings, but one end is savory and the other is sweet. This side is a rustic cashew cheese with a sprinkling of fresh basil leaves, and the other side is a sweet berry compote with a delightful hint of rosemary.
I even got fancy and marked the savory side with an S!
Or was the S for the sweet side? Darn it. I can't remember. Can you take a few bites and let me know?
FAKE
BITES
FLIP
Mmmm. Yeah. Delicious. So good I'm full already.
What side was the S on?
Uh . . . sweet?
That's what I thought!

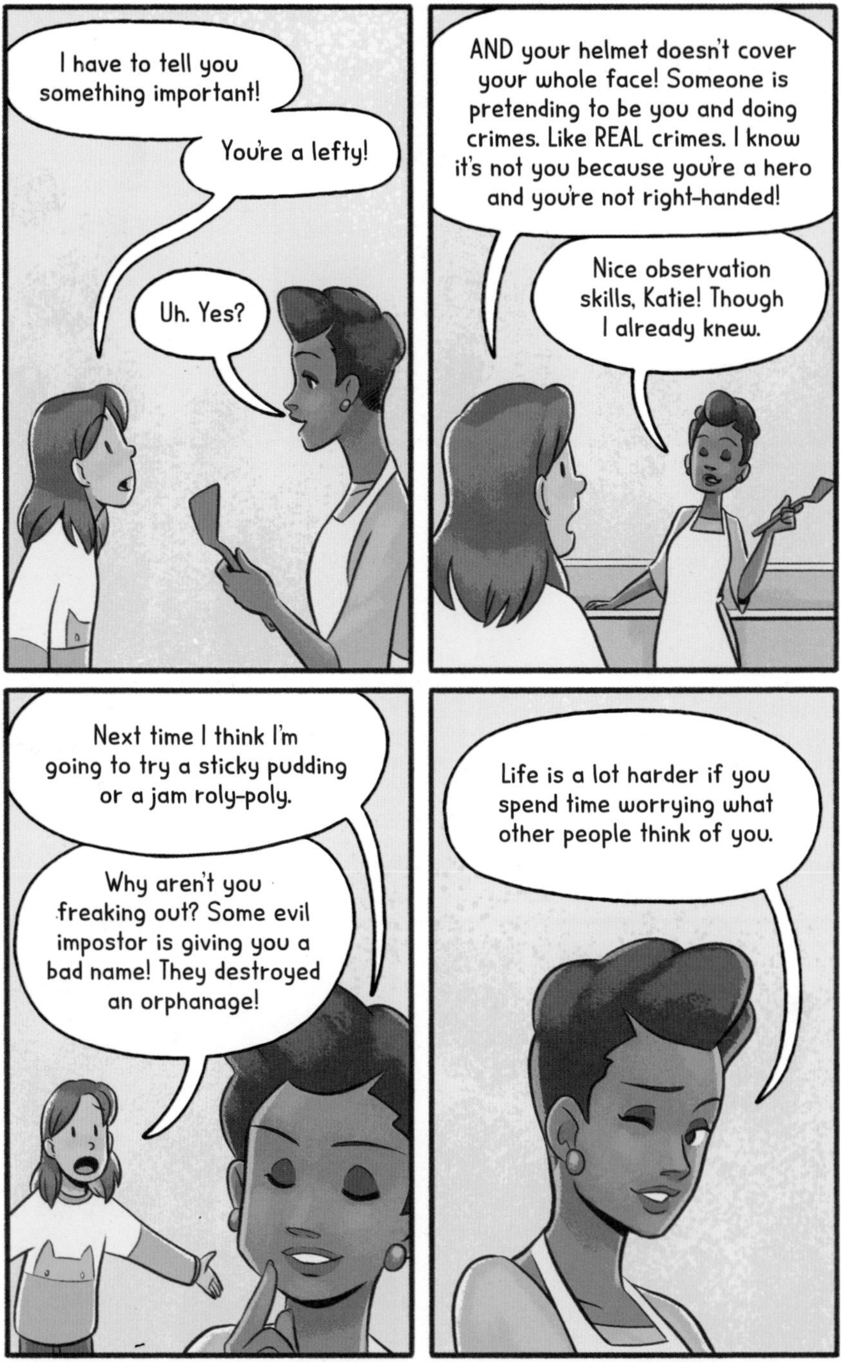
I have to tell you something important!
You're a lefty!
Uh. Yes?
AND your helmet doesn't cover your whole face! Someone is pretending to be you and doing crimes. Like REAL crimes. I know it's not you because you're a hero and you're not right-handed!
Nice observation skills, Katie! Though I already knew.
Next time I think I'm going to try a sticky pudding or a jam roly-poly.
Why aren't you freaking out? Some evil impostor is giving you a bad name! They destroyed an orphanage!
Life is a lot harder if you spend time worrying what other people think of you.

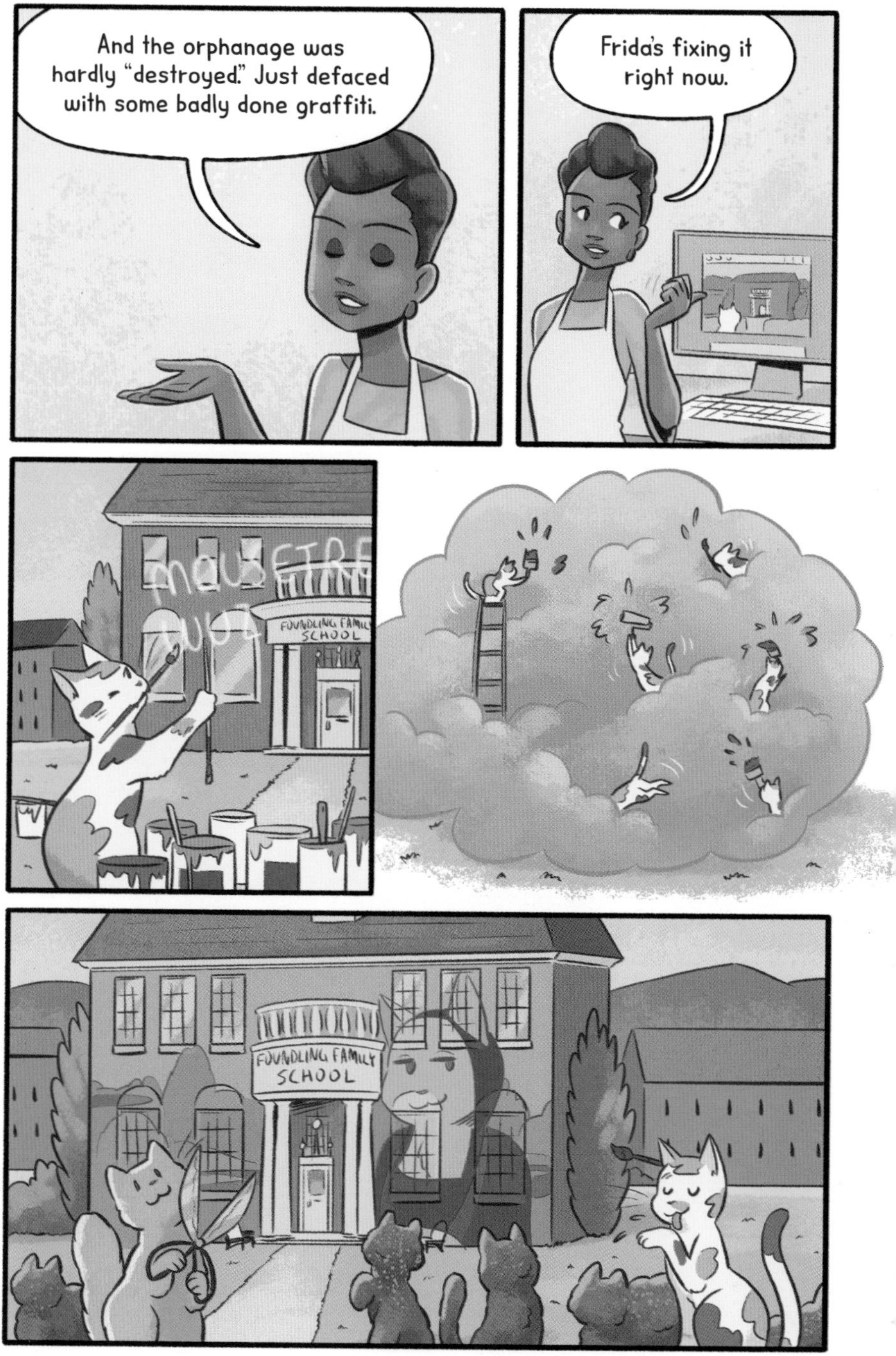
And the orphanage was hardly "destroyed." Just defaced with some badly done graffiti.
Frida's fixing it right now.
MOUSETRE WUZ
FOUNDLING FAMILY SCHOOL
FOUNDLING FAMILY SCHOOL

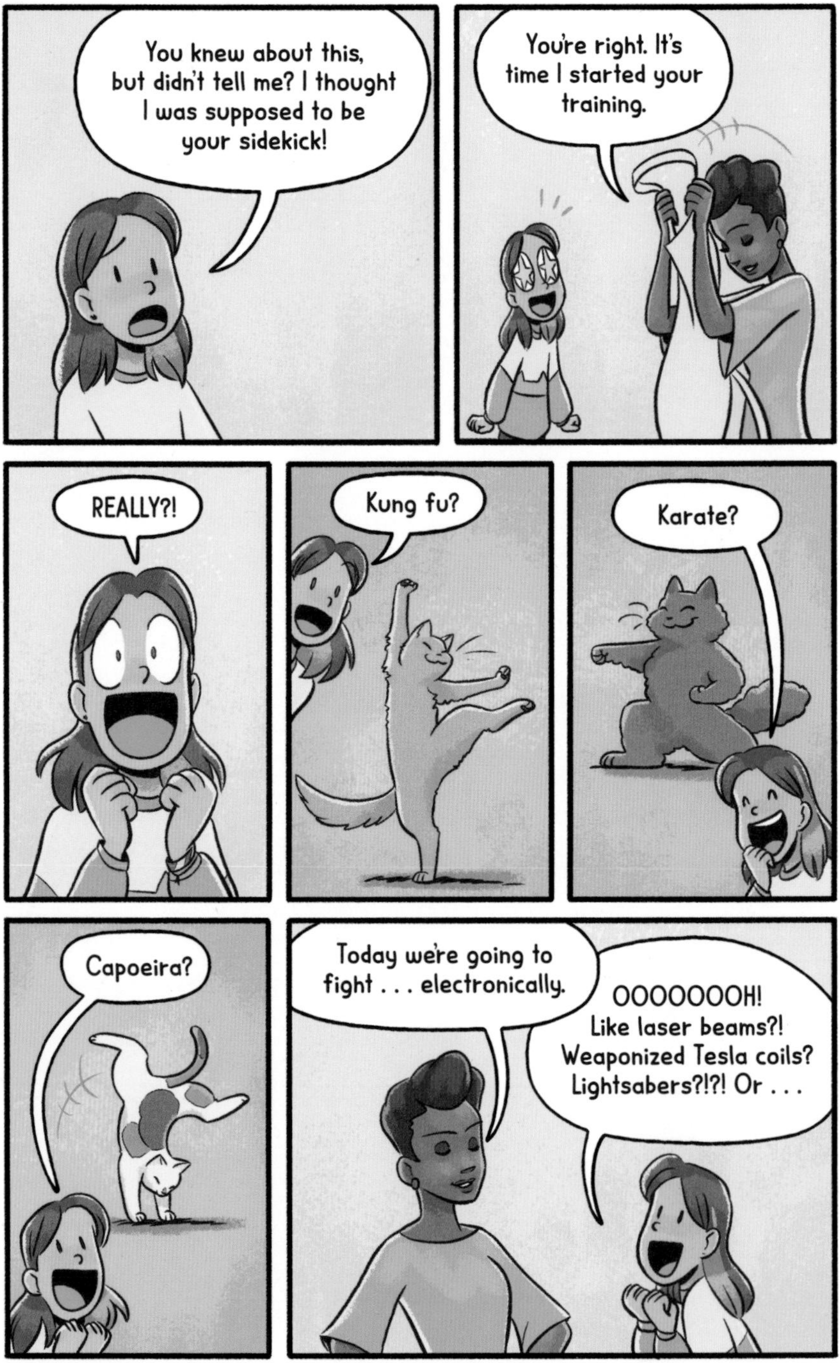
You knew about this, but didn't tell me? I thought I was supposed to be your sidekick!
You're right. It's time I started your training.
REALLY?!
Kung fu?
Karate?
Capoeira?
Today we're going to fight . . . electronically.
OOOOOOOH! Like laser beams?! Weaponized Tesla coils? Lightsabers?!?! Or . . .

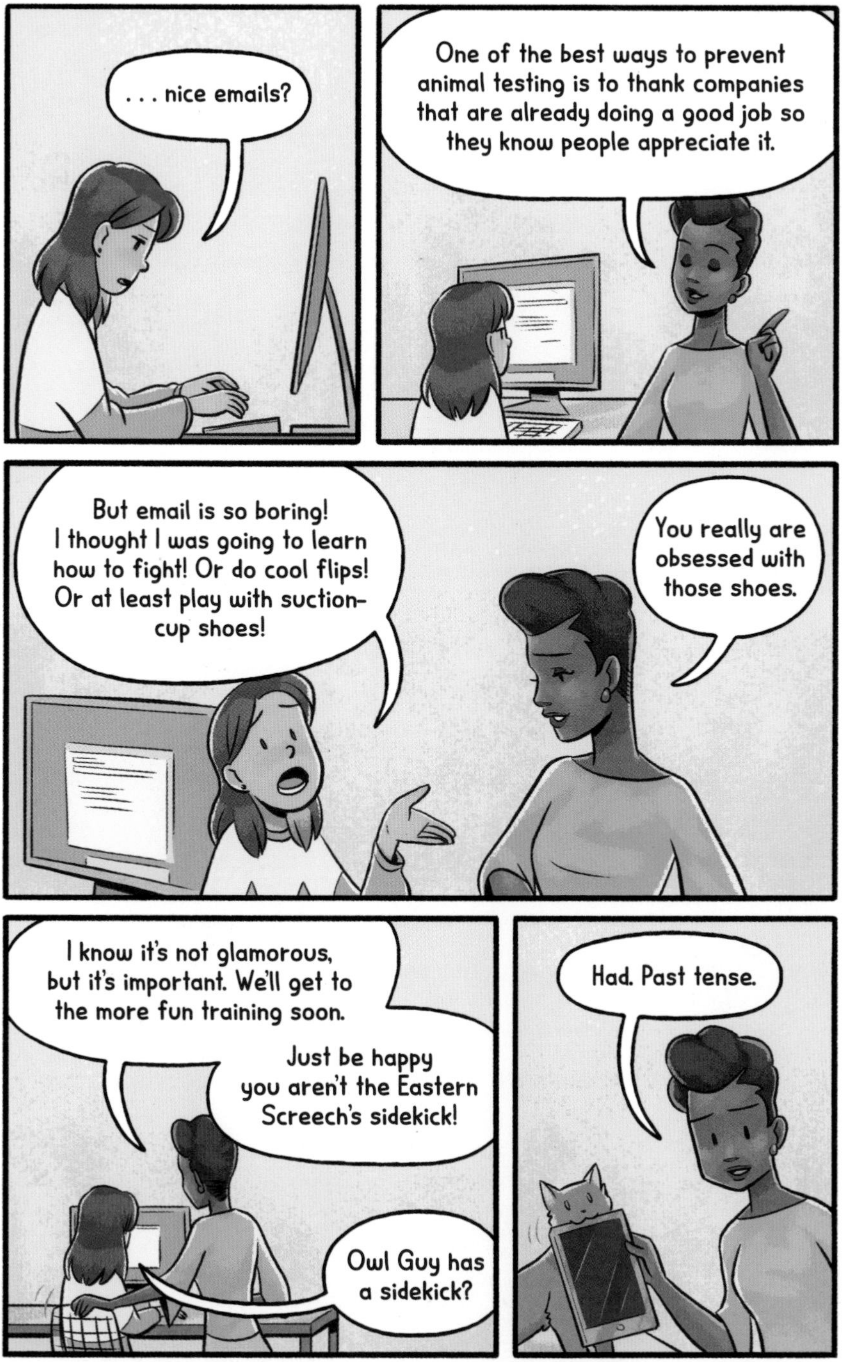
. . . nice emails?
One of the best ways to prevent animal testing is to thank companies that are already doing a good job so they know people appreciate it.
But email is so boring! I thought I was going to learn how to fight! Or do cool flips! Or at least play with suction-cup shoes!
You really are obsessed with those shoes.
I know it's not glamorous, but it's important. We'll get to the more fun training soon.
Just be happy you aren't the Eastern Screech's sidekick!
Owl Guy has a sidekick?
Had. Past tense.

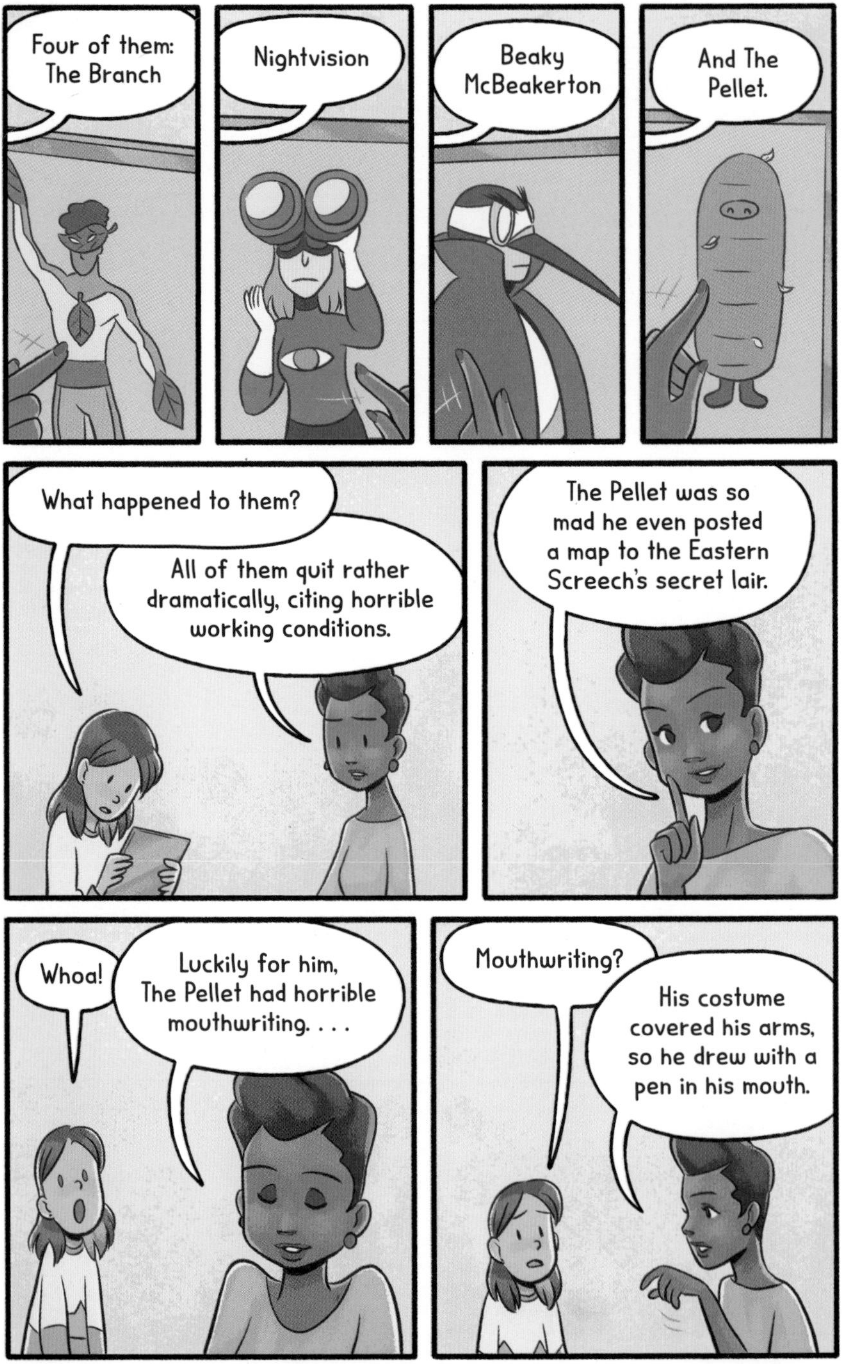

Four of them: The Branch
Nightvision
Beaky McBeakerton
And The Pellet.
What happened to them?
All of them quit rather dramatically, citing horrible working conditions.
The Pellet was so mad he even posted a map to the Eastern Screech's secret lair.
Whoa!
Luckily for him, The Pellet had horrible mouthwriting. . . .
Mouthwriting?
His costume covered his arms, so he drew with a pen in his mouth.

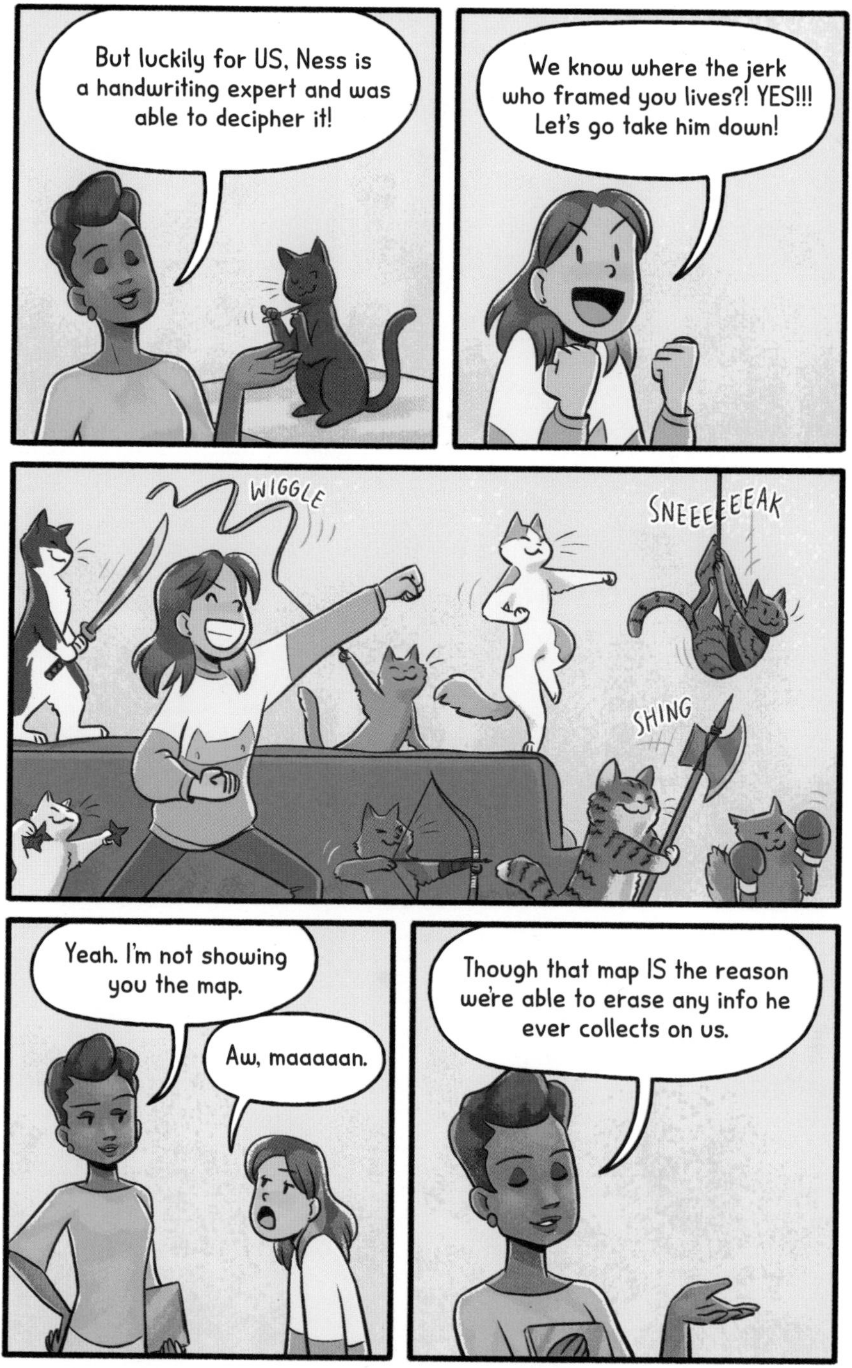
But luckily for US, Ness is a handwriting expert and was able to decipher it!
We know where the jerk who framed you lives?! YES!!! Let's go take him down!
WIGGLE
SNEEEEEEAK
SHING
Yeah. I'm not showing you the map.
Aw, maaaaan.
Though that map IS the reason we're able to erase any info he ever collects on us.

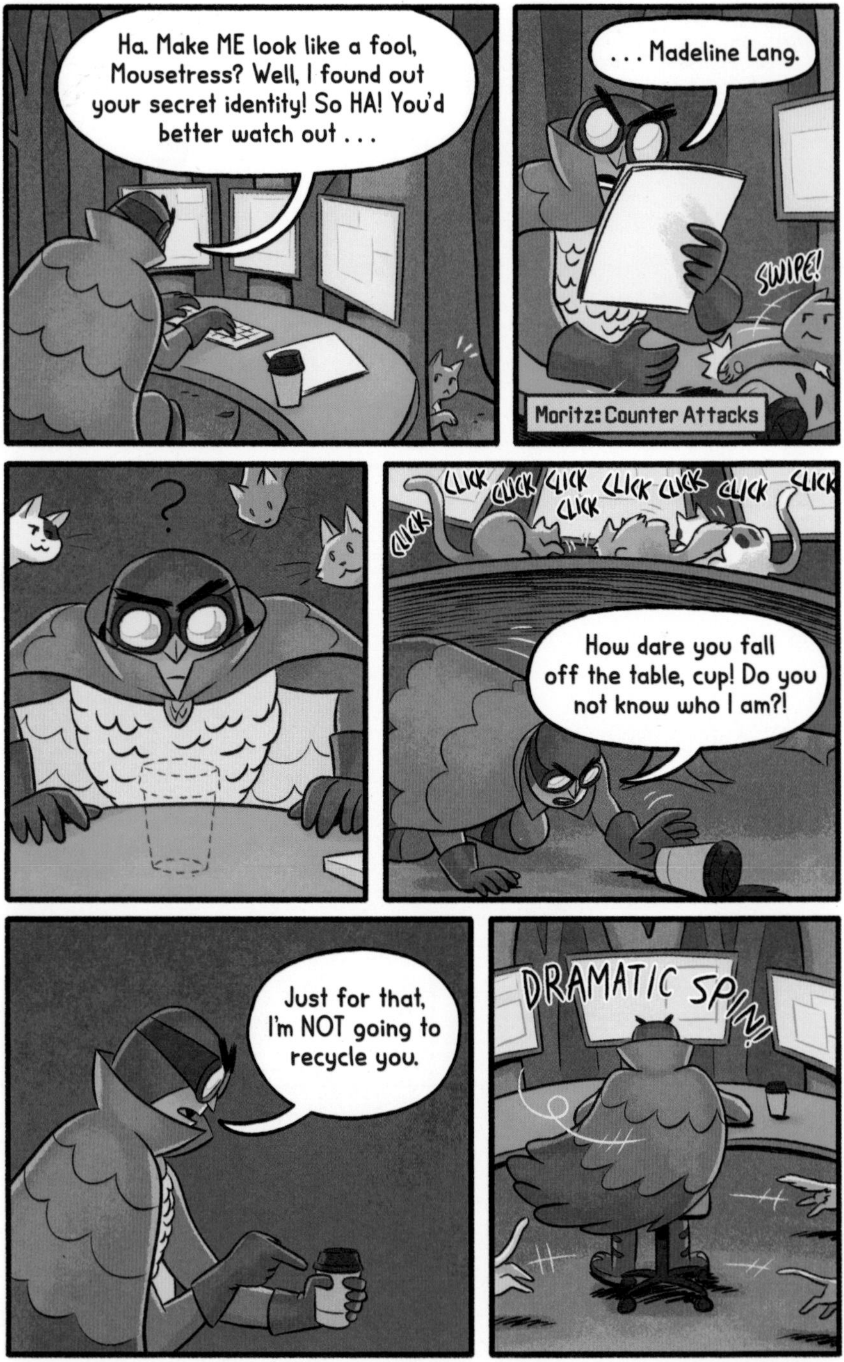

Ha. Make ME look like a fool, Mousetress? Well, I found out your secret identity! So HA! You'd better watch out . . .
. . . Madeline Lang.
SWIPE!
Moritz: Counter Attacks
?
CLICK CLICK CLICK CLICK CLICK CLICK CLICK CLICK CLICK
How dare you fall off the table, cup! Do you not know who I am?!
Just for that, I'm NOT going to recycle you.
DRAMATIC SPIN!

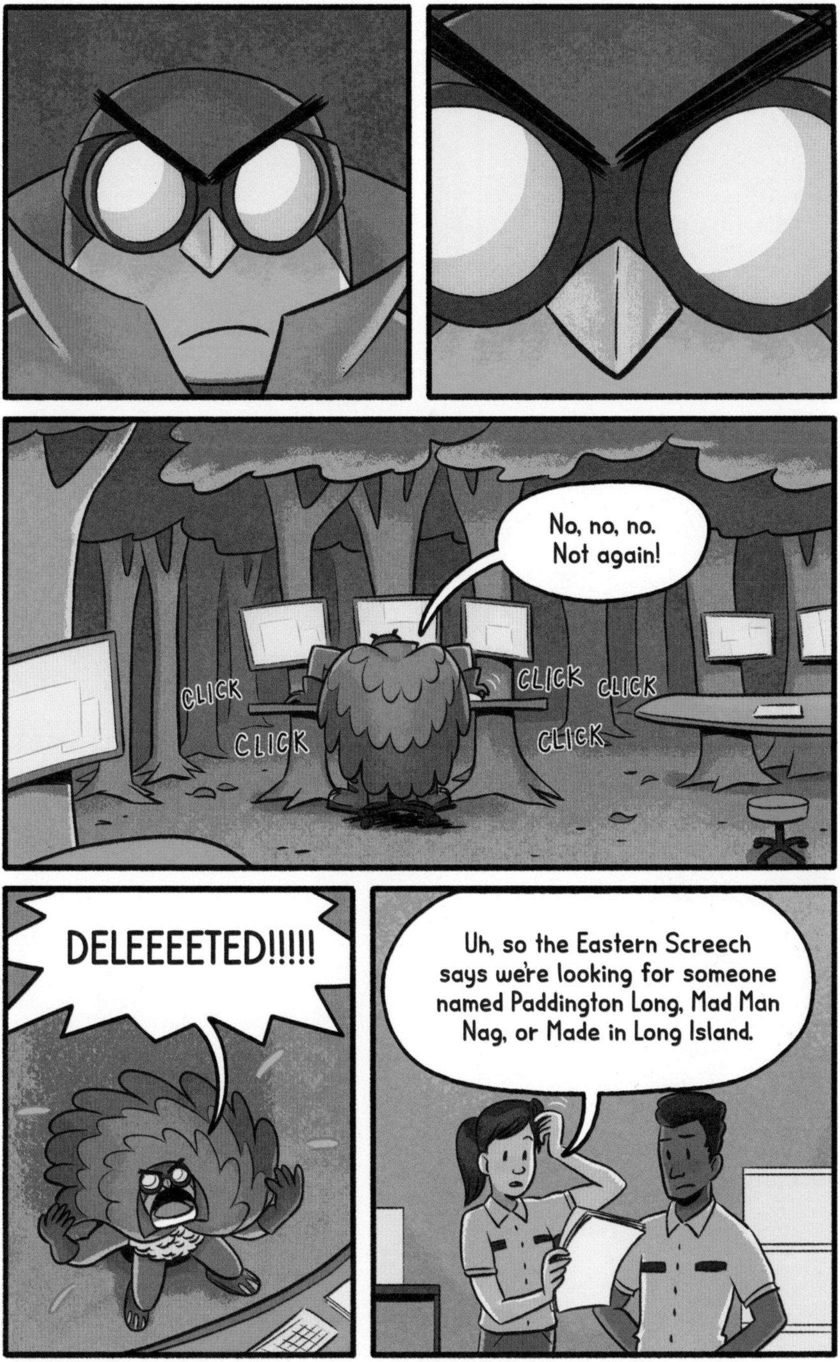
No, no, no.
Not again!
CLICK
CLICK
CLICK
CLICK
CLICK
DELEEEETED!!!!!
Uh, so the Eastern Screech says we're looking for someone named Paddington Long, Mad Man Nag, or Made in Long Island.

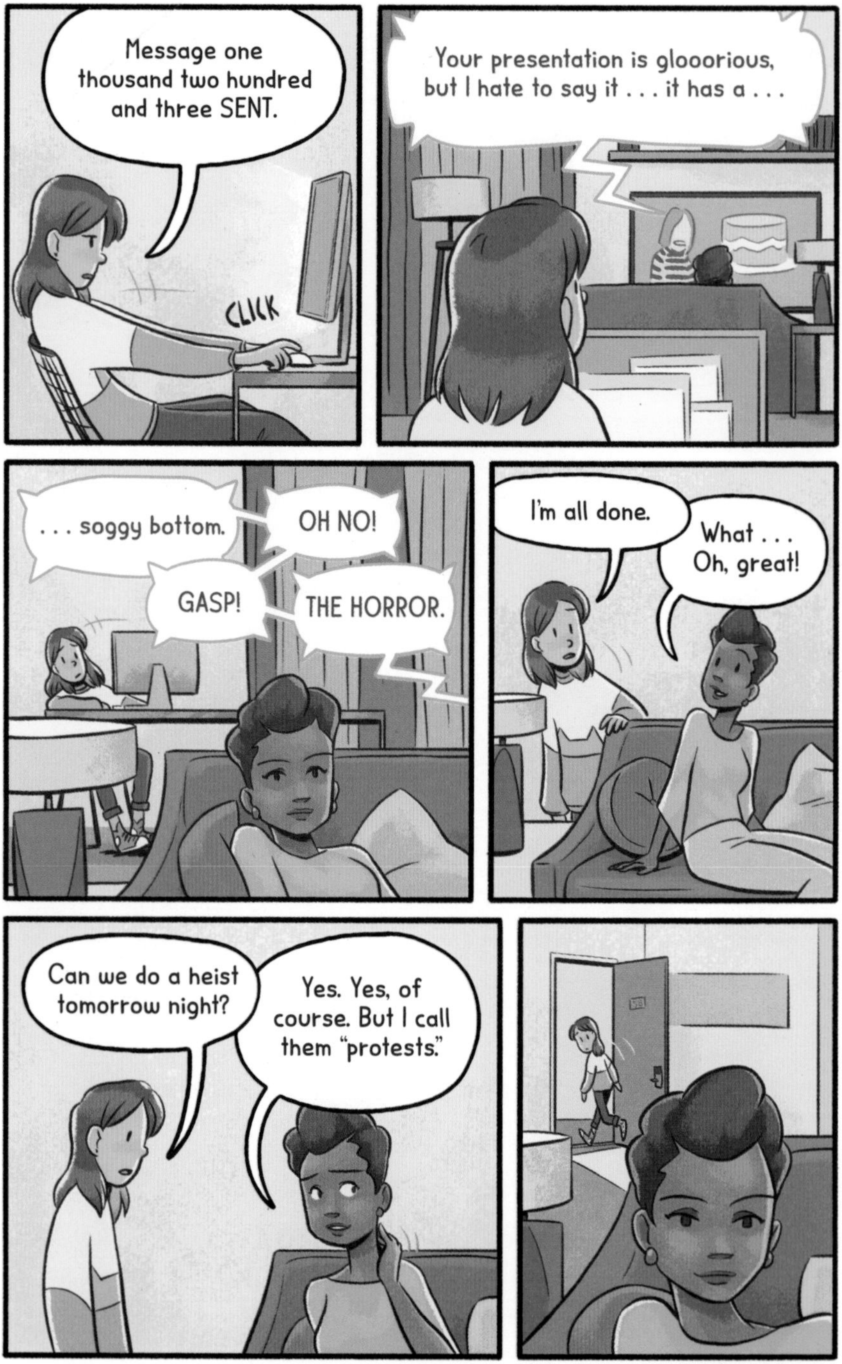
Message one thousand two hundred and three SENT.
CLICK
Your presentation is glooorious, but I hate to say it . . . it has a . . .
. . . soggy bottom.
OH NO!
GASP!
THE HORROR.
I'm all done.
What . . . Oh, great!
Can we do a heist tomorrow night?
Yes. Yes, of course. But I call them "protests."

CHAPTER THREE

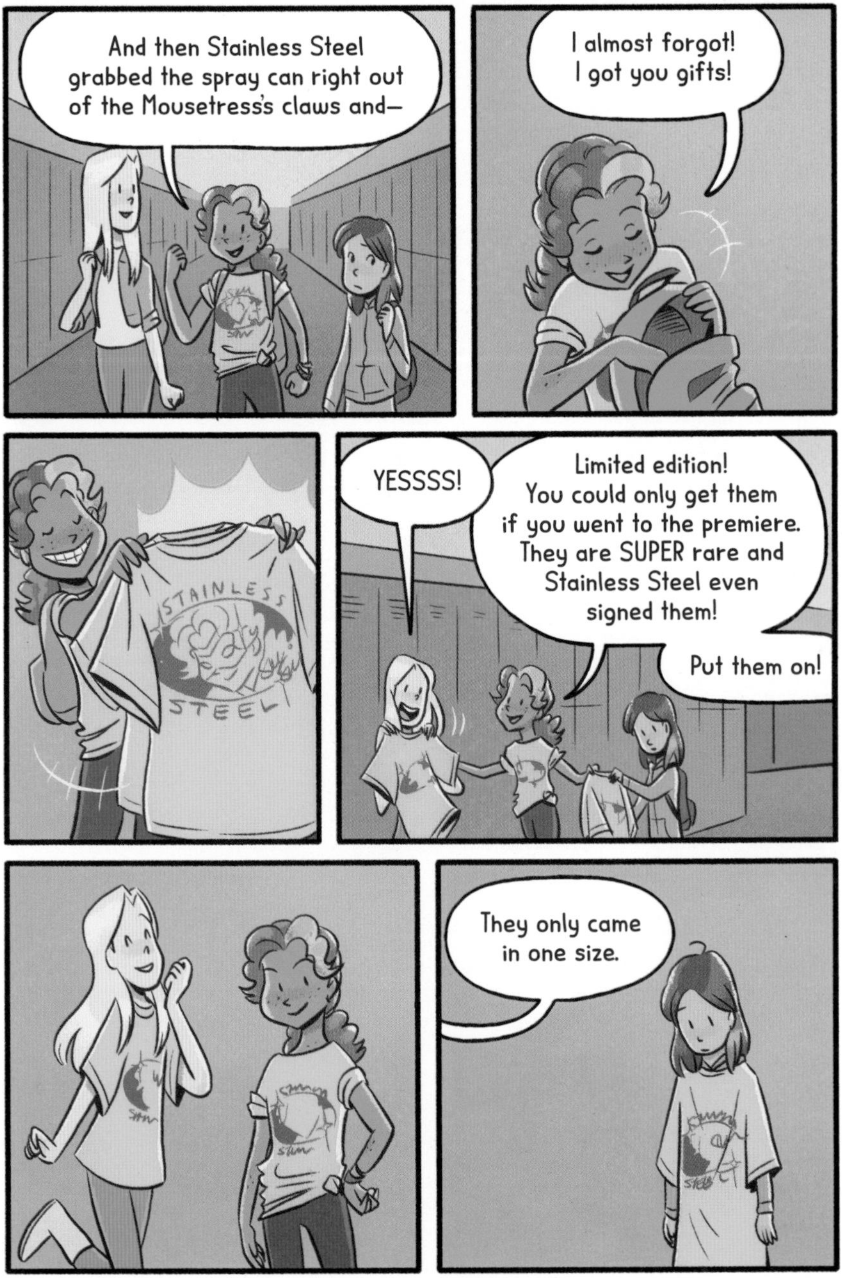

And then Stainless Steel grabbed the spray can right out of the Mousetress's claws and—
I almost forgot! I got you gifts!
STAINLESS
STEEL
YESSSS!
Limited edition! You could only get them if you went to the premiere. They are SUPER rare and Stainless Steel even signed them!
Put them on!
They only came in one size.

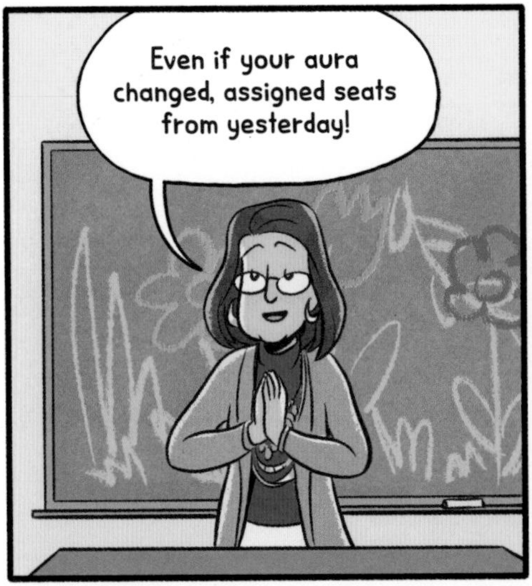
Even if your aura changed, assigned seats from yesterday!

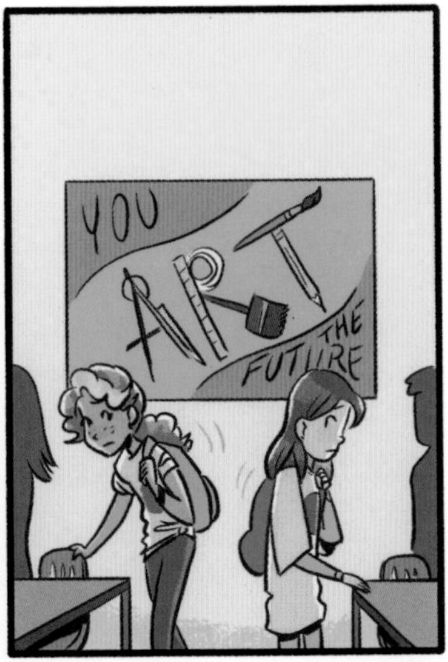
YOU ART THE FUTURE

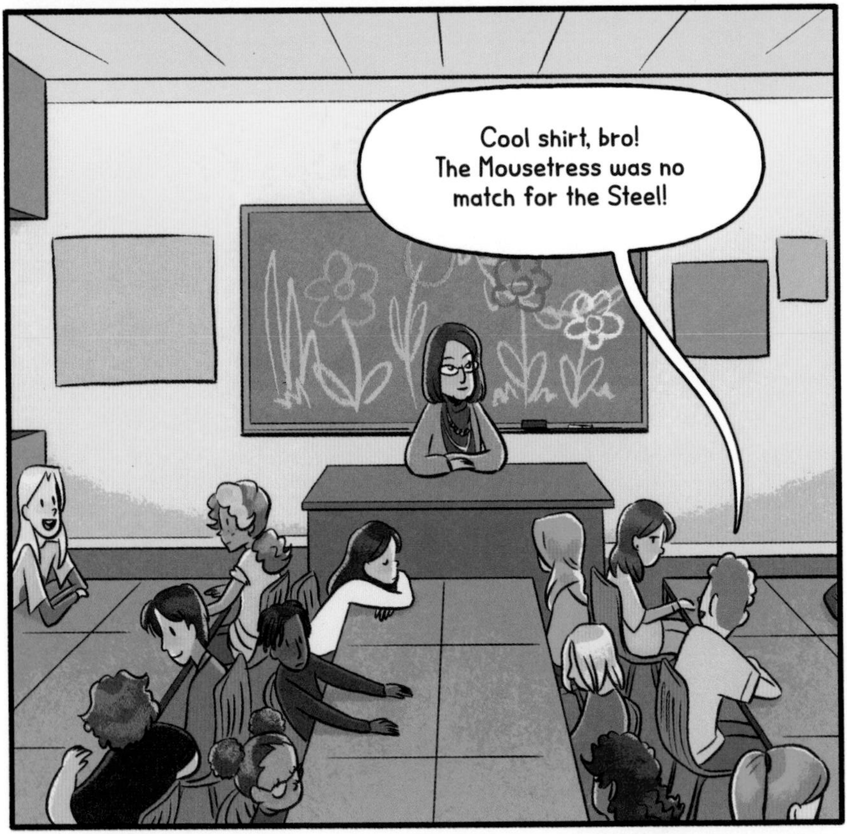
Cool shirt, bro!
The Mousetress was no match for the Steel!

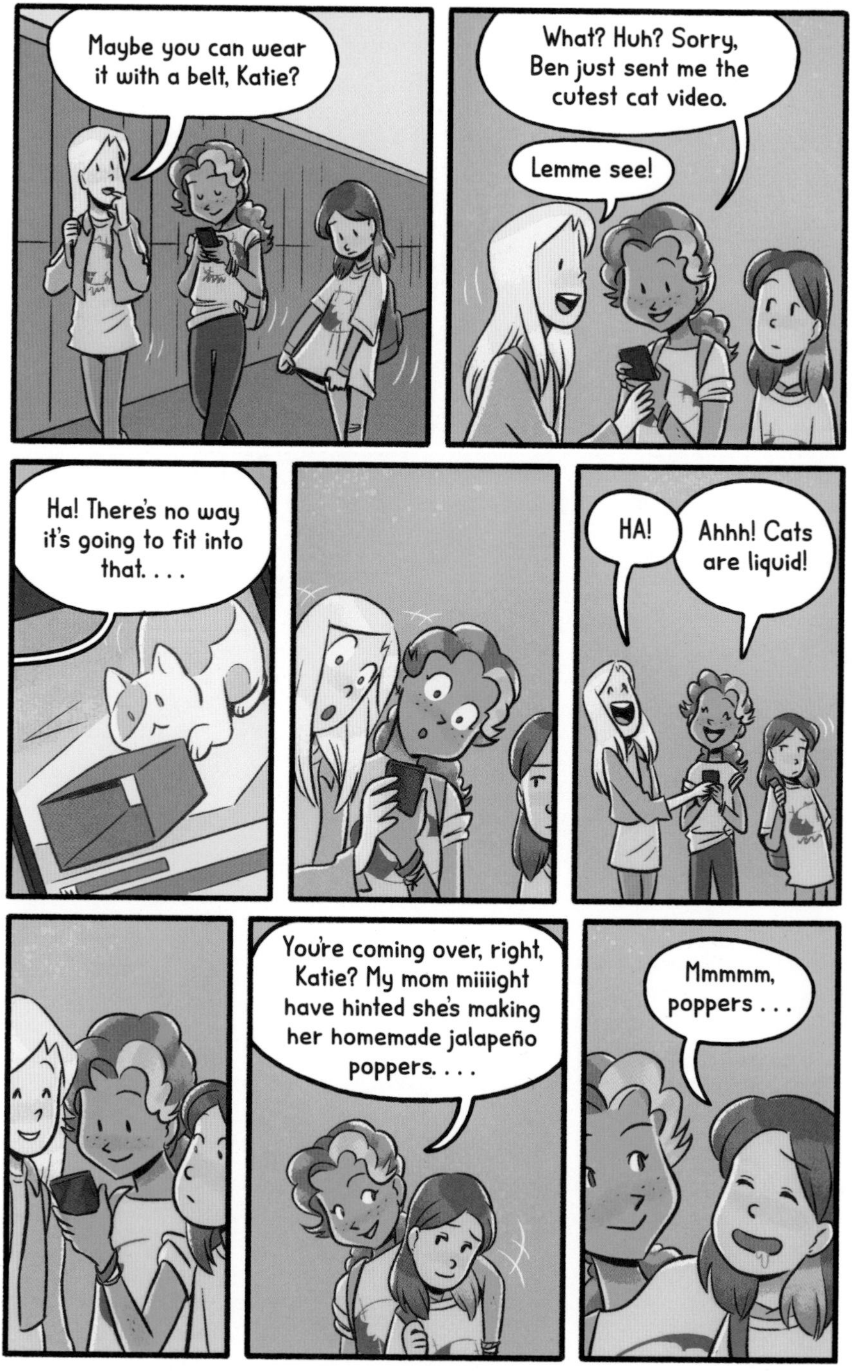

Maybe you can wear it with a belt, Katie?
What? Huh? Sorry, Ben just sent me the cutest cat video.
Lemme see!
Ha! There's no way it's going to fit into that. . . .
HA!
Ahhh! Cats are liquid!
You're coming over, right, Katie? My mom miiiight have hinted she's making her homemade jalapeño poppers. . . .
Mmmmm, poppers . . .

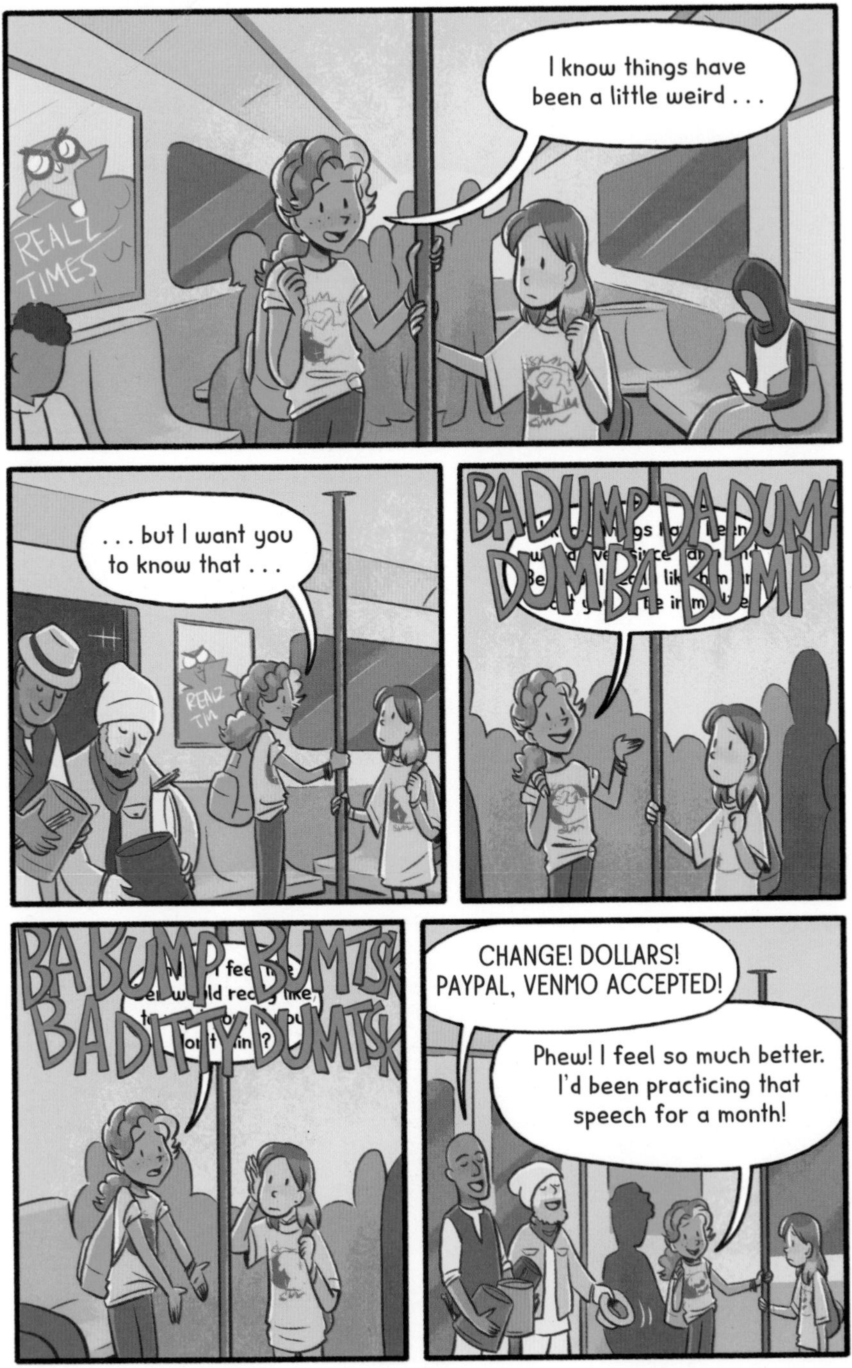
I know things have been a little weird . . .
. . . but I want you to know that . . .
BADUMP DA DUM
DUM BA BUMP
BA BUMP BUMTSK
BA DITTY DUMTSK
CHANGE! DOLLARS! PAYPAL, VENMO ACCEPTED!
Phew! I feel so much better. I'd been practicing that speech for a month!
REALZ TIMES

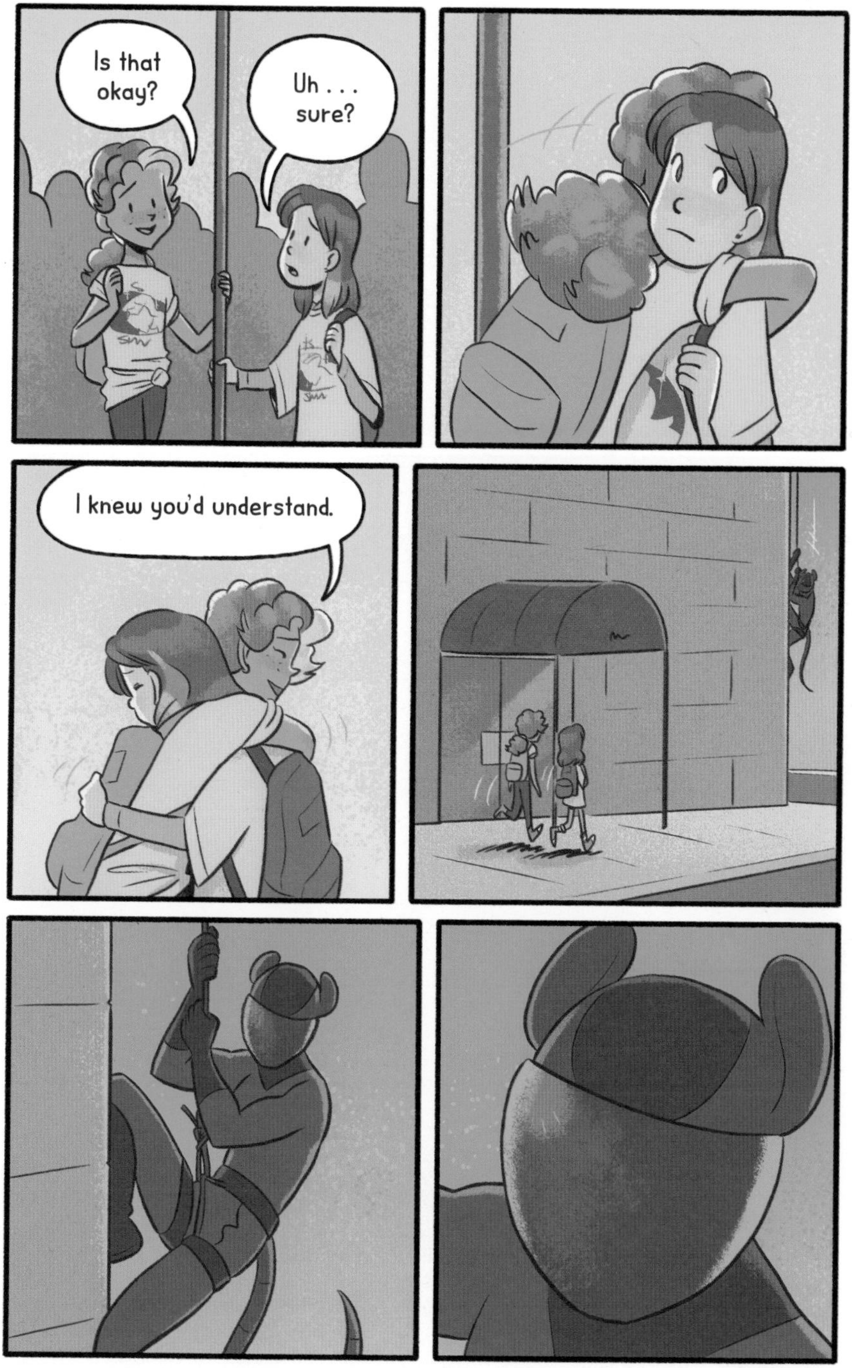

Is that okay?
Uh . . . sure?
I knew you'd understand.

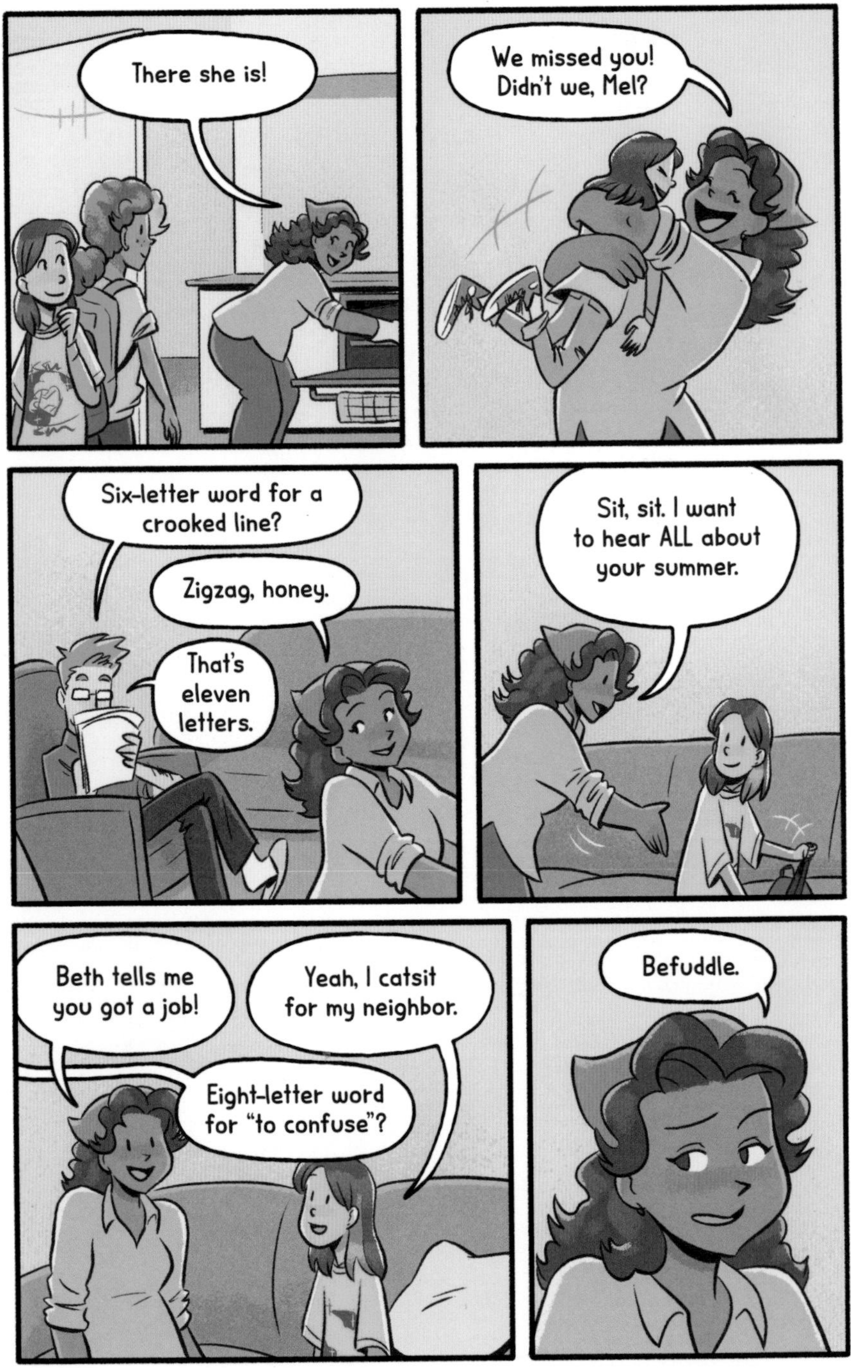

There she is!
We missed you! Didn't we, Mel?
Six-letter word for a crooked line?
Zigzag, honey.
That's eleven letters.
Sit, sit. I want to hear ALL about your summer.
Beth tells me you got a job!
Yeah, I catsit for my neighbor.
Eight-letter word for "to confuse"?
Befuddle.

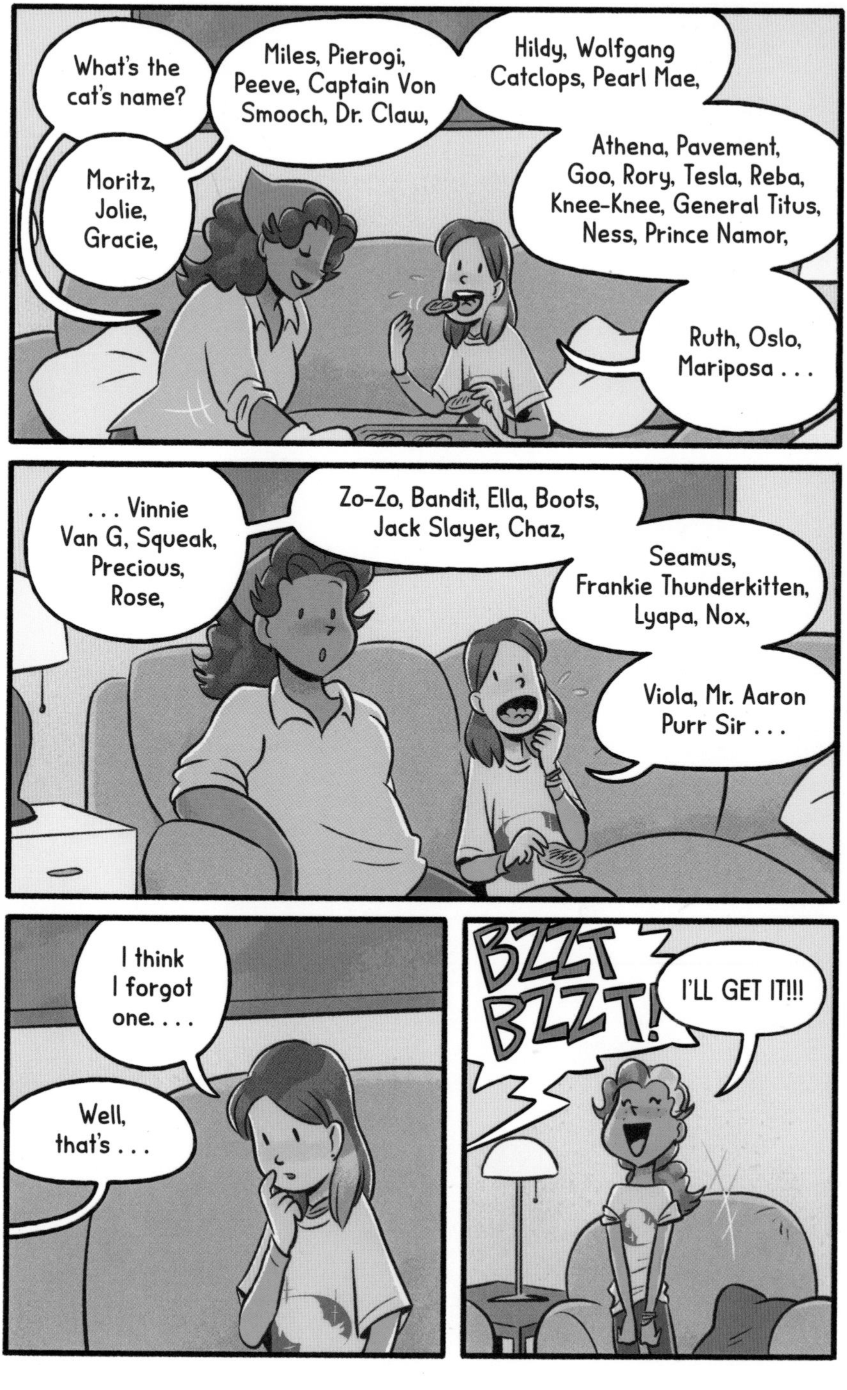
What's the cat's name?
Miles, Pierogi, Peeve, Captain Von Smooch, Dr. Claw,
Hildy, Wolfgang Catclops, Pearl Mae,
Moritz, Jolie, Gracie,
Athena, Pavement, Goo, Rory, Tesla, Reba, Knee-Knee, General Titus, Ness, Prince Namor,
Ruth, Oslo, Mariposa . . .
. . . Vinnie Van G, Squeak, Precious, Rose,
Zo-Zo, Bandit, Ella, Boots, Jack Slayer, Chaz,
Seamus, Frankie Thunderkitten, Lyapa, Nox,
Viola, Mr. Aaron Purr Sir . . .
I think I forgot one. . . .
Well, that's . . .
BZZT BZZT!
I'LL GET IT!!!

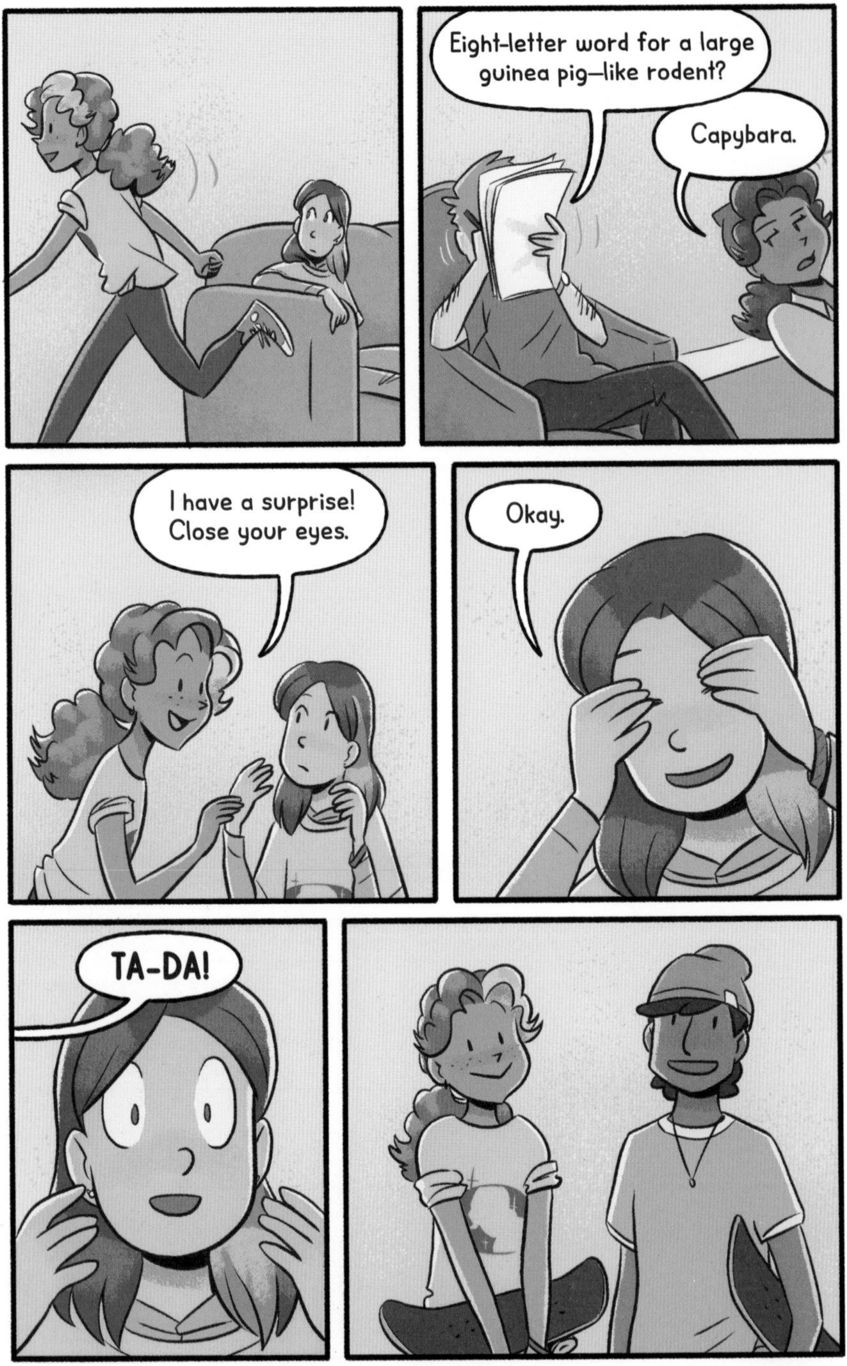
Eight-letter word for a large guinea pig—like rodent?
Capybara.
I have a surprise! Close your eyes.
Okay.
TA-DA!

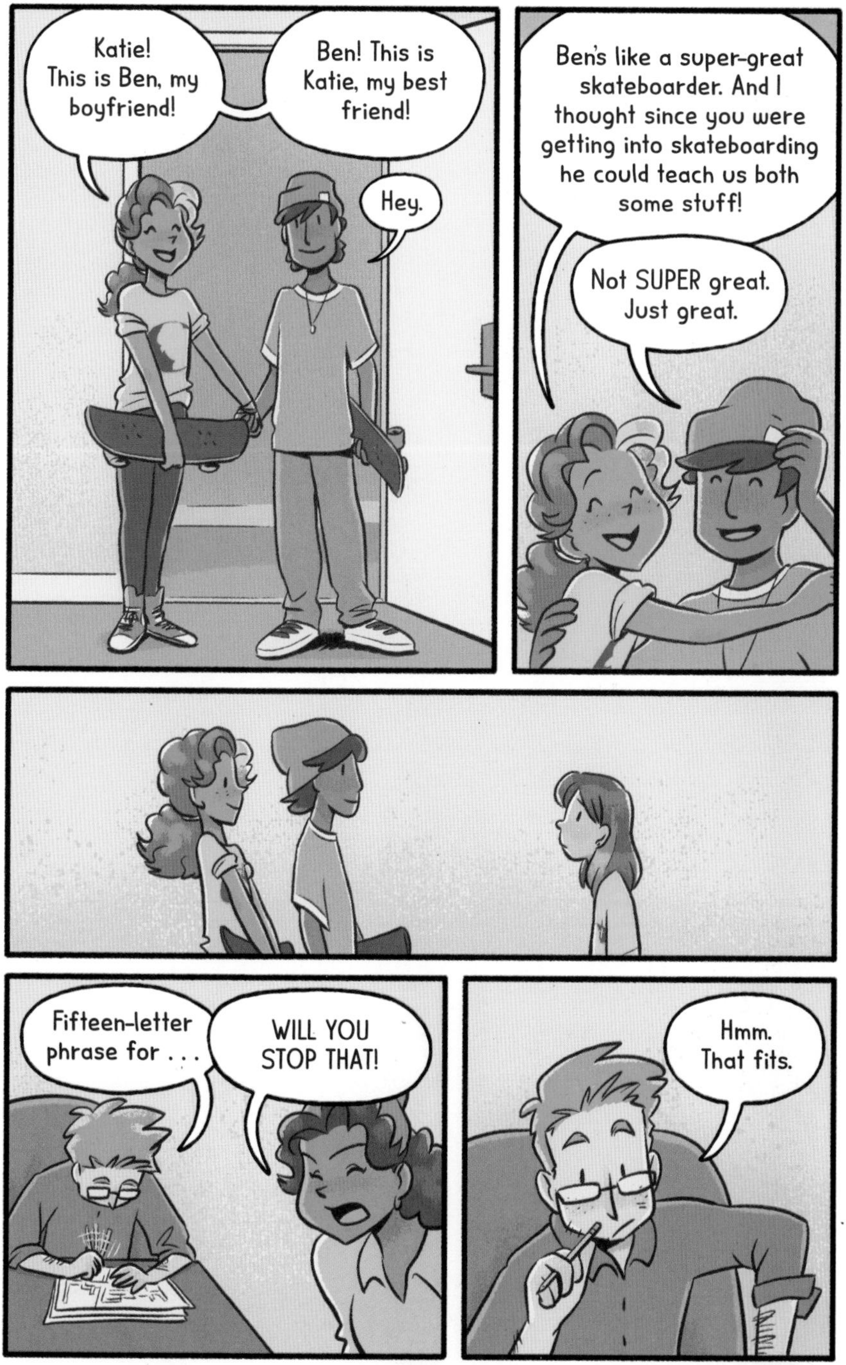
Katie!
This is Ben, my boyfriend!
Ben! This is Katie, my best friend!
Hey.
Ben's like a super-great skateboarder. And I thought since you were getting into skateboarding he could teach us both some stuff!
Not SUPER great. Just great.
Fifteen-letter phrase for . . .
WILL YOU STOP THAT!
Hmm. That fits.

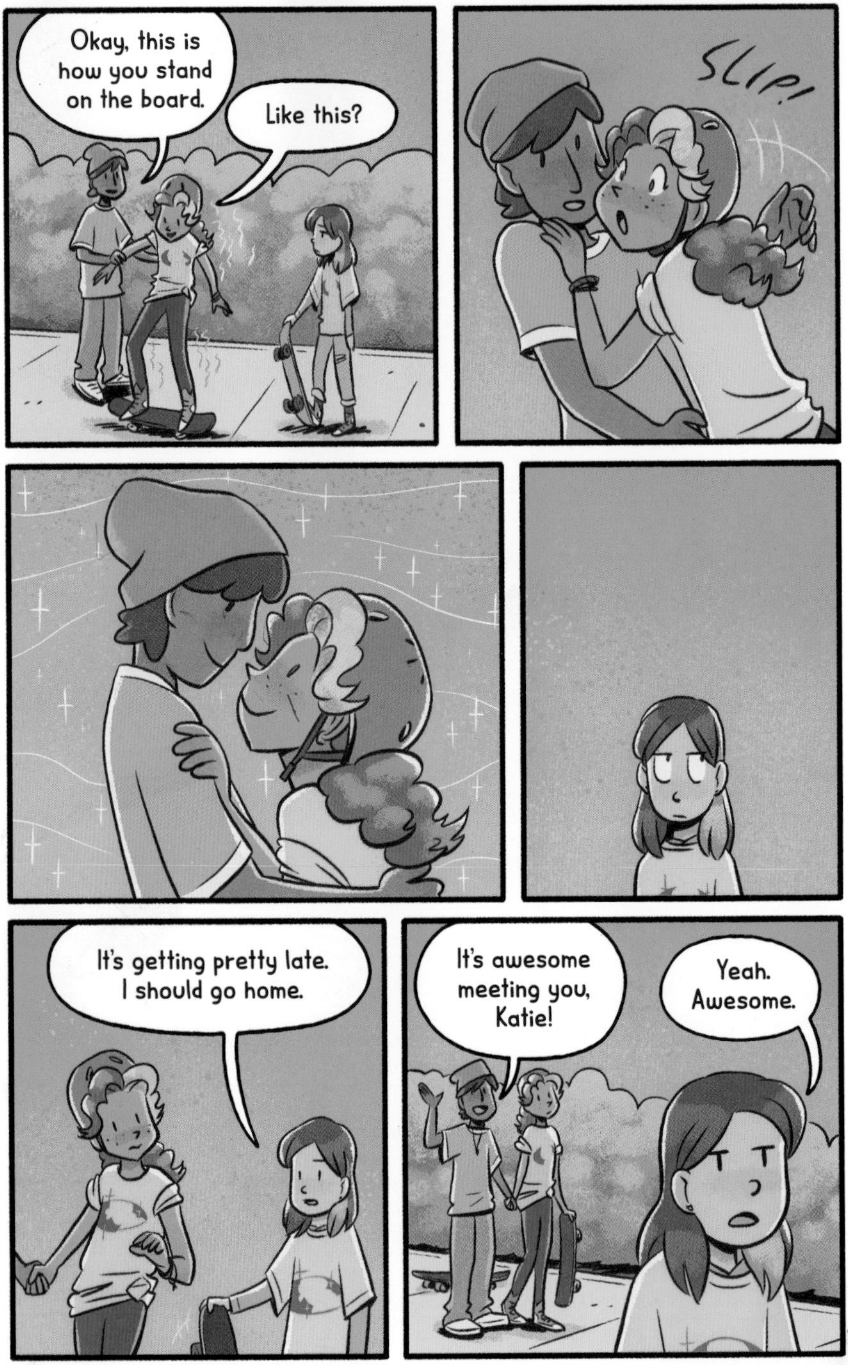
Okay, this is how you stand on the board.
Like this?
SLIP!
It's getting pretty late. I should go home.
It's awesome meeting you, Katie!
Yeah. Awesome.

CHAPTER FOUR

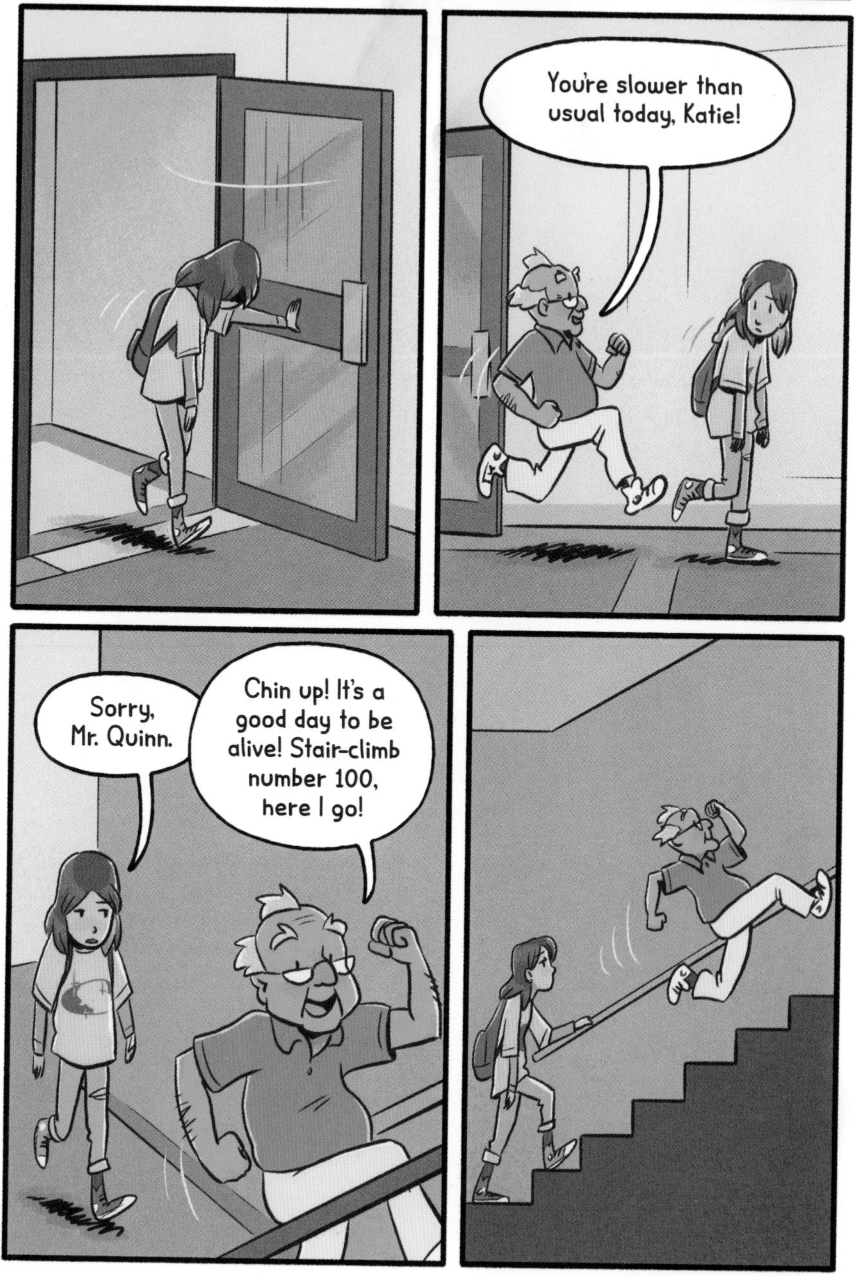

You're slower than usual today, Katie!
Sorry, Mr. Quinn.
Chin up! It's a good day to be alive! Stair-climb number 100, here I go!

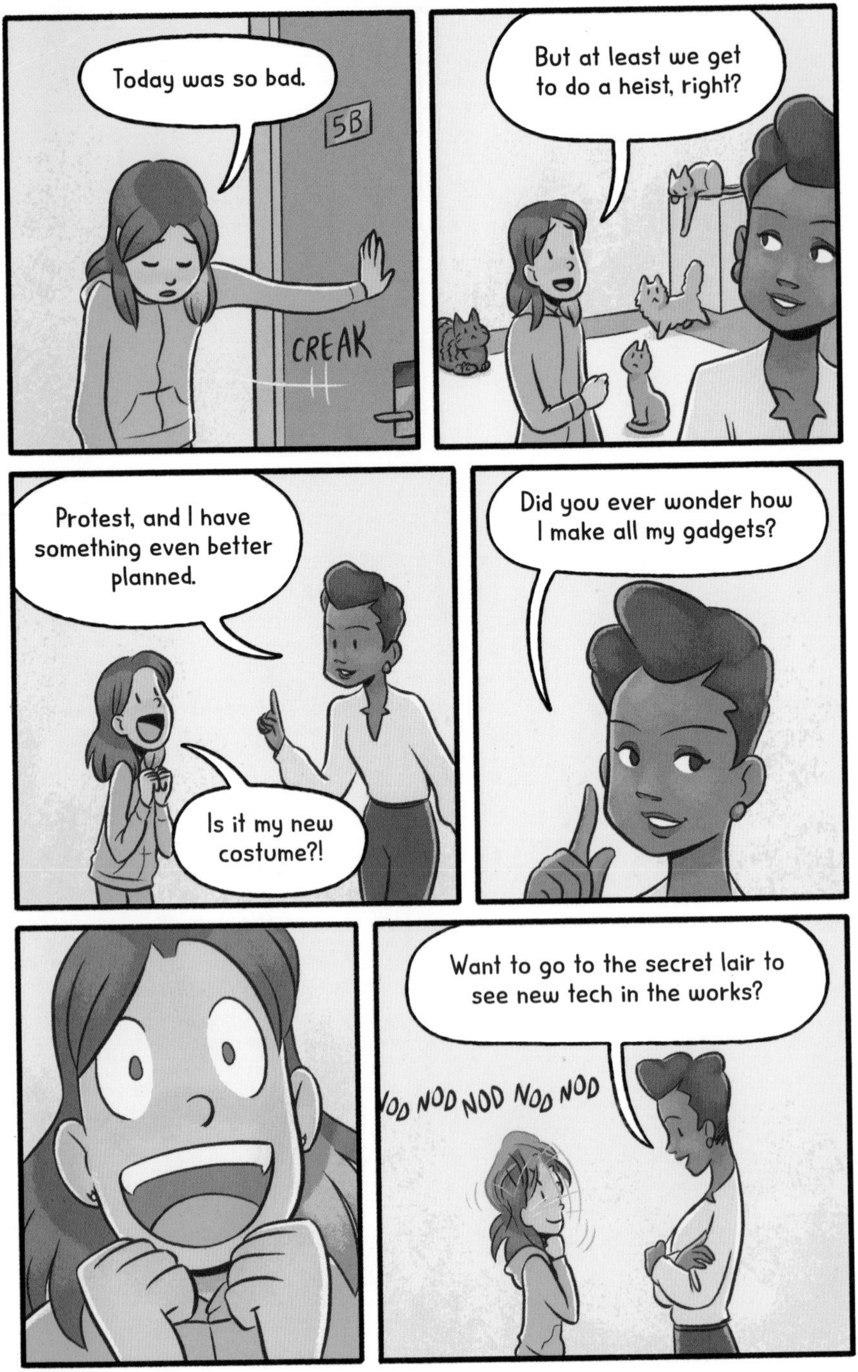
Today was so bad.
5B
CREAK
But at least we get to do a heist, right?
Protest, and I have something even better planned.
Is it my new costume?!
Did you ever wonder how I make all my gadgets?
Want to go to the secret lair to see new tech in the works?
NOD NOD NOD NOD NOD

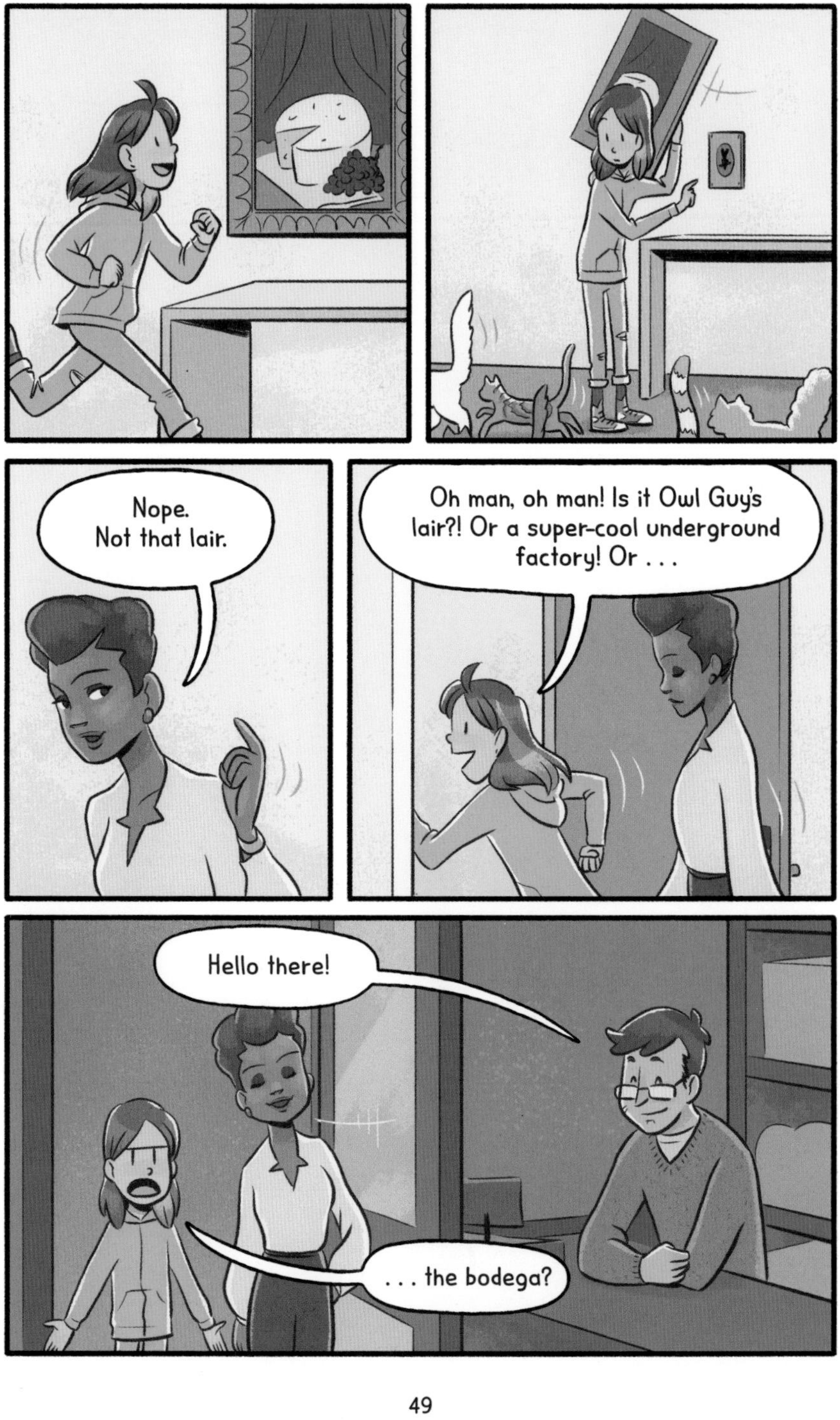
Nope.
Not that lair.
Oh man, oh man! Is it Owl Guy's lair?! Or a super-cool underground factory! Or . . .
Hello there!
. . . the bodega?

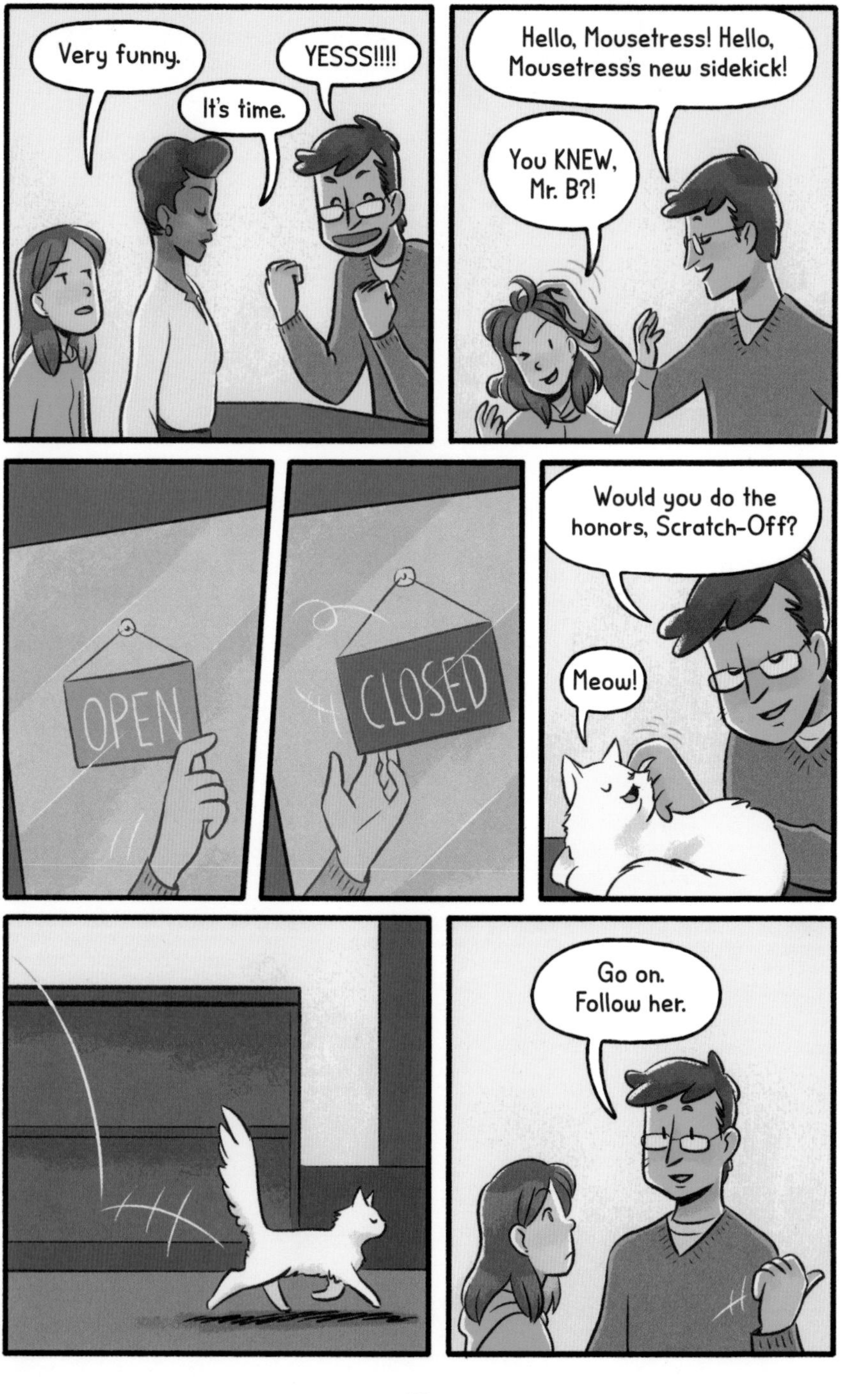
Very funny.
It's time.
YESSS!!!!
Hello, Mousetress! Hello, Mousetress's new sidekick!
You KNEW, Mr. B?!
OPEN
CLOSED
Would you do the honors, Scratch-Off?
Meow!
Go on. Follow her.

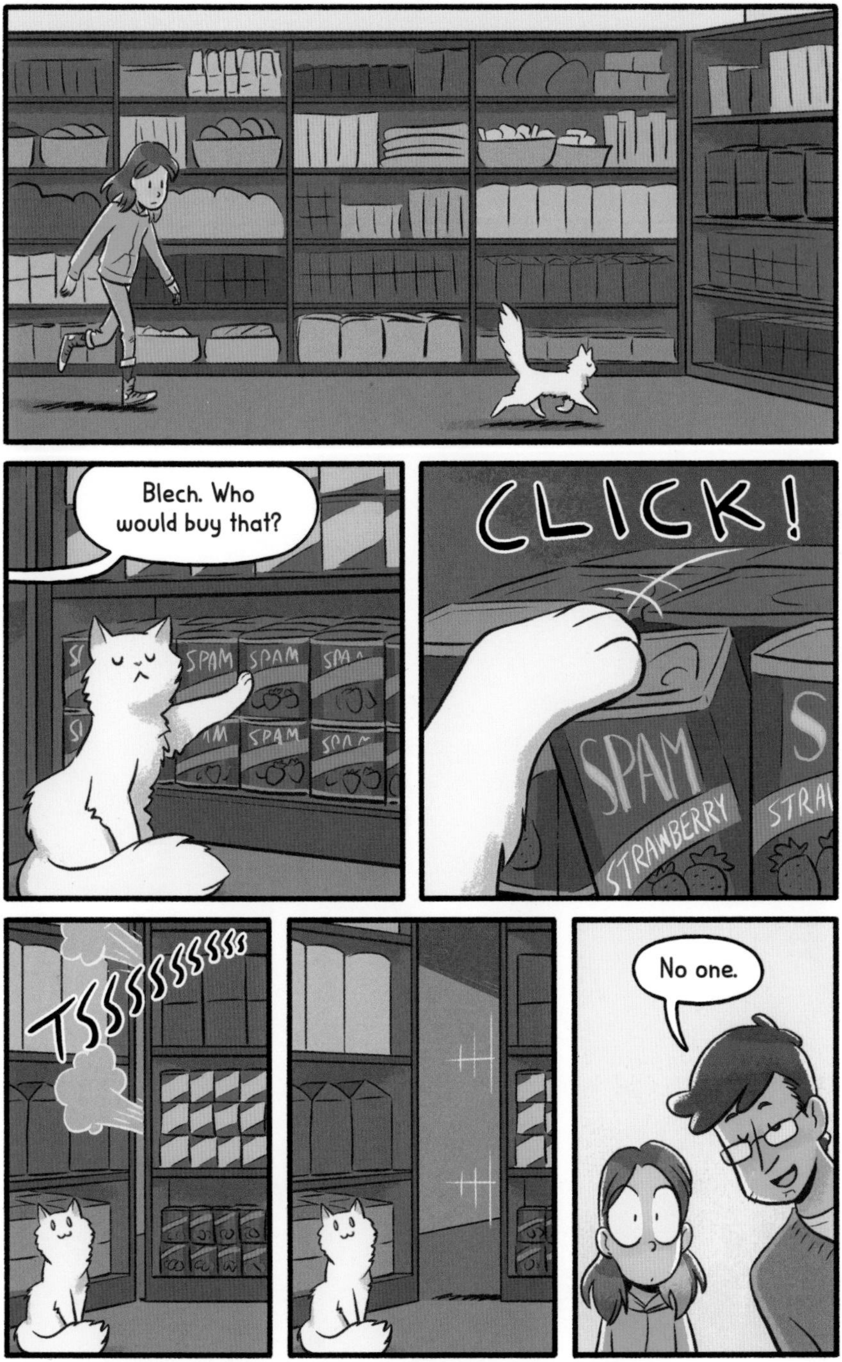
Blech. Who would buy that?
CLICK!
SPAM
STRAWBERRY
TSSSSSSSSSS
No one.

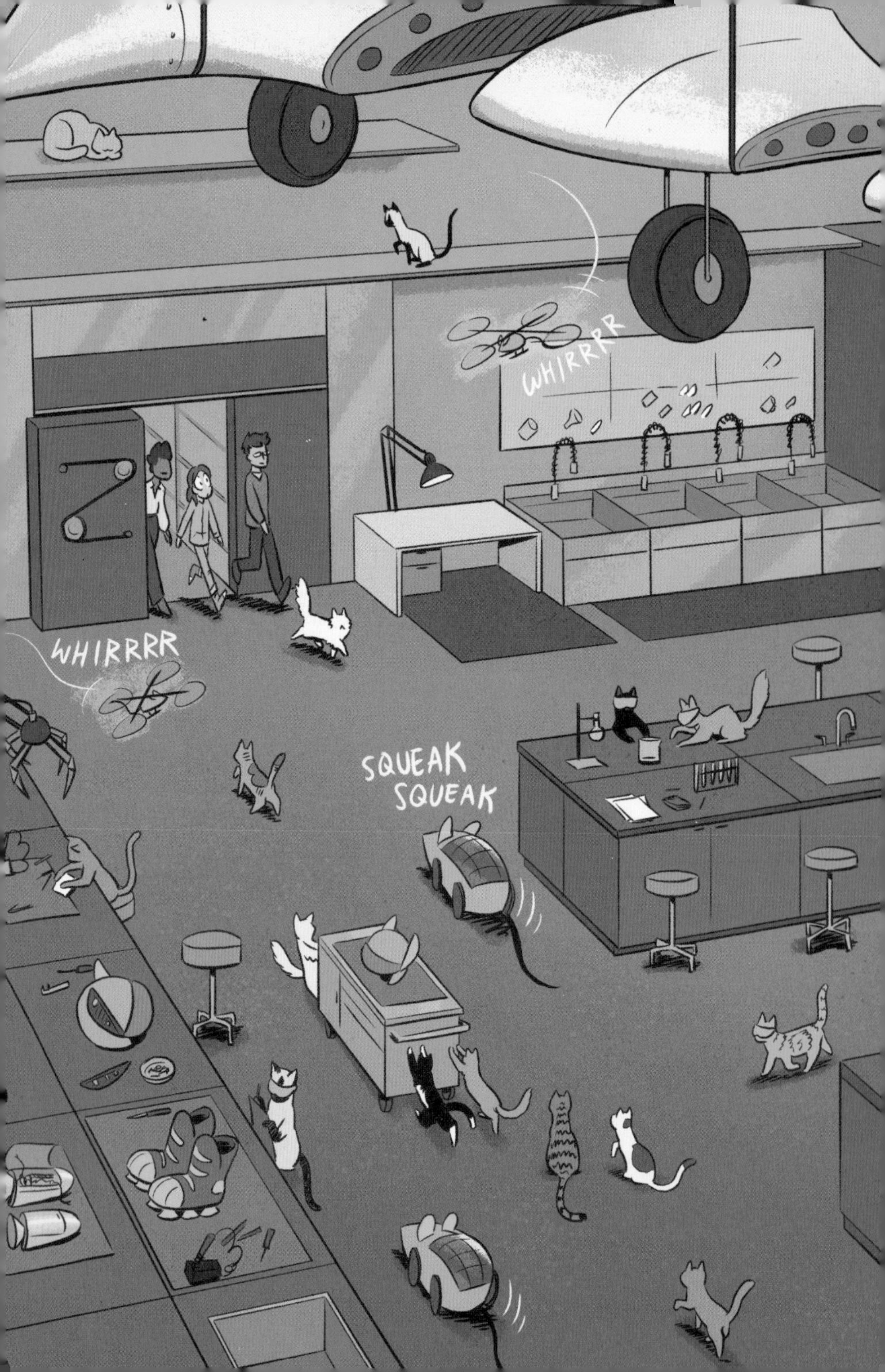
WHIRRRR
WHIRRRR
SQUEAK
SQUEAK

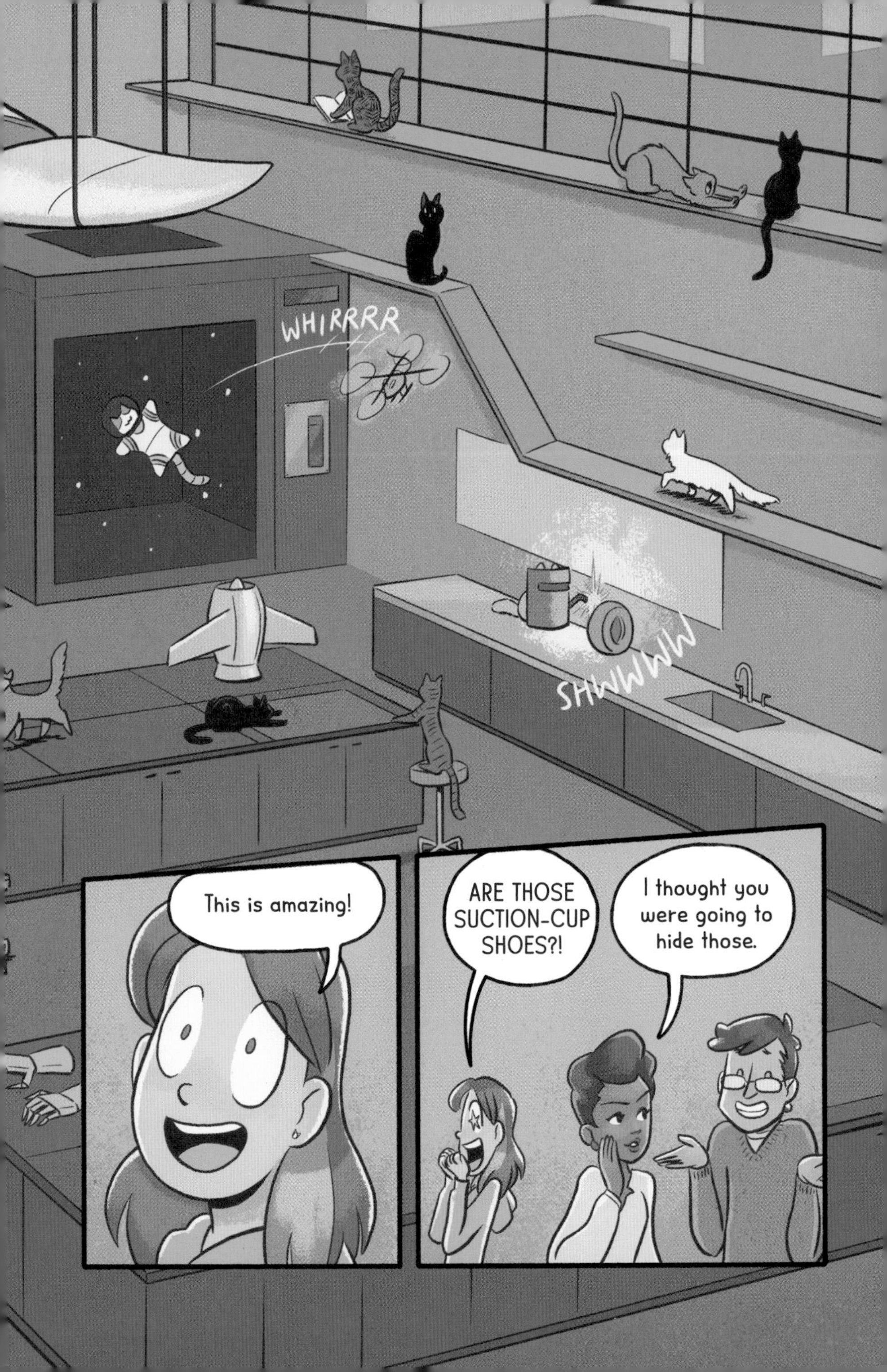
WHIRRRR
SHWWWW
This is amazing!
ARE THOSE SUCTION-CUP SHOES?!
I thought you were going to hide those.

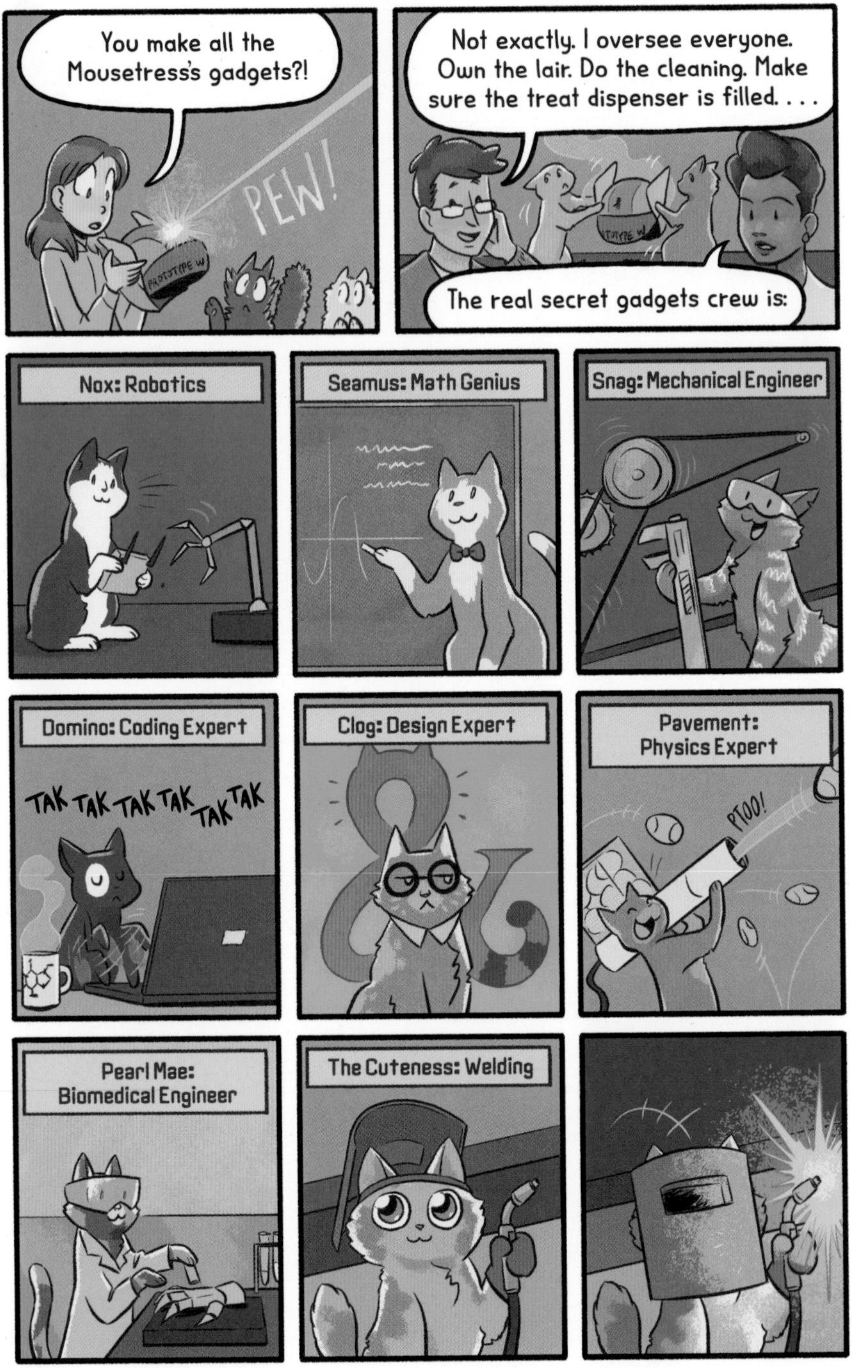
You make all the Mousetress's gadgets?!
PEW!
Not exactly. I oversee everyone. Own the lair. Do the cleaning. Make sure the treat dispenser is filled. . . .
The real secret gadgets crew is:
Nox: Robotics
Seamus: Math Genius
Snag: Mechanical Engineer
Domino: Coding Expert
TAK TAK TAK TAK TAK TAK
Clog: Design Expert
Pavement: Physics Expert
PTOO!
Pearl Mae: Biomedical Engineer
The Cuteness: Welding

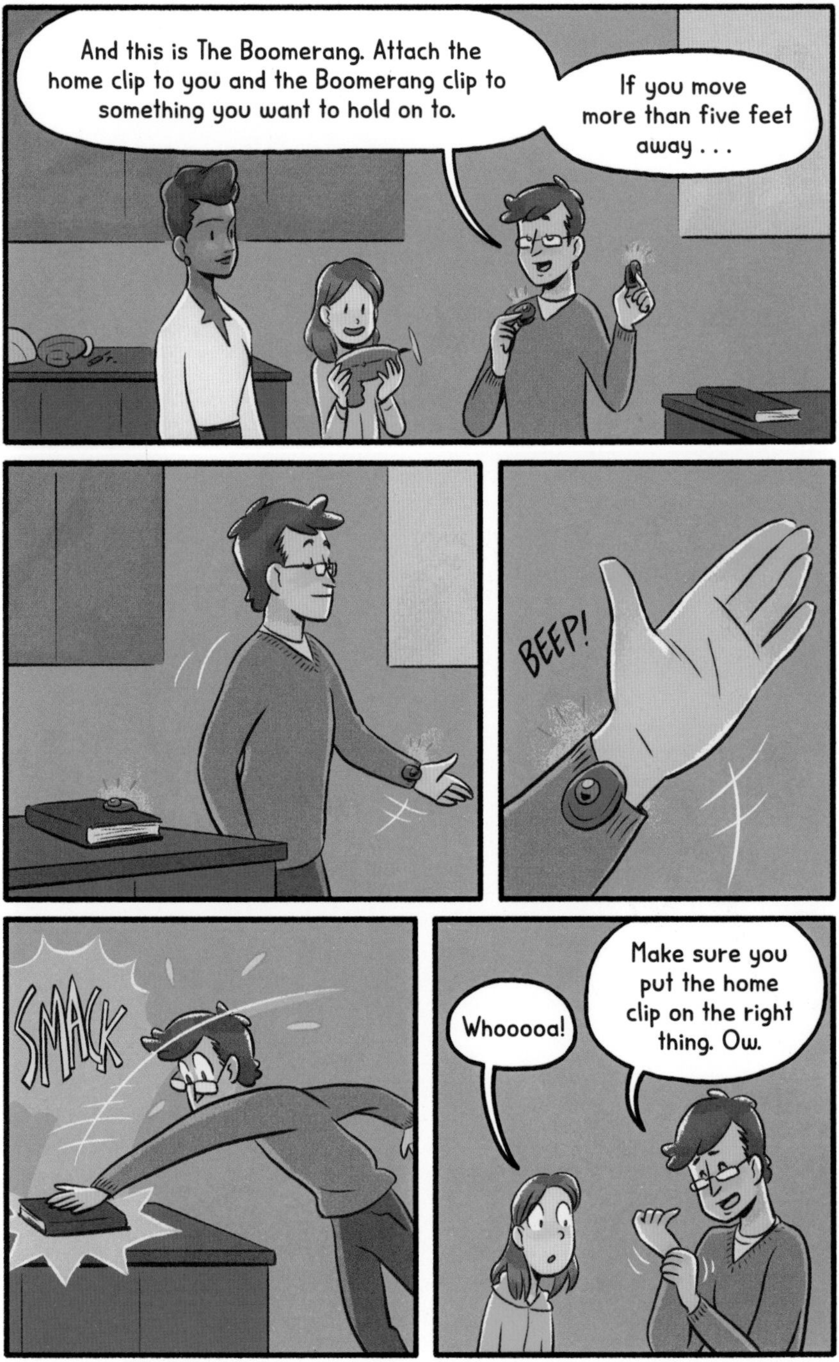
And this is The Boomerang. Attach the home clip to you and the Boomerang clip to something you want to hold on to.
If you move more than five feet away . . .
BEEP!
SMACK
Whoooooa!
Make sure you put the home clip on the right thing. Ow.

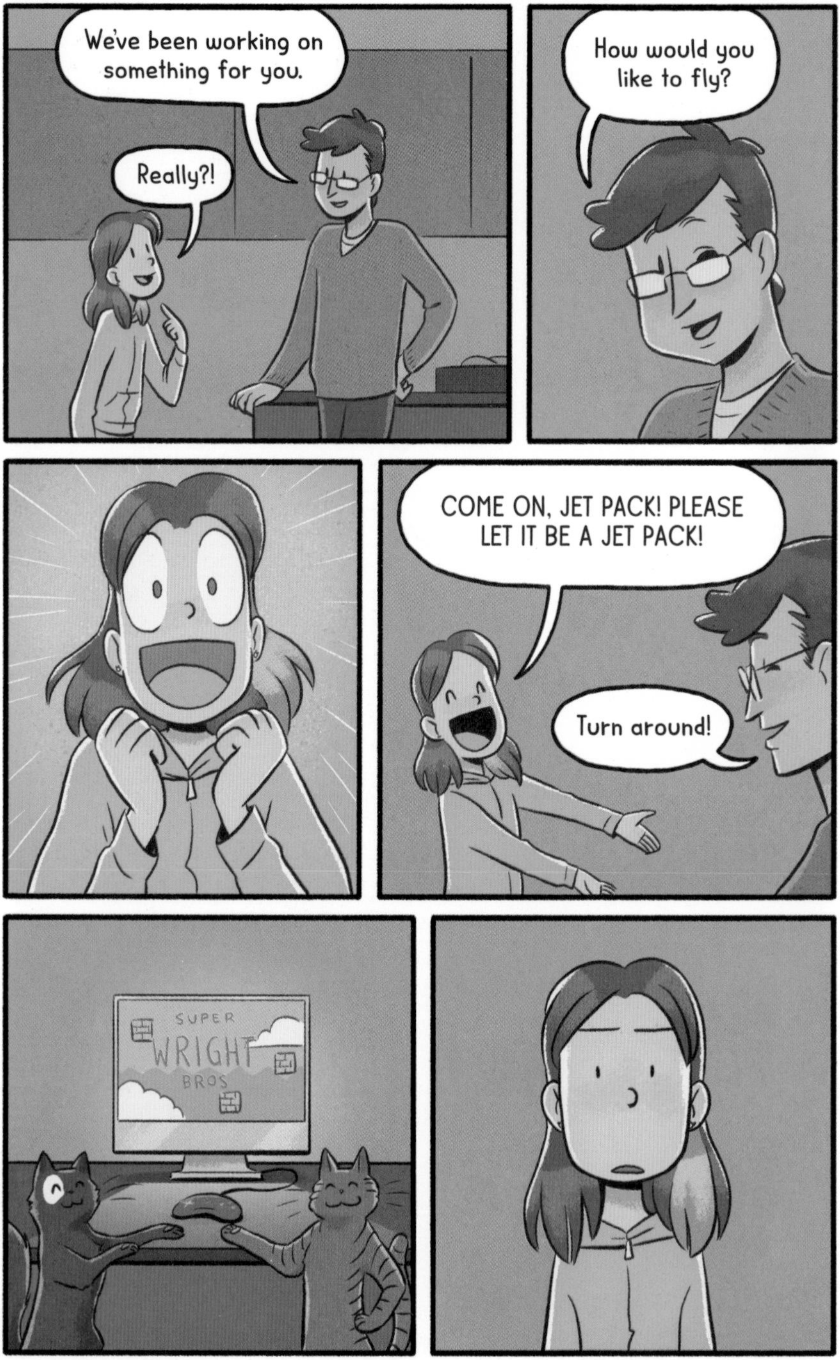
We've been working on something for you.
Really?!
How would you like to fly?
COME ON, JET PACK! PLEASE LET IT BE A JET PACK!
Turn around!
SUPER
WRIGHT
BROS

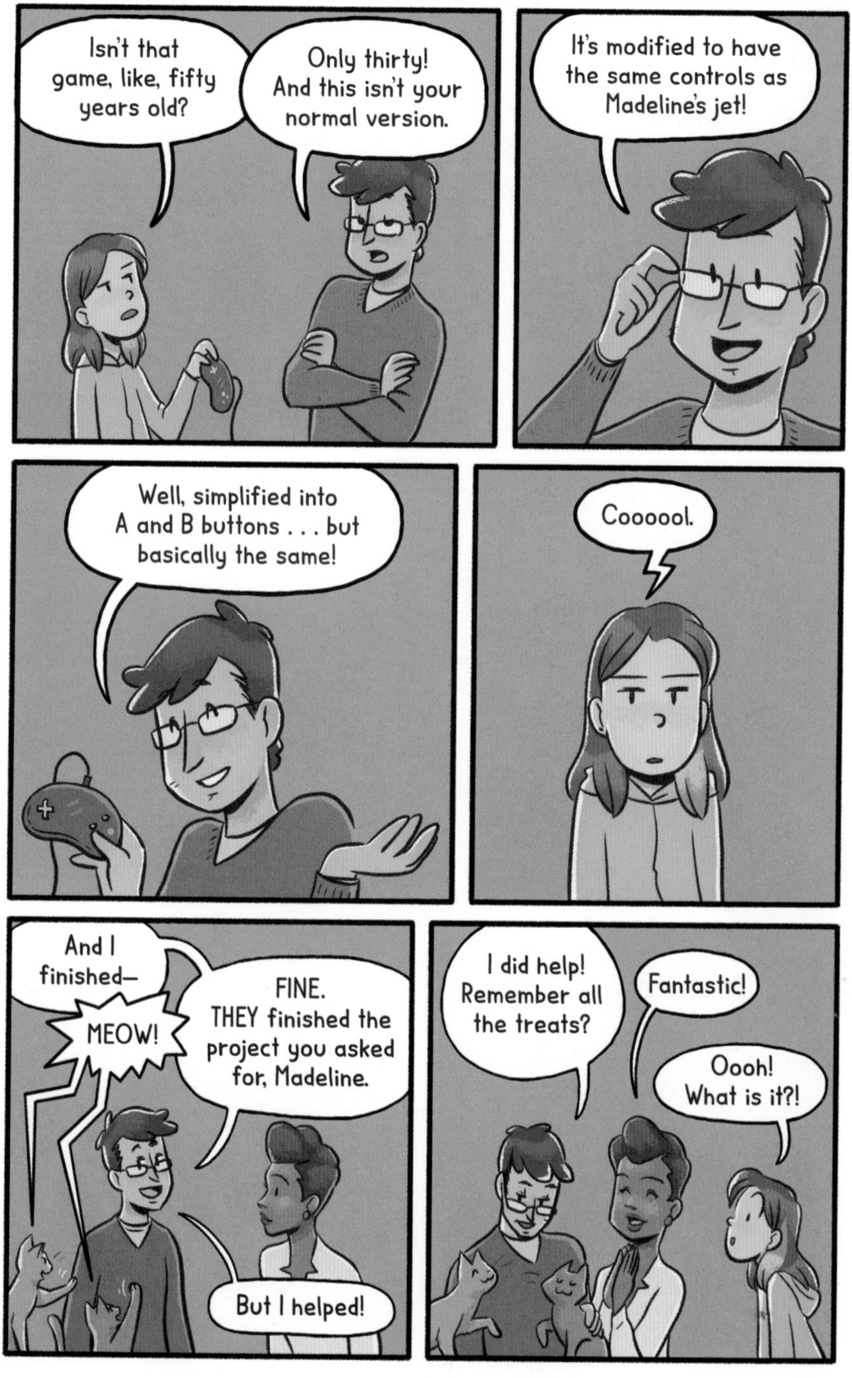
Isn't that game, like, fifty years old?
Only thirty! And this isn't your normal version.
It's modified to have the same controls as Madeline's jet!
Well, simplified into A and B buttons . . . but basically the same!
Coooool.
And I finished—
MEOW!
FINE. THEY finished the project you asked for, Madeline.
But I helped!
I did help! Remember all the treats?
Fantastic!
Oooh! What is it?!

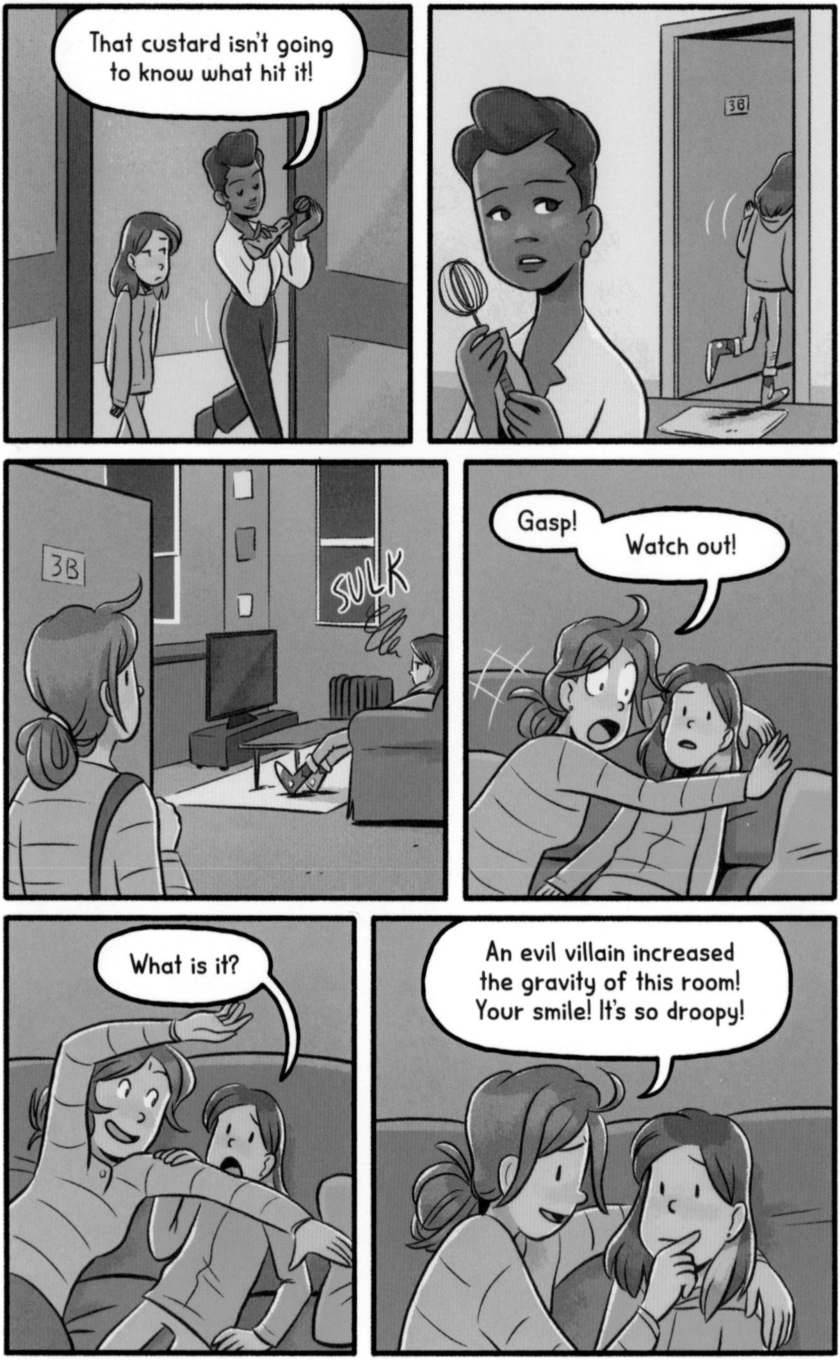

That custard isn't going to know what hit it!
3B
3B
SULK
Gasp!
Watch out!
What is it?
An evil villain increased the gravity of this room! Your smile! It's so droopy!

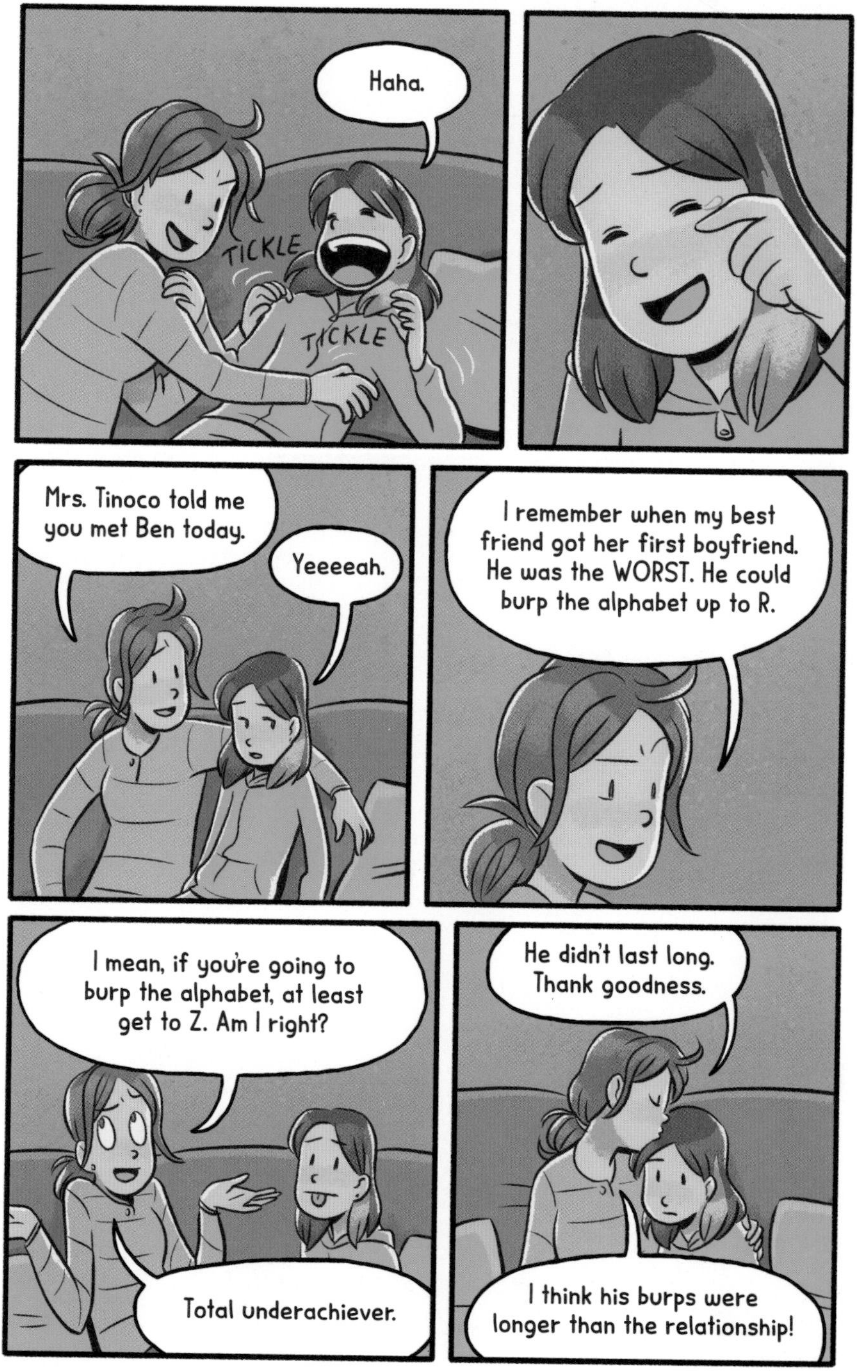
Haha.
TICKLE
TICKLE
Mrs. Tinoco told me you met Ben today.
Yeeeeah.
I remember when my best friend got her first boyfriend. He was the WORST. He could burp the alphabet up to R.
I mean, if you're going to burp the alphabet, at least get to Z. Am I right?
Total underachiever.
He didn't last long. Thank goodness.
I think his burps were longer than the relationship!

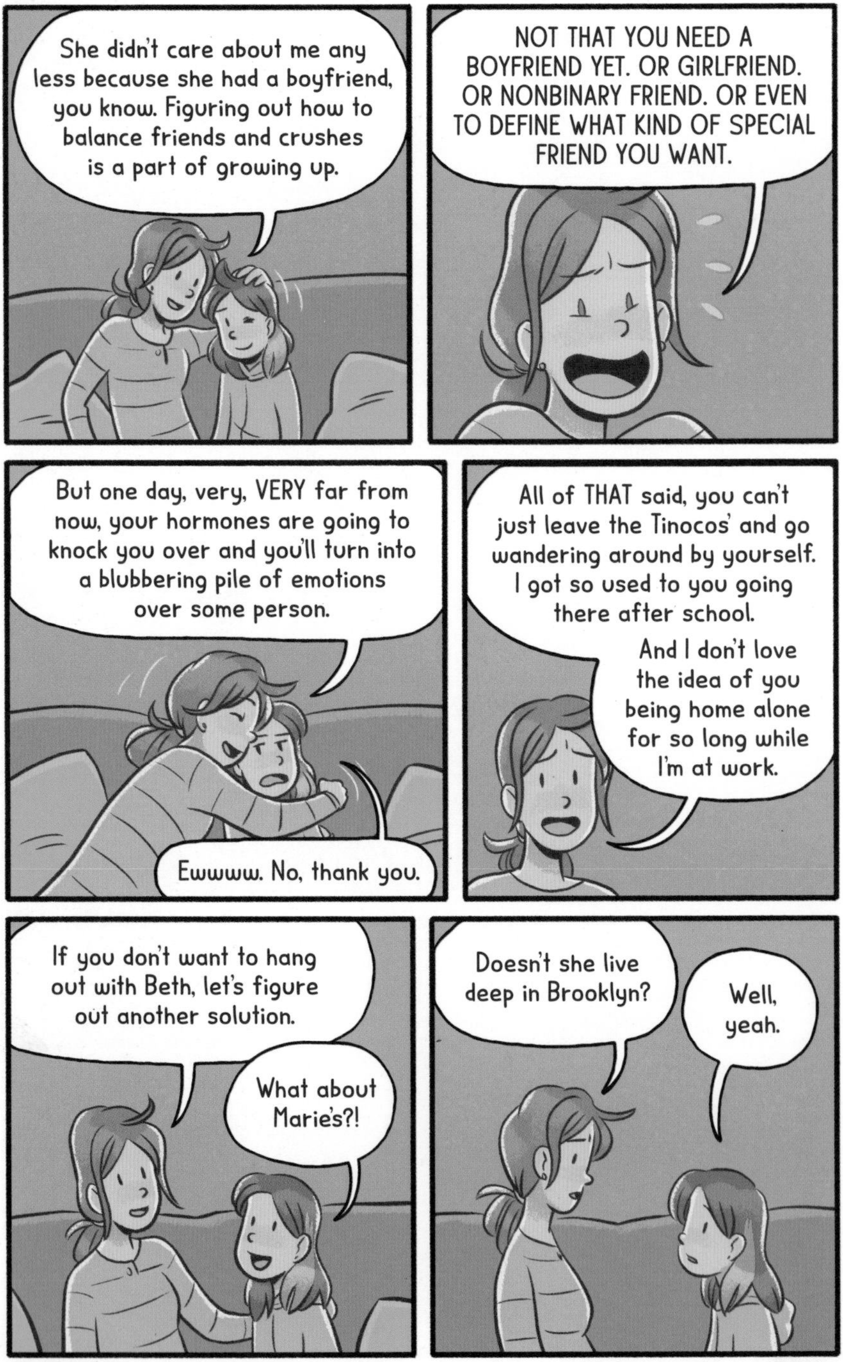
She didn't care about me any less because she had a boyfriend, you know. Figuring out how to balance friends and crushes is a part of growing up.
NOT THAT YOU NEED A BOYFRIEND YET. OR GIRLFRIEND. OR NONBINARY FRIEND. OR EVEN TO DEFINE WHAT KIND OF SPECIAL FRIEND YOU WANT.
But one day, very, VERY far from now, your hormones are going to knock you over and you'll turn into a blubbering pile of emotions over some person.
Ewwww. No, thank you.
All of THAT said, you can't just leave the Tinocos' and go wandering around by yourself. I got so used to you going there after school.
And I don't love the idea of you being home alone for so long while I'm at work.
If you don't want to hang out with Beth, let's figure out another solution.
What about Marie's?!
Doesn't she live deep in Brooklyn?
Well, yeah.

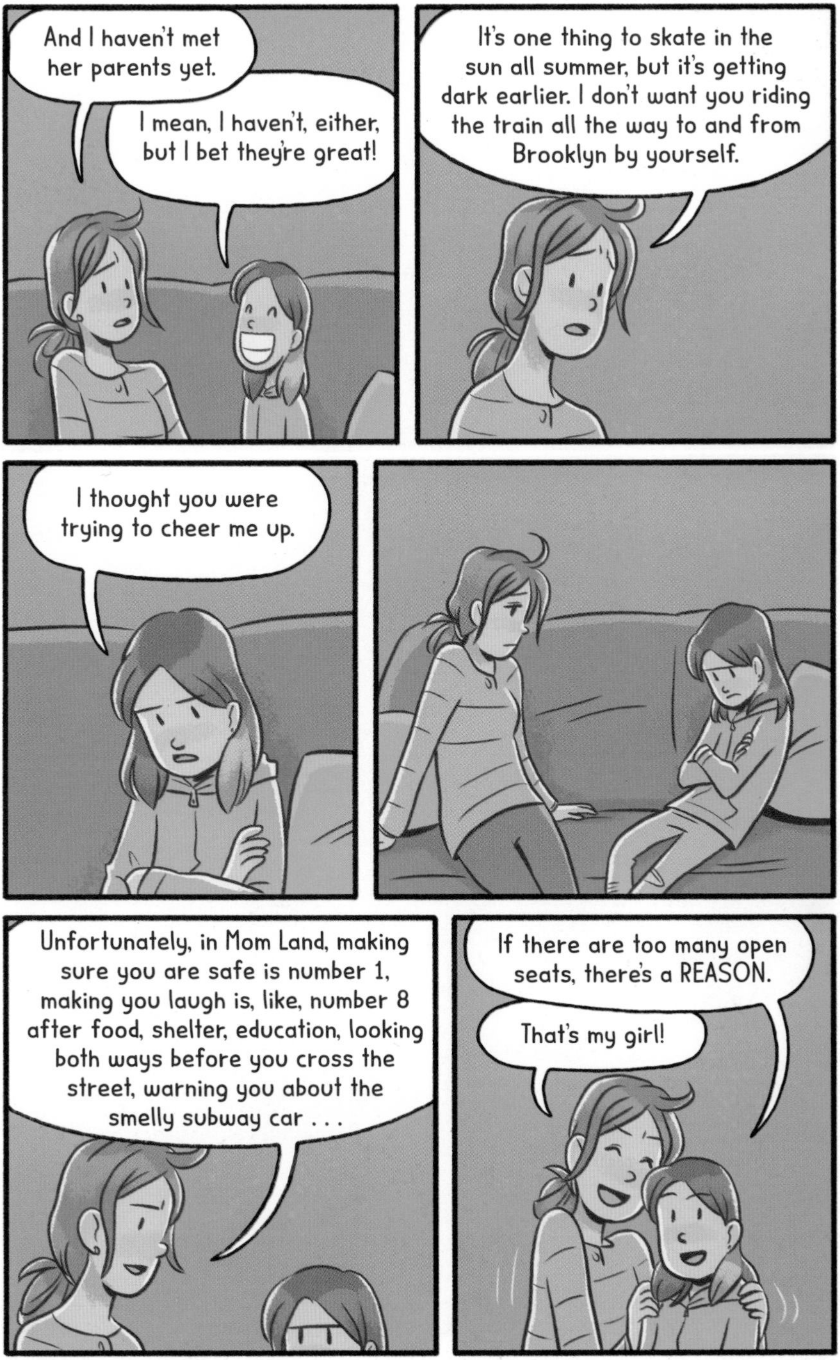
And I haven't met her parents yet.
I mean, I haven't, either, but I bet they're great!
It's one thing to skate in the sun all summer, but it's getting dark earlier. I don't want you riding the train all the way to and from Brooklyn by yourself.
I thought you were trying to cheer me up.
Unfortunately, in Mom Land, making sure you are safe is number 1, making you laugh is, like, number 8 after food, shelter, education, looking both ways before you cross the street, warning you about the smelly subway car . . .
If there are too many open seats, there's a REASON.
That's my girl!

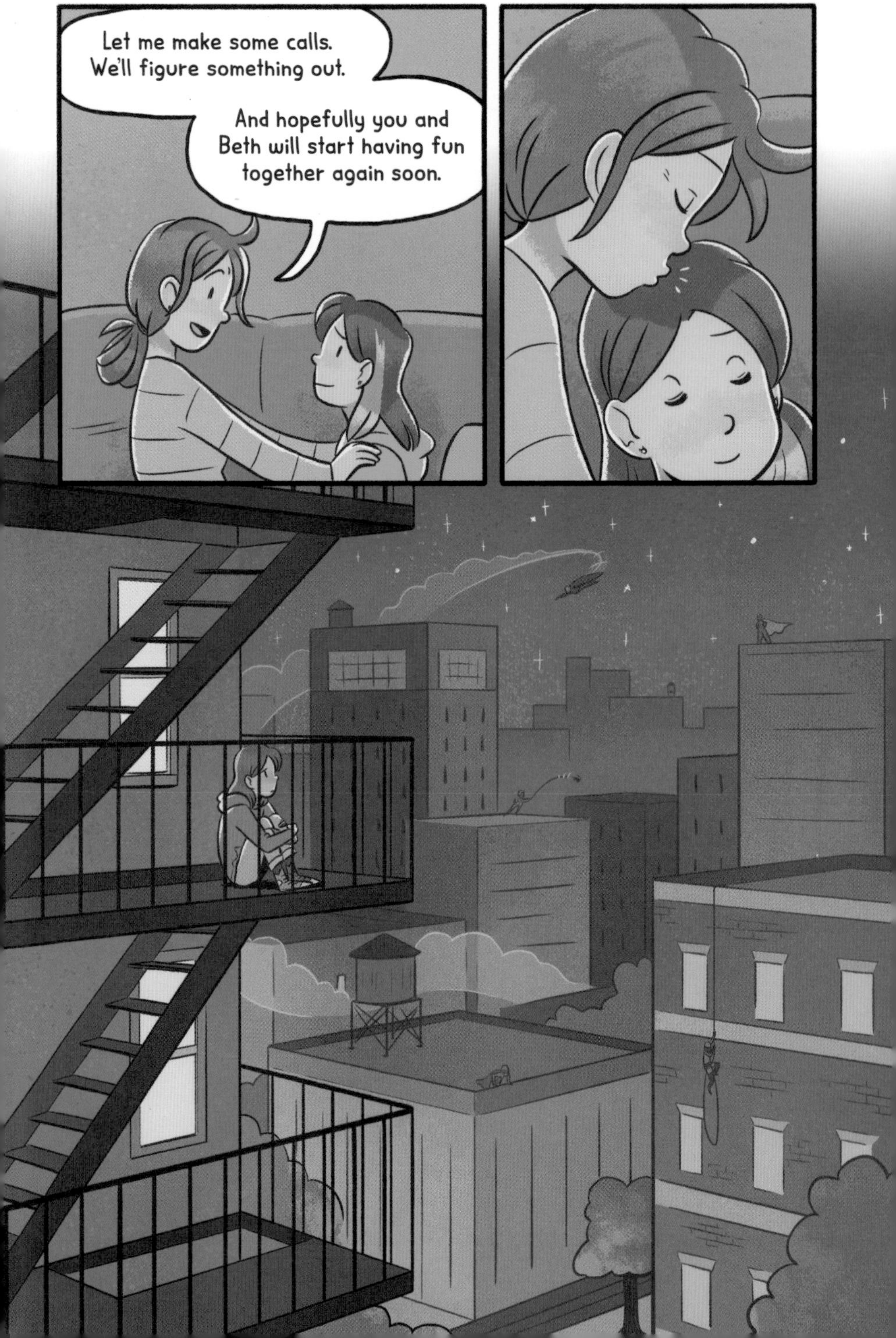
Let me make some calls. We'll figure something out.
And hopefully you and Beth will start having fun together again soon.

CHAPTER FIVE

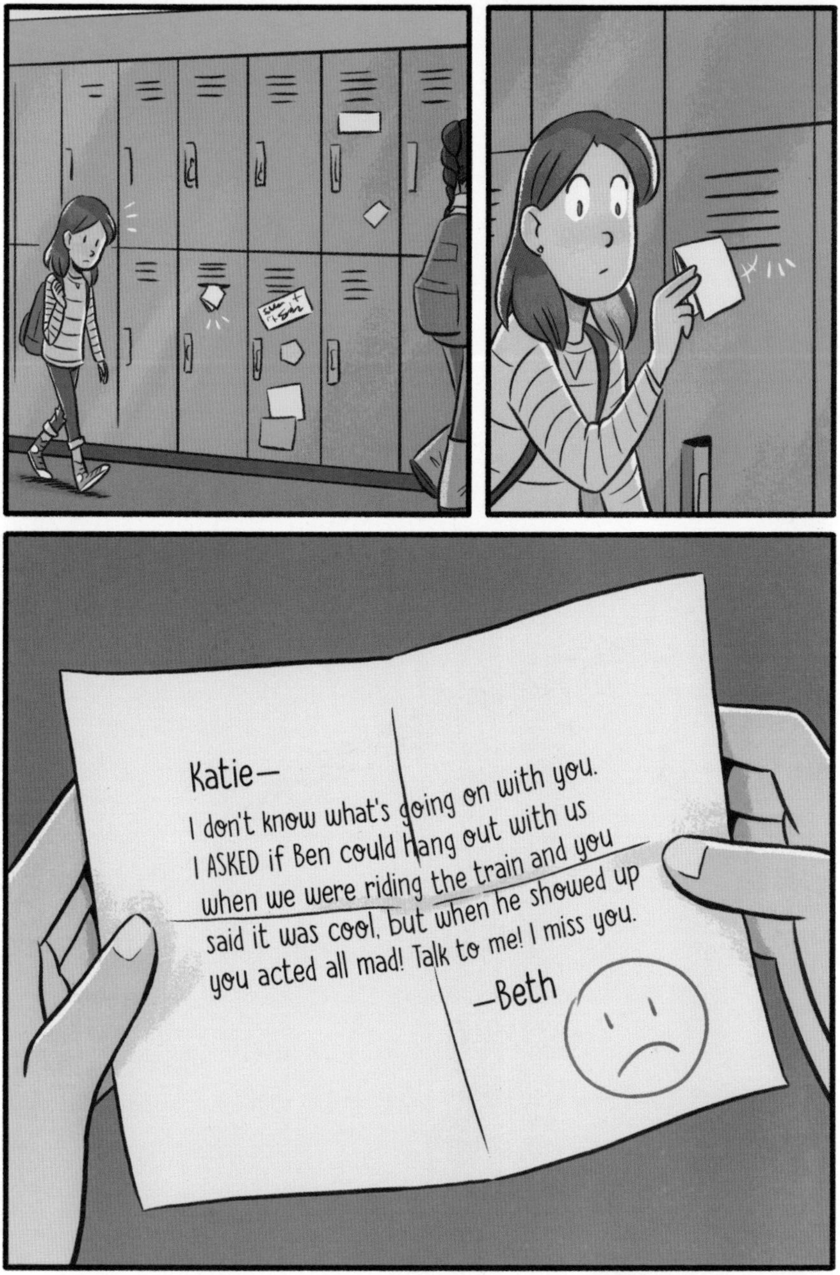

Katie—
I don't know what's going on with you.
I ASKED if Ben could hang out with us
when we were riding the train and you
said it was cool, but when he showed up
you acted all mad! Talk to me! I miss you.
—Beth

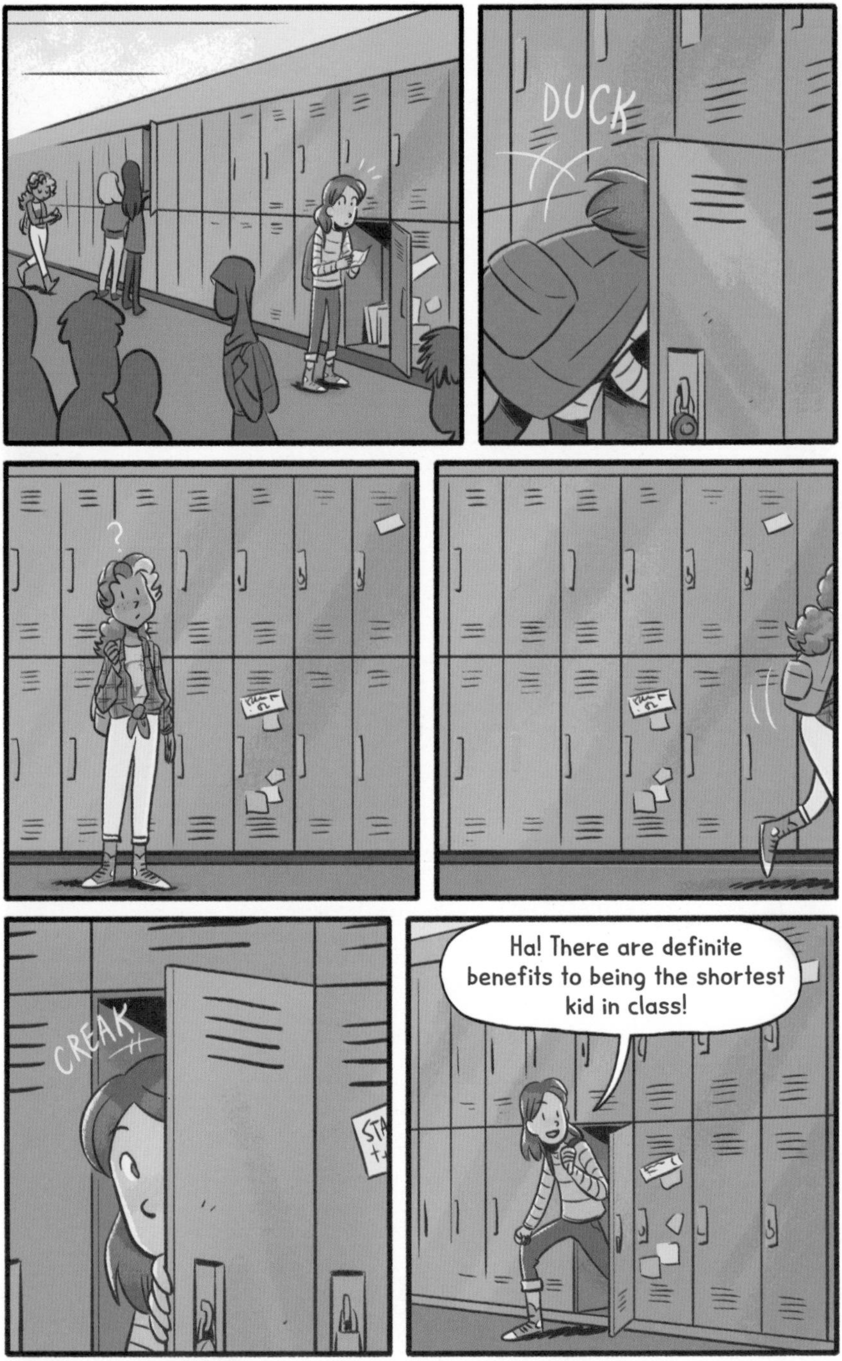
DUCK
CREAK
Ha! There are definite benefits to being the shortest kid in class!

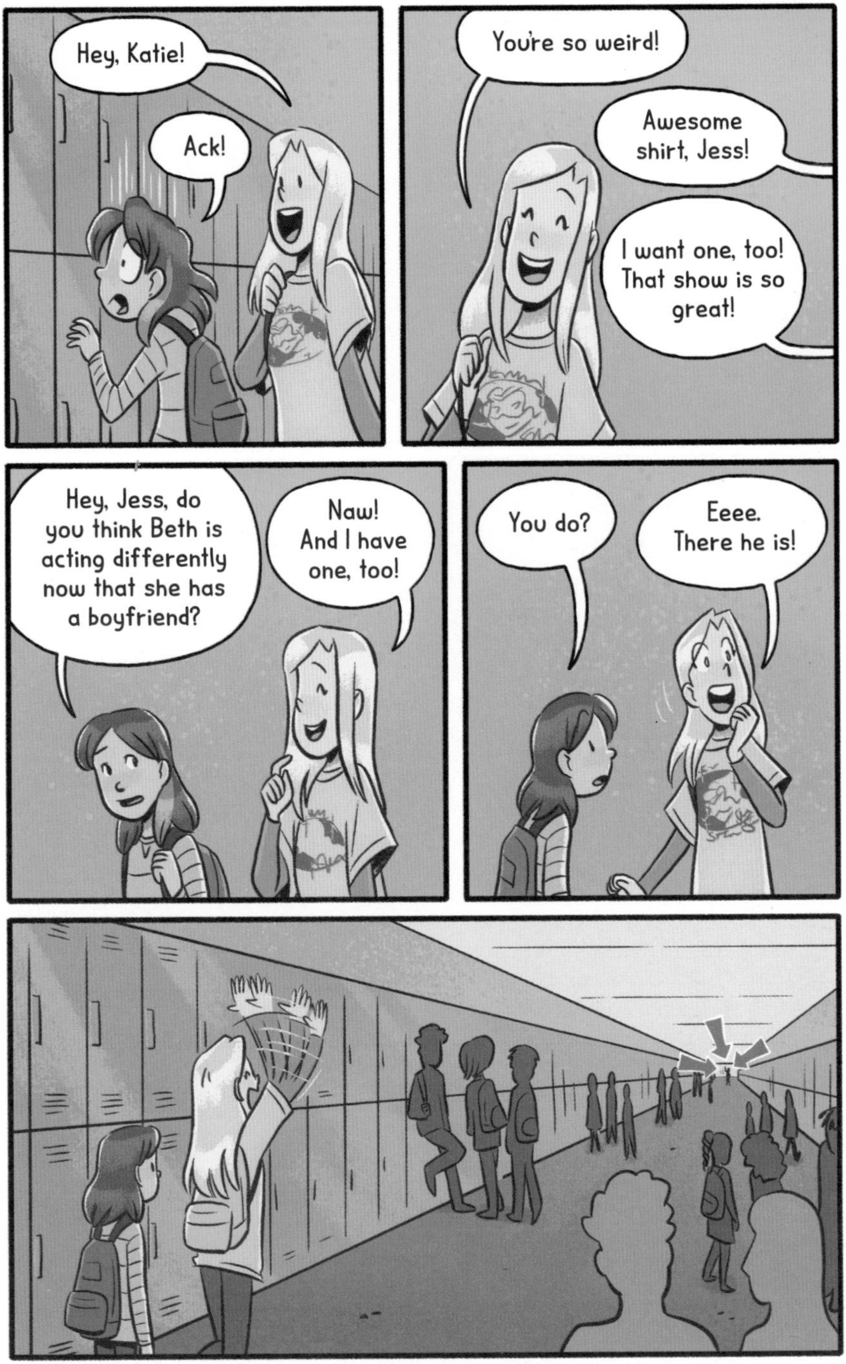
Hey, Katie!
Ack!
You're so weird!
Awesome shirt, Jess!
I want one, too! That show is so great!
Hey, Jess, do you think Beth is acting differently now that she has a boyfriend?
Naw! And I have one, too!
You do?
Eeee. There he is!

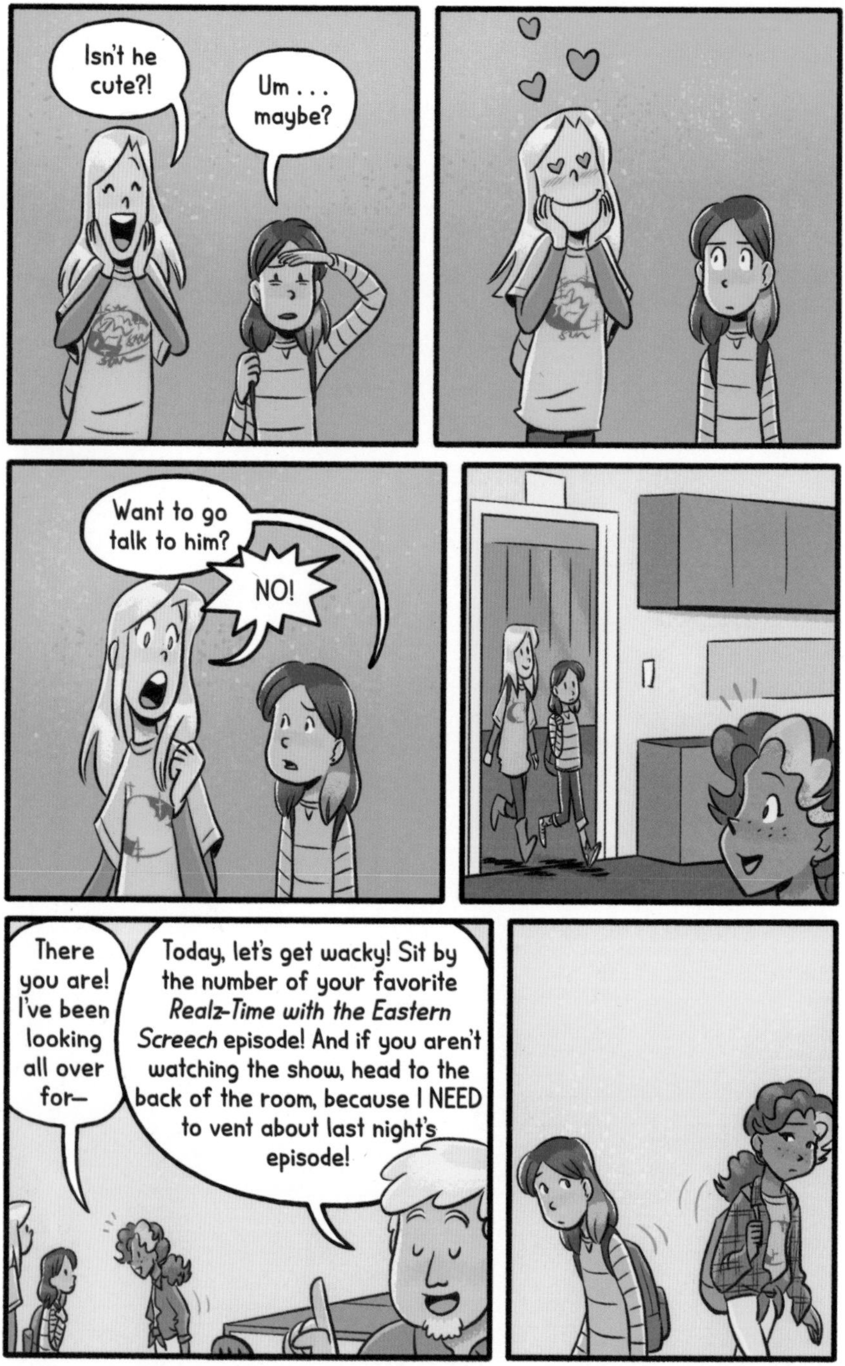
Isn't he cute?!
Um . . . maybe?
Want to go talk to him?
NO!
There you are! I've been looking all over for—
Today, let's get wacky! Sit by the number of your favorite *Realz-Time with the Eastern Screech* episode! And if you aren't watching the show, head to the back of the room, because I NEED to vent about last night's episode!

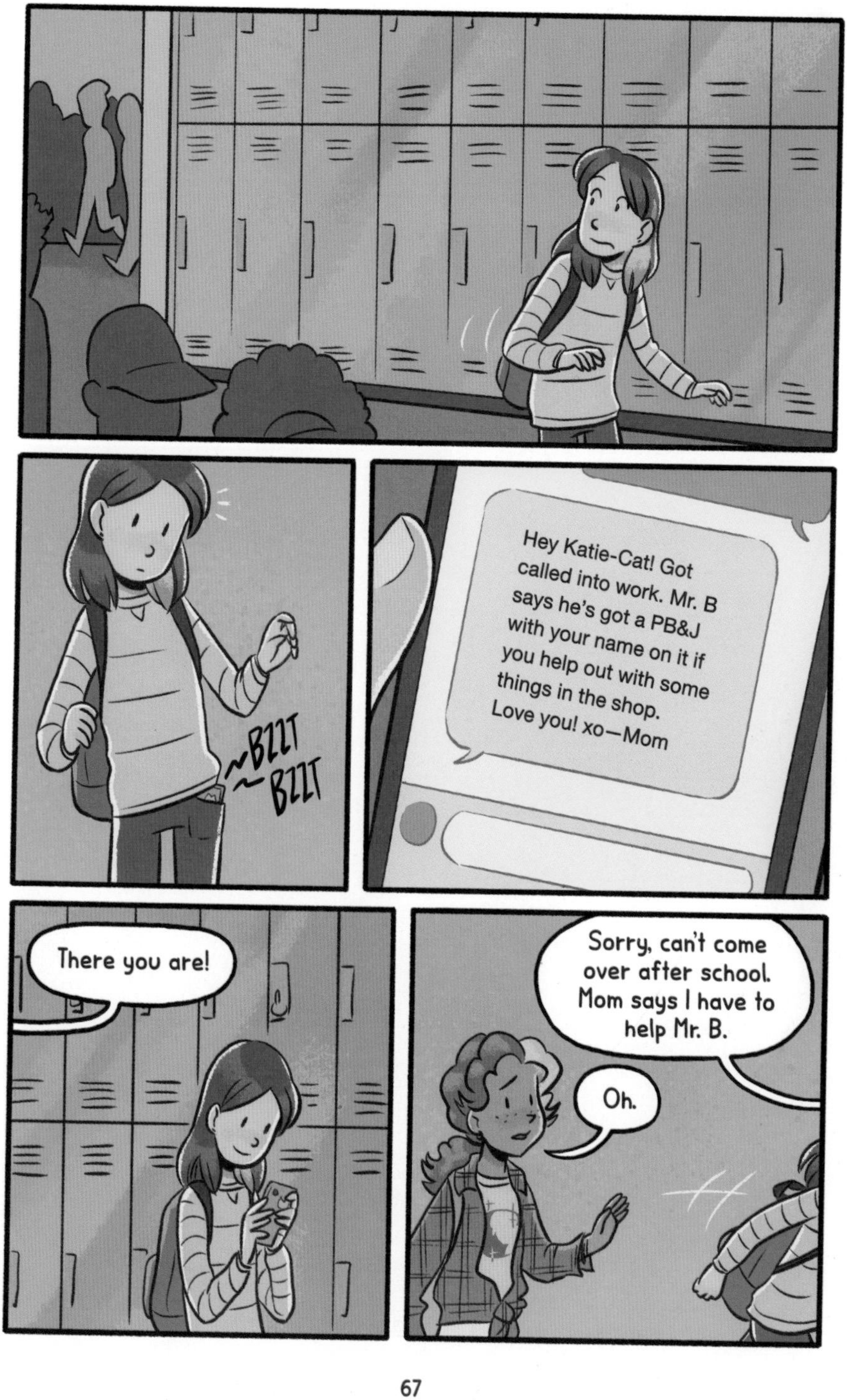
~BZZT
~BZZT
Hey Katie-Cat! Got called into work. Mr. B says he's got a PB&J with your name on it if you help out with some things in the shop. Love you! xo—Mom
There you are!
Sorry, can't come over after school. Mom says I have to help Mr. B.
Oh.

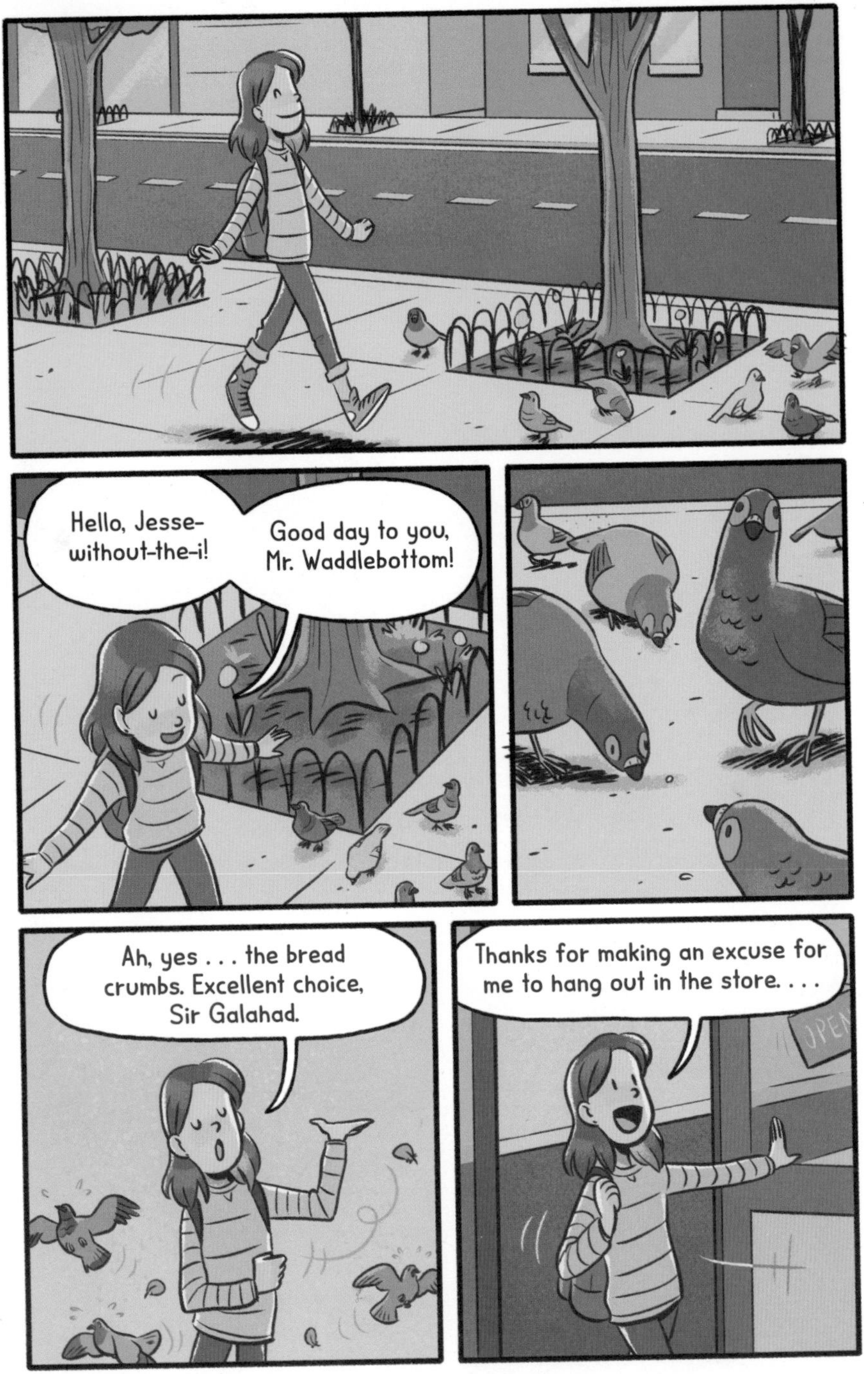

Hello, Jesse-without-the-i!
Good day to you, Mr. Waddlebottom!
Ah, yes . . . the bread crumbs. Excellent choice, Sir Galahad.
Thanks for making an excuse for me to hang out in the store. . . .

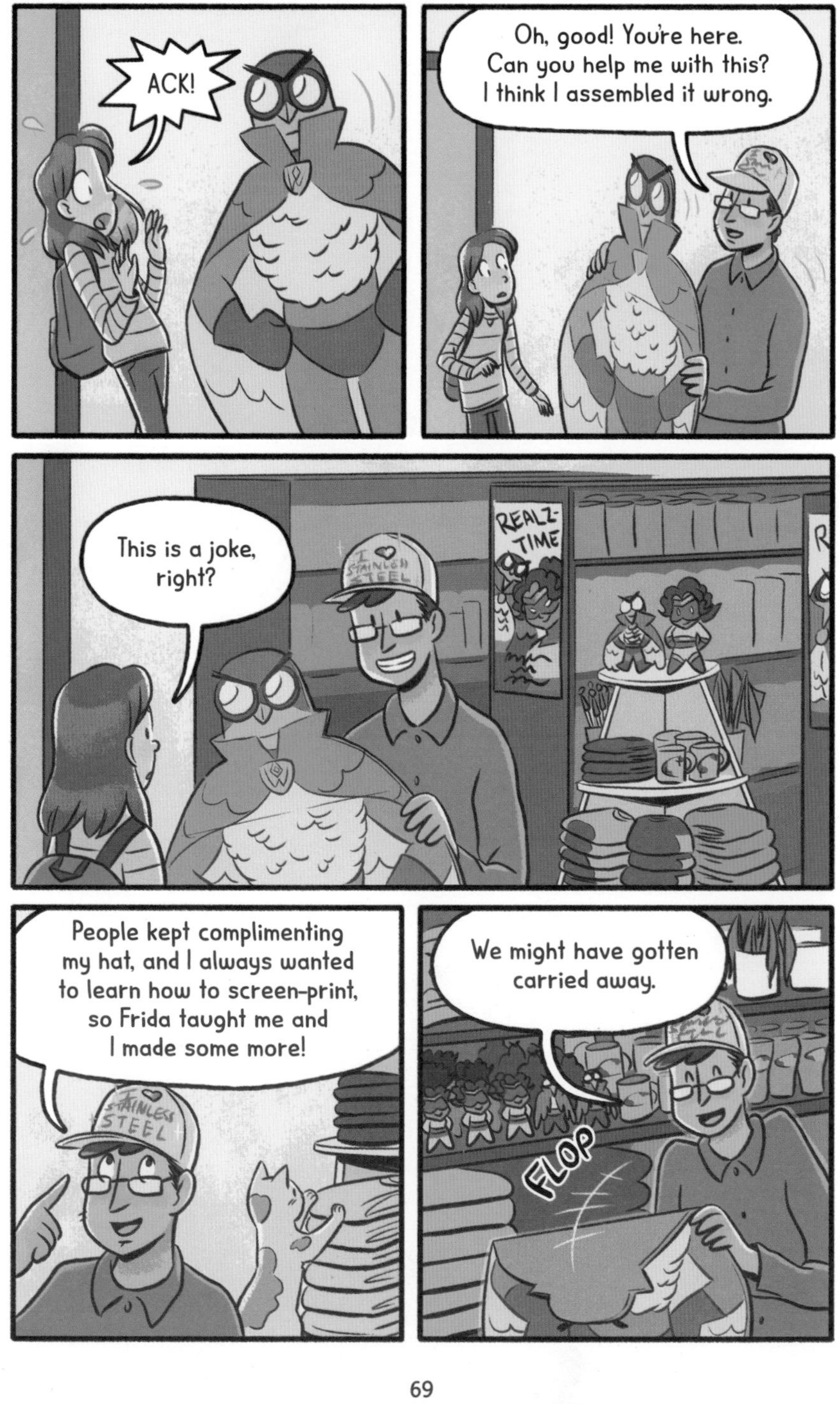
ACK!
Oh, good! You're here. Can you help me with this? I think I assembled it wrong.
REALZ-TIME
This is a joke, right?
People kept complimenting my hat, and I always wanted to learn how to screen-print, so Frida taught me and I made some more!
STAINLESS STEEL
We might have gotten carried away.
FLOP

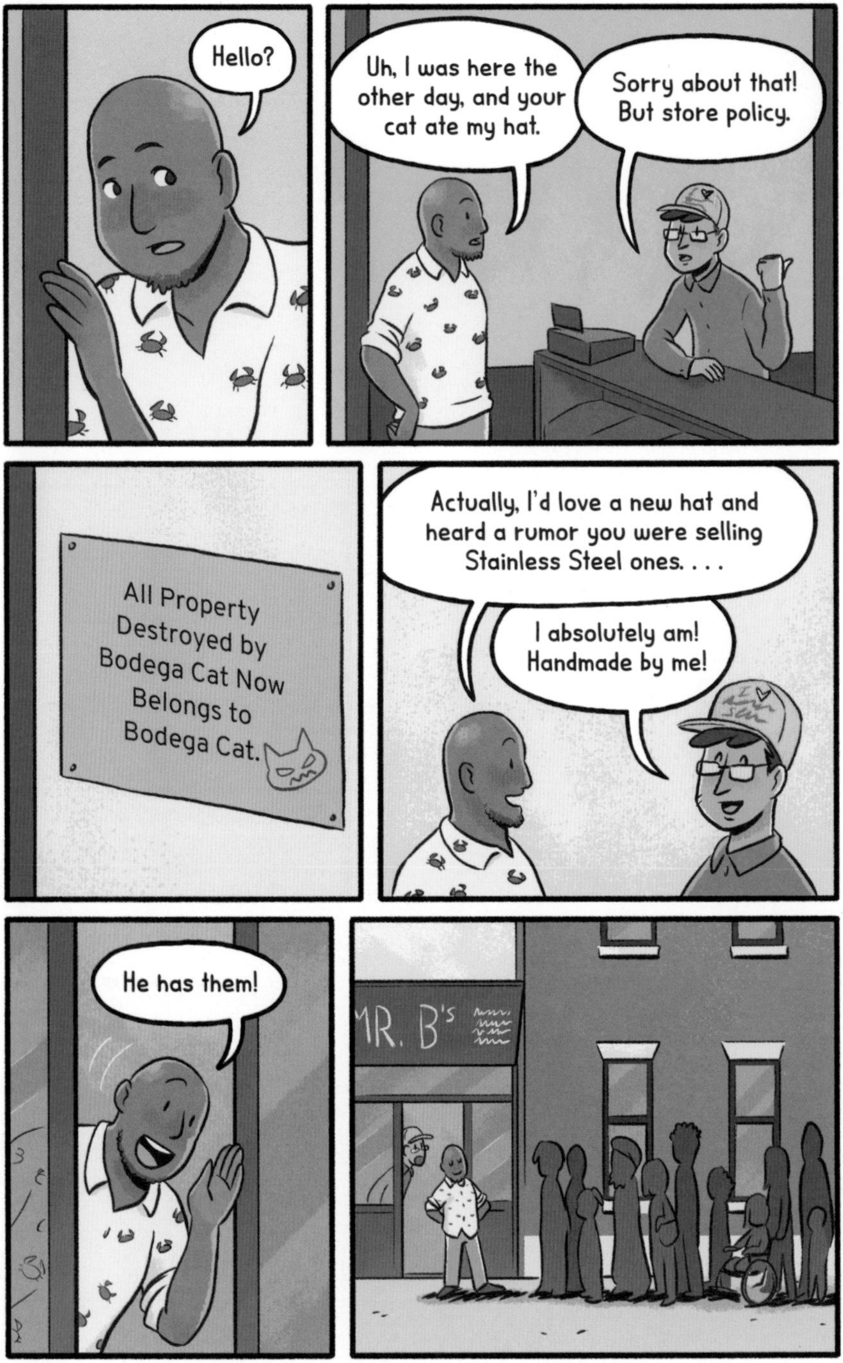
Hello?
Uh, I was here the other day, and your cat ate my hat.
Sorry about that! But store policy.
All Property Destroyed by Bodega Cat Now Belongs to Bodega Cat.
Actually, I'd love a new hat and heard a rumor you were selling Stainless Steel ones. . . .
I absolutely am! Handmade by me!
He has them!
MR. B's

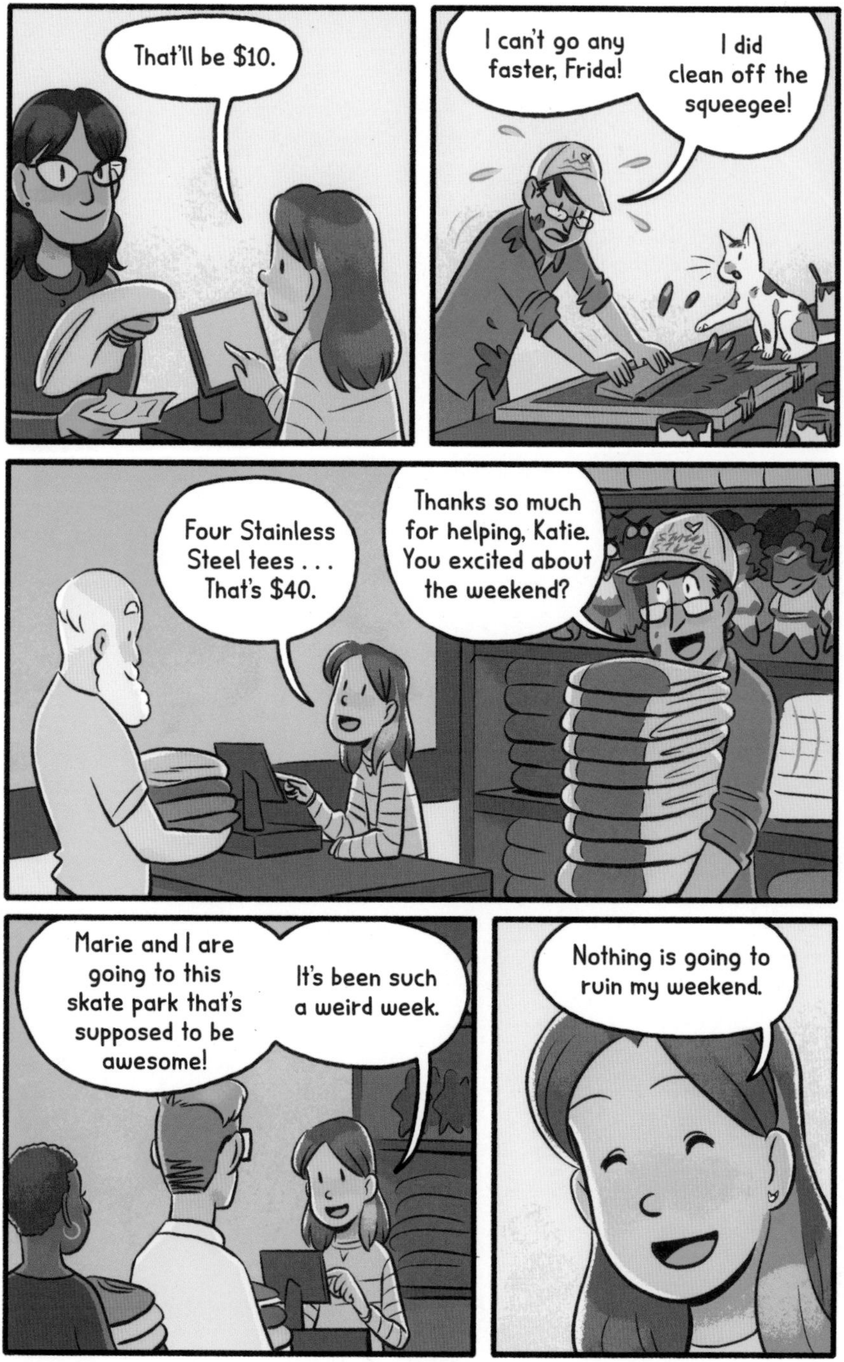
That'll be $10.
I can't go any faster, Frida!
I did clean off the squeegee!
Four Stainless Steel tees . . . That's $40.
Thanks so much for helping, Katie. You excited about the weekend?
Marie and I are going to this skate park that's supposed to be awesome!
It's been such a weird week.
Nothing is going to ruin my weekend.

FRIDAY EVENING
SMASH
THE HEROES & KIDS CLUB OF AMERICA

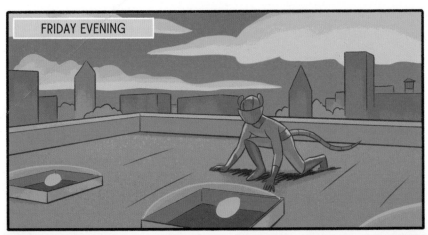

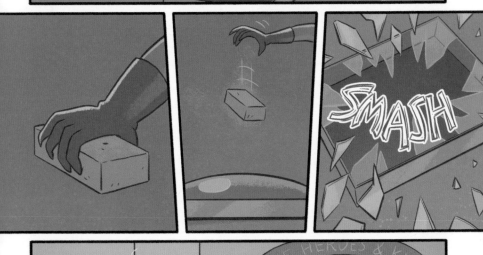

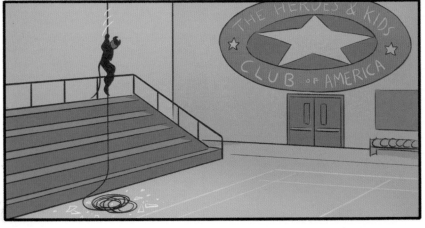

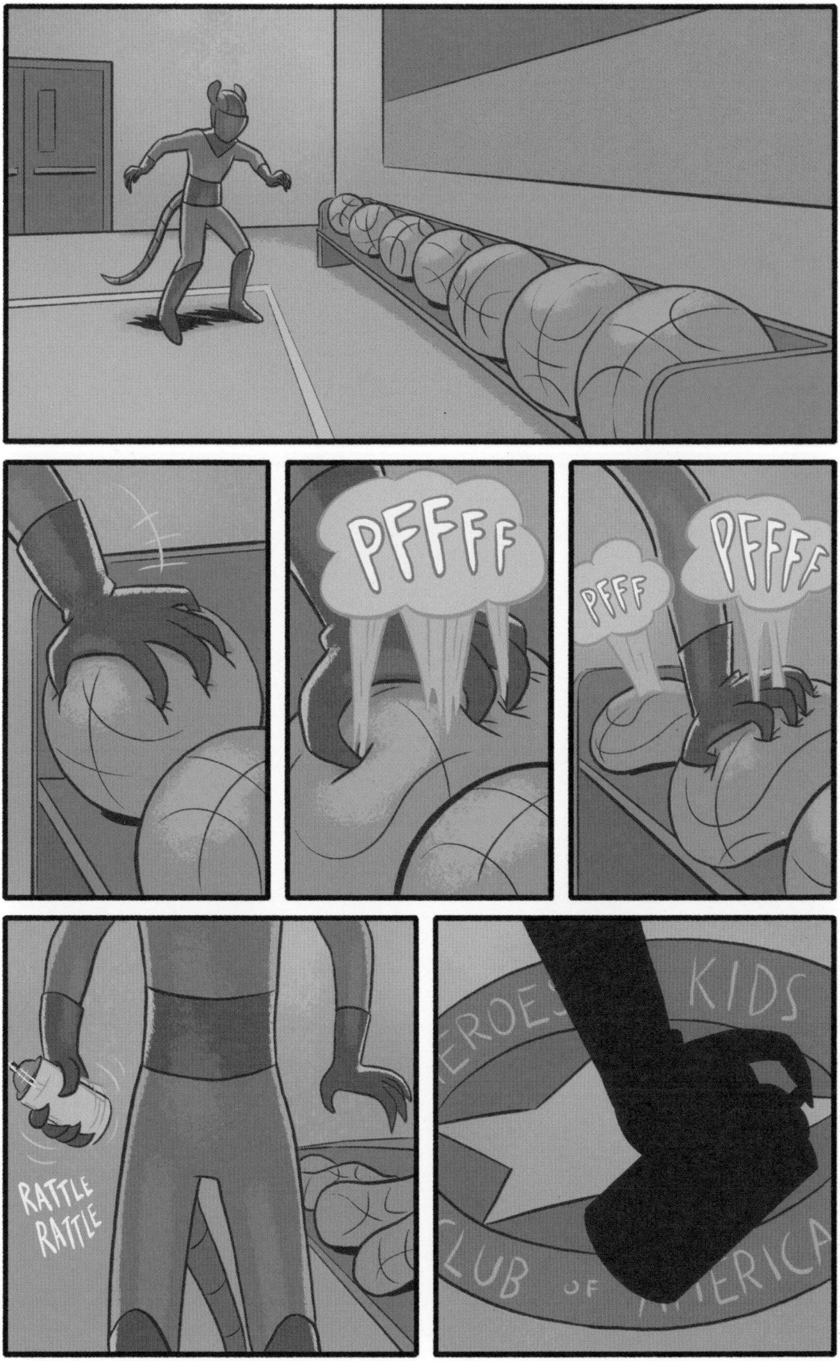
PFFFF
PFFF
PFFFF
RATTLE RATTLE
KIDS
CLUB OF

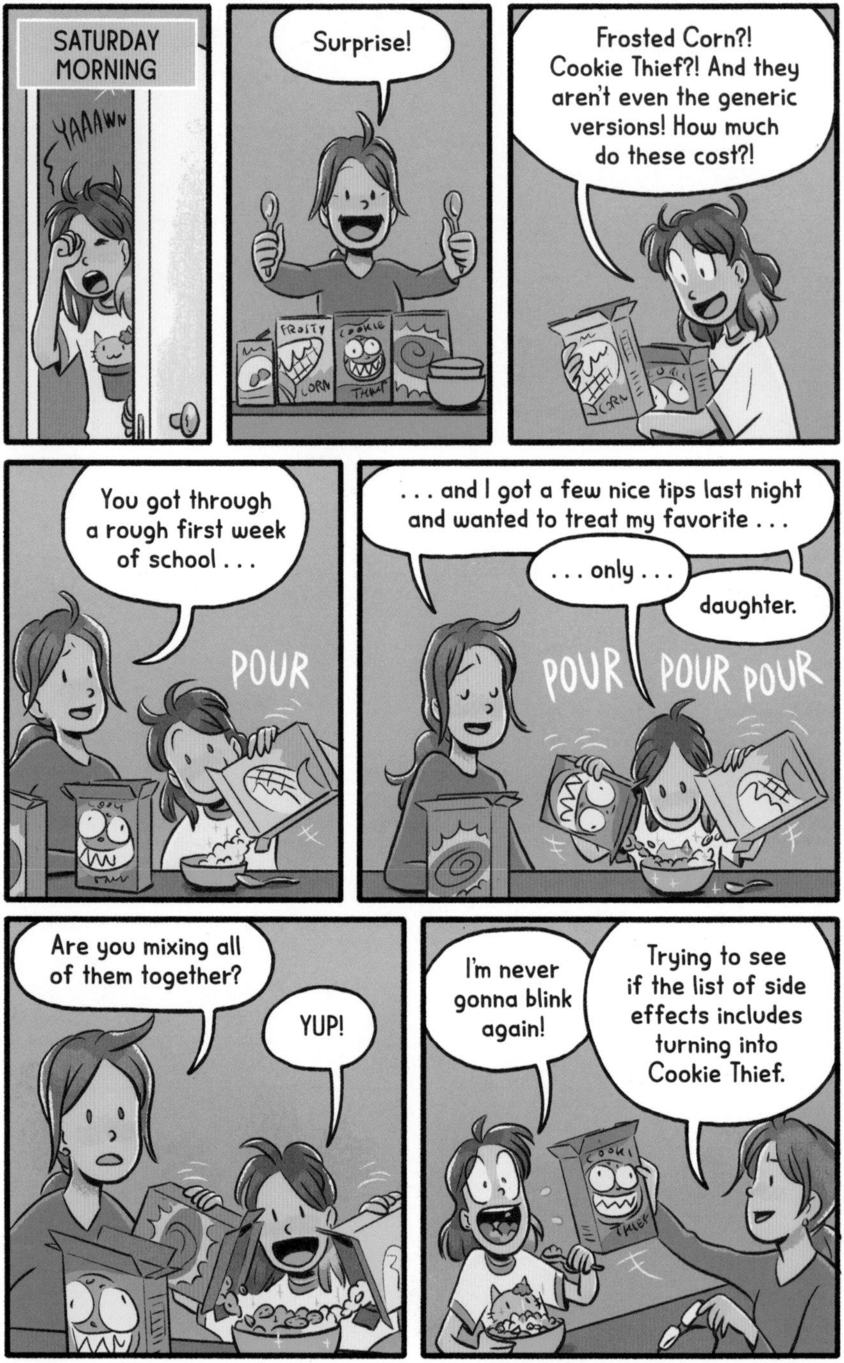
SATURDAY MORNING
YAAAWN
Surprise!
FROSTY CORN
COOKIE THIEF
Frosted Corn?! Cookie Thief?! And they aren't even the generic versions! How much do these cost?!
You got through a rough first week of school . . .
POUR
. . . and I got a few nice tips last night and wanted to treat my favorite . . .
. . . only . . .
daughter.
POUR
POUR POUR
Are you mixing all of them together?
YUP!
I'm never gonna blink again!
Trying to see if the list of side effects includes turning into Cookie Thief.
COOKI THIEF

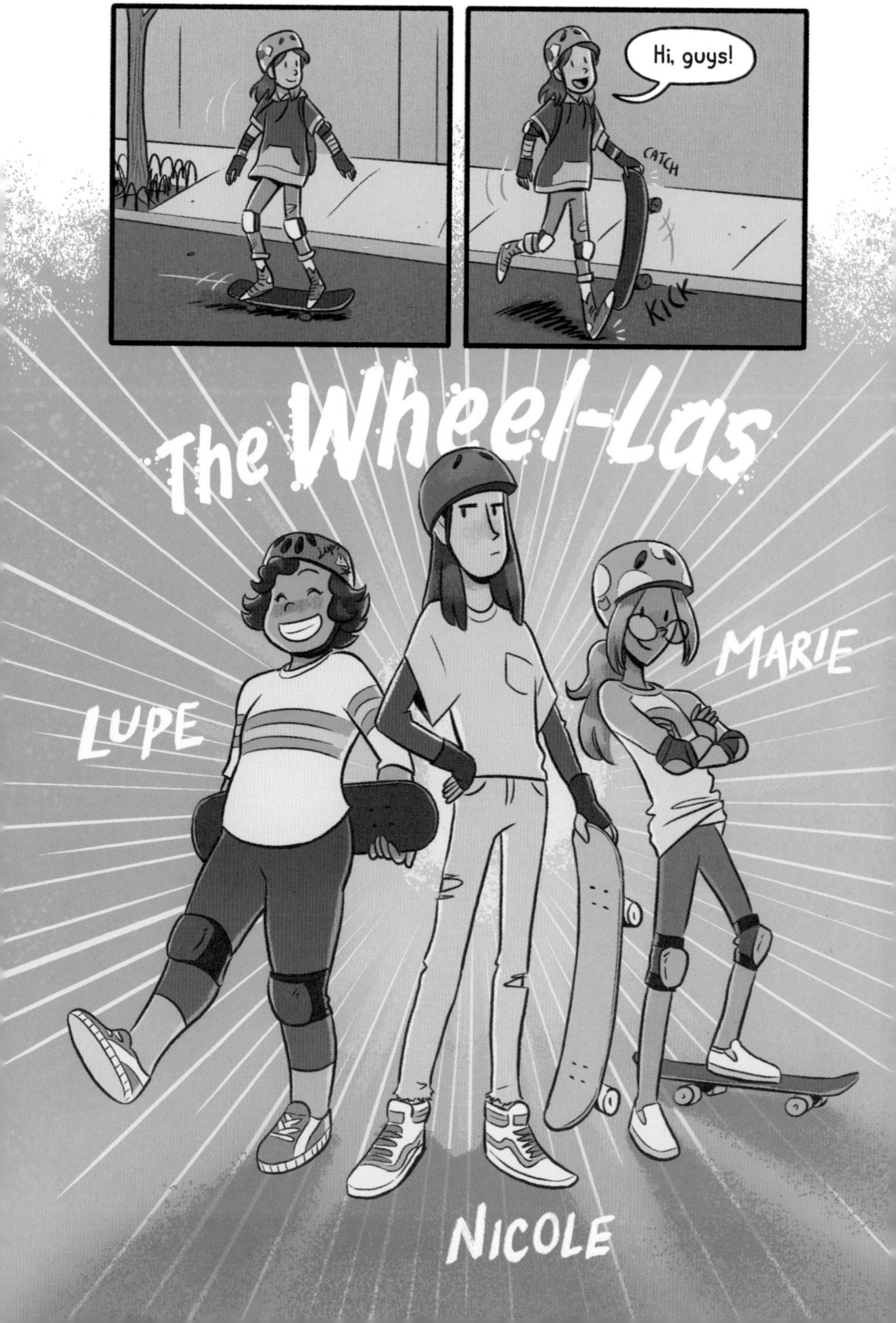
Hi, guys!
CATCH
KICK
The Wheel-Las
LUPE
MARIE
NICOLE

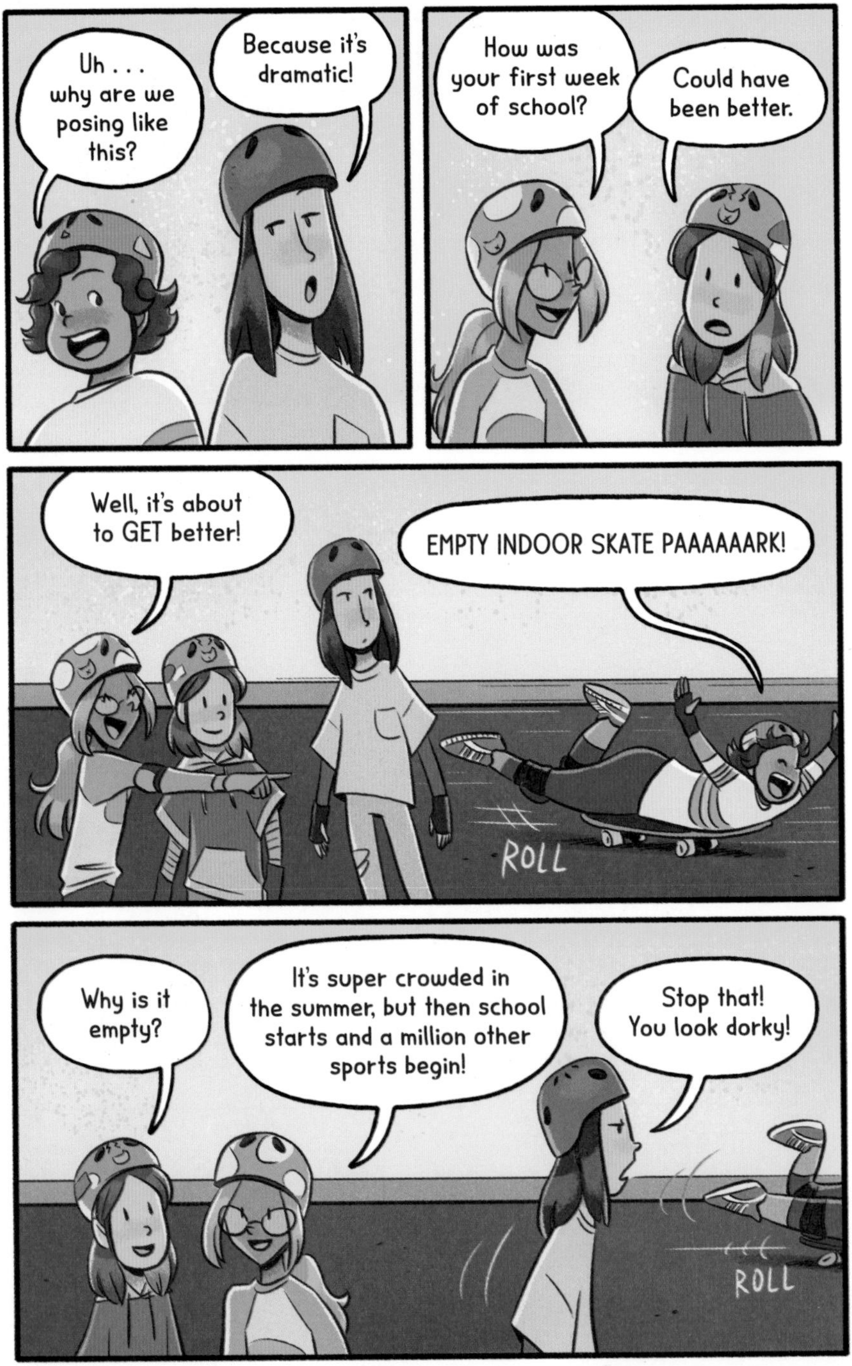
Uh . . . why are we posing like this?
Because it's dramatic!
How was your first week of school?
Could have been better.
Well, it's about to GET better!
EMPTY INDOOR SKATE PAAAAAARK!
ROLL
Why is it empty?
It's super crowded in the summer, but then school starts and a million other sports begin!
Stop that! You look dorky!
ROLL

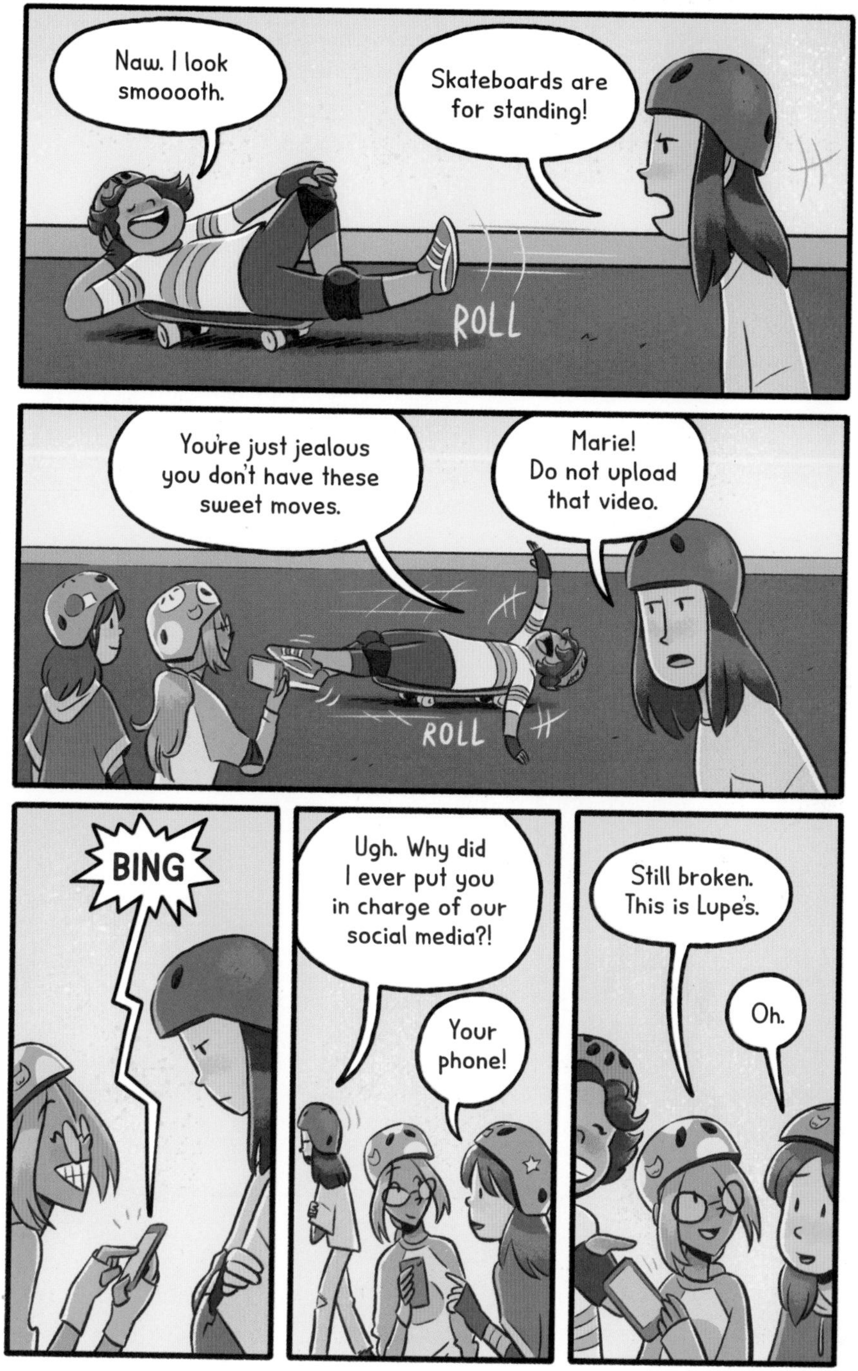
Naw. I look smoooooth.
Skateboards are for standing!
ROLL
You're just jealous you don't have these sweet moves.
Marie! Do not upload that video.
ROLL
BING
Ugh. Why did I ever put you in charge of our social media?!
Your phone!
Still broken. This is Lupe's.
Oh.

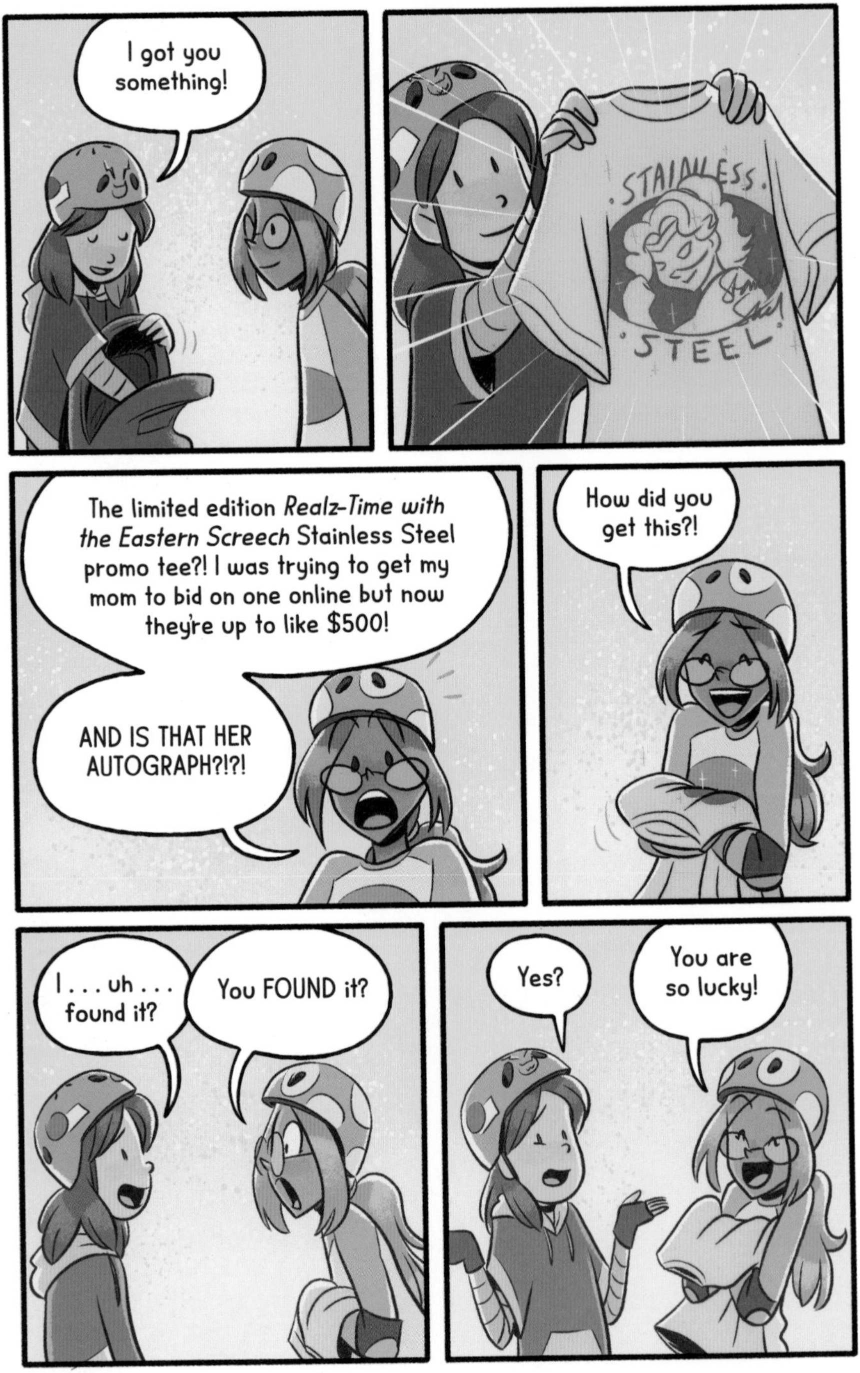
I got you something!
STAINLESS STEEL
The limited edition *Realz-Time with the Eastern Screech* Stainless Steel promo tee?! I was trying to get my mom to bid on one online but now they're up to like $500!
AND IS THAT HER AUTOGRAPH?!?!
How did you get this?!
I . . . uh . . . found it?
You FOUND it?
Yes?
You are so lucky!

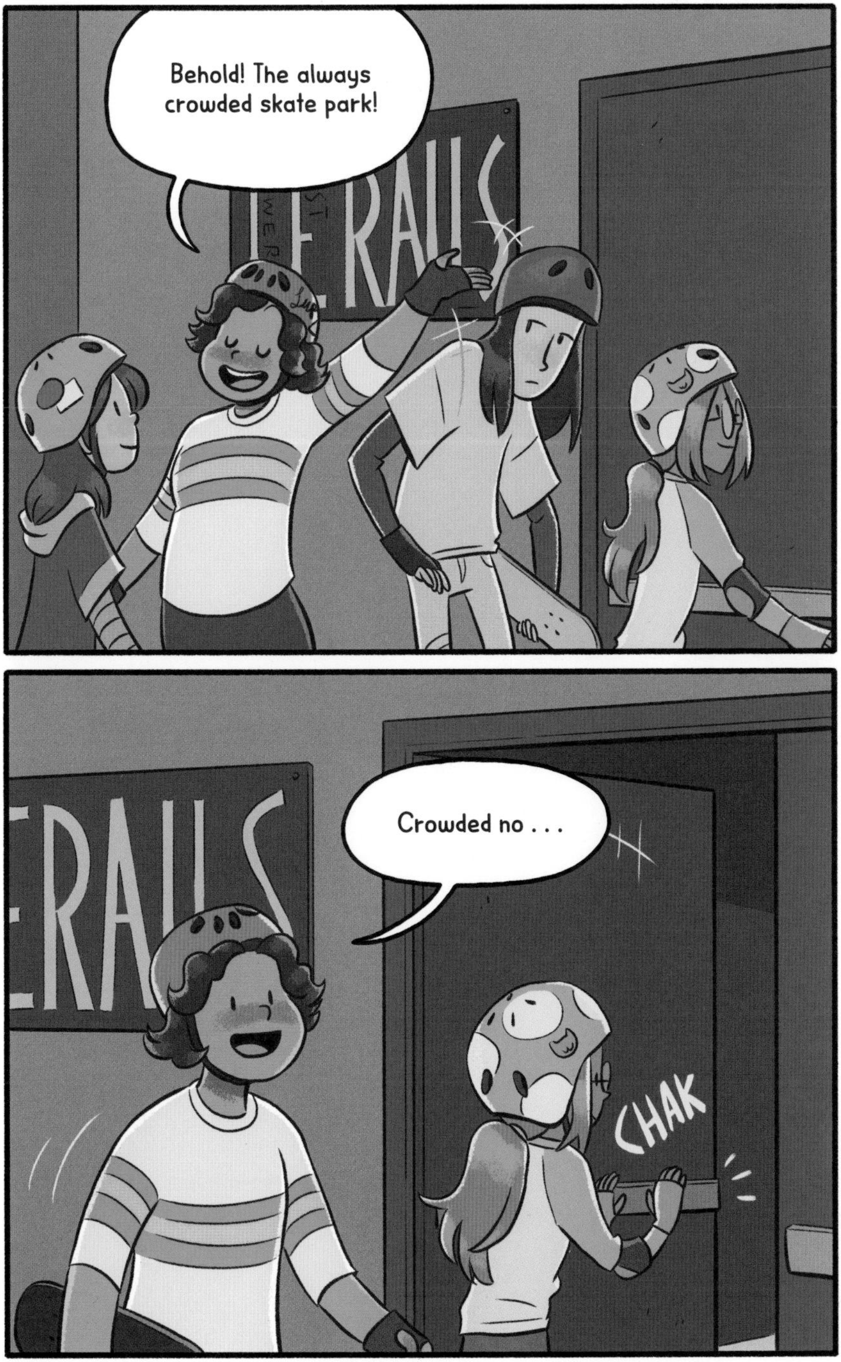
Behold! The always crowded skate park!
Crowded no . . .
CHAK

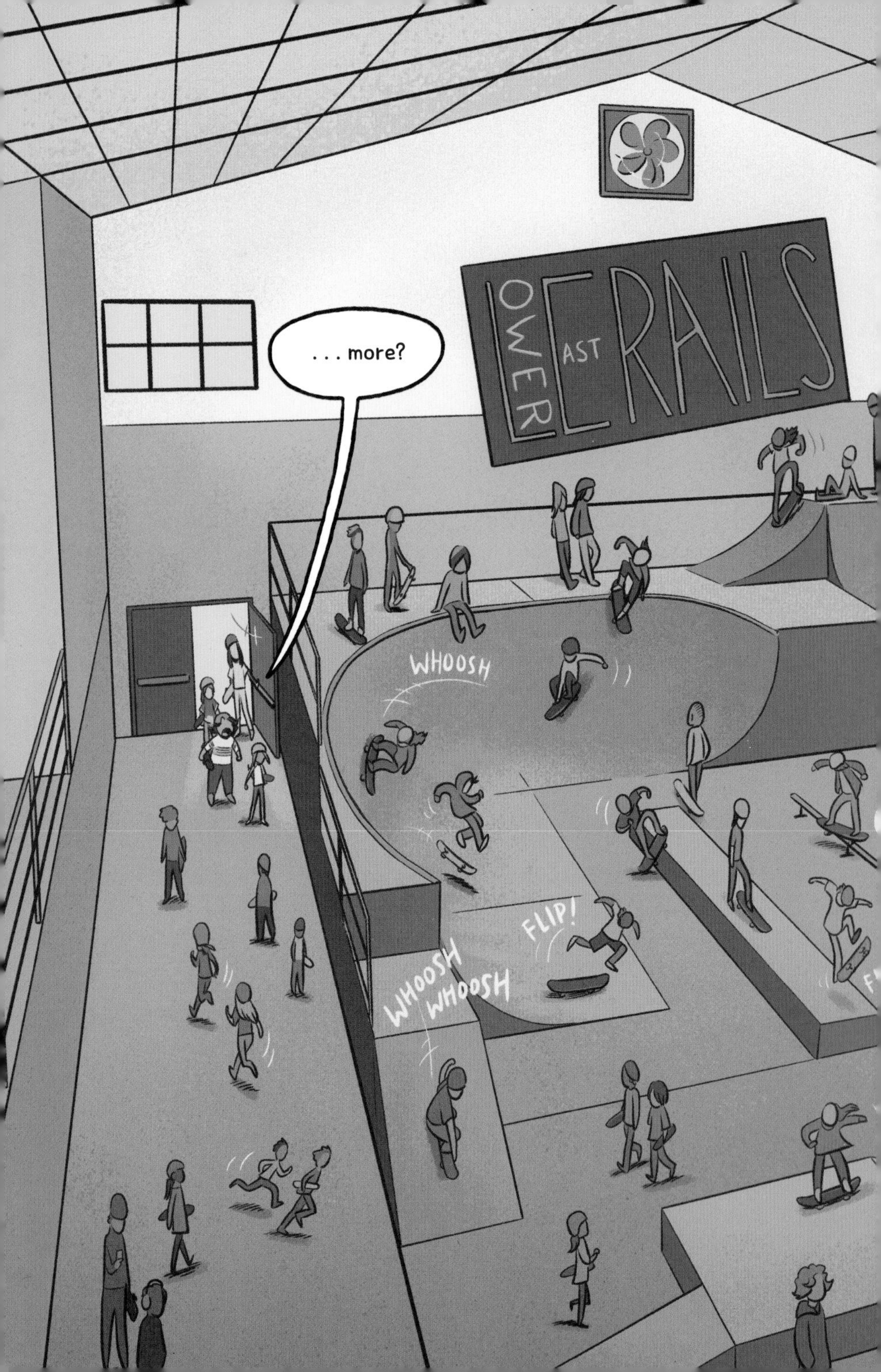

LOWER EAST RAILS
. . . more?
WHOOSH
WHOOSH WHOOSH
FLIP!

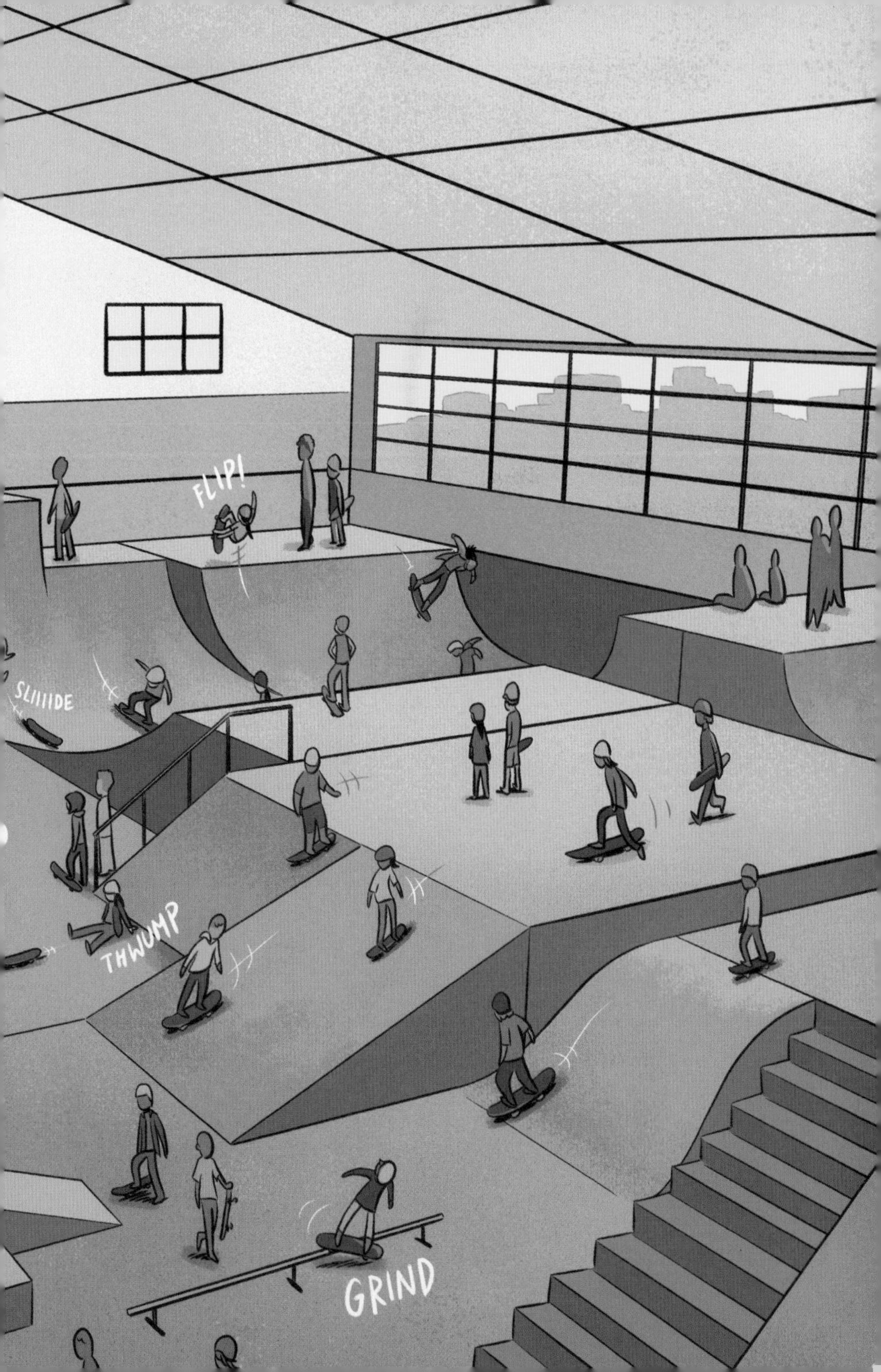
FLIP!
SLIIIIDE
THWUMP
GRIND

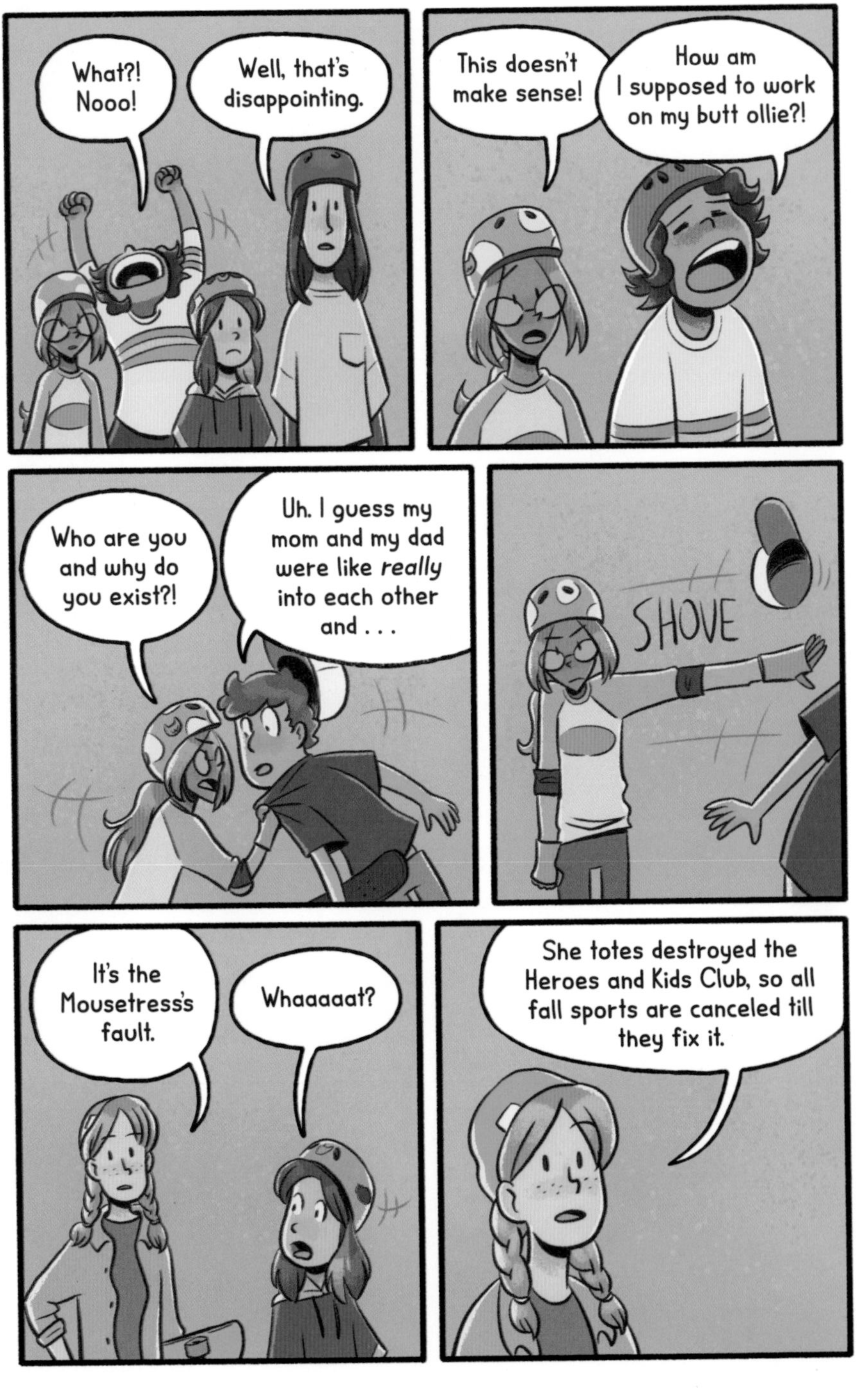
What?! Nooo!
Well, that's disappointing.
This doesn't make sense!
How am I supposed to work on my butt ollie?!
Who are you and why do you exist?!
Uh. I guess my mom and my dad were like *really* into each other and . . .
SHOVE
It's the Mousetress's fault.
Whaaaaat?
She totes destroyed the Heroes and Kids Club, so all fall sports are canceled till they fix it.

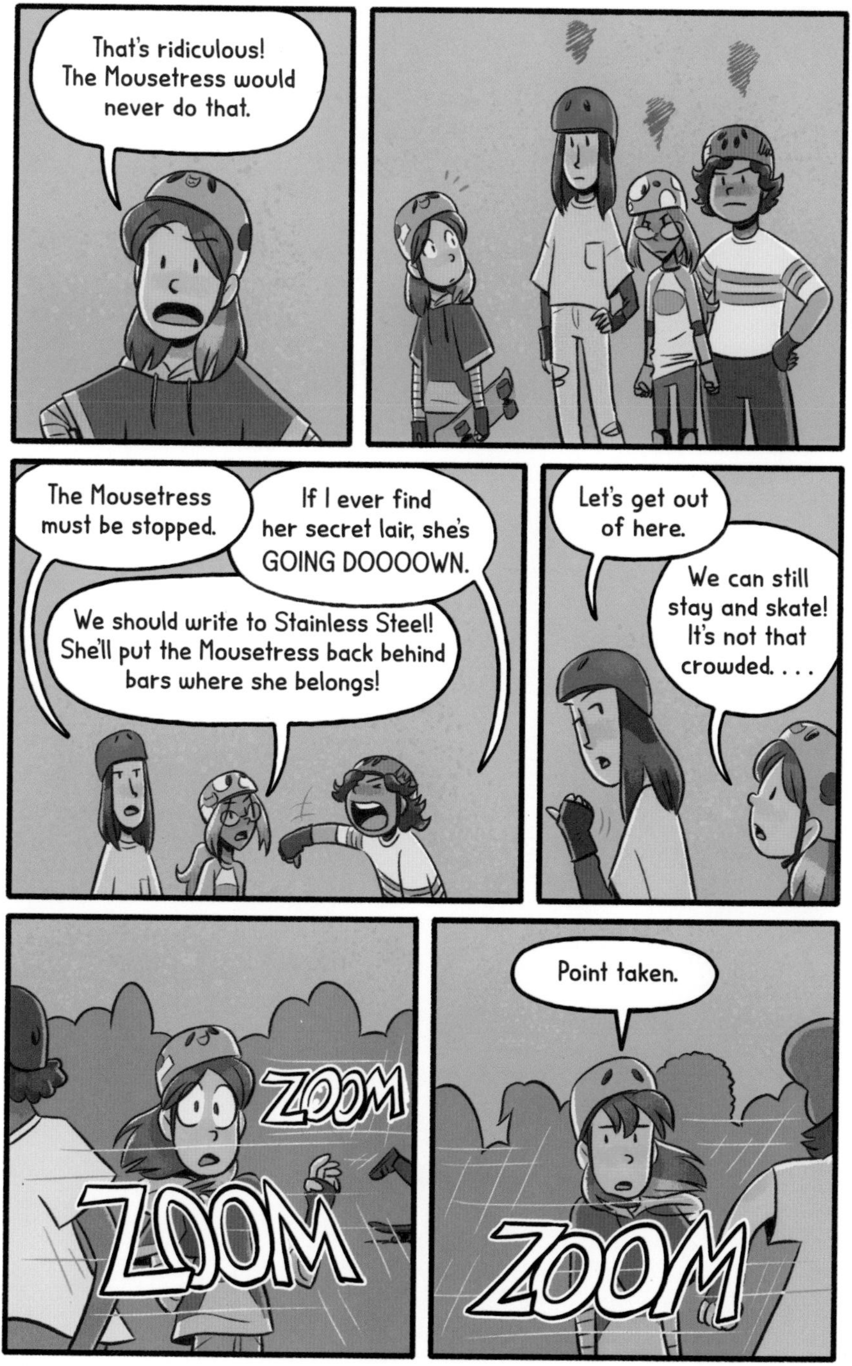
That's ridiculous! The Mousetress would never do that.
The Mousetress must be stopped.
If I ever find her secret lair, she's GOING DOOOOWN.
We should write to Stainless Steel! She'll put the Mousetress back behind bars where she belongs!
Let's get out of here.
We can still stay and skate! It's not that crowded. . . .
ZOOM
ZOOM
Point taken.
ZOOM

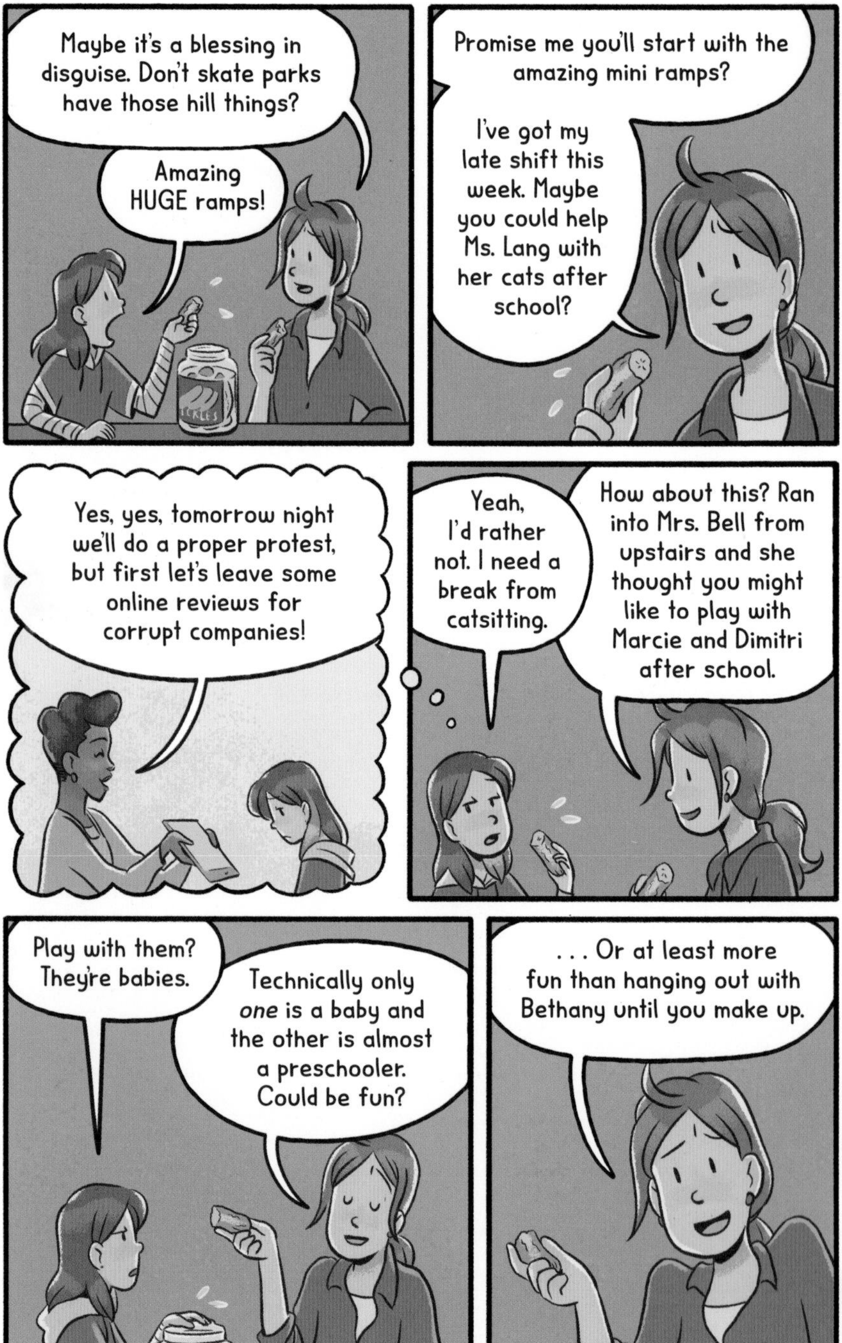
Maybe it's a blessing in disguise. Don't skate parks have those hill things?
Amazing HUGE ramps!
Promise me you'll start with the amazing mini ramps?
I've got my late shift this week. Maybe you could help Ms. Lang with her cats after school?
Yes, yes, tomorrow night we'll do a proper protest, but first let's leave some online reviews for corrupt companies!
Yeah, I'd rather not. I need a break from catsitting.
How about this? Ran into Mrs. Bell from upstairs and she thought you might like to play with Marcie and Dimitri after school.
Play with them? They're babies.
Technically only *one* is a baby and the other is almost a preschooler. Could be fun?
. . . Or at least more fun than hanging out with Bethany until you make up.

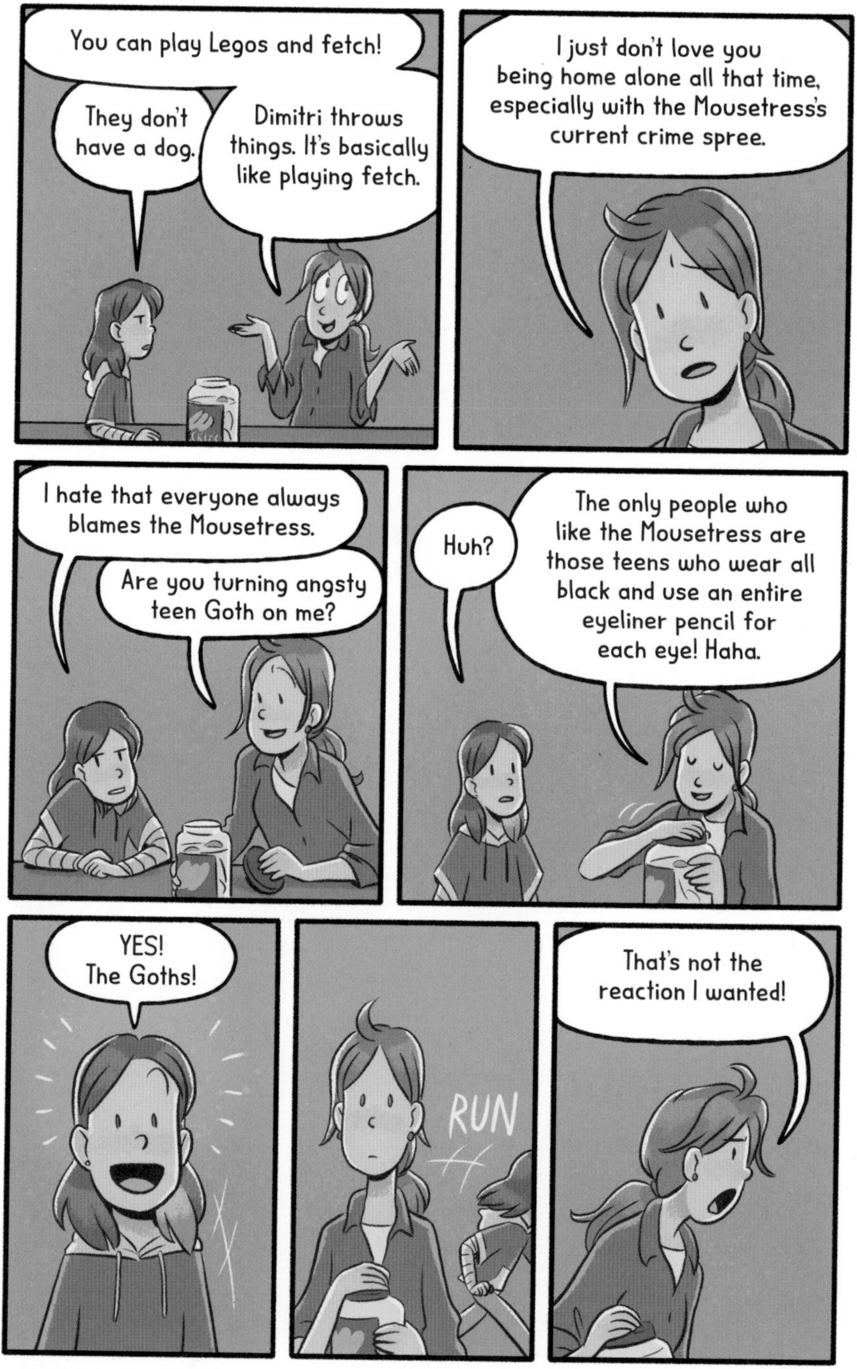
You can play Legos and fetch!
They don't have a dog.
Dimitri throws things. It's basically like playing fetch.
I just don't love you being home alone all that time, especially with the Mousetress's current crime spree.
I hate that everyone always blames the Mousetress.
Are you turning angsty teen Goth on me?
Huh?
The only people who like the Mousetress are those teens who wear all black and use an entire eyeliner pencil for each eye! Haha.
YES! The Goths!
RUN
That's not the reaction I wanted!

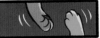

CHAPTER SIX

Ugh, the sun. Why aren't our meetings at night?

Walk faster. We're going to be late.

My boots make my toes bleed!

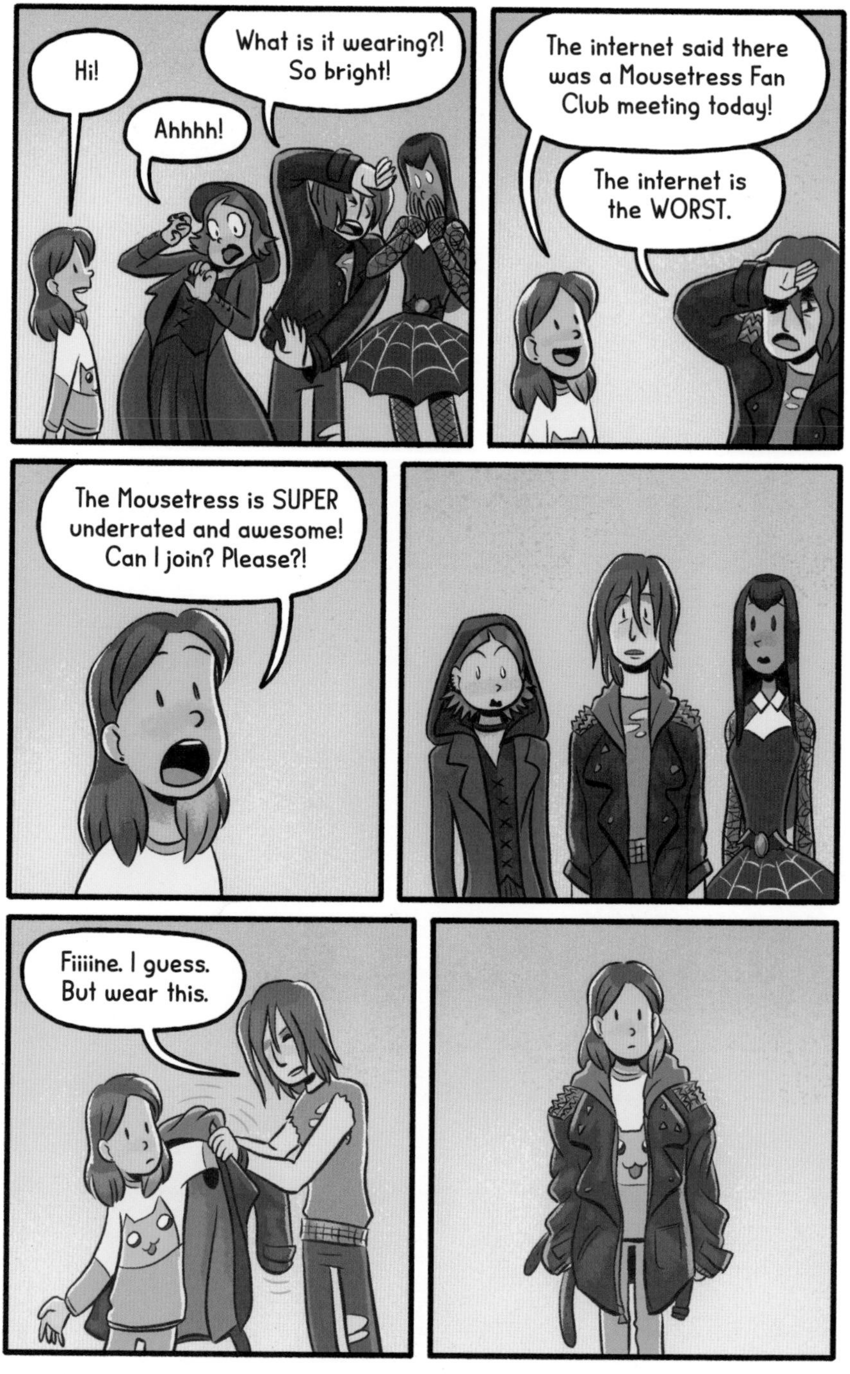
Hi!
Ahhhh!
What is it wearing?! So bright!
The internet said there was a Mousetress Fan Club meeting today!
The internet is the WORST.
The Mousetress is SUPER underrated and awesome! Can I join? Please?!
Fiiiine. I guess. But wear this.

Are the lights broken?

We're here.

Fan Club Meeting Room
Schedule for Saturdays

9 a.m.	Eastern Screech
10 a.m.	Eastern Screech
11 a.m.	Eastern Screech
12 p.m.	Eastern Screech
1 p.m.	*new* Stainless Steel
2 p.m.	Eastern Screech
3 p.m.	Misc Villains
4 p.m.	Eastern Screech

Where is everyone?

This is everyone.

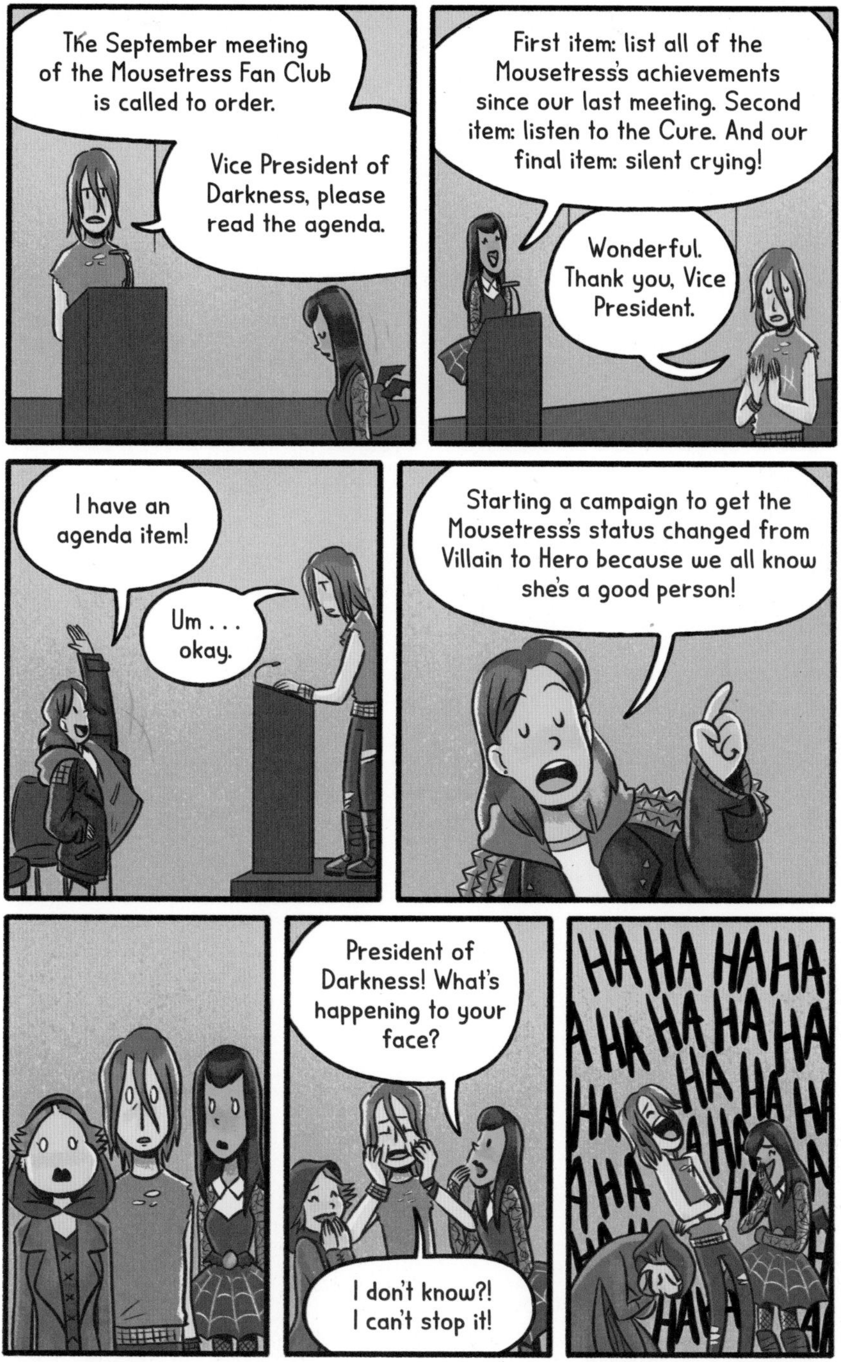
The September meeting of the Mousetress Fan Club is called to order.
Vice President of Darkness, please read the agenda.
First item: list all of the Mousetress's achievements since our last meeting. Second item: listen to the Cure. And our final item: silent crying!
Wonderful. Thank you, Vice President.
I have an agenda item!
Um . . . okay.
Starting a campaign to get the Mousetress's status changed from Villain to Hero because we all know she's a good person!
President of Darkness! What's happening to your face?
I don't know?! I can't stop it!
HA HA HA HA HA HA HA HA HA HA HA HA HA HA HA HA HA HA HA

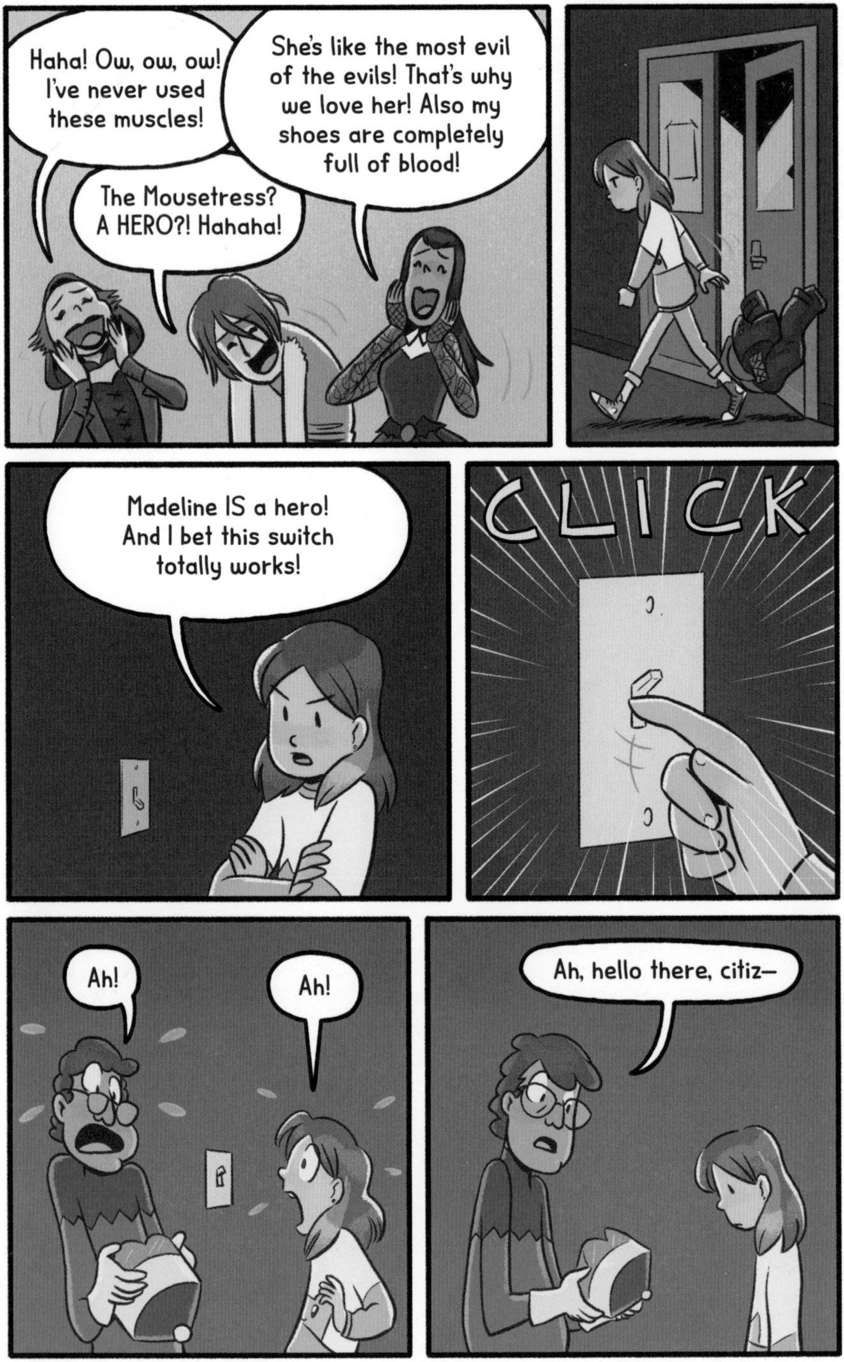
Haha! Ow, ow, ow! I've never used these muscles!
The Mousetress? A HERO?! Hahaha!
She's like the most evil of the evils! That's why we love her! Also my shoes are completely full of blood!
Madeline IS a hero! And I bet this switch totally works!
CLICK
Ah!
Ah!
Ah, hello there, citiz—

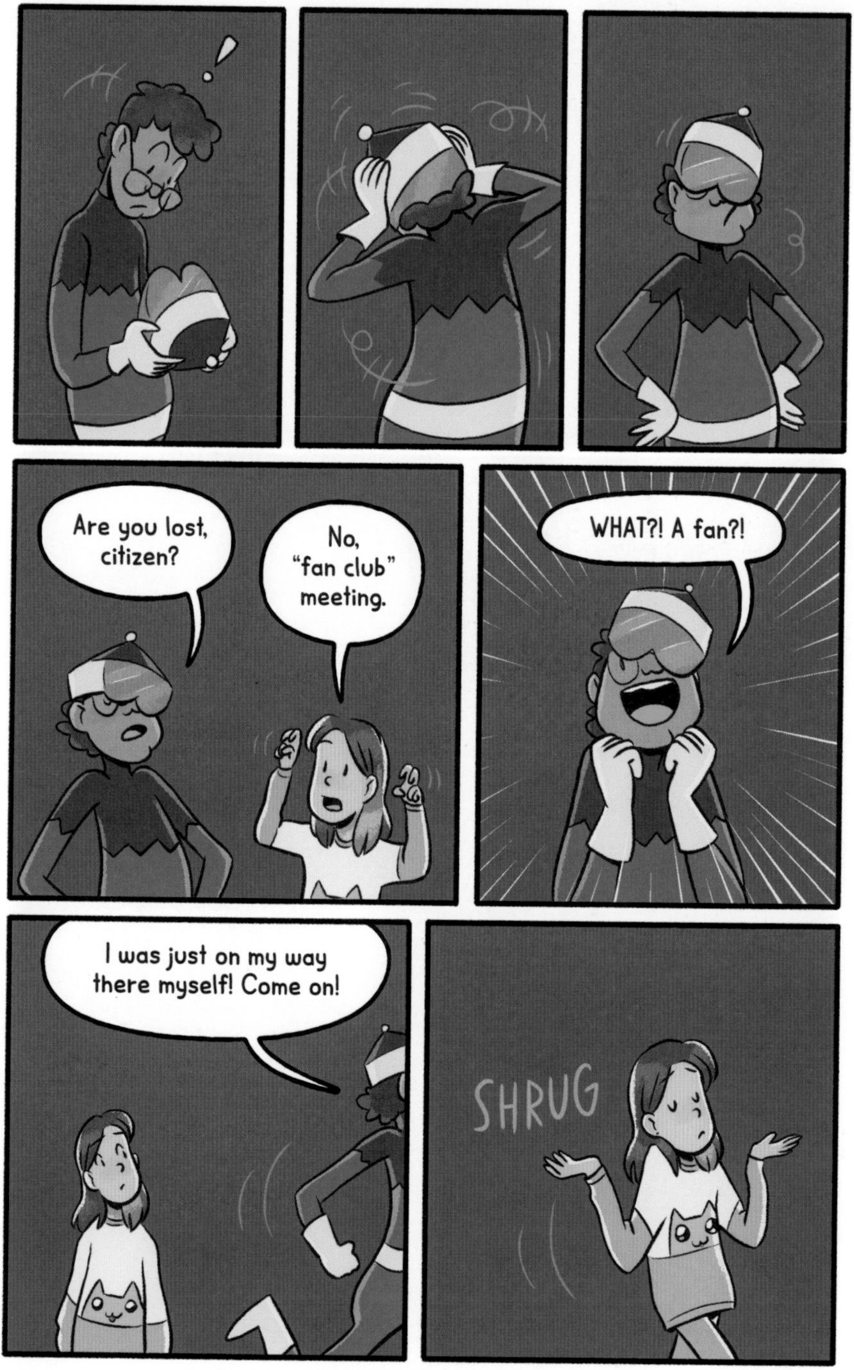
!
Are you lost, citizen?
No, "fan club" meeting.
WHAT?! A fan?!
I was just on my way there myself! Come on!
SHRUG

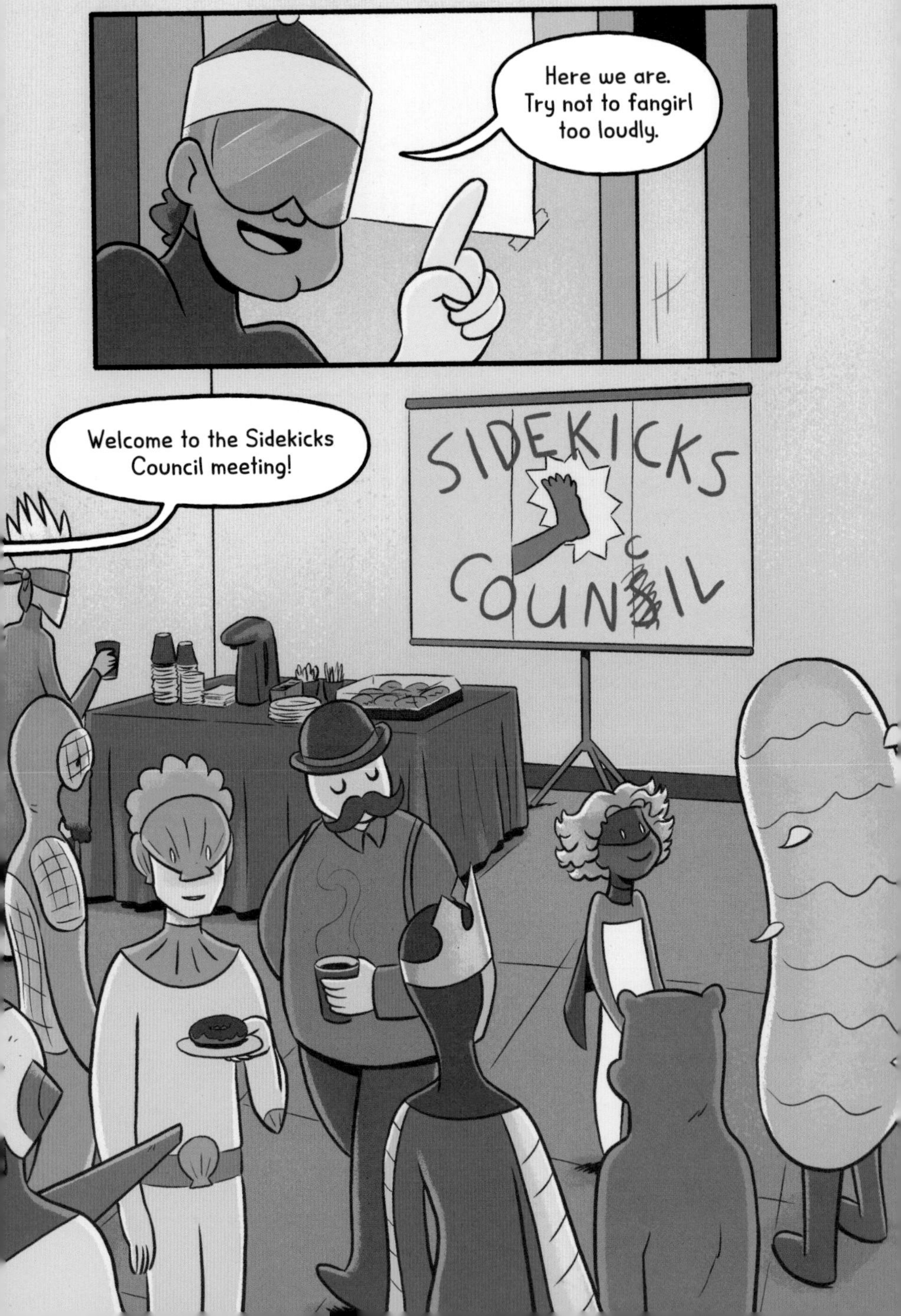
Here we are. Try not to fangirl too loudly.
Welcome to the Sidekicks Council meeting!
SIDEKICKS
COUNCIL

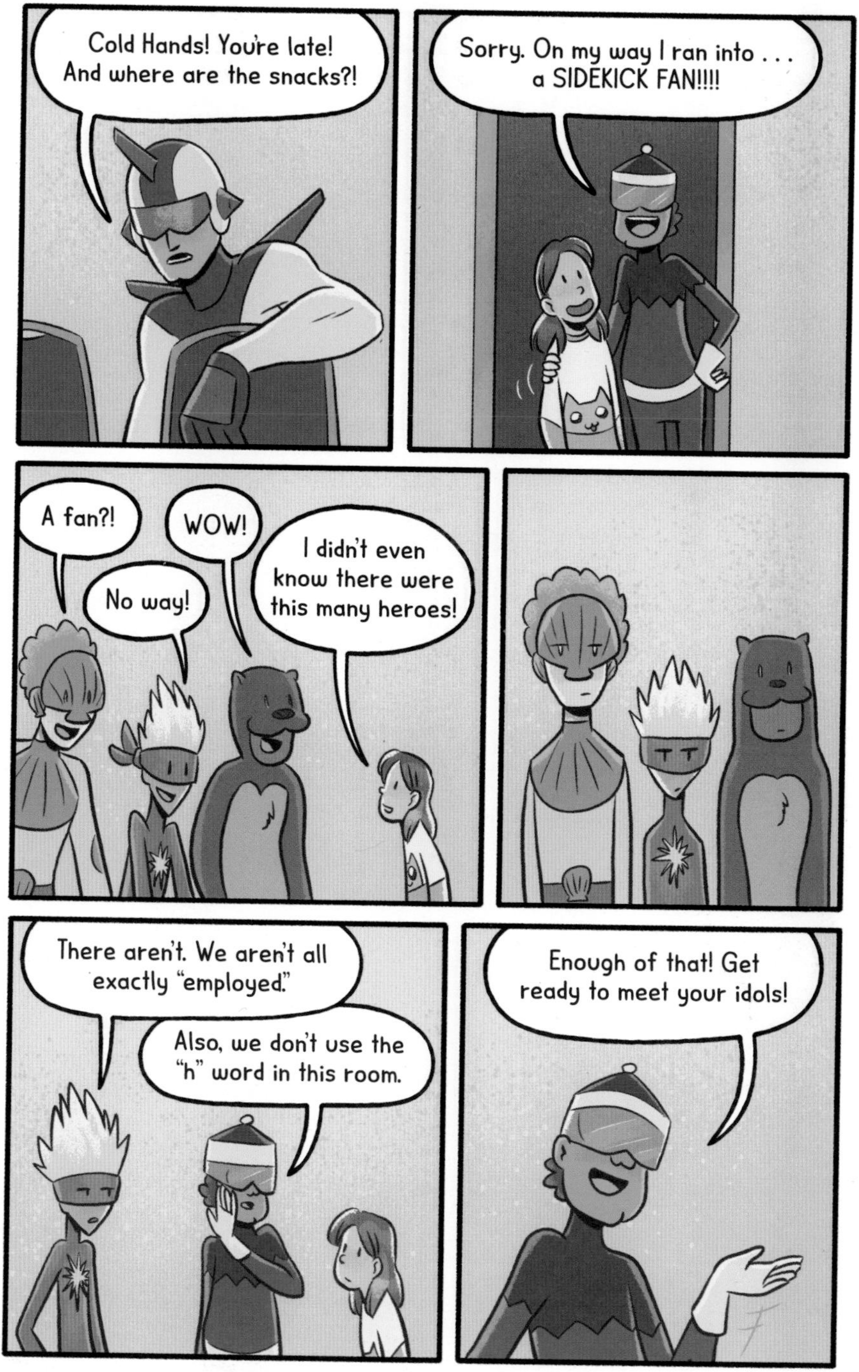
Cold Hands! You're late! And where are the snacks?!
Sorry. On my way I ran into . . . a SIDEKICK FAN!!!!
A fan?!
WOW!
No way!
I didn't even know there were this many heroes!
There aren't. We aren't all exactly "employed."
Also, we don't use the "h" word in this room.
Enough of that! Get ready to meet your idols!

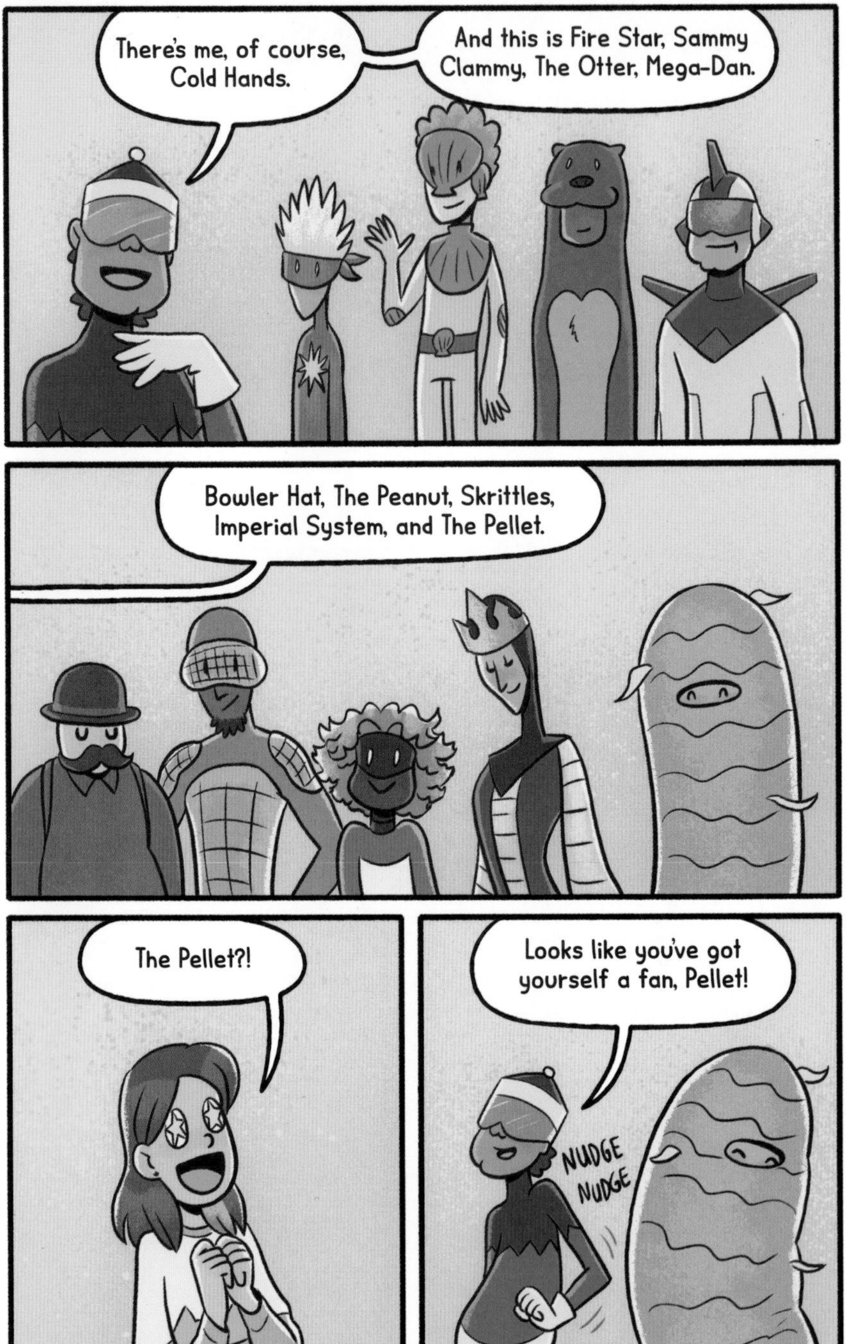
There's me, of course, Cold Hands.
And this is Fire Star, Sammy Clammy, The Otter, Mega-Dan.
Bowler Hat, The Peanut, Skrittles, Imperial System, and The Pellet.
The Pellet?!
Looks like you've got yourself a fan, Pellet!
NUDGE NUDGE

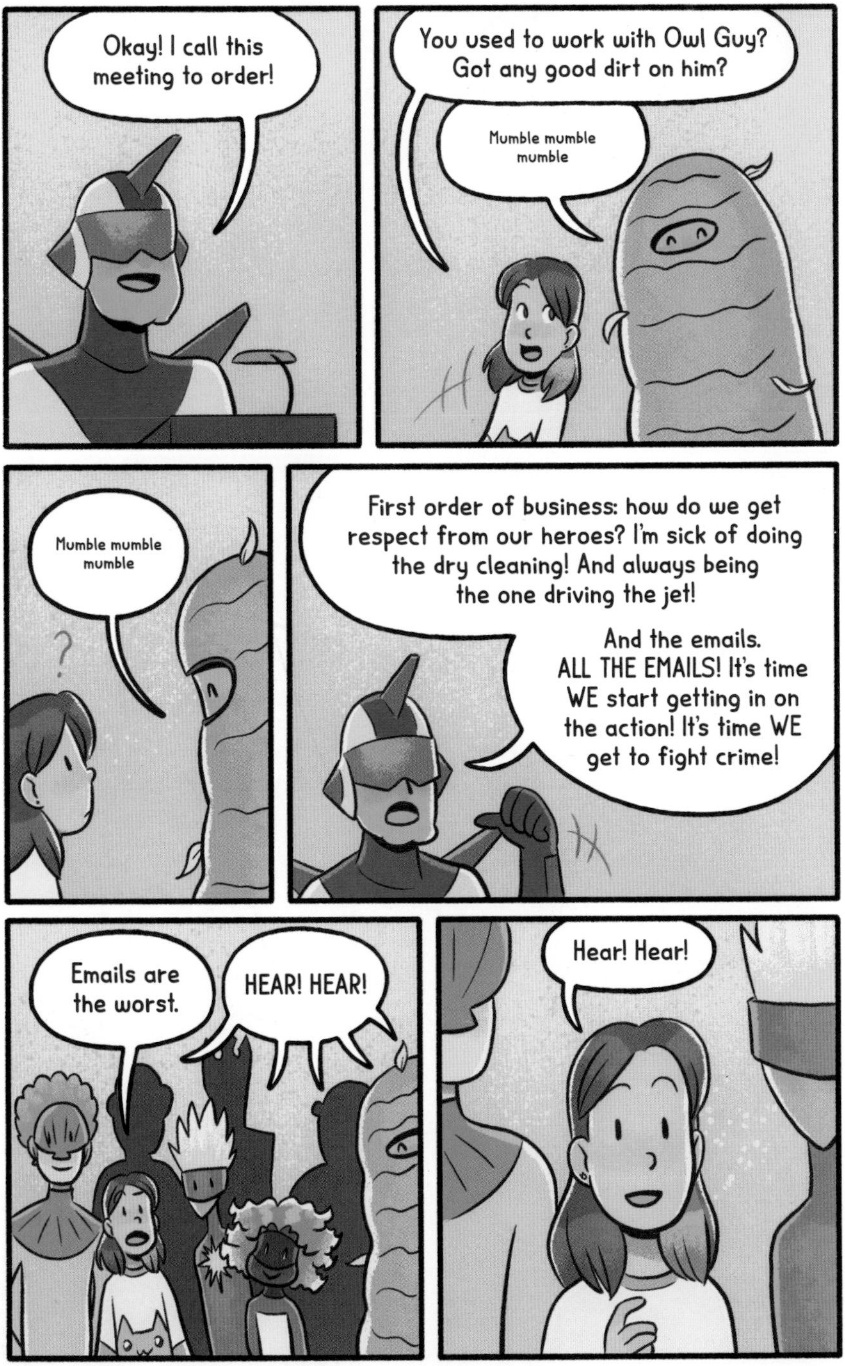
Okay! I call this meeting to order!
You used to work with Owl Guy? Got any good dirt on him?
Mumble mumble mumble
Mumble mumble mumble
?
First order of business: how do we get respect from our heroes? I'm sick of doing the dry cleaning! And always being the one driving the jet!
And the emails. ALL THE EMAILS! It's time WE start getting in on the action! It's time WE get to fight crime!
Emails are the worst.
HEAR! HEAR!
Hear! Hear!

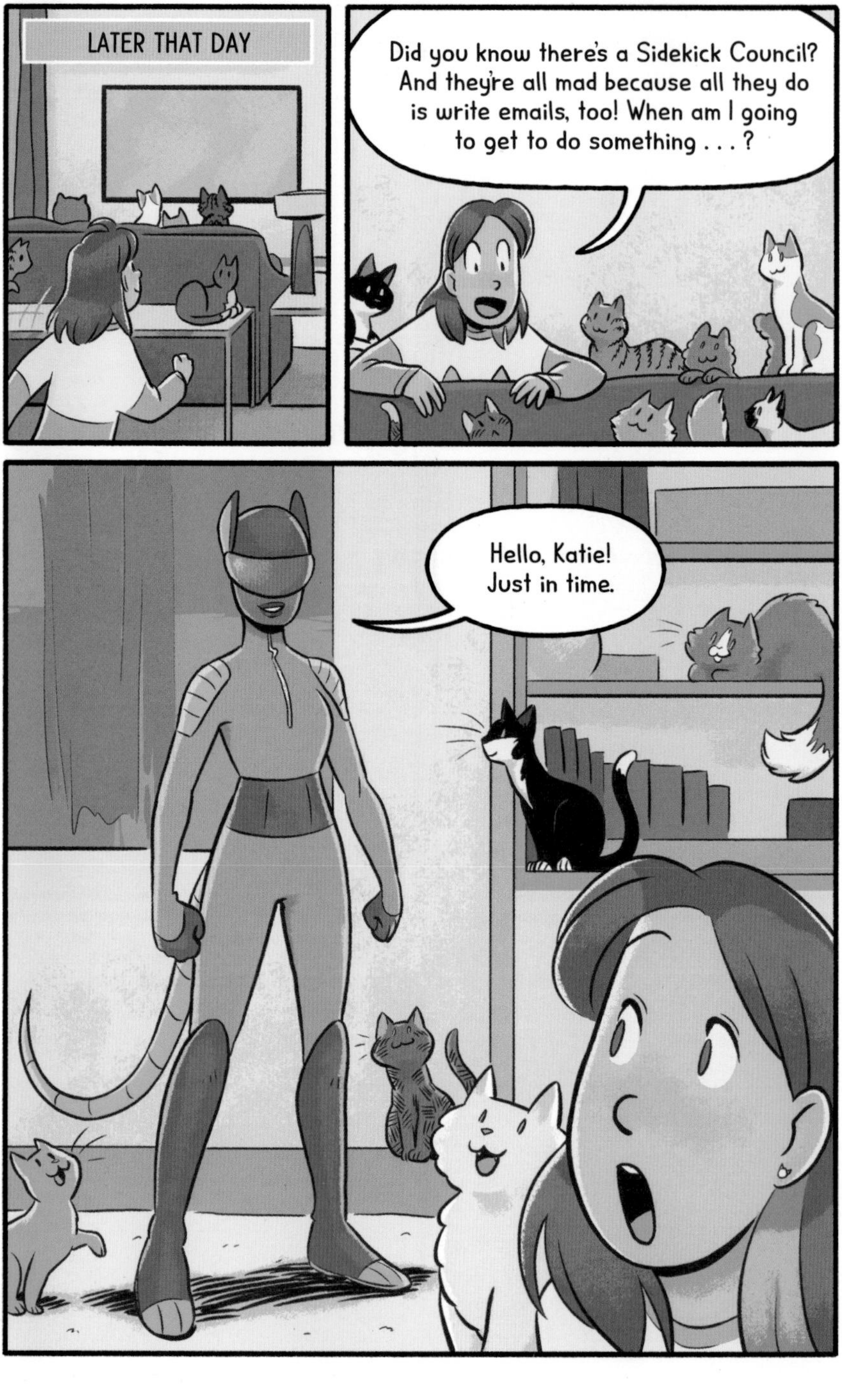
LATER THAT DAY
Did you know there's a Sidekick Council? And they're all mad because all they do is write emails, too! When am I going to get to do something . . . ?
Hello, Katie! Just in time.

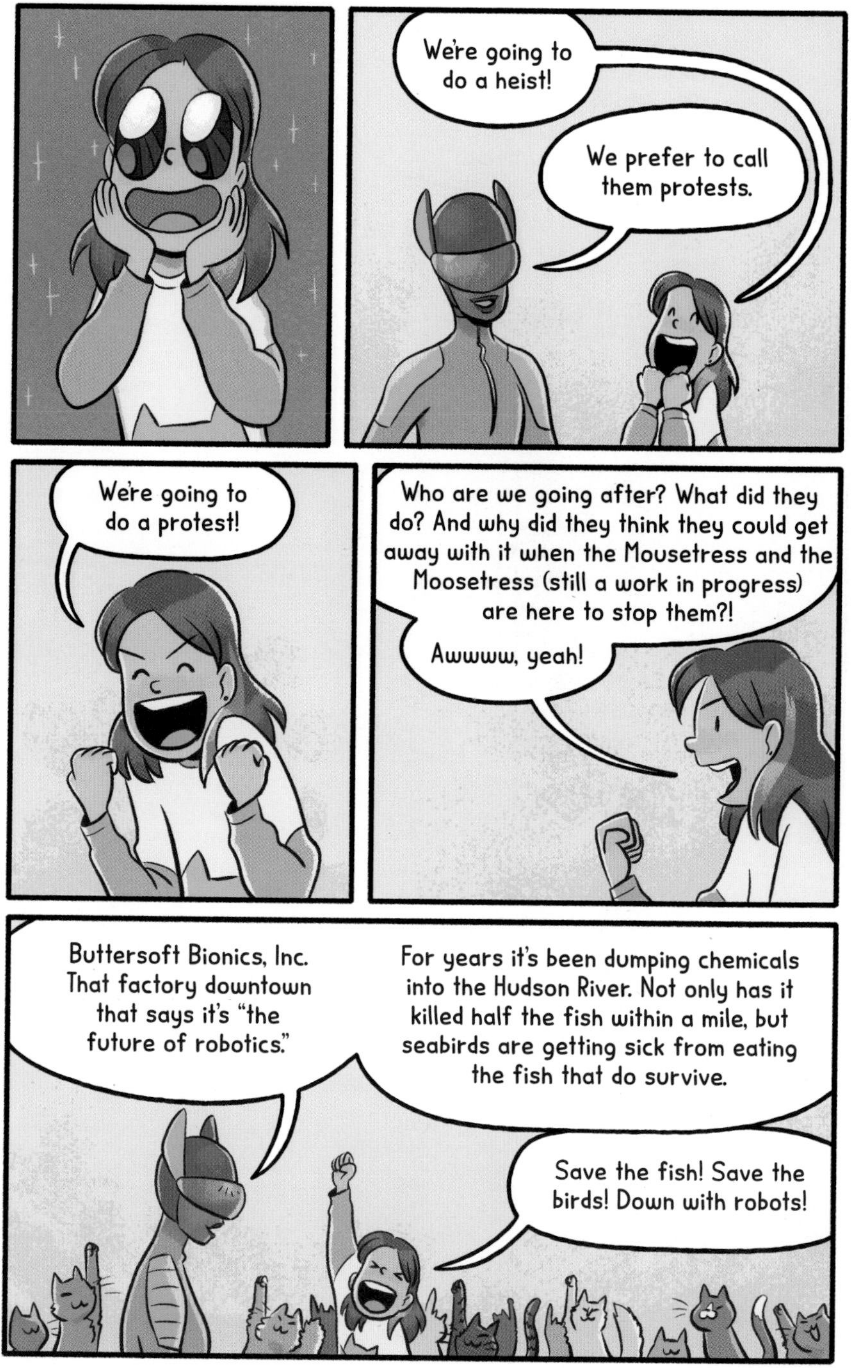
We're going to do a heist!
We prefer to call them protests.
We're going to do a protest!
Who are we going after? What did they do? And why did they think they could get away with it when the Mousetress and the Moosetress (still a work in progress) are here to stop them?!
Awwww, yeah!
Buttersoft Bionics, Inc. That factory downtown that says it's "the future of robotics."
For years it's been dumping chemicals into the Hudson River. Not only has it killed half the fish within a mile, but seabirds are getting sick from eating the fish that do survive.
Save the fish! Save the birds! Down with robots!

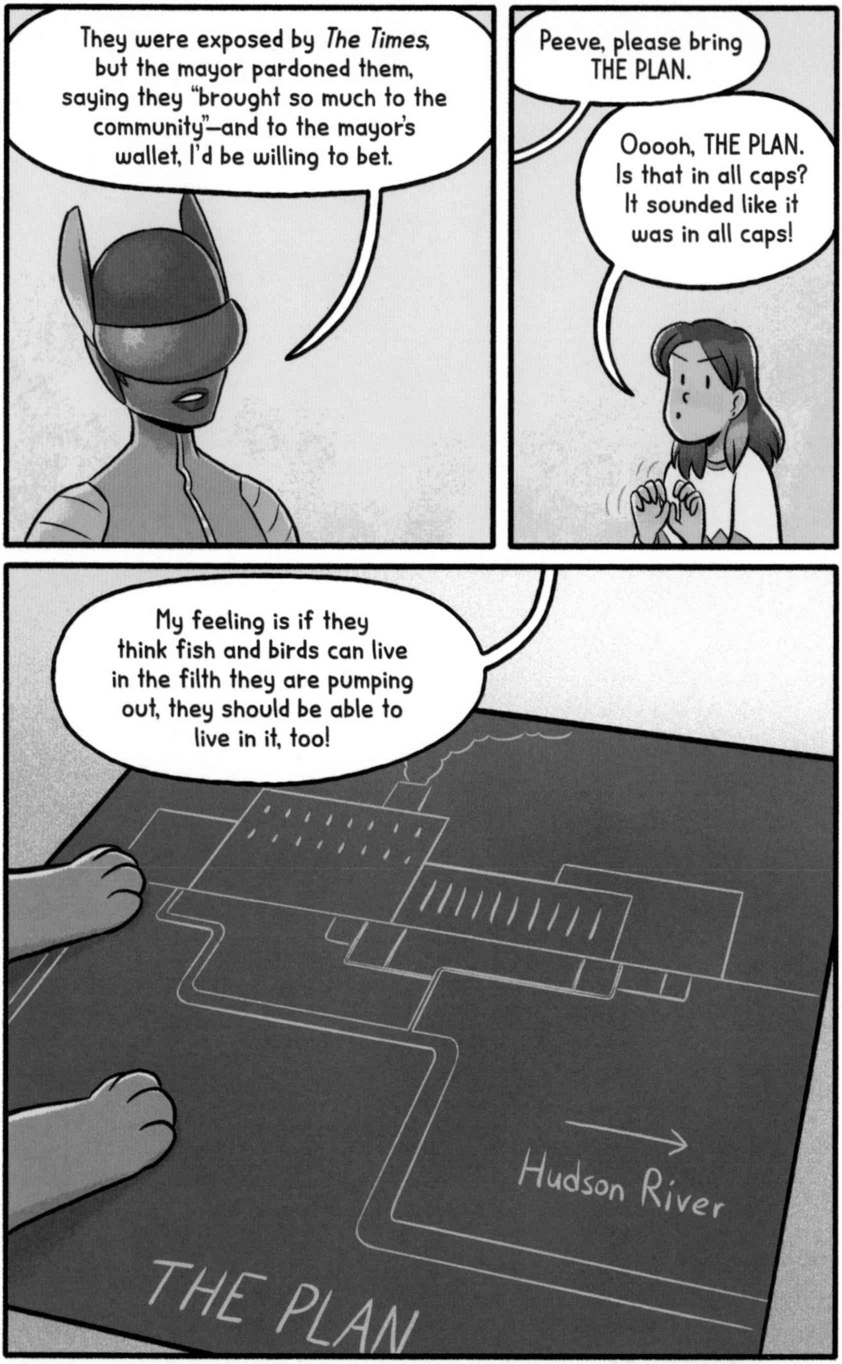

They were exposed by *The Times*, but the mayor pardoned them, saying they "brought so much to the community"—and to the mayor's wallet, I'd be willing to bet.
Peeve, please bring THE PLAN.
Ooooh, THE PLAN. Is that in all caps? It sounded like it was in all caps!
My feeling is if they think fish and birds can live in the filth they are pumping out, they should be able to live in it, too!
Hudson River
THE PLAN

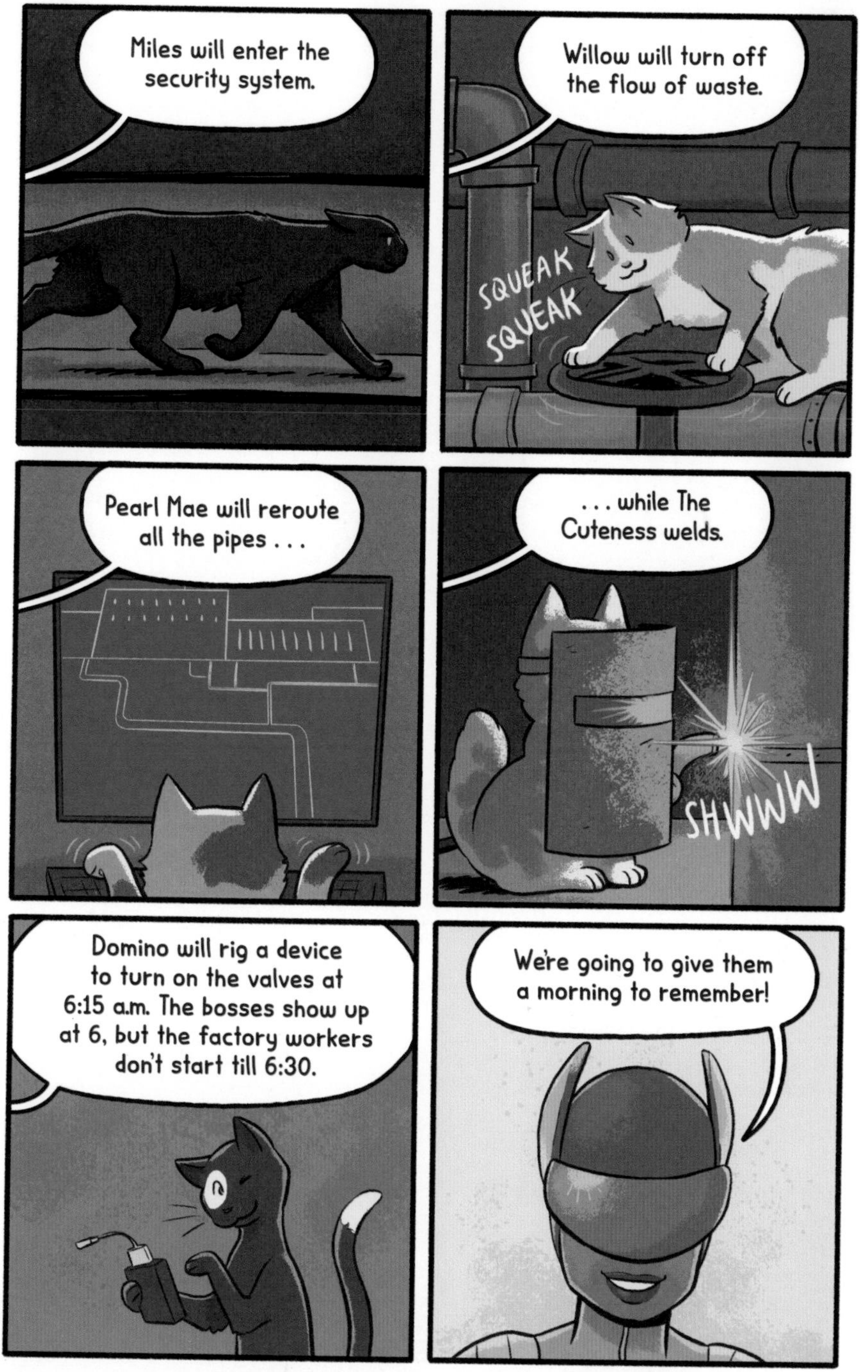
Miles will enter the security system.
Willow will turn off the flow of waste.
SQUEAK SQUEAK
Pearl Mae will reroute all the pipes . . .
. . . while The Cuteness welds.
SHWWW
Domino will rig a device to turn on the valves at 6:15 a.m. The bosses show up at 6, but the factory workers don't start till 6:30.
We're going to give them a morning to remember!

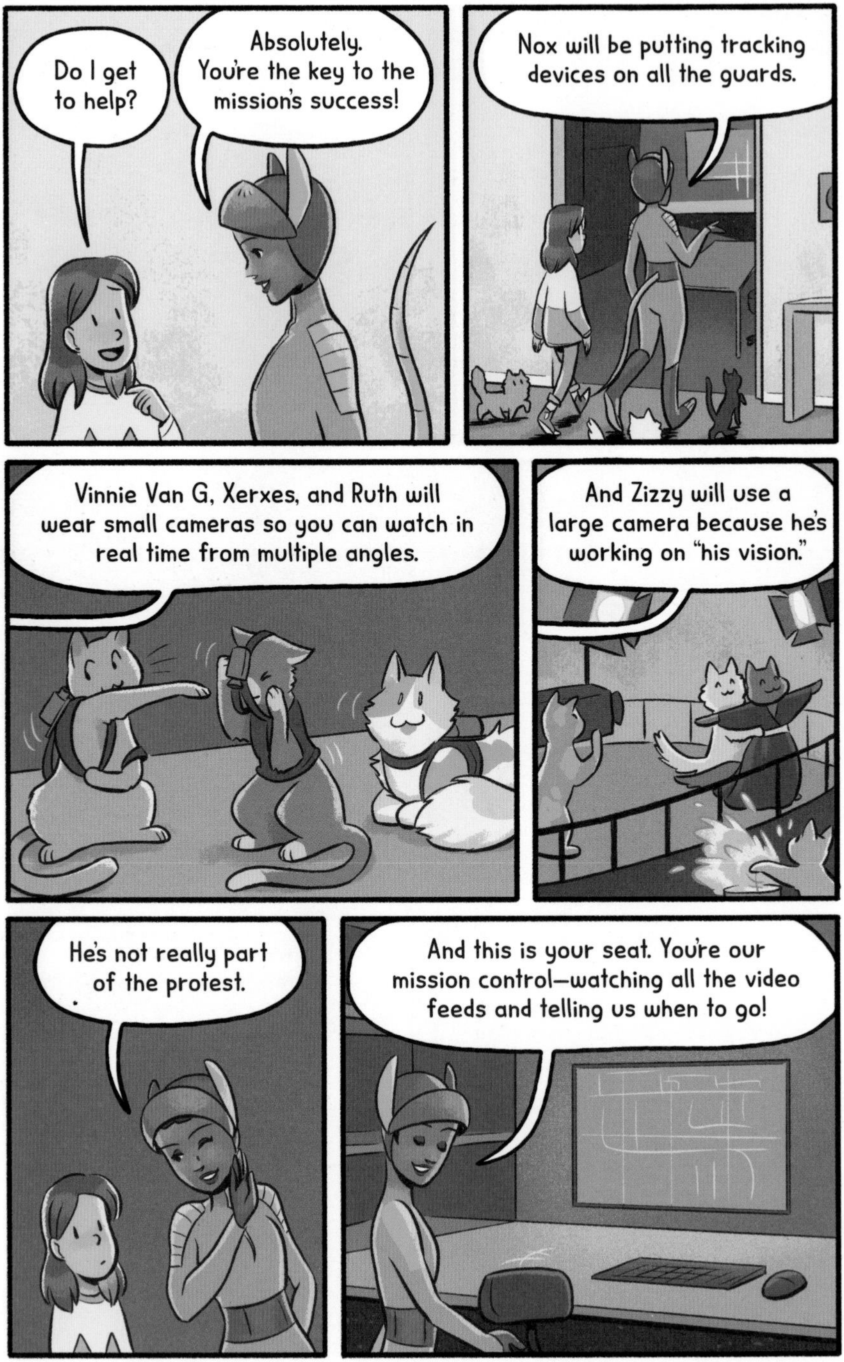
Do I get to help?
Absolutely. You're the key to the mission's success!
Nox will be putting tracking devices on all the guards.
Vinnie Van G, Xerxes, and Ruth will wear small cameras so you can watch in real time from multiple angles.
And Zizzy will use a large camera because he's working on "his vision."
He's not really part of the protest.
And this is your seat. You're our mission control—watching all the video feeds and telling us when to go!

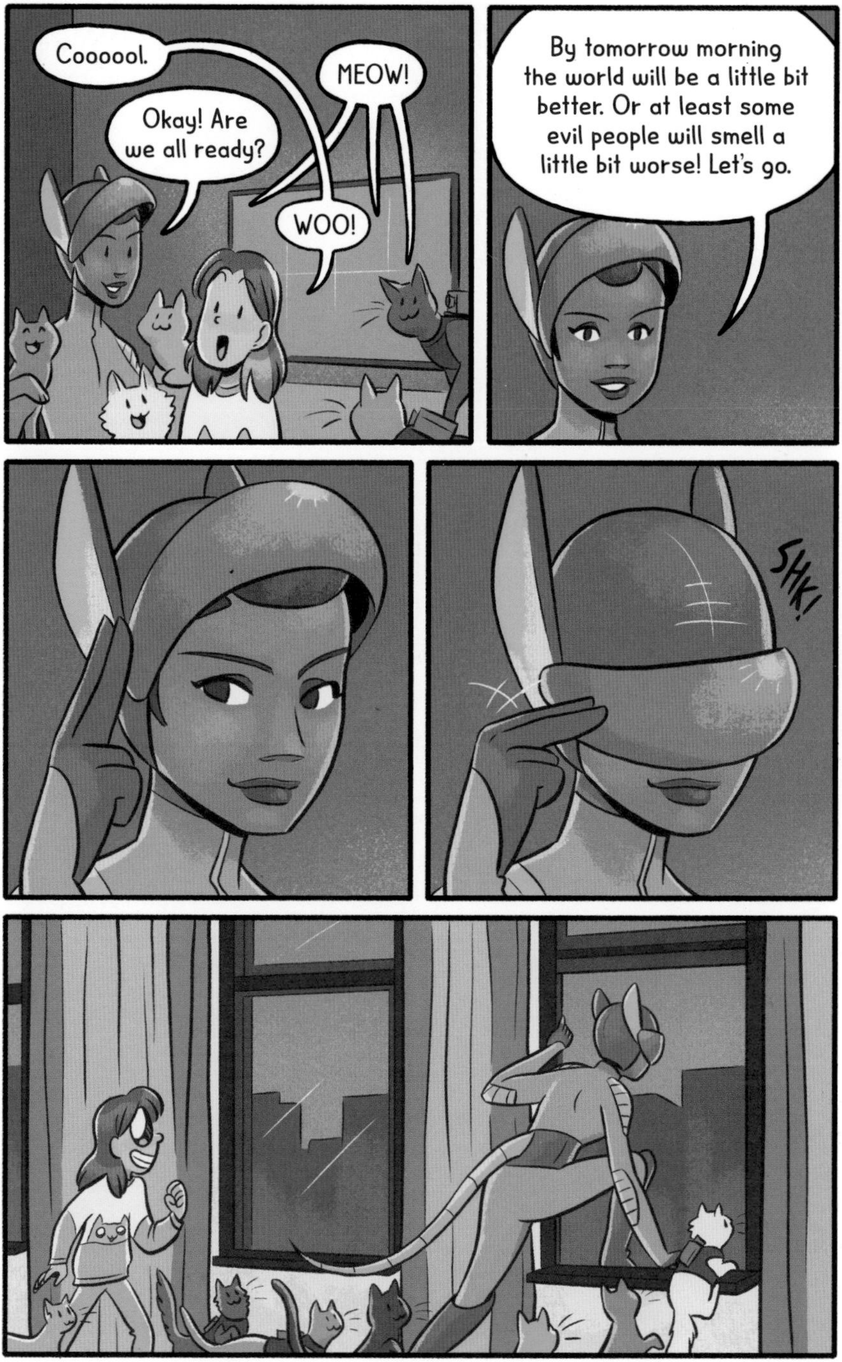
Coooool.
Okay! Are we all ready?
MEOW!
WOO!
By tomorrow morning the world will be a little bit better. Or at least some evil people will smell a little bit worse! Let's go.
SHK!

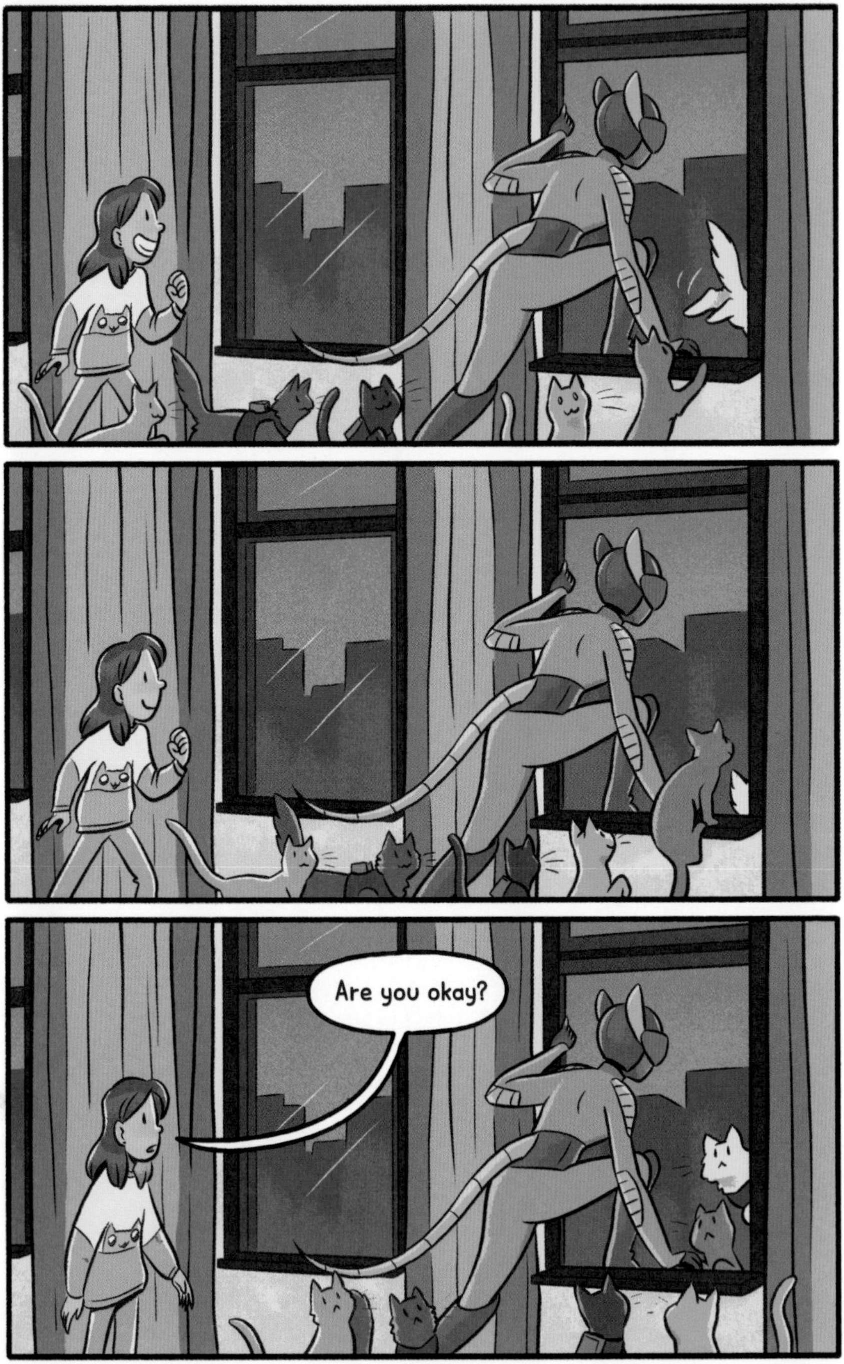
Are you okay?

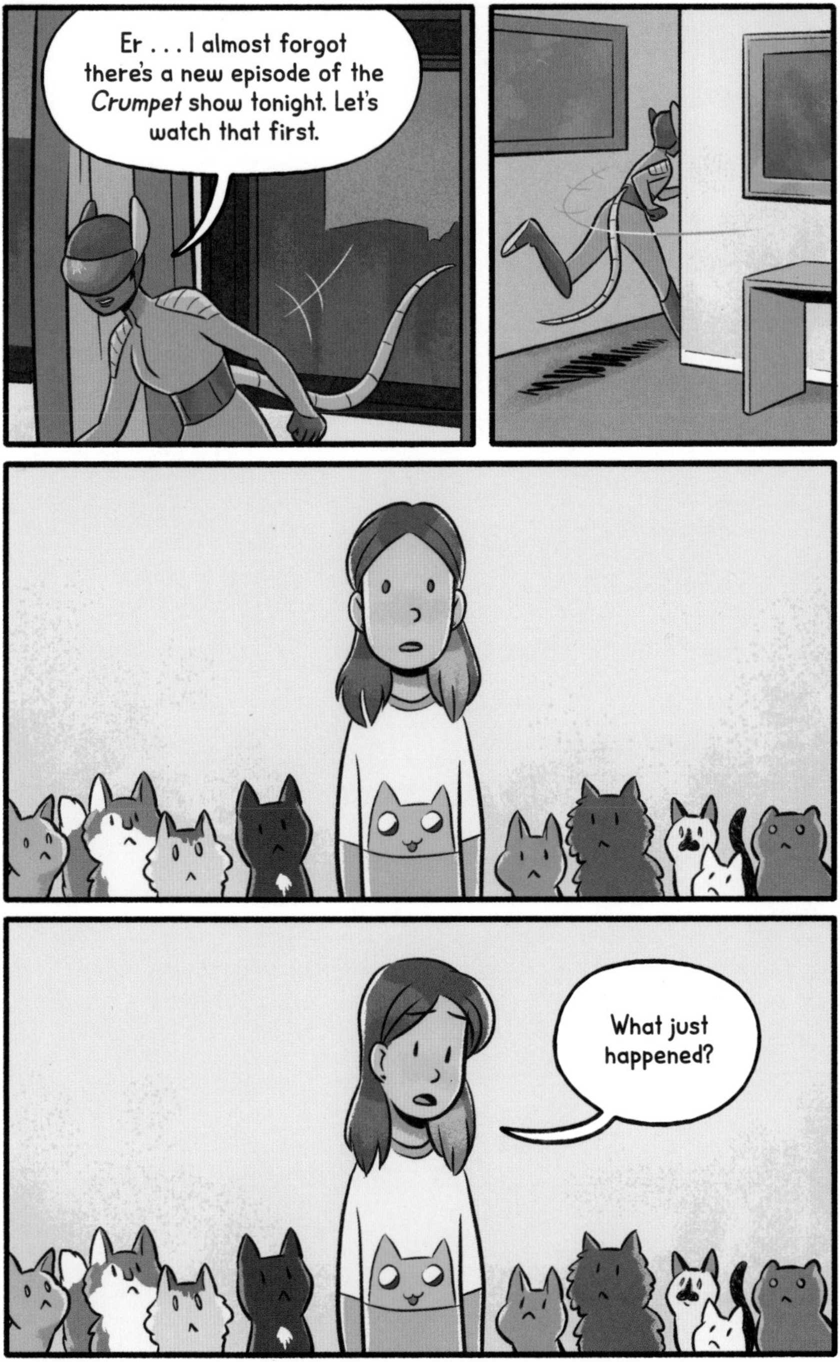
Er . . . I almost forgot there's a new episode of the *Crumpet* show tonight. Let's watch that first.
What just happened?

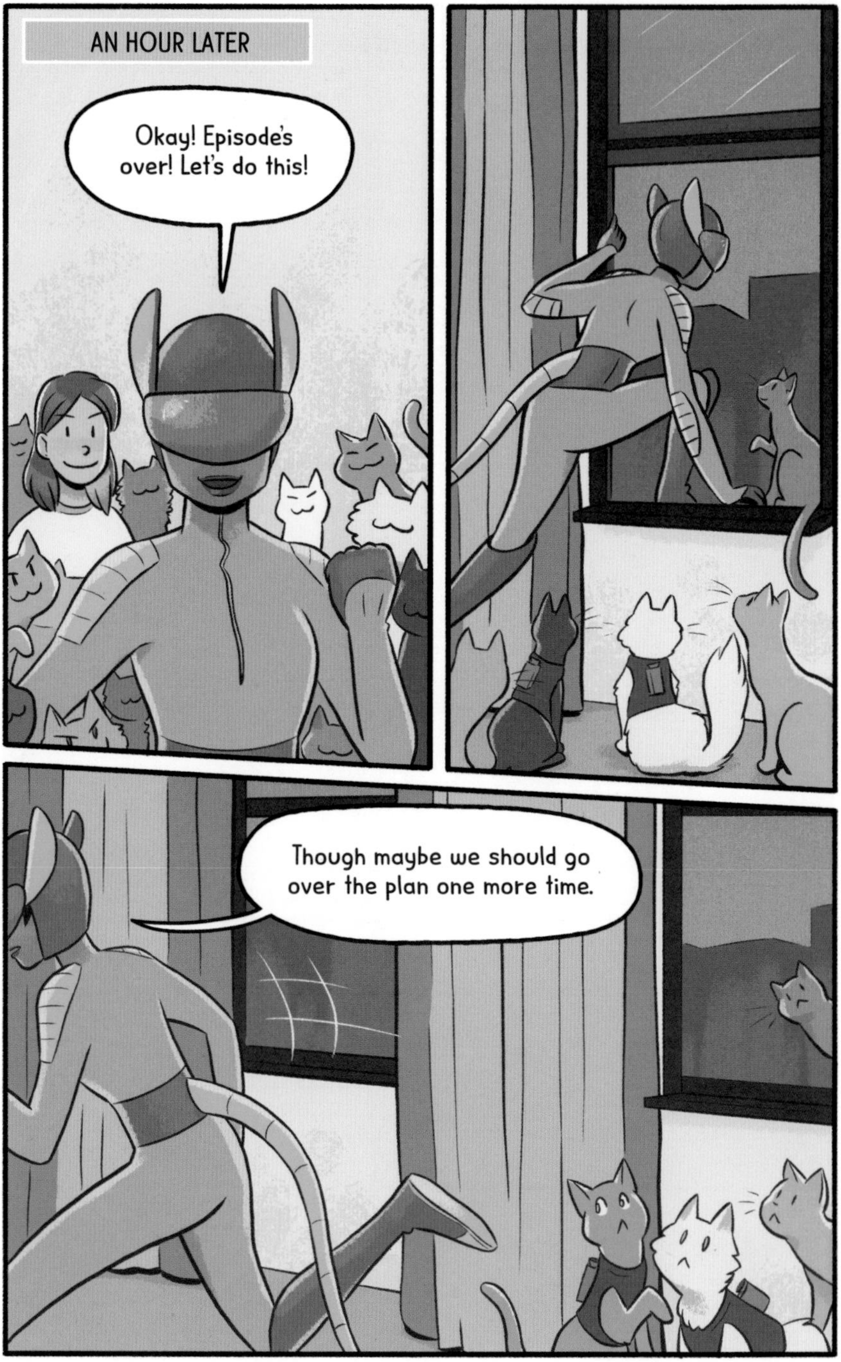
AN HOUR LATER
Okay! Episode's over! Let's do this!
Though maybe we should go over the plan one more time.

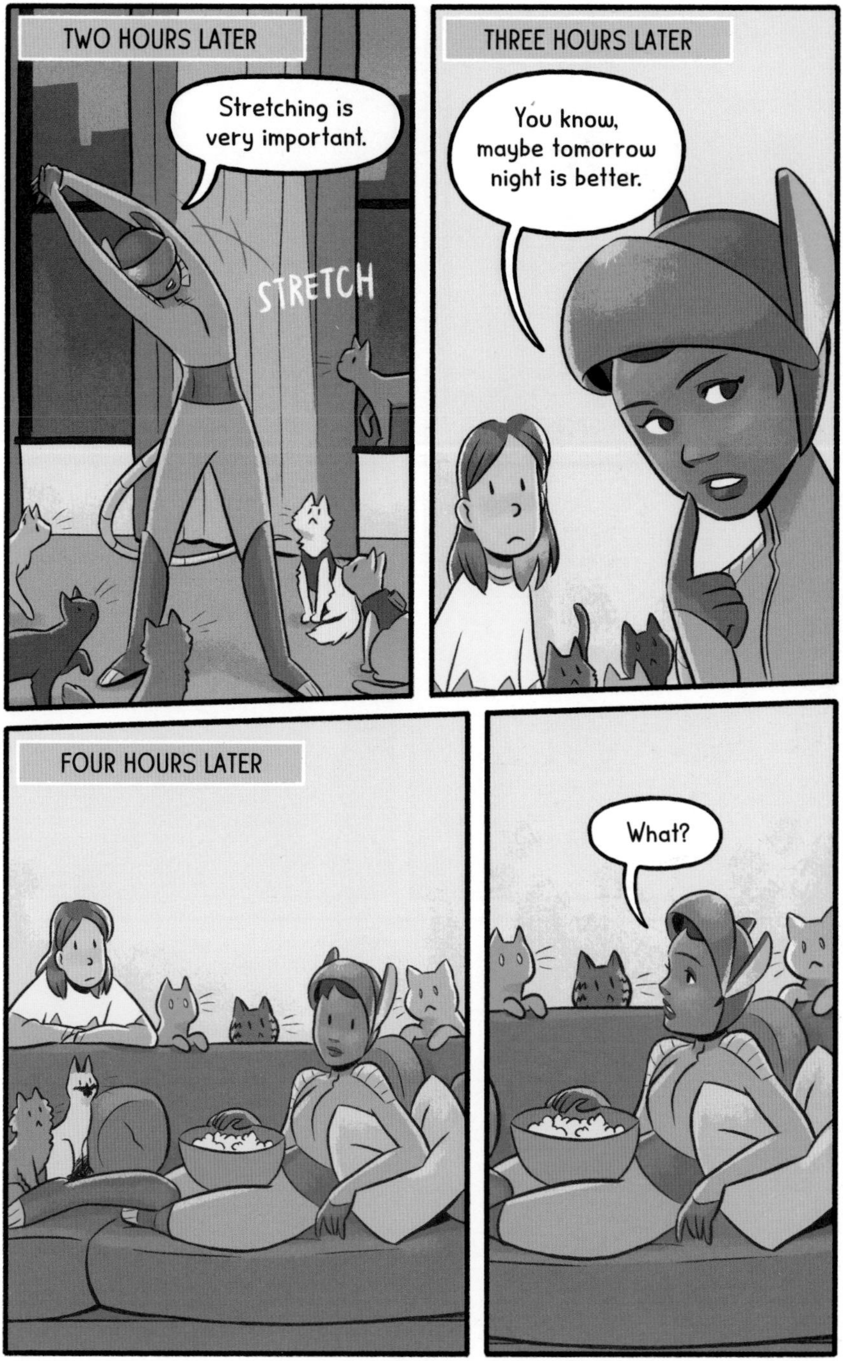
TWO HOURS LATER
Stretching is very important.
STRETCH
THREE HOURS LATER
You know, maybe tomorrow night is better.
FOUR HOURS LATER
What?

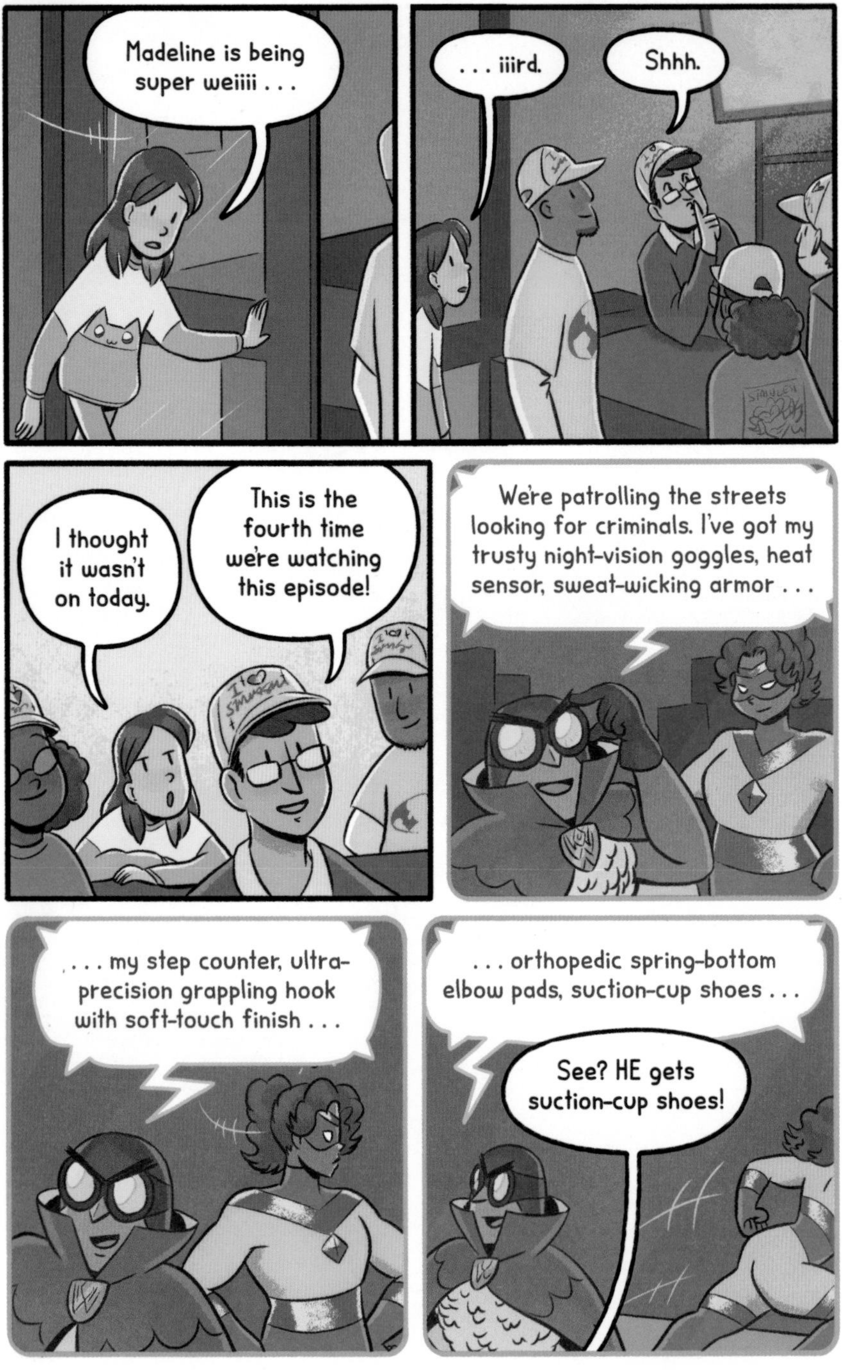

Madeline is being super weiiii . . .
. . . iiird.
Shhh.
I thought it wasn't on today.
This is the fourth time we're watching this episode!
We're patrolling the streets looking for criminals. I've got my trusty night-vision goggles, heat sensor, sweat-wicking armor . . .
. . . my step counter, ultra-precision grappling hook with soft-touch finish . . .
. . . orthopedic spring-bottom elbow pads, suction-cup shoes . . .
See? HE gets suction-cup shoes!

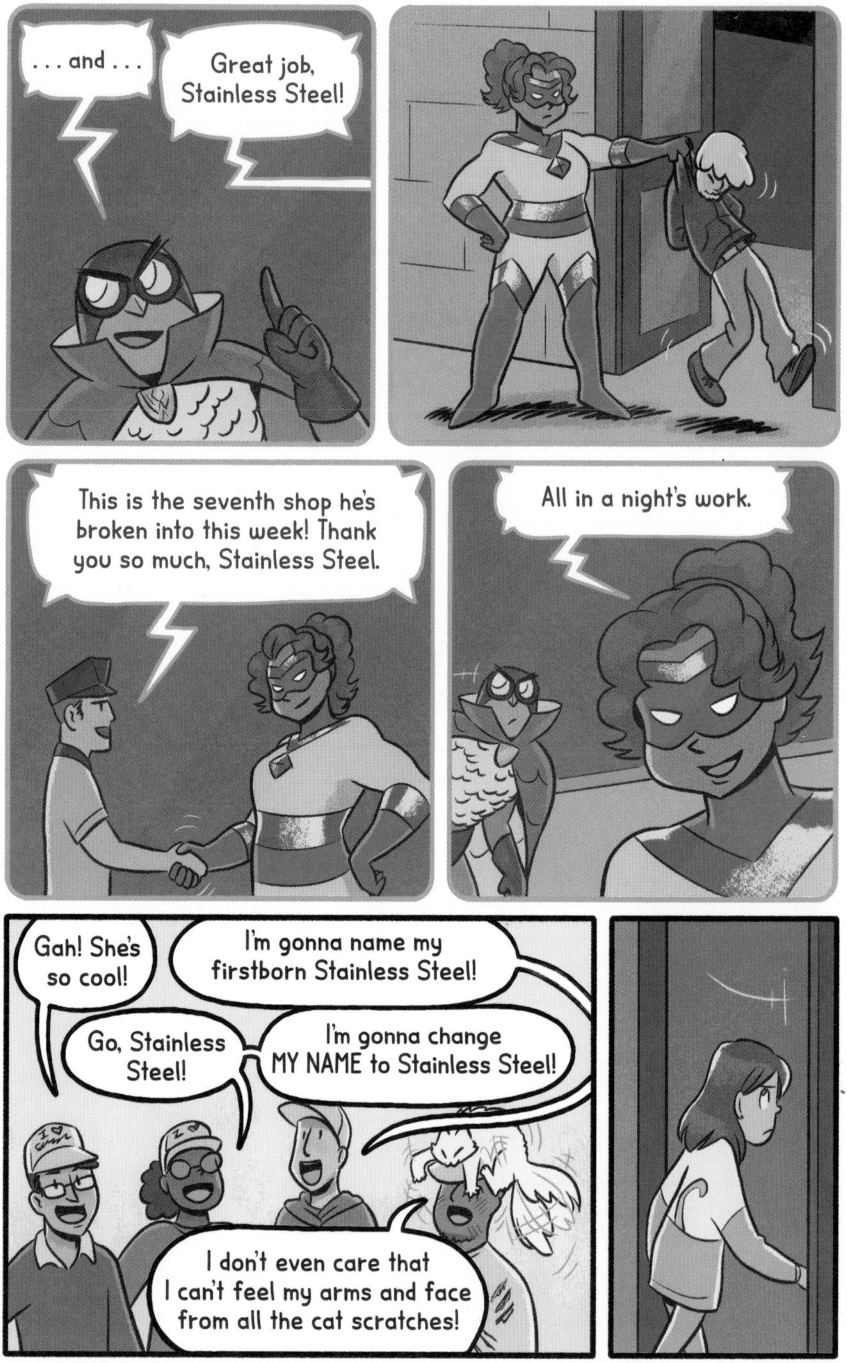
. . . and . . .
Great job, Stainless Steel!
This is the seventh shop he's broken into this week! Thank you so much, Stainless Steel.
All in a night's work.
Gah! She's so cool!
I'm gonna name my firstborn Stainless Steel!
Go, Stainless Steel!
I'm gonna change MY NAME to Stainless Steel!
I don't even care that I can't feel my arms and face from all the cat scratches!

CHAPTER SEVEN

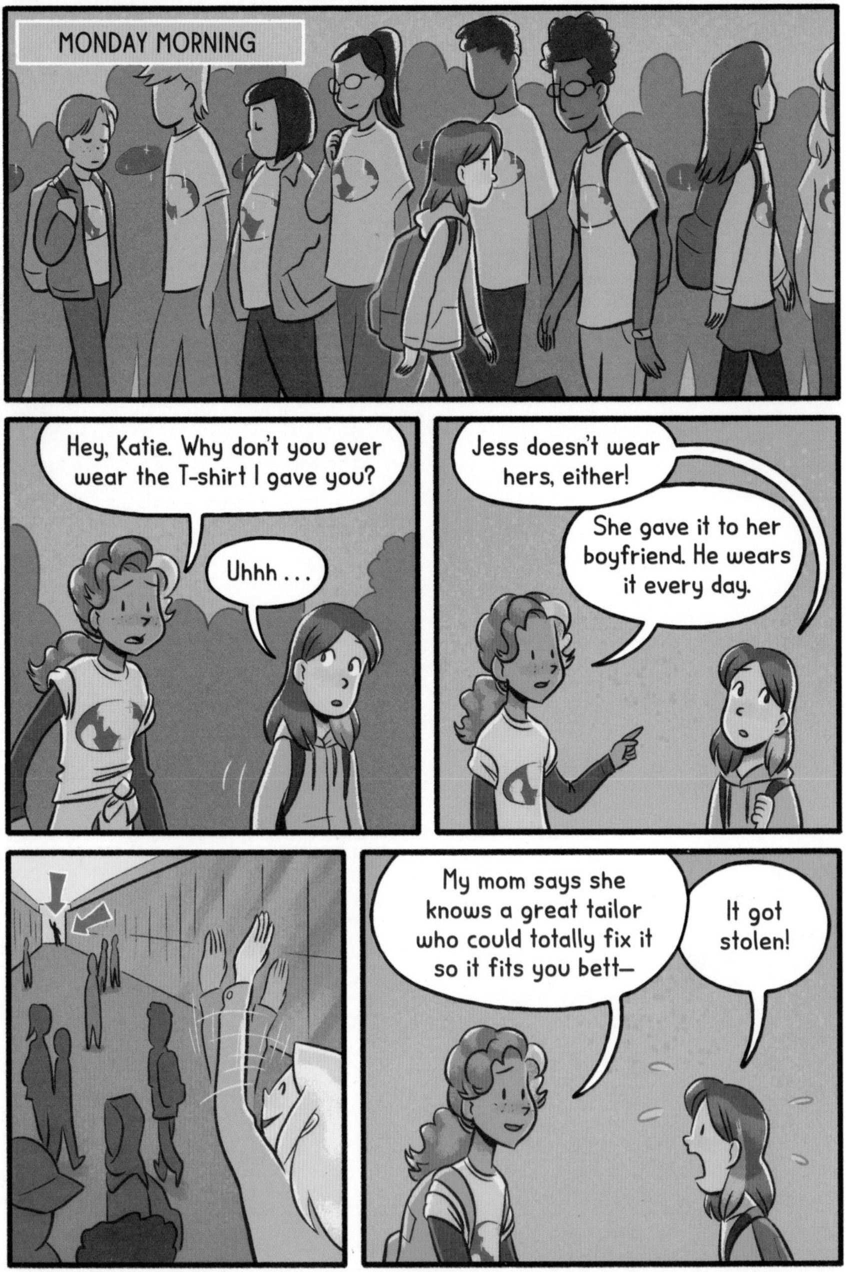

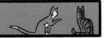

MONDAY MORNING
Hey, Katie. Why don't you ever wear the T-shirt I gave you?
Uhhh . . .
Jess doesn't wear hers, either!
She gave it to her boyfriend. He wears it every day.
My mom says she knows a great tailor who could totally fix it so it fits you bett—
It got stolen!

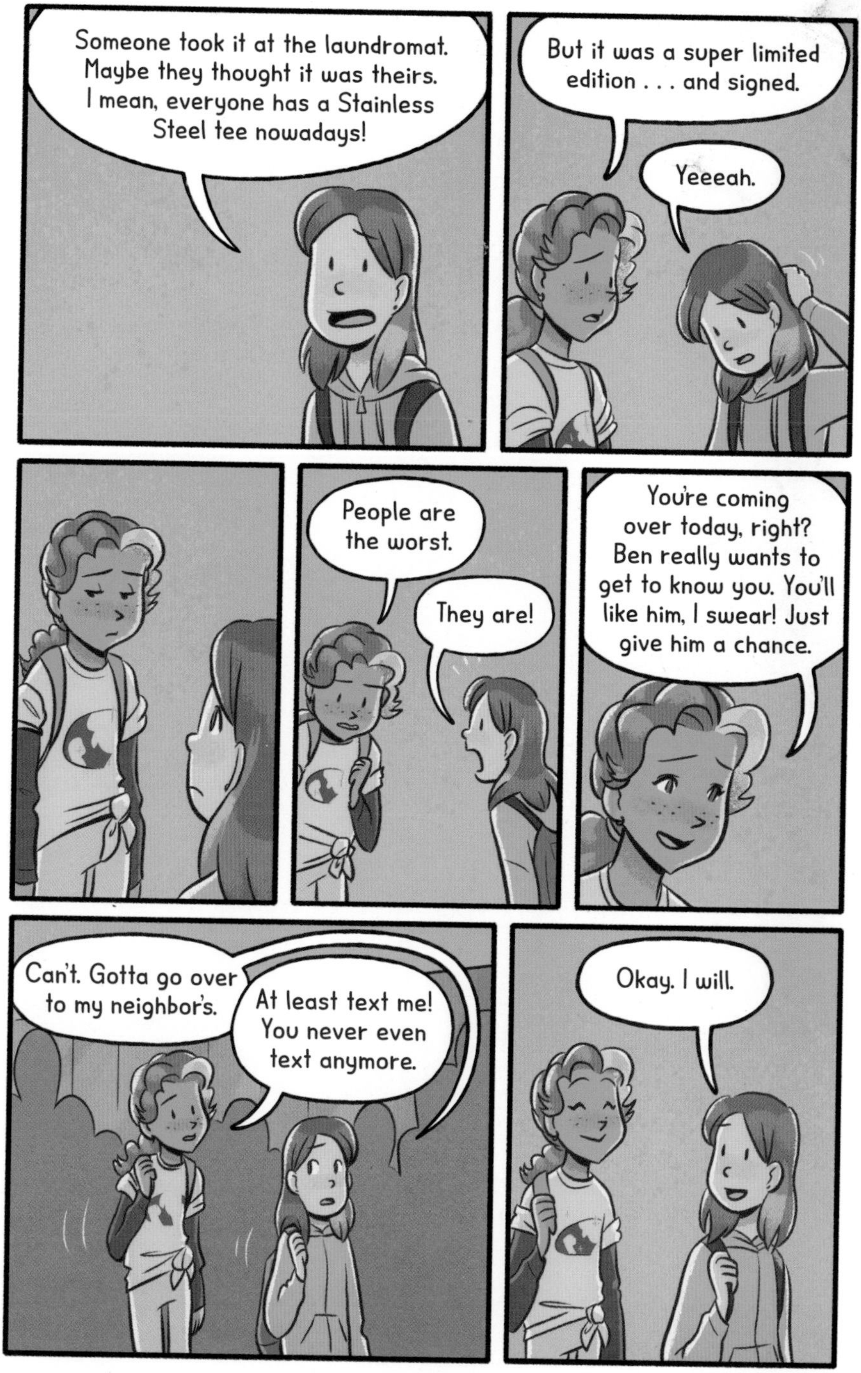
Someone took it at the laundromat. Maybe they thought it was theirs. I mean, everyone has a Stainless Steel tee nowadays!
But it was a super limited edition . . . and signed.
Yeeeah.
People are the worst.
They are!
You're coming over today, right? Ben really wants to get to know you. You'll like him, I swear! Just give him a chance.
Can't. Gotta go over to my neighbor's.
At least text me! You never even text anymore.
Okay. I will.

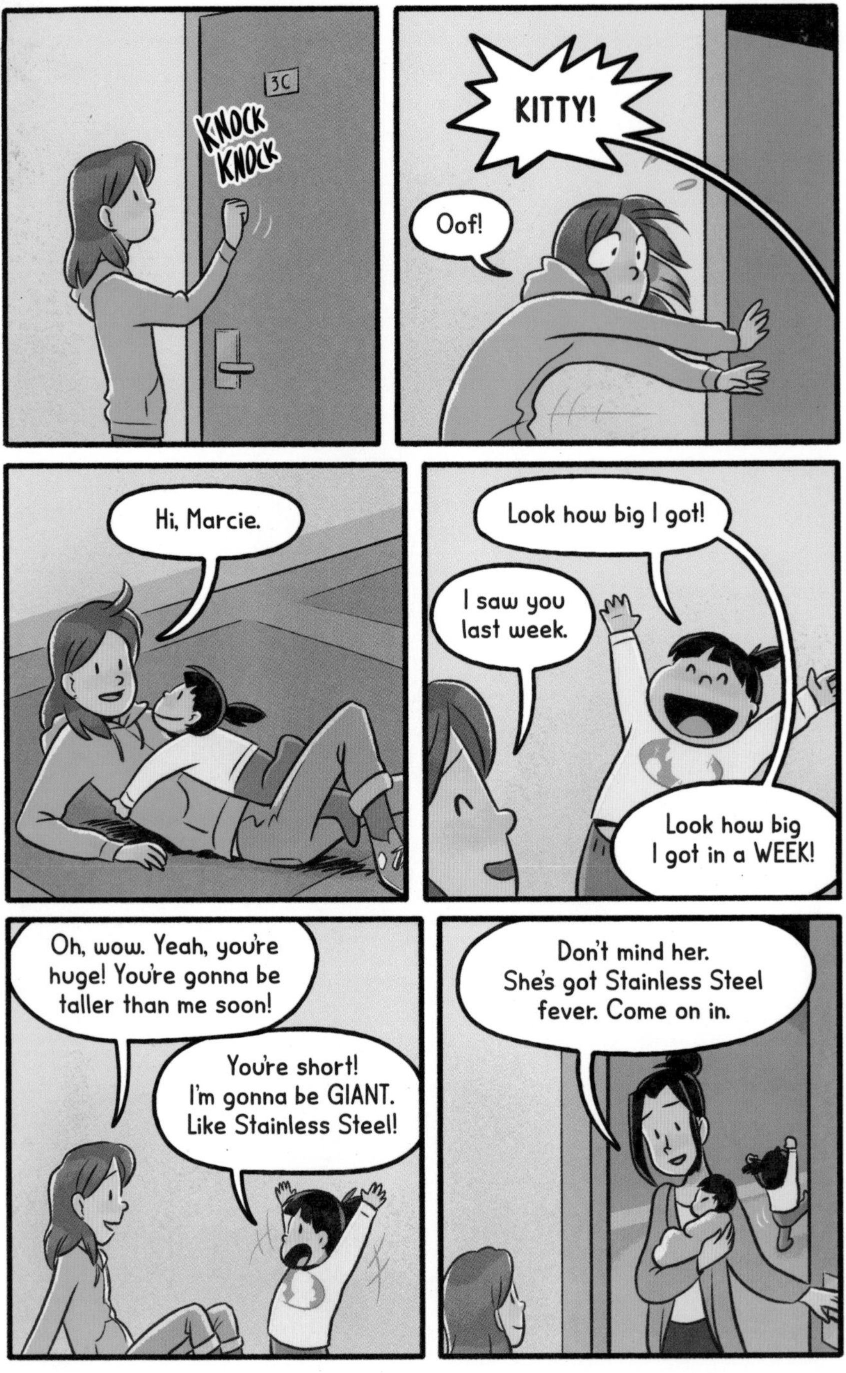
3C
KNOCK KNOCK
KITTY!
Oof!
Hi, Marcie.
Look how big I got!
I saw you last week.
Look how big I got in a WEEK!
Oh, wow. Yeah, you're huge! You're gonna be taller than me soon!
You're short! I'm gonna be GIANT. Like Stainless Steel!
Don't mind her. She's got Stainless Steel fever. Come on in.

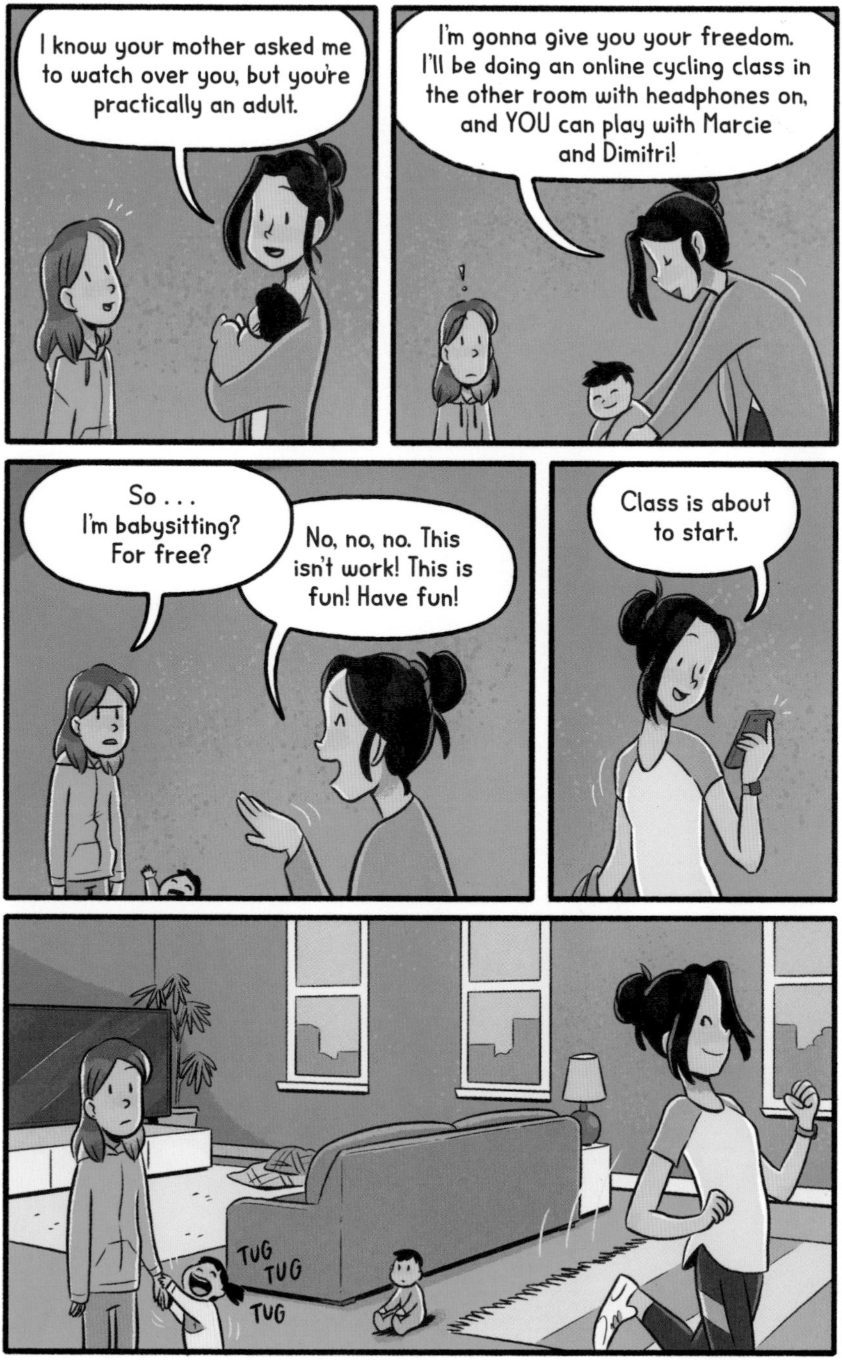
I know your mother asked me to watch over you, but you're practically an adult.
I'm gonna give you your freedom. I'll be doing an online cycling class in the other room with headphones on, and YOU can play with Marcie and Dimitri!
!
So . . . I'm babysitting? For free?
No, no, no. This isn't work! This is fun! Have fun!
Class is about to start.
TUG TUG
TUG

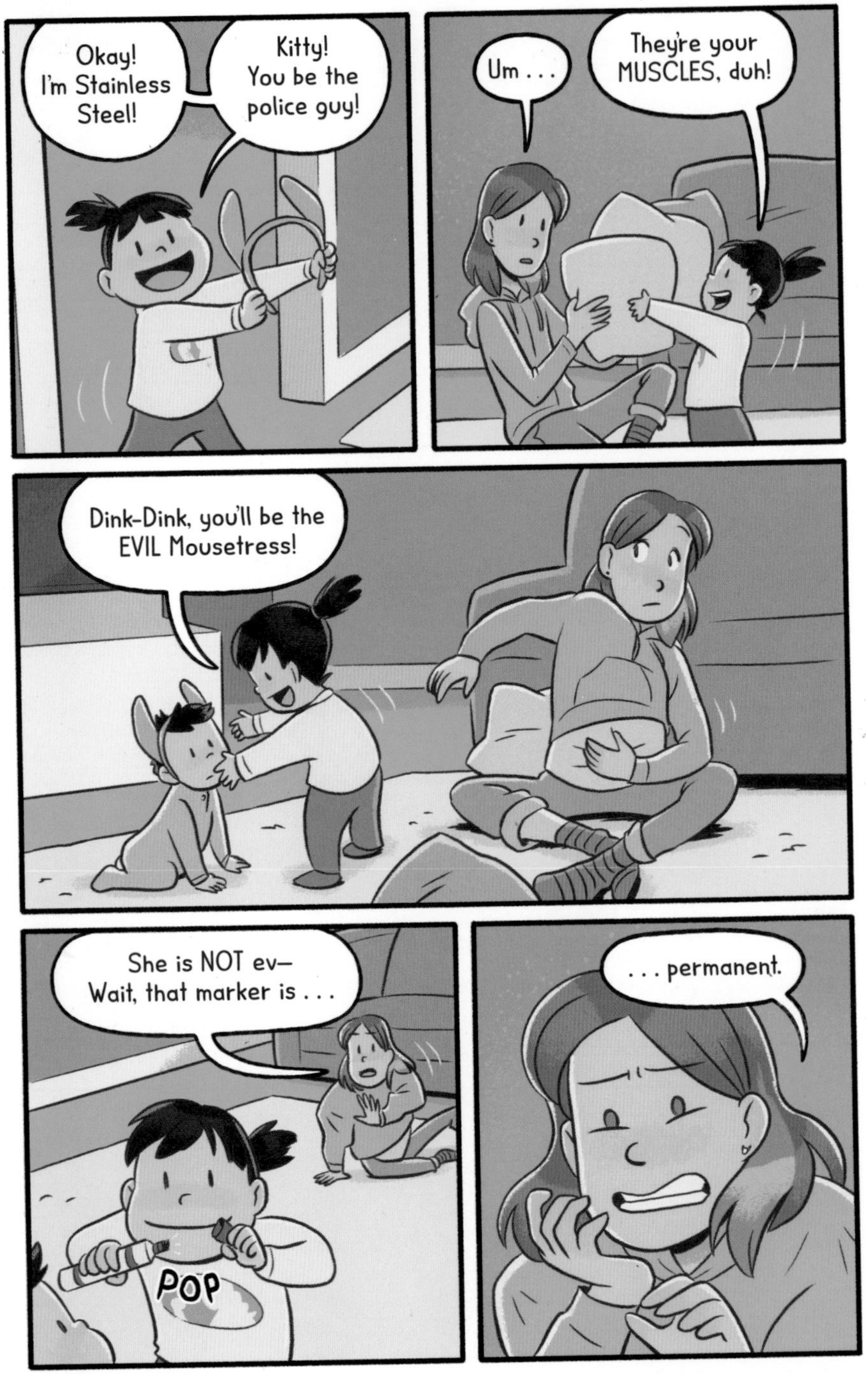
Okay! I'm Stainless Steel!
Kitty! You be the police guy!
Um . . .
They're your MUSCLES, duh!
Dink-Dink, you'll be the EVIL Mousetress!
She is NOT ev— Wait, that marker is . . .
POP
. . . permanent.

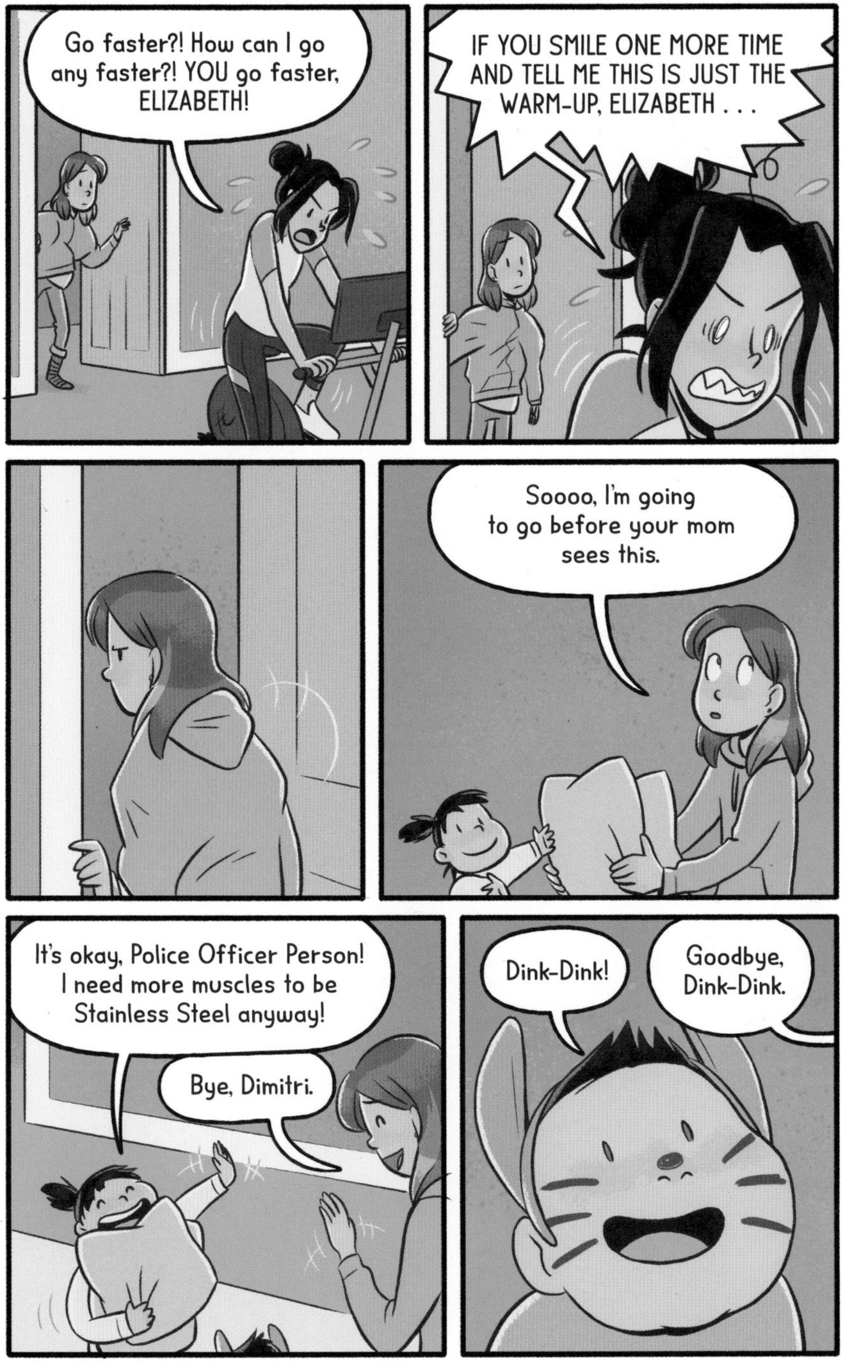
Go faster?! How can I go any faster?! YOU go faster, ELIZABETH!
IF YOU SMILE ONE MORE TIME AND TELL ME THIS IS JUST THE WARM-UP, ELIZABETH . . .
Soooo, I'm going to go before your mom sees this.
It's okay, Police Officer Person! I need more muscles to be Stainless Steel anyway!
Bye, Dimitri.
Dink-Dink!
Goodbye, Dink-Dink.

SATURDAY MORNING

Blah! I don't like museums!

I promise you, you'll like this exhibit!

Hey, Katie.

Where are your boards?

Too cold. No more skateboarding till the spring. Didn't Marie text you?

Ugh, yeah. I might have gone for one last ride with my new phone in my pocket. Sorry.

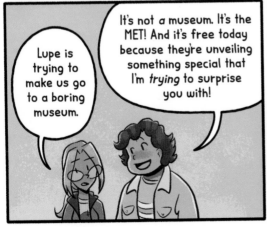

Lupe is trying to make us go to a boring museum.

It's not a museum. It's the MET! And it's free today because they're unveiling something special that I'm *trying* to surprise you with!

I like museums.

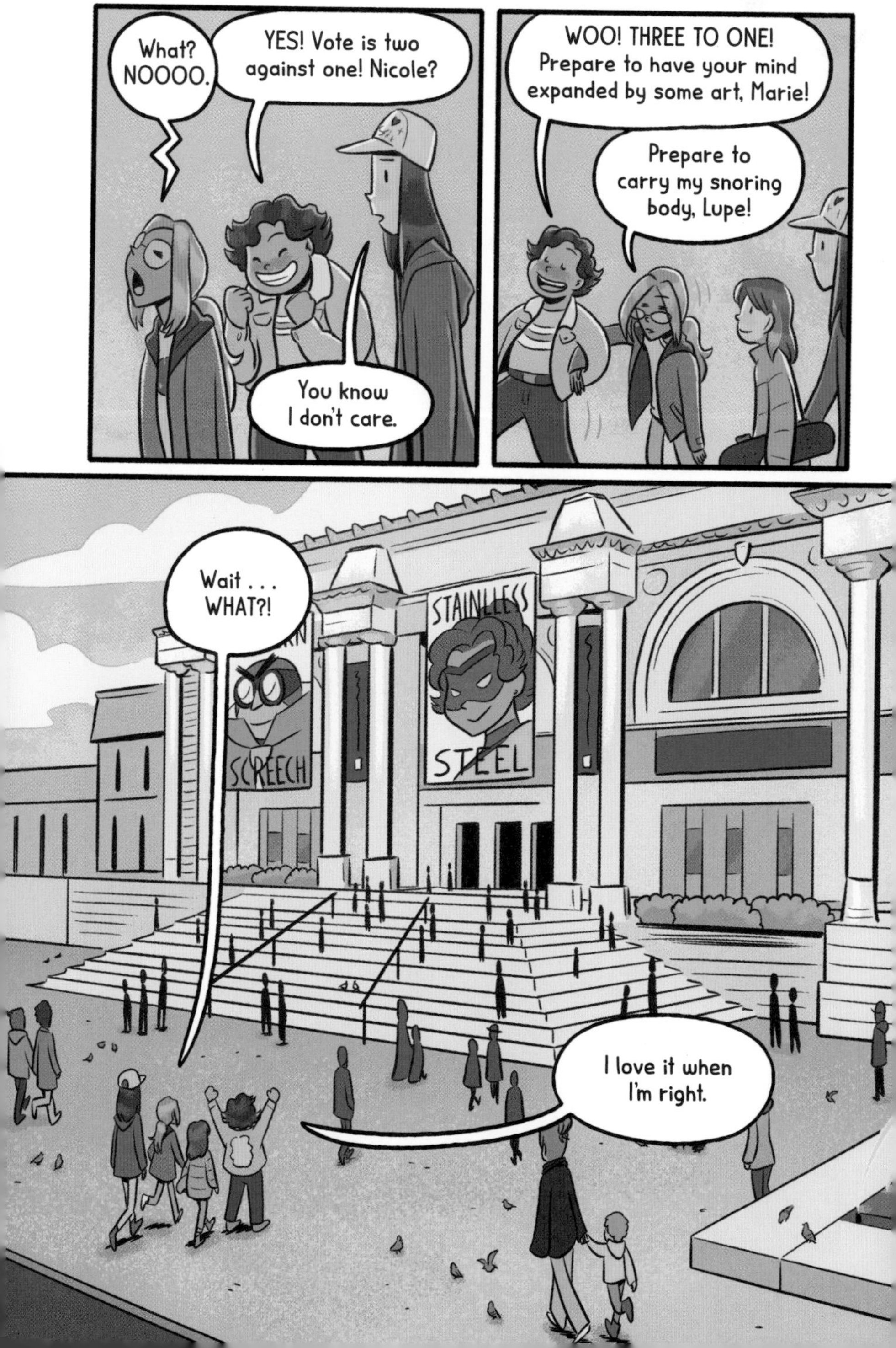
What? NOOOO.
YES! Vote is two against one! Nicole?
You know I don't care.
WOO! THREE TO ONE! Prepare to have your mind expanded by some art, Marie!
Prepare to carry my snoring body, Lupe!
Wait . . . WHAT?!
STAINLESS STEEL
SCREECH
I love it when I'm right.

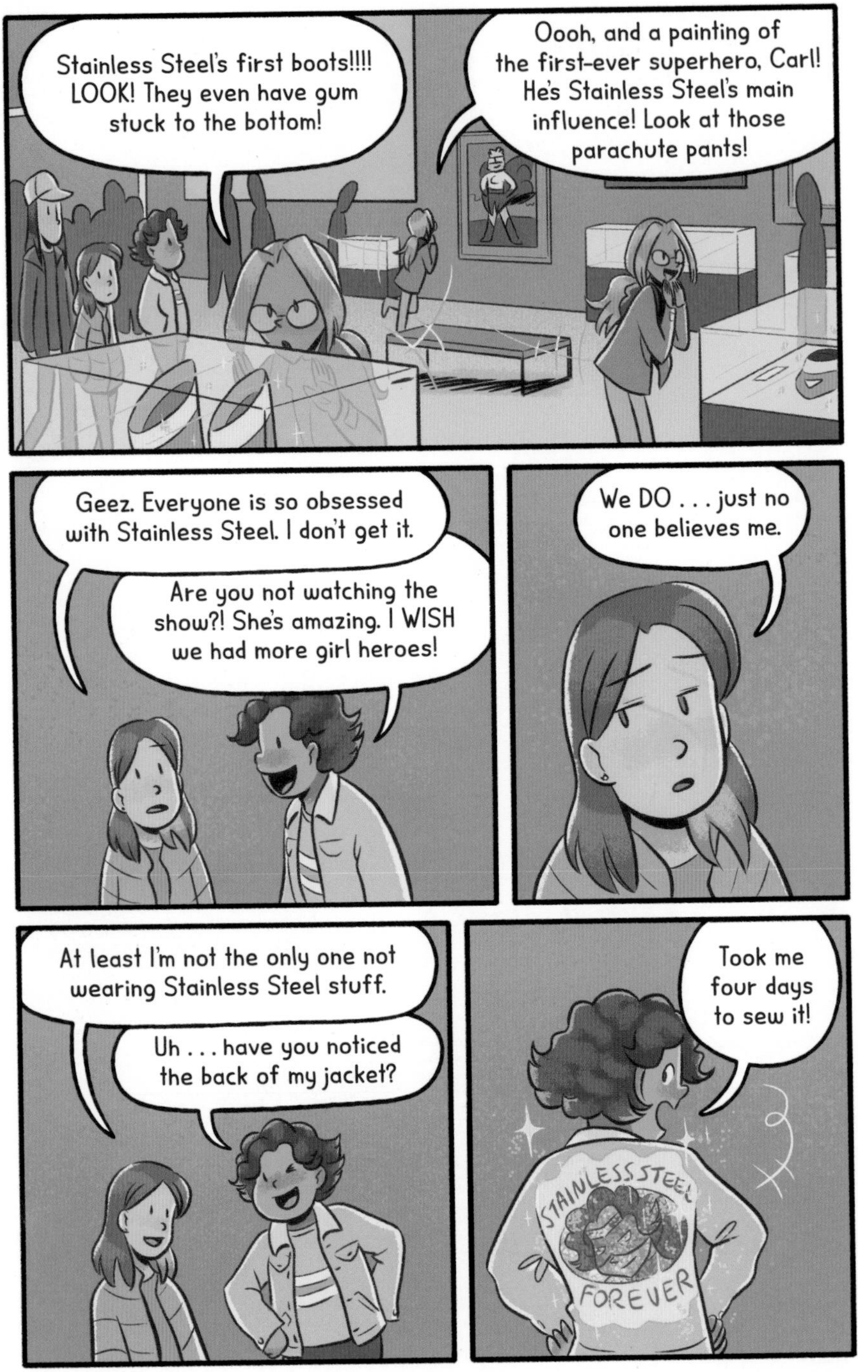

Stainless Steel's first boots!!!! LOOK! They even have gum stuck to the bottom!
Oooh, and a painting of the first-ever superhero, Carl! He's Stainless Steel's main influence! Look at those parachute pants!
Geez. Everyone is so obsessed with Stainless Steel. I don't get it.
Are you not watching the show?! She's amazing. I WISH we had more girl heroes!
We DO . . . just no one believes me.
At least I'm not the only one not wearing Stainless Steel stuff.
Uh . . . have you noticed the back of my jacket?
Took me four days to sew it!
STAINLESS STEEL
FOREVER

Oh. Cool.

Okay, folks. The big moment is here! The unveiling of a new painting for our permanent collection!

WHOOSH

No pushing. Everyone behind the line.

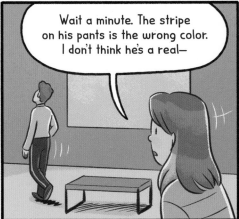

Wait a minute. The stripe on his pants is the wrong color. I don't think he's a real—

Katie!

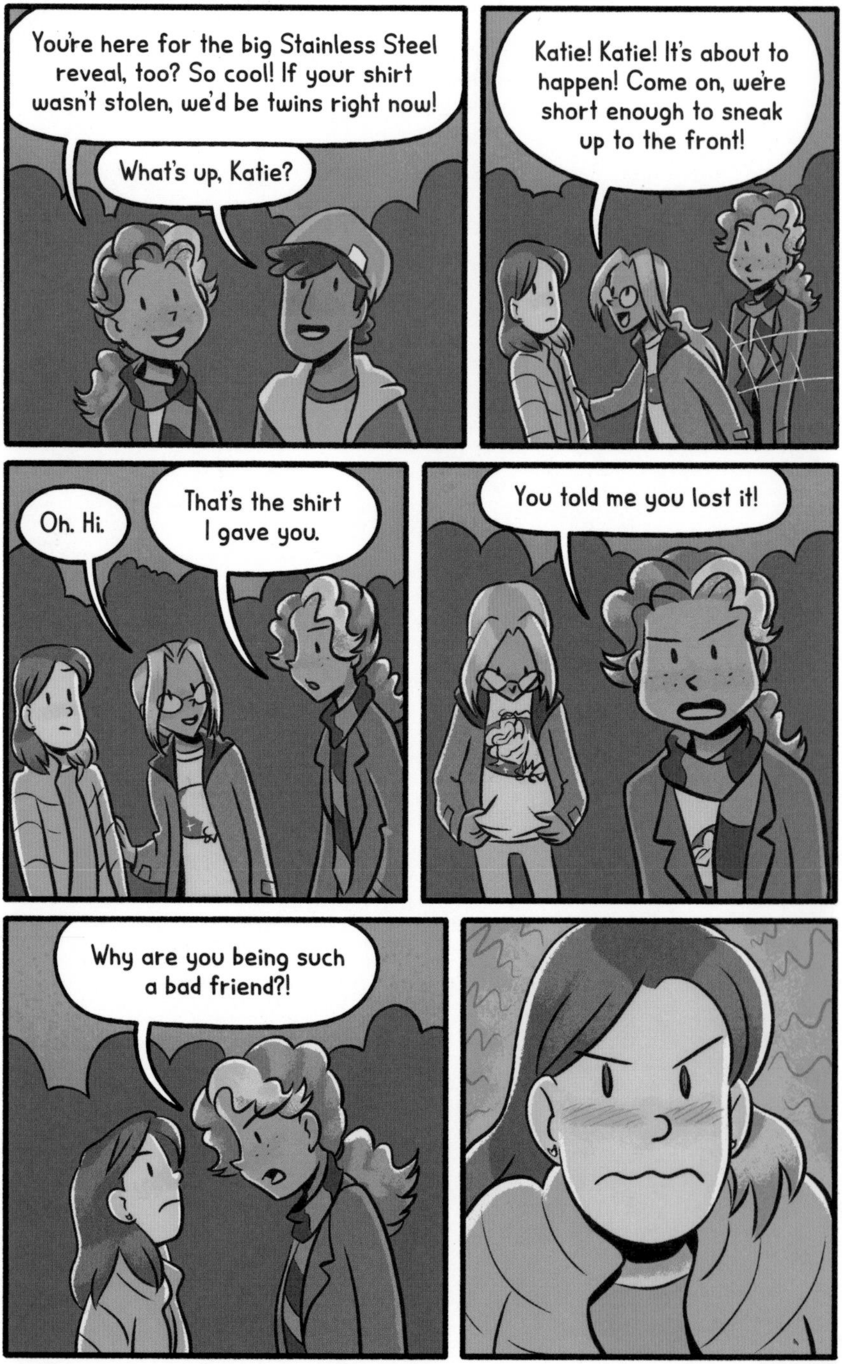
You're here for the big Stainless Steel reveal, too? So cool! If your shirt wasn't stolen, we'd be twins right now!
What's up, Katie?
Katie! Katie! It's about to happen! Come on, we're short enough to sneak up to the front!
Oh. Hi.
That's the shirt I gave you.
You told me you lost it!
Why are you being such a bad friend?!

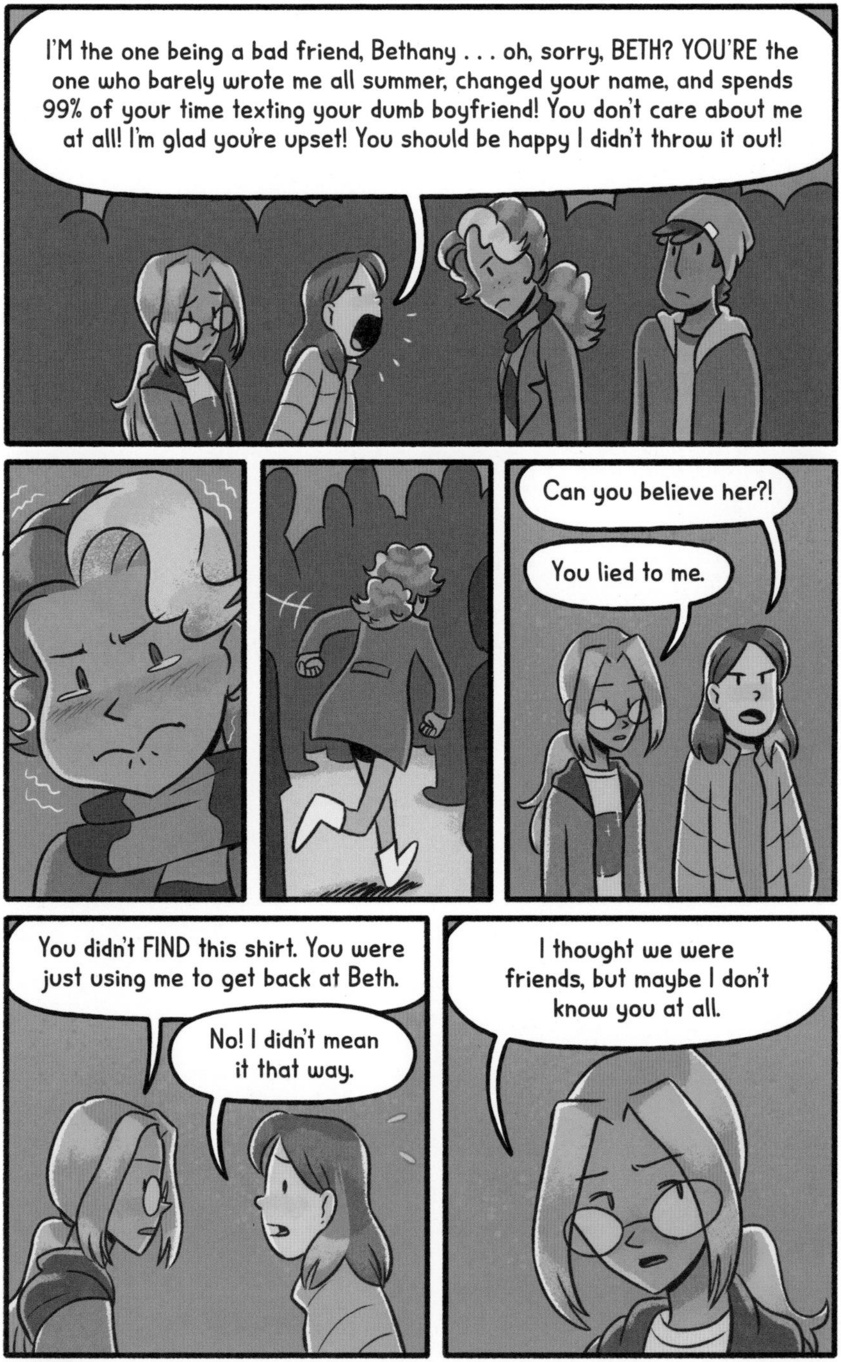
I'M the one being a bad friend, Bethany . . . oh, sorry, BETH? YOU'RE the one who barely wrote me all summer, changed your name, and spends 99% of your time texting your dumb boyfriend! You don't care about me at all! I'm glad you're upset! You should be happy I didn't throw it out!
Can you believe her?!
You lied to me.
You didn't FIND this shirt. You were just using me to get back at Beth.
No! I didn't mean it that way.
I thought we were friends, but maybe I don't know you at all.

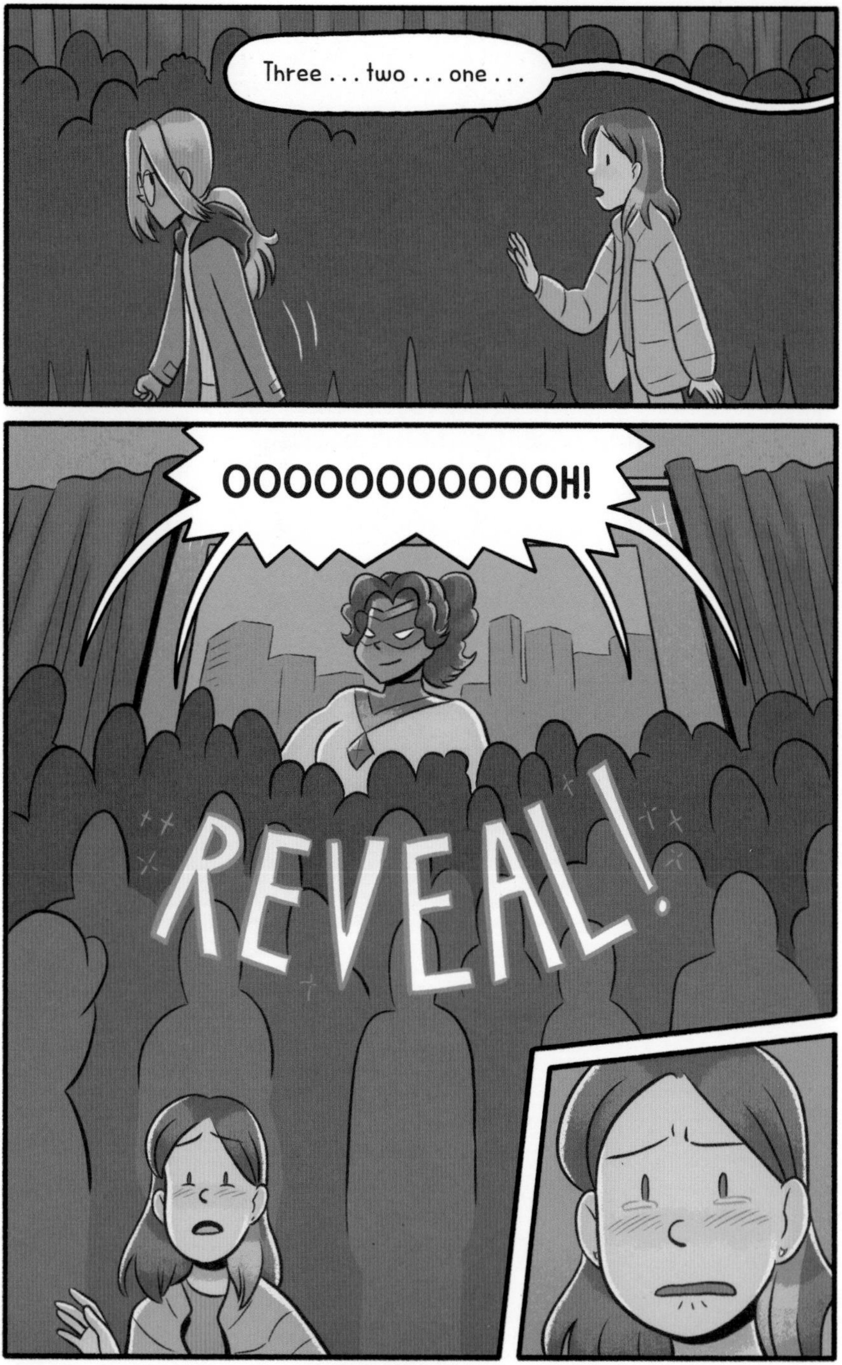
Three . . . two . . . one . . .
OOOOOOOOOOOOH!
REVEAL!

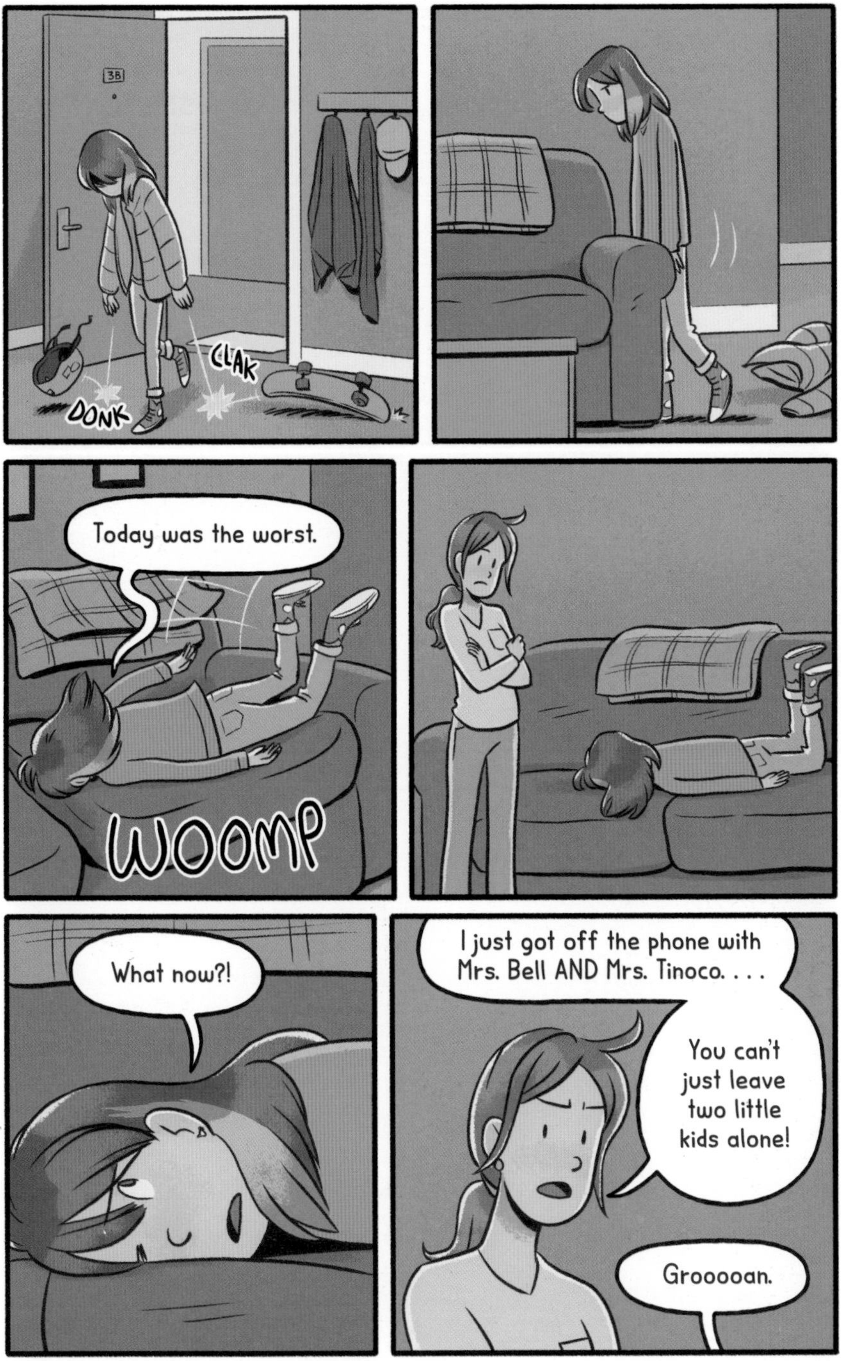
DONK
CLAK
Today was the worst.
WOOMP
What now?!
I just got off the phone with Mrs. Bell AND Mrs. Tinoco. . . .
You can't just leave two little kids alone!
Groooan.

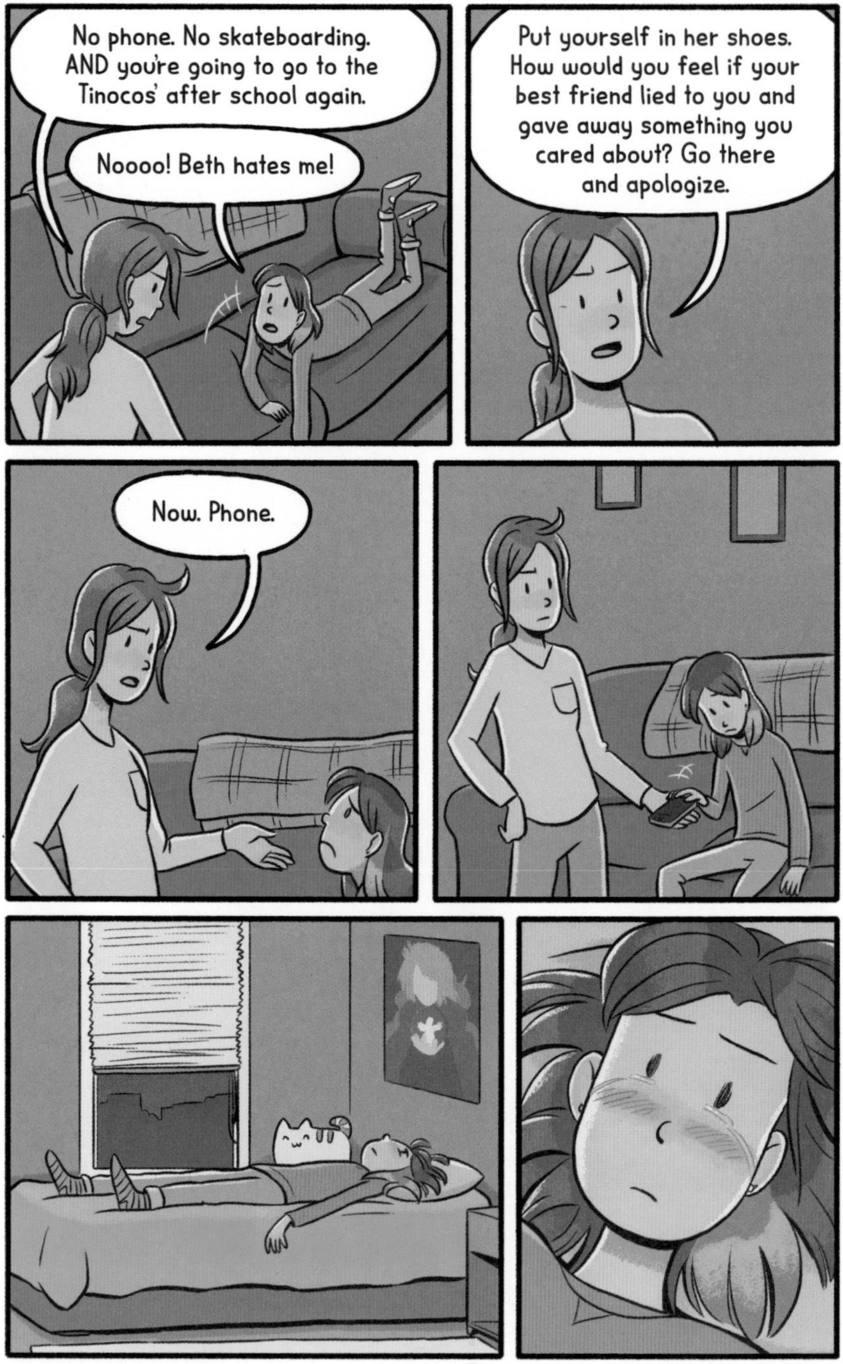
No phone. No skateboarding. AND you're going to go to the Tinocos' after school again.
Noooo! Beth hates me!
Put yourself in her shoes. How would you feel if your best friend lied to you and gave away something you cared about? Go there and apologize.
Now. Phone.

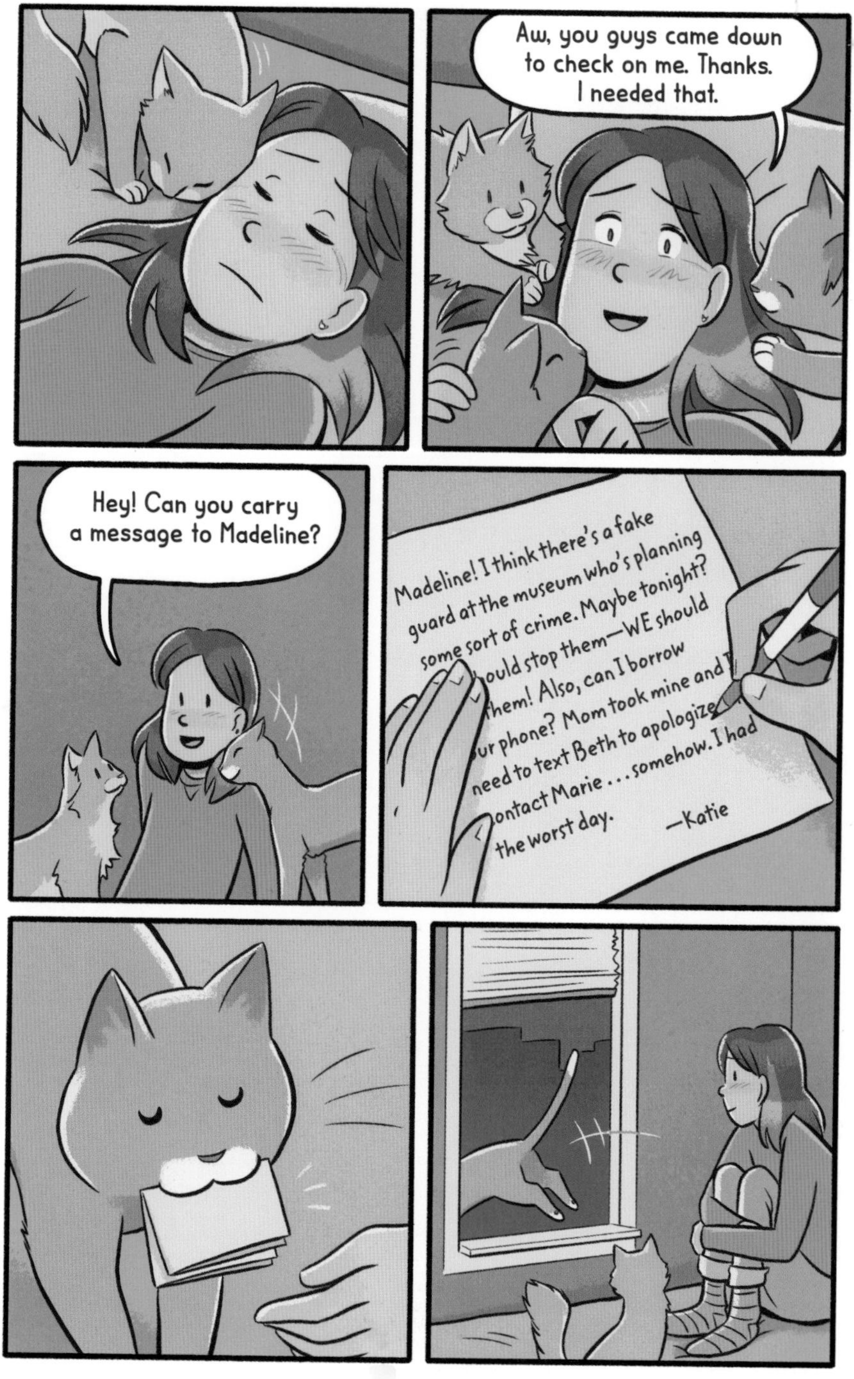
Aw, you guys came down to check on me. Thanks. I needed that.
Hey! Can you carry a message to Madeline?
Madeline! I think there's a fake
guard at the museum who's planning
some sort of crime. Maybe tonight?
hould stop them—WE should
them! Also, can I borrow
ur phone? Mom took mine and
need to text Beth to apologize
ontact Marie . . . somehow. I had
the worst day.
—Katie

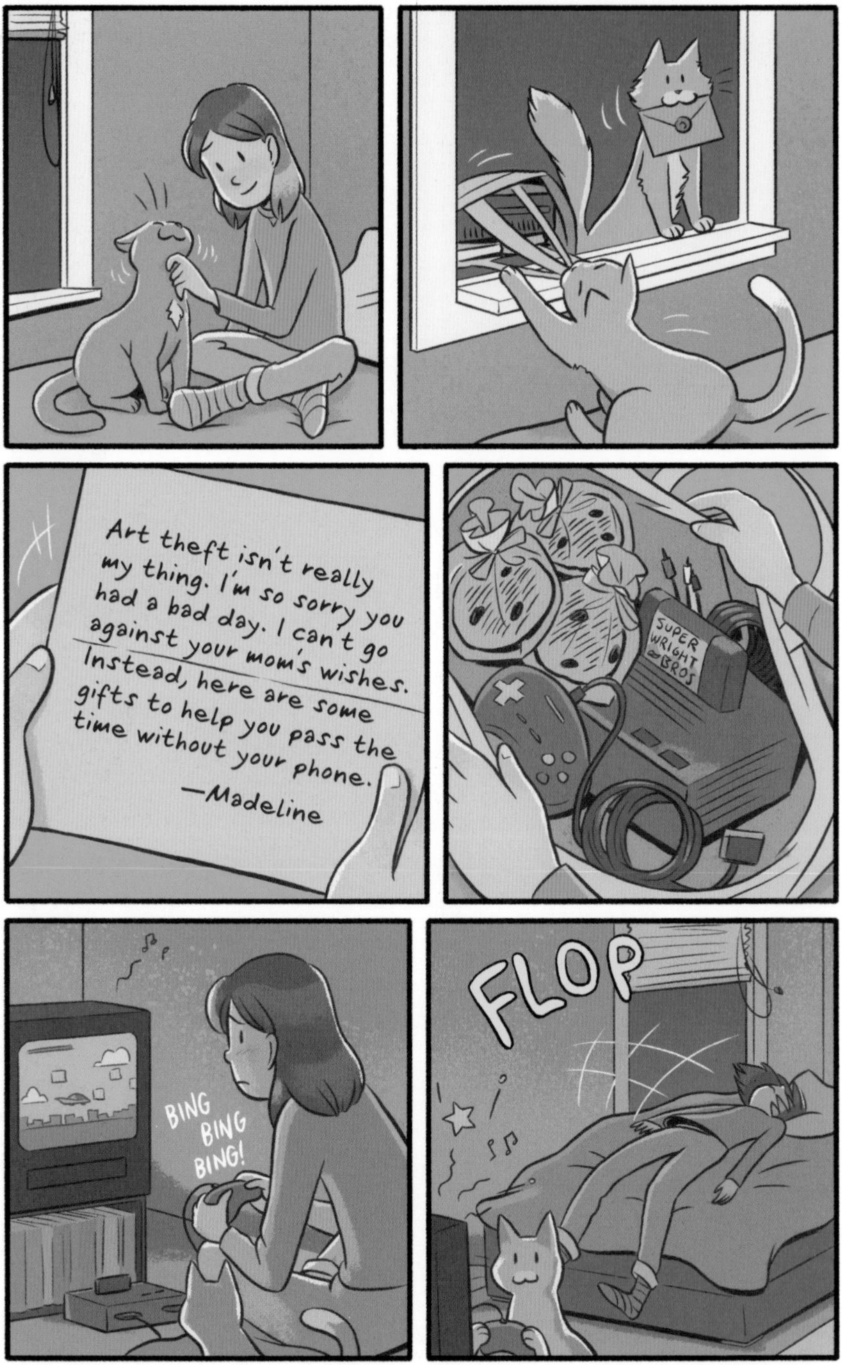
Art theft isn't really my thing. I'm so sorry you had a bad day. I can't go against your mom's wishes. Instead, here are some gifts to help you pass the time without your phone.
—Madeline
SUPER WRIGHT BROS
BING BING BING!
FLOP

LATER THAT EVENING . . .

CRACK

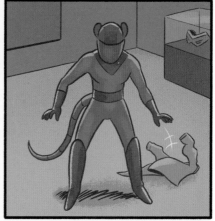

SCRAAAAAAATCH

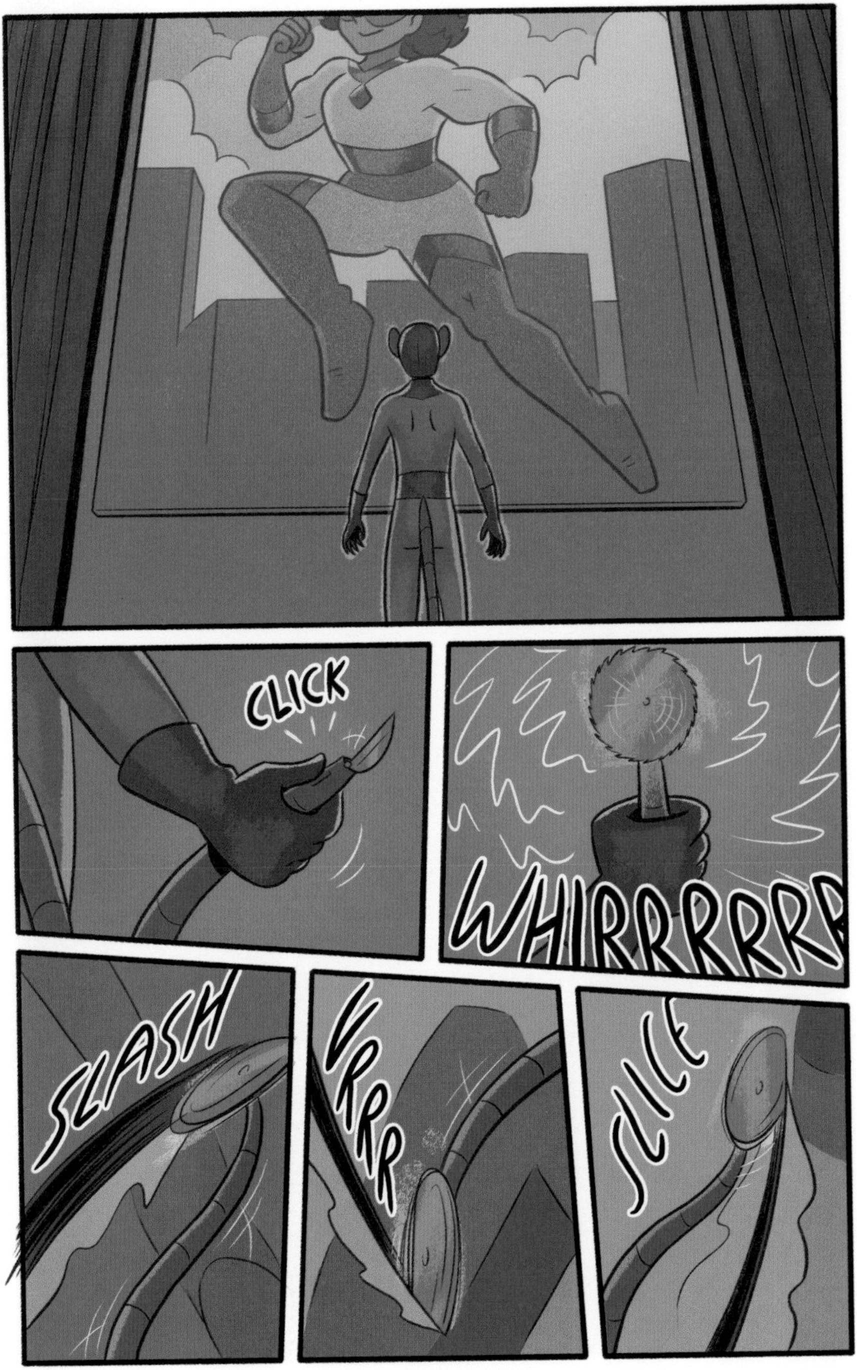
CLICK
WHIRRRRRR
SLASH
VRRR
SLICE

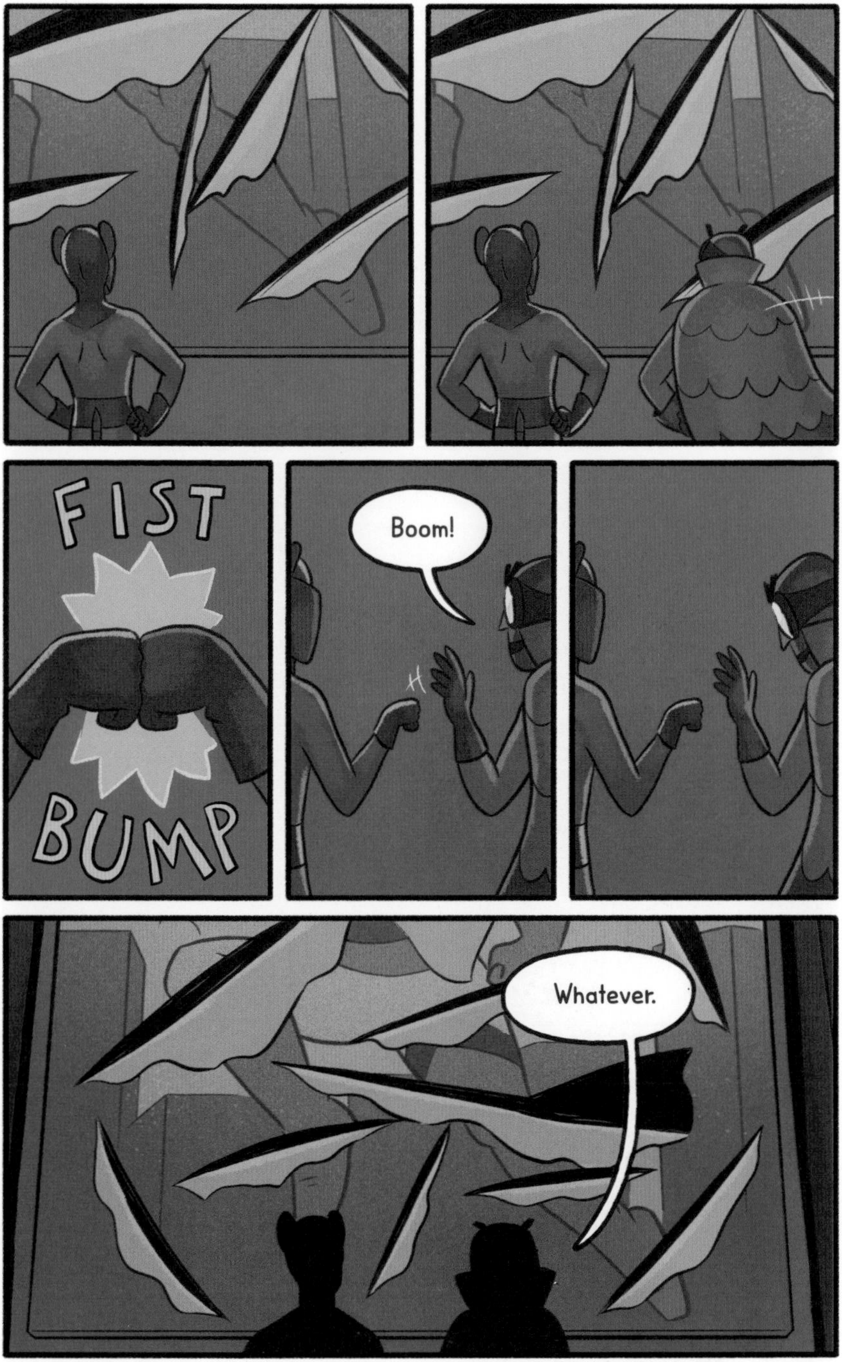
FIST
BUMP
Boom!
Whatever.

CHAPTER EIGHT

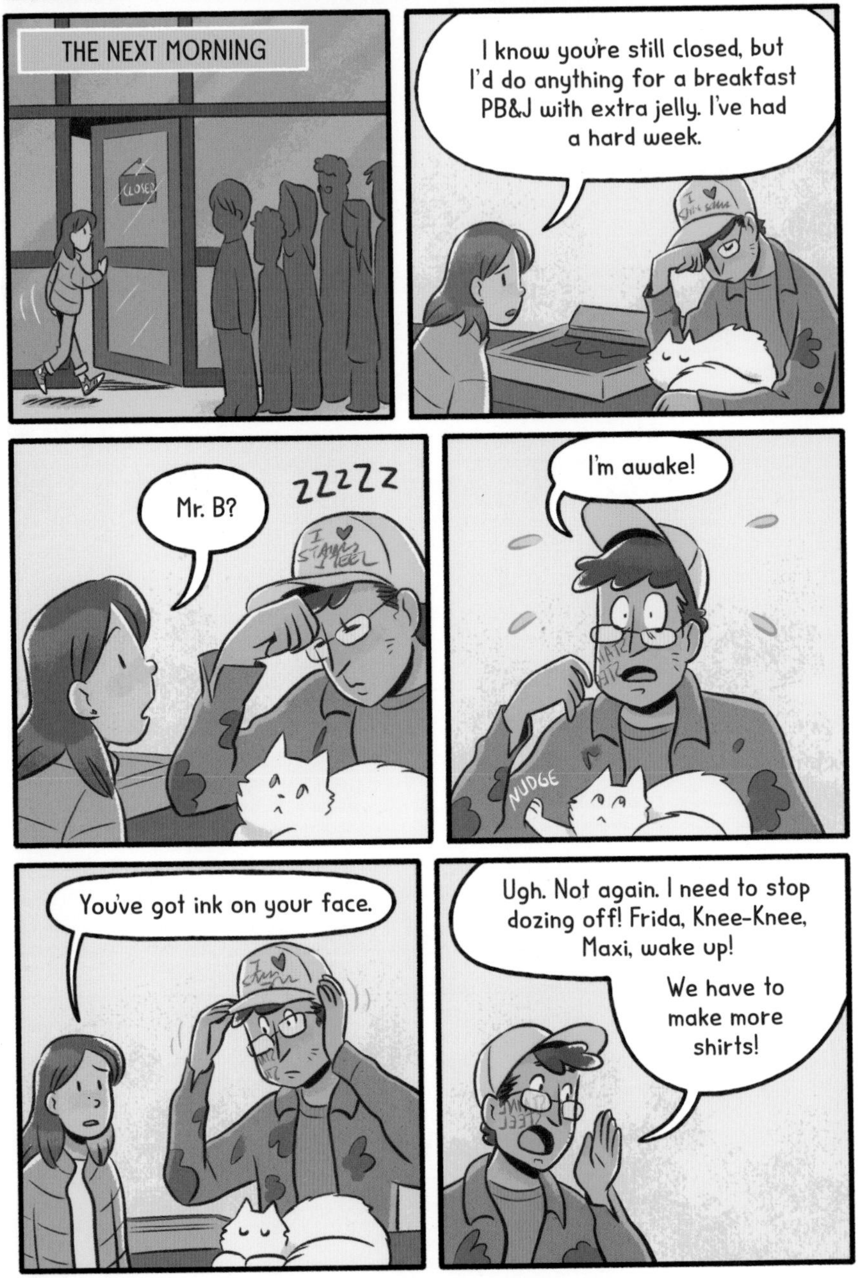
THE NEXT MORNING
CLOSED
I know you're still closed, but I'd do anything for a breakfast PB&J with extra jelly. I've had a hard week.
Mr. B?
ZZZZZ
I'm awake!
NUDGE
You've got ink on your face.
Ugh. Not again. I need to stop dozing off! Frida, Knee-Knee, Maxi, wake up!
We have to make more shirts!

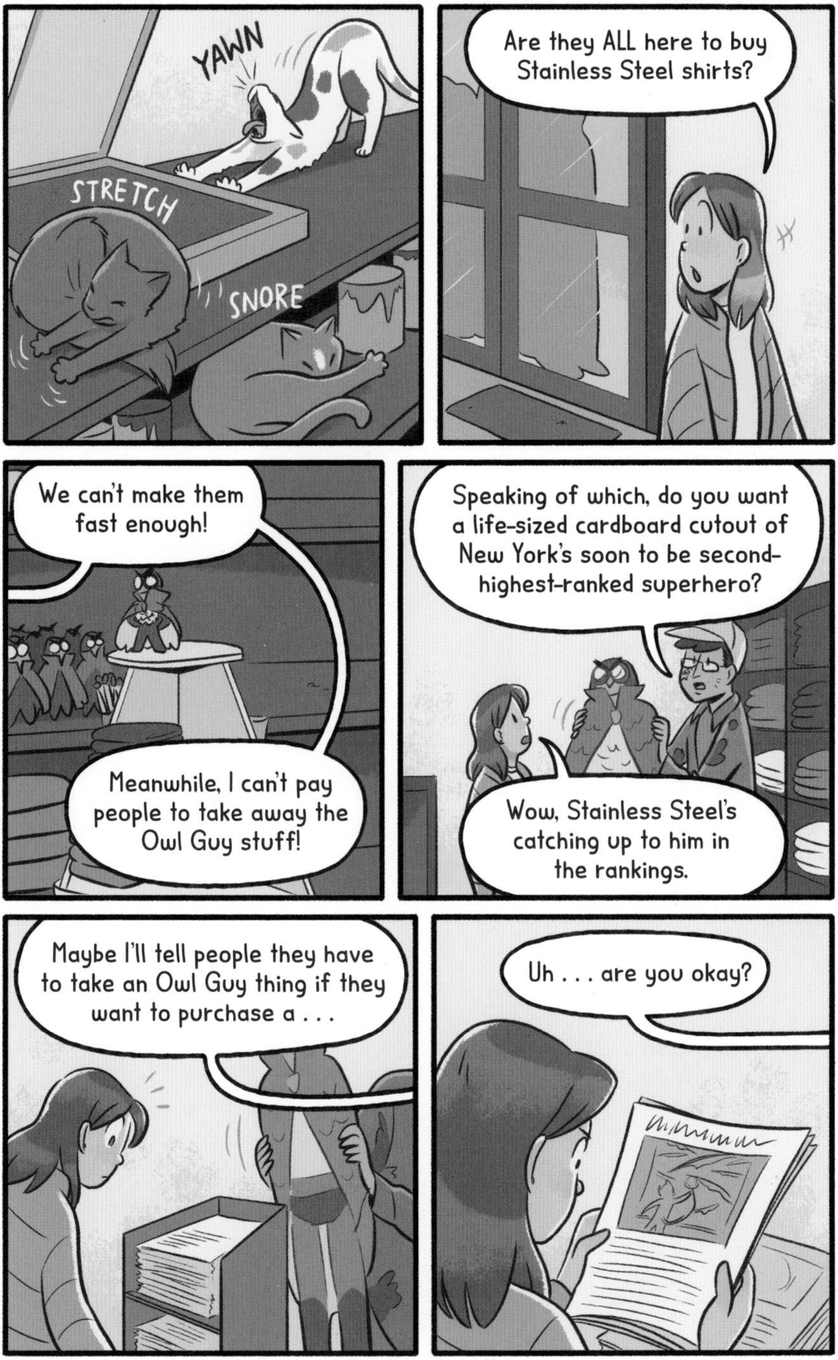
YAWN
STRETCH
SNORE
Are they ALL here to buy Stainless Steel shirts?
We can't make them fast enough!
Meanwhile, I can't pay people to take away the Owl Guy stuff!
Speaking of which, do you want a life-sized cardboard cutout of New York's soon to be second-highest-ranked superhero?
Wow, Stainless Steel's catching up to him in the rankings.
Maybe I'll tell people they have to take an Owl Guy thing if they want to purchase a . . .
Uh . . . are you okay?

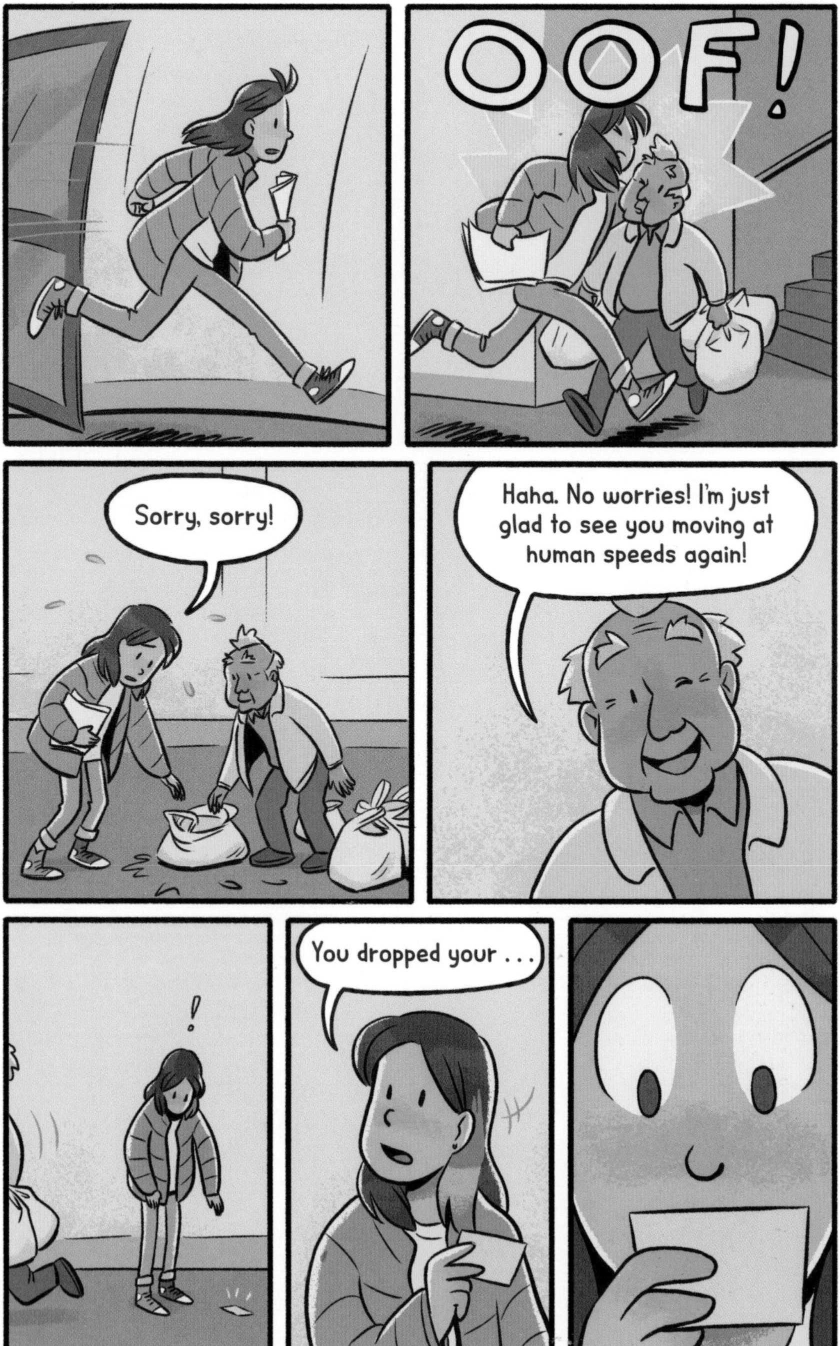
OOF!
Sorry, sorry!
Haha. No worries! I'm just glad to see you moving at human speeds again!
!
You dropped your . . .

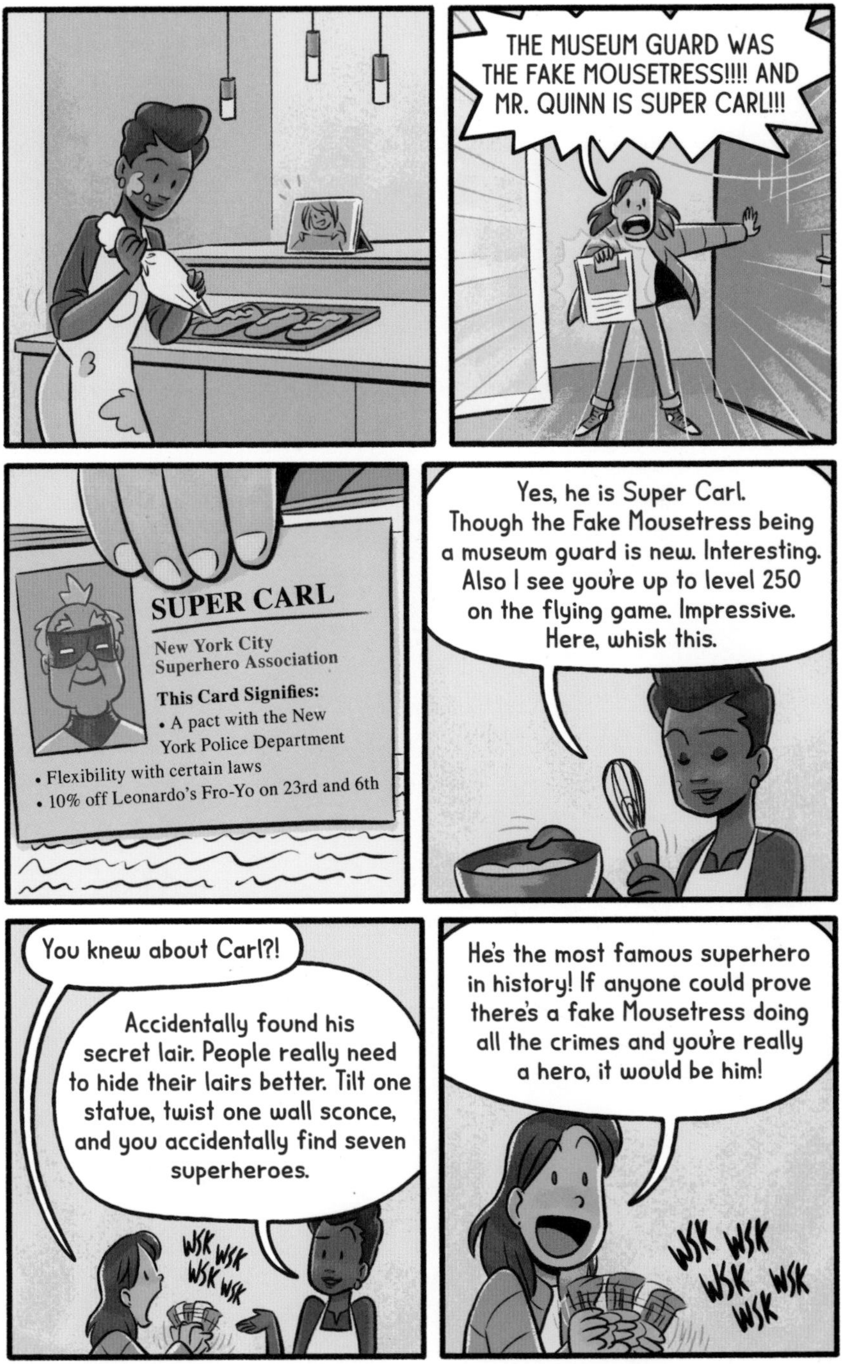
THE MUSEUM GUARD WAS THE FAKE MOUSETRESS!!!! AND MR. QUINN IS SUPER CARL!!!
SUPER CARL
New York City Superhero Association
This Card Signifies:
• A pact with the New York Police Department
• Flexibility with certain laws
• 10% off Leonardo's Fro-Yo on 23rd and 6th
Yes, he is Super Carl. Though the Fake Mousetress being a museum guard is new. Interesting. Also I see you're up to level 250 on the flying game. Impressive. Here, whisk this.
You knew about Carl?!
Accidentally found his secret lair. People really need to hide their lairs better. Tilt one statue, twist one wall sconce, and you accidentally find seven superheroes.
WSK WSK WSK WSK
He's the most famous superhero in history! If anyone could prove there's a fake Mousetress doing all the crimes and you're really a hero, it would be him!
WSK WSK WSK WSK WSK

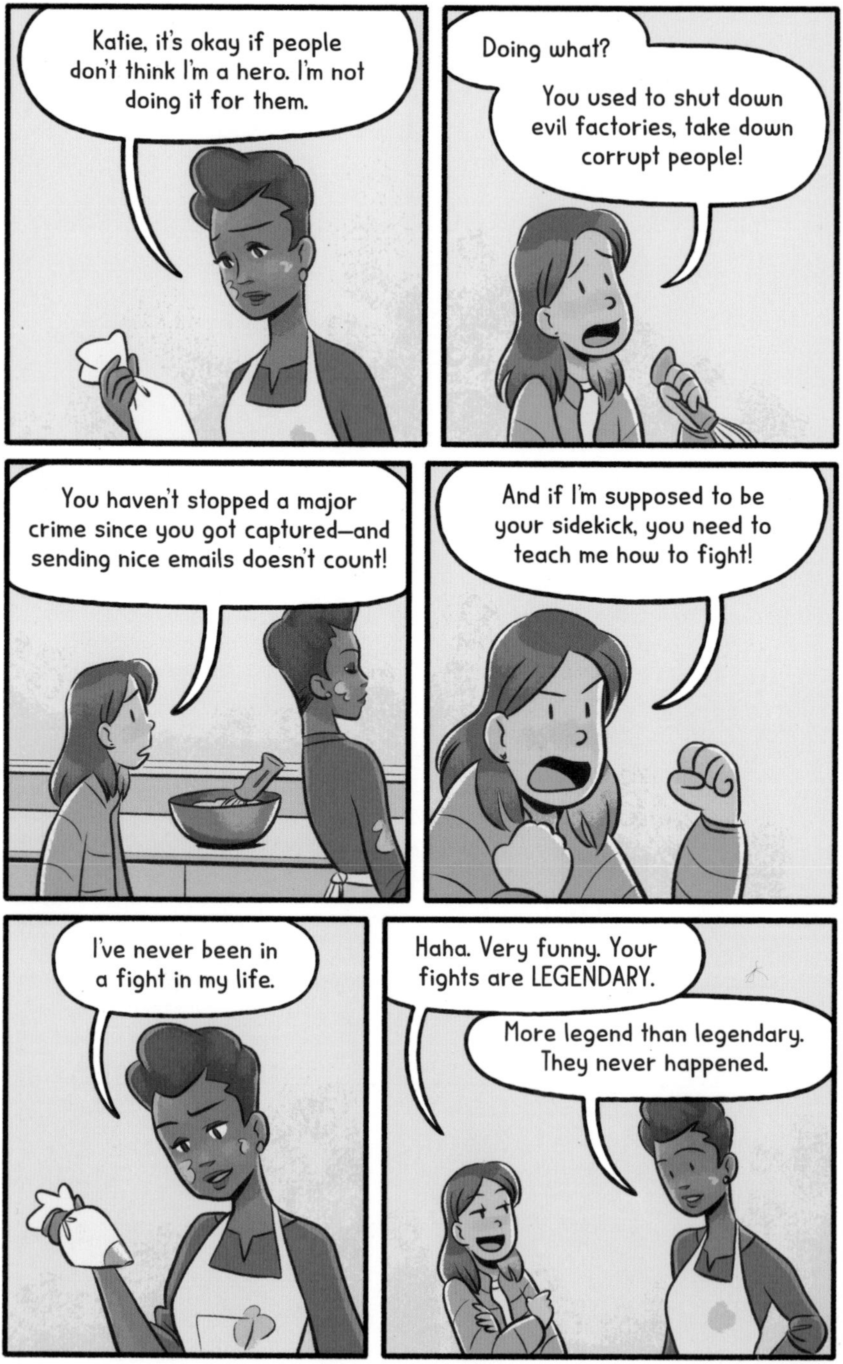
Katie, it's okay if people don't think I'm a hero. I'm not doing it for them.
Doing what?
You used to shut down evil factories, take down corrupt people!
You haven't stopped a major crime since you got captured—and sending nice emails doesn't count!
And if I'm supposed to be your sidekick, you need to teach me how to fight!
I've never been in a fight in my life.
Haha. Very funny. Your fights are LEGENDARY.
More legend than legendary. They never happened.

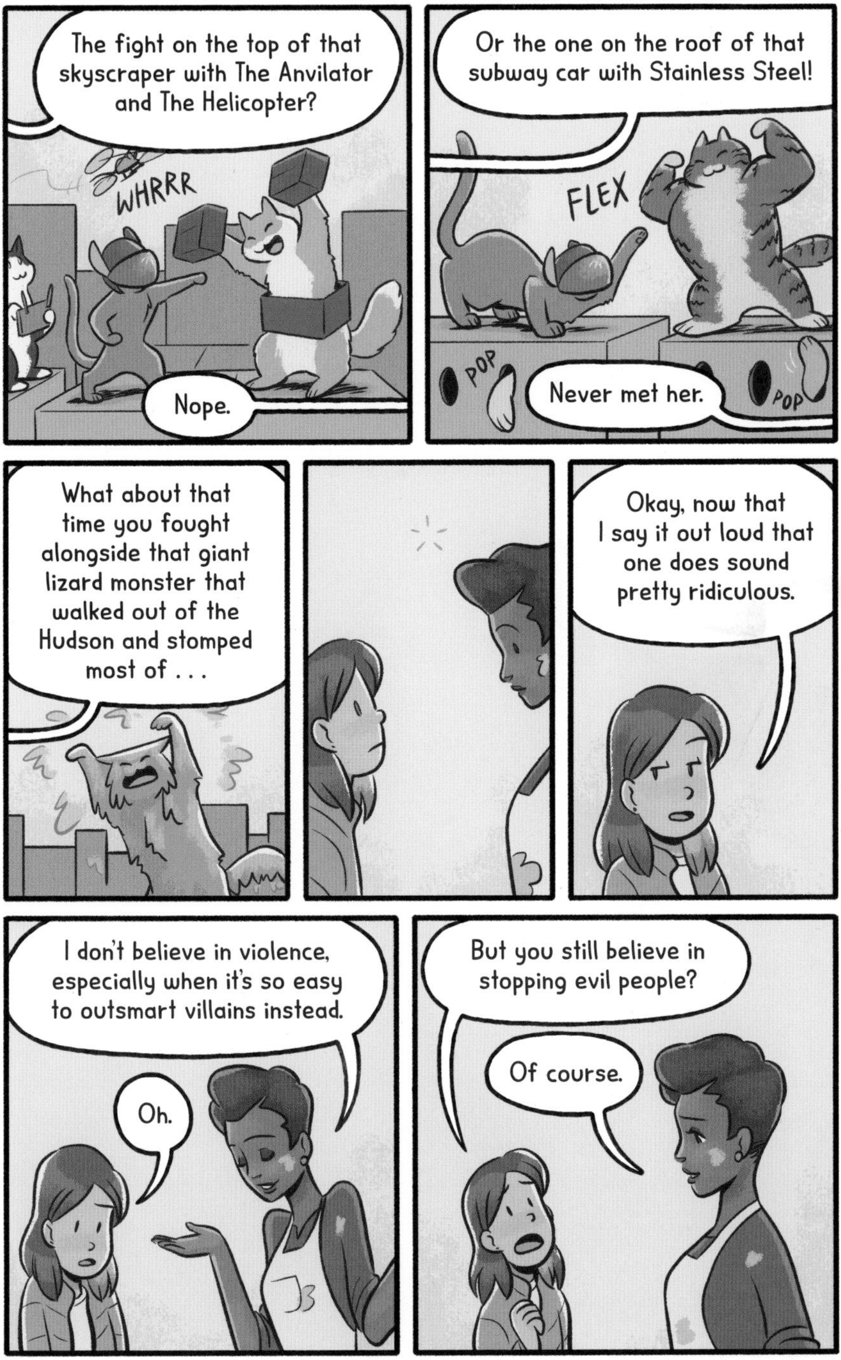
The fight on the top of that skyscraper with The Anvilator and The Helicopter?
WHRRR
Nope.
Or the one on the roof of that subway car with Stainless Steel!
FLEX
POP
Never met her.
POP
What about that time you fought alongside that giant lizard monster that walked out of the Hudson and stomped most of . . .
Okay, now that I say it out loud that one does sound pretty ridiculous.
I don't believe in violence, especially when it's so easy to outsmart villains instead.
Oh.
But you still believe in stopping evil people?
Of course.

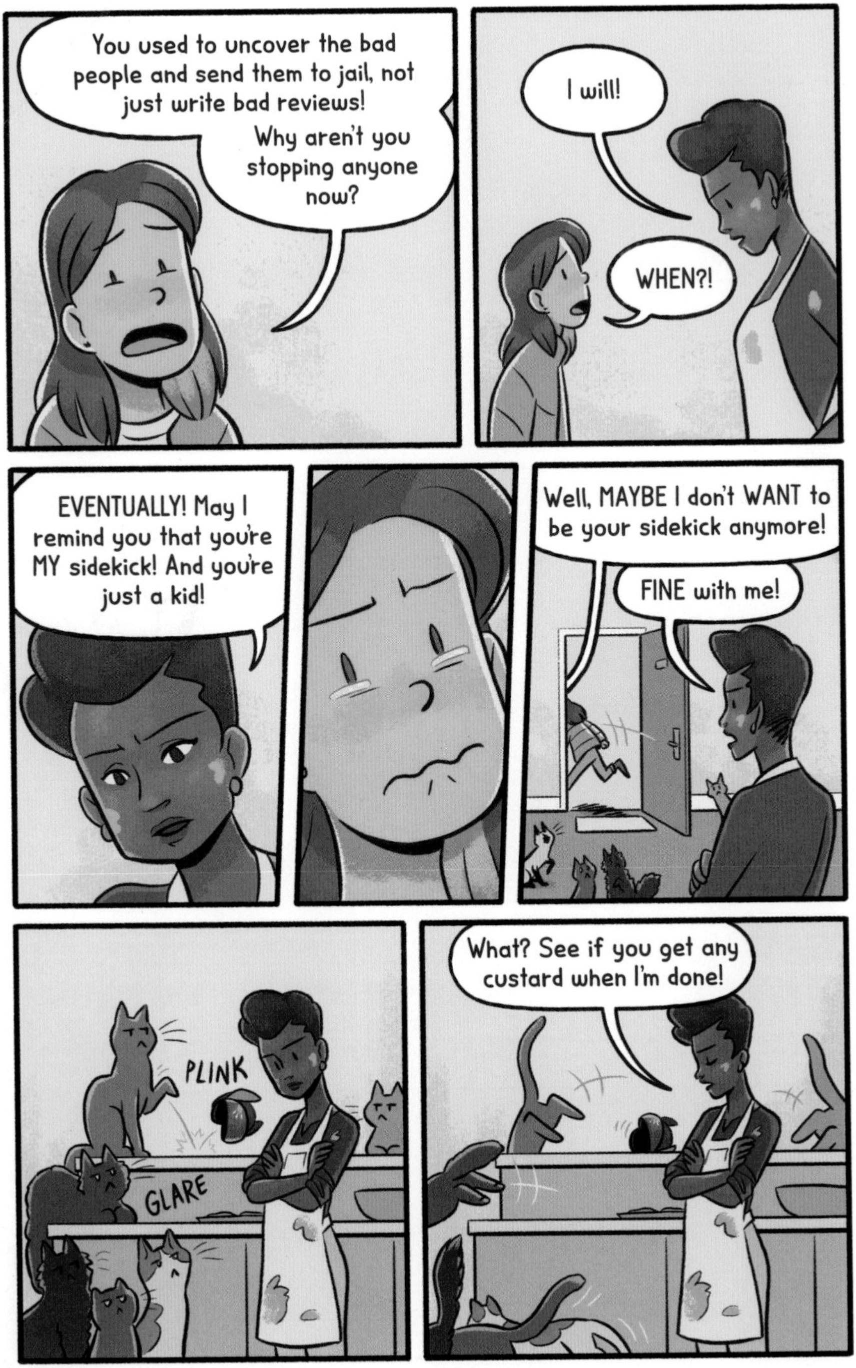
You used to uncover the bad people and send them to jail, not just write bad reviews!
Why aren't you stopping anyone now?
I will!
WHEN?!
EVENTUALLY! May I remind you that you're MY sidekick! And you're just a kid!
Well, MAYBE I don't WANT to be your sidekick anymore!
FINE with me!
PLINK
GLARE
What? See if you get any custard when I'm done!

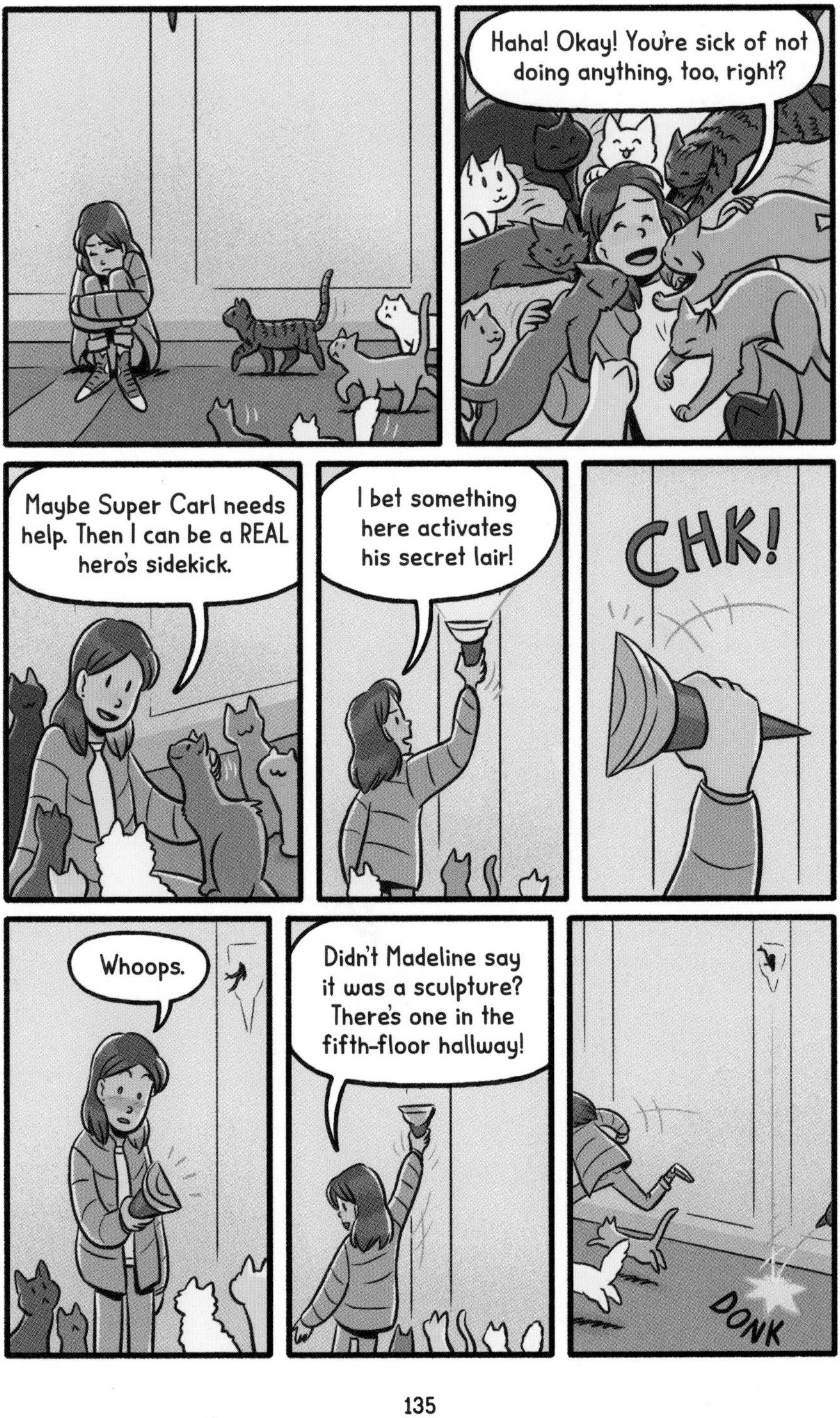
Haha! Okay! You're sick of not doing anything, too, right?
Maybe Super Carl needs help. Then I can be a REAL hero's sidekick.
I bet something here activates his secret lair!
CHK!
Whoops.
Didn't Madeline say it was a sculpture? There's one in the fifth-floor hallway!
DONK

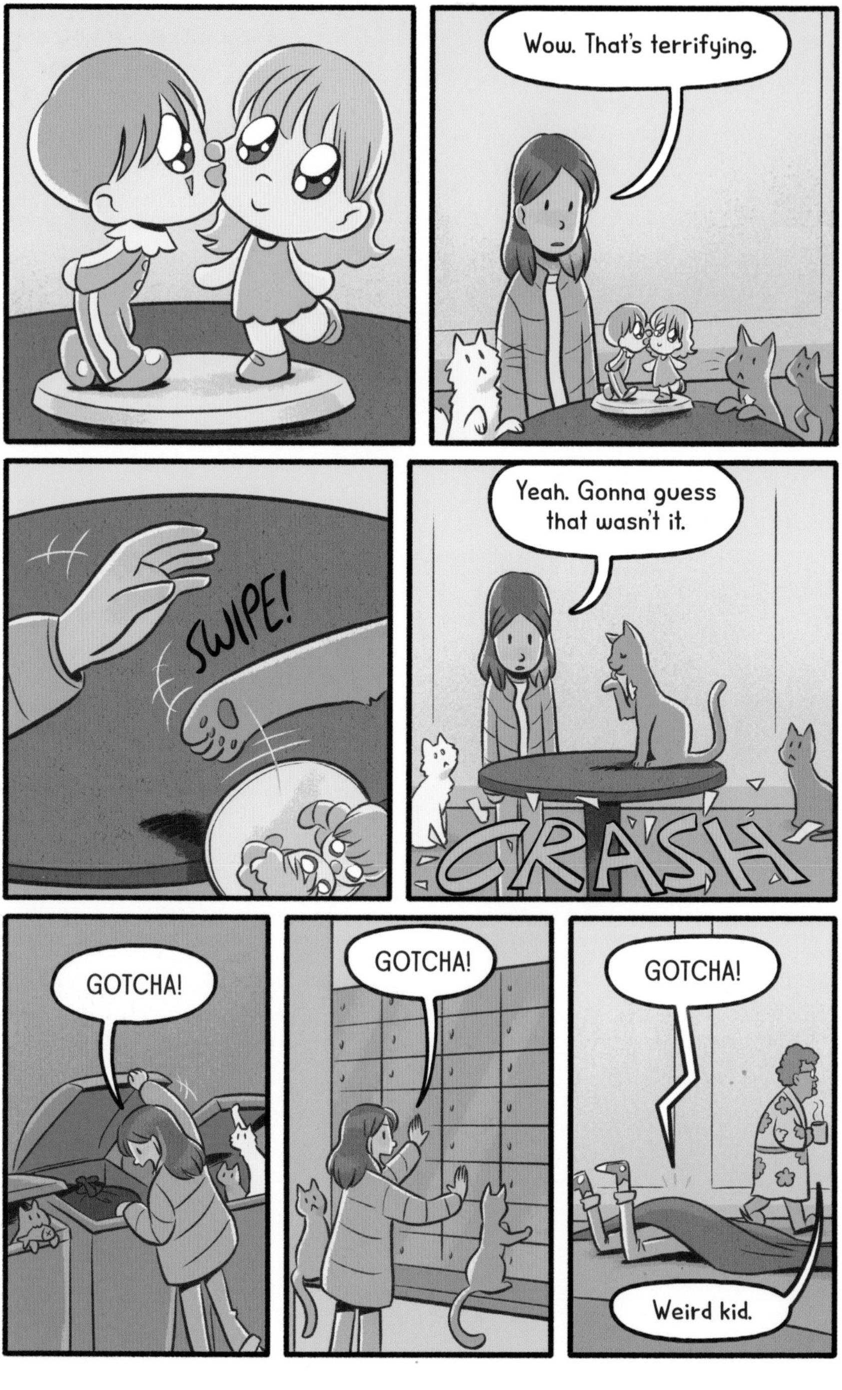
Wow. That's terrifying.
SWIPE!
Yeah. Gonna guess that wasn't it.
CRASH
GOTCHA!
GOTCHA!
GOTCHA!
Weird kid.

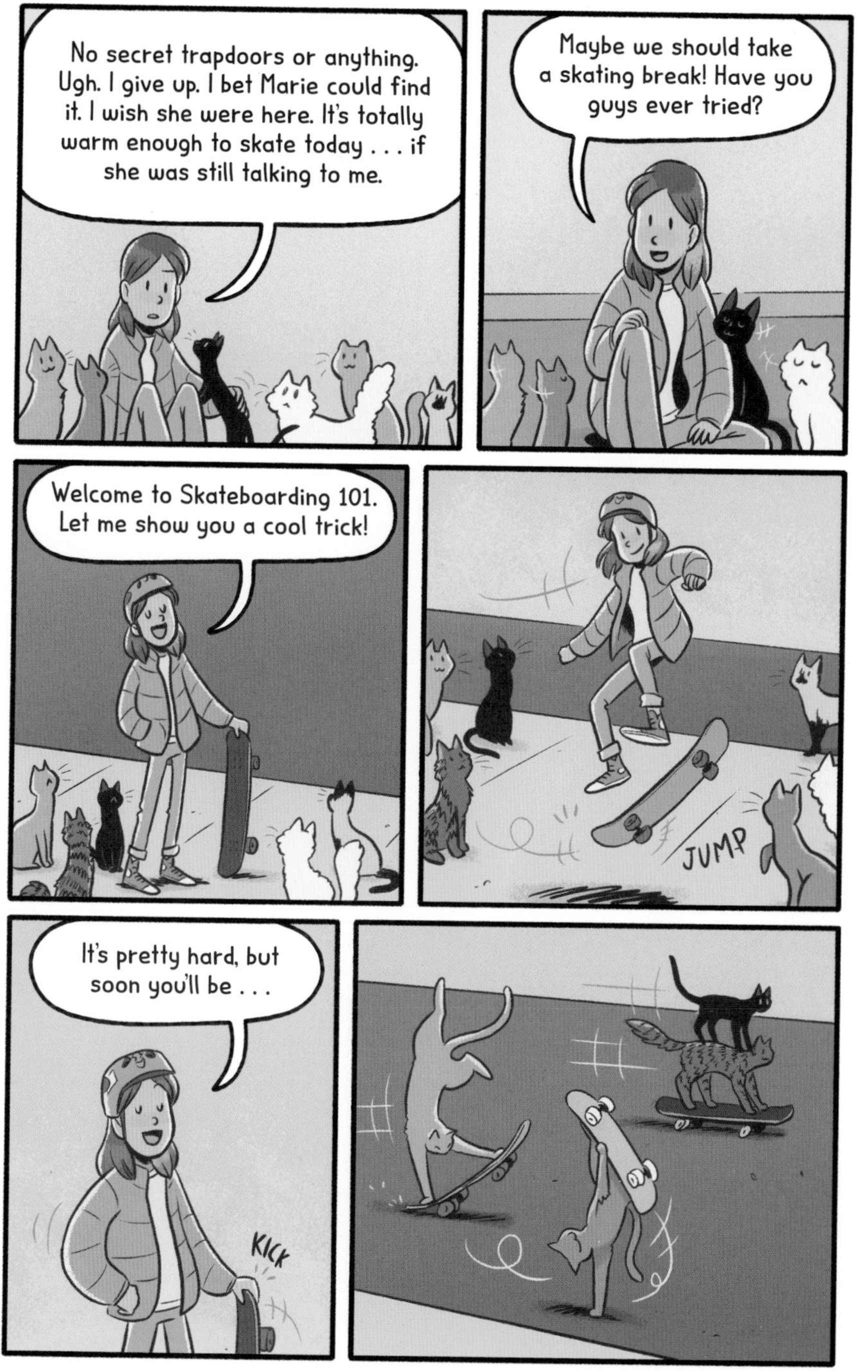
No secret trapdoors or anything. Ugh. I give up. I bet Marie could find it. I wish she were here. It's totally warm enough to skate today . . . if she was still talking to me.
Maybe we should take a skating break! Have you guys ever tried?
Welcome to Skateboarding 101. Let me show you a cool trick!
JUMP
It's pretty hard, but soon you'll be . . .
KICK

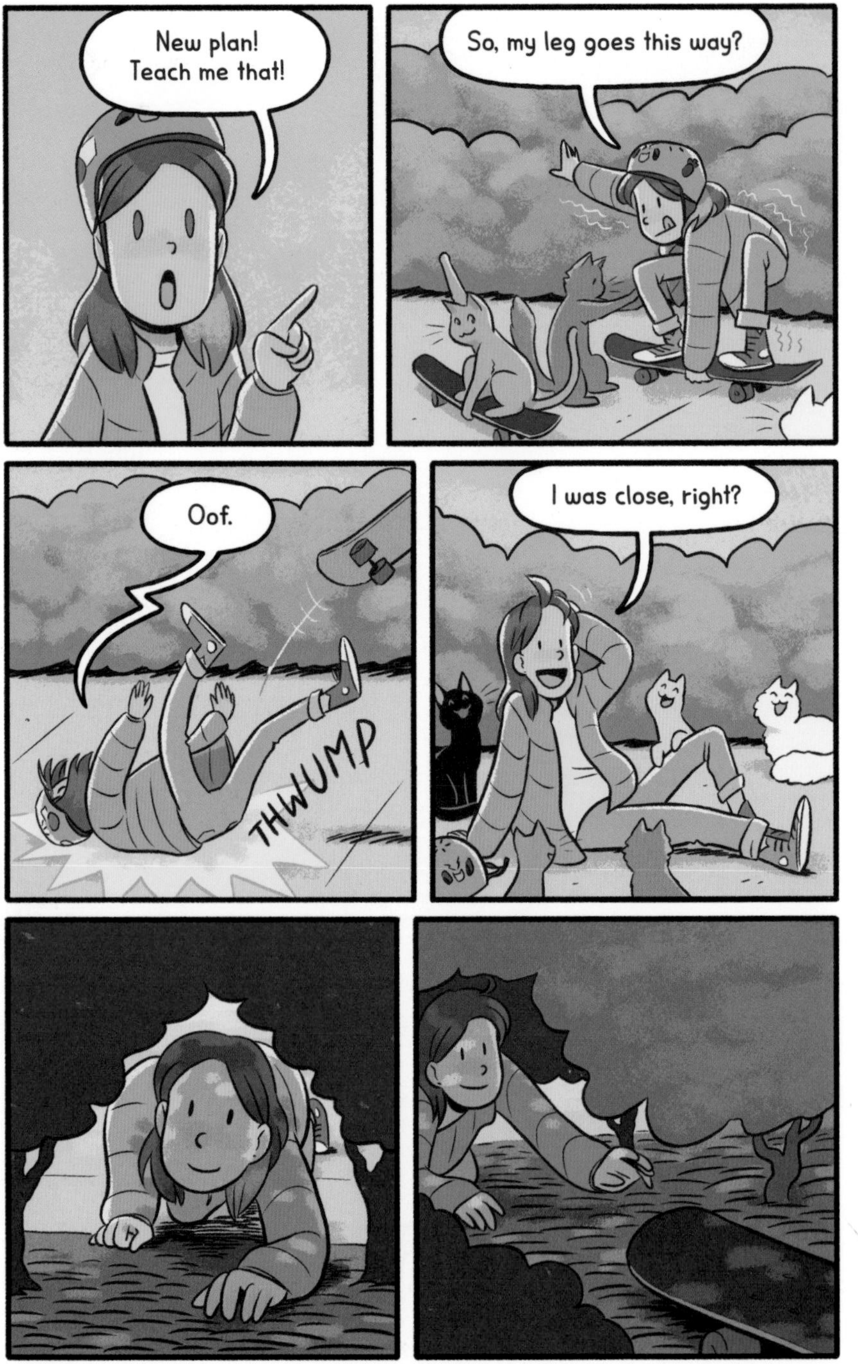
New plan! Teach me that!
So, my leg goes this way?
Oof.
THWUMP
I was close, right?

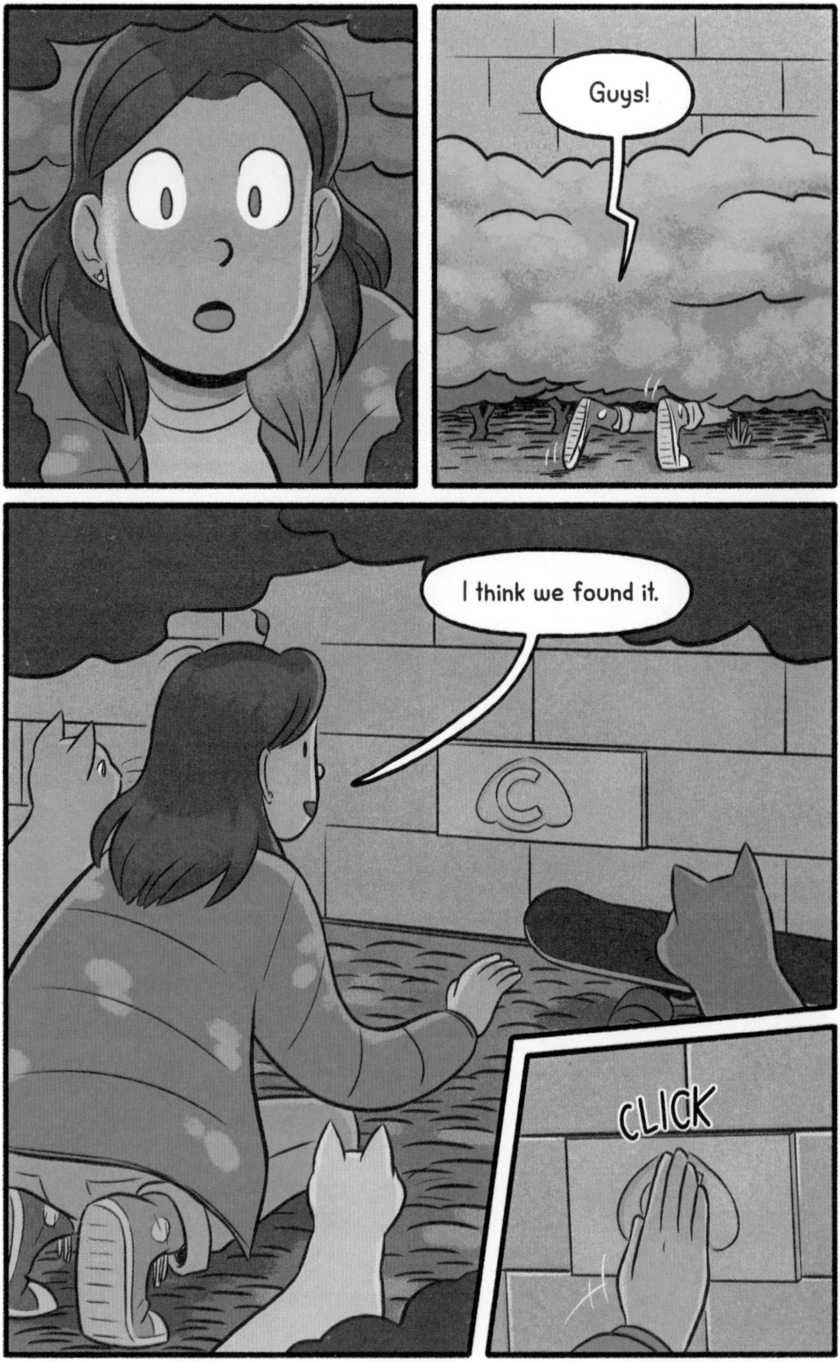
Guys!
I think we found it.
CLICK

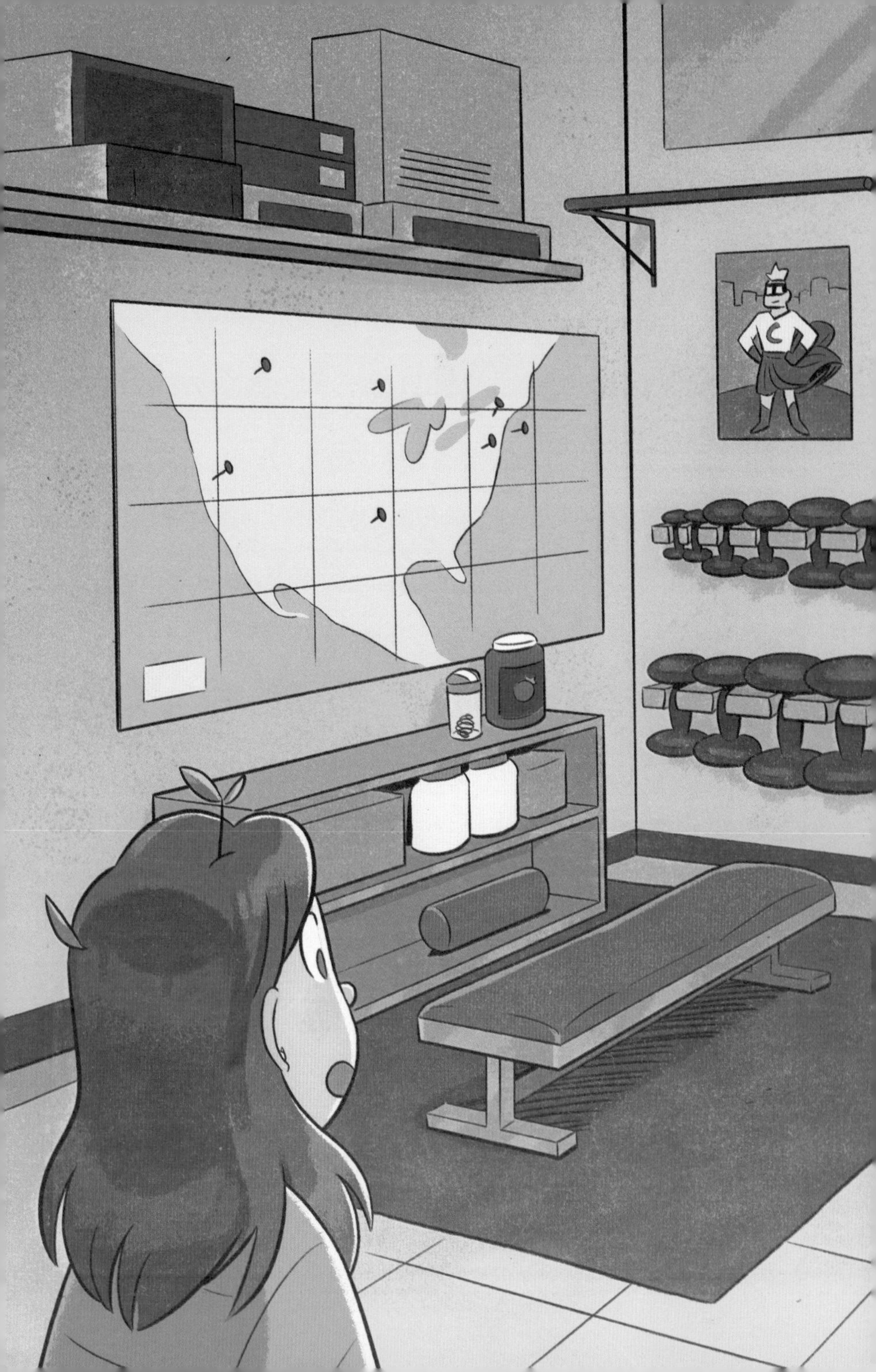

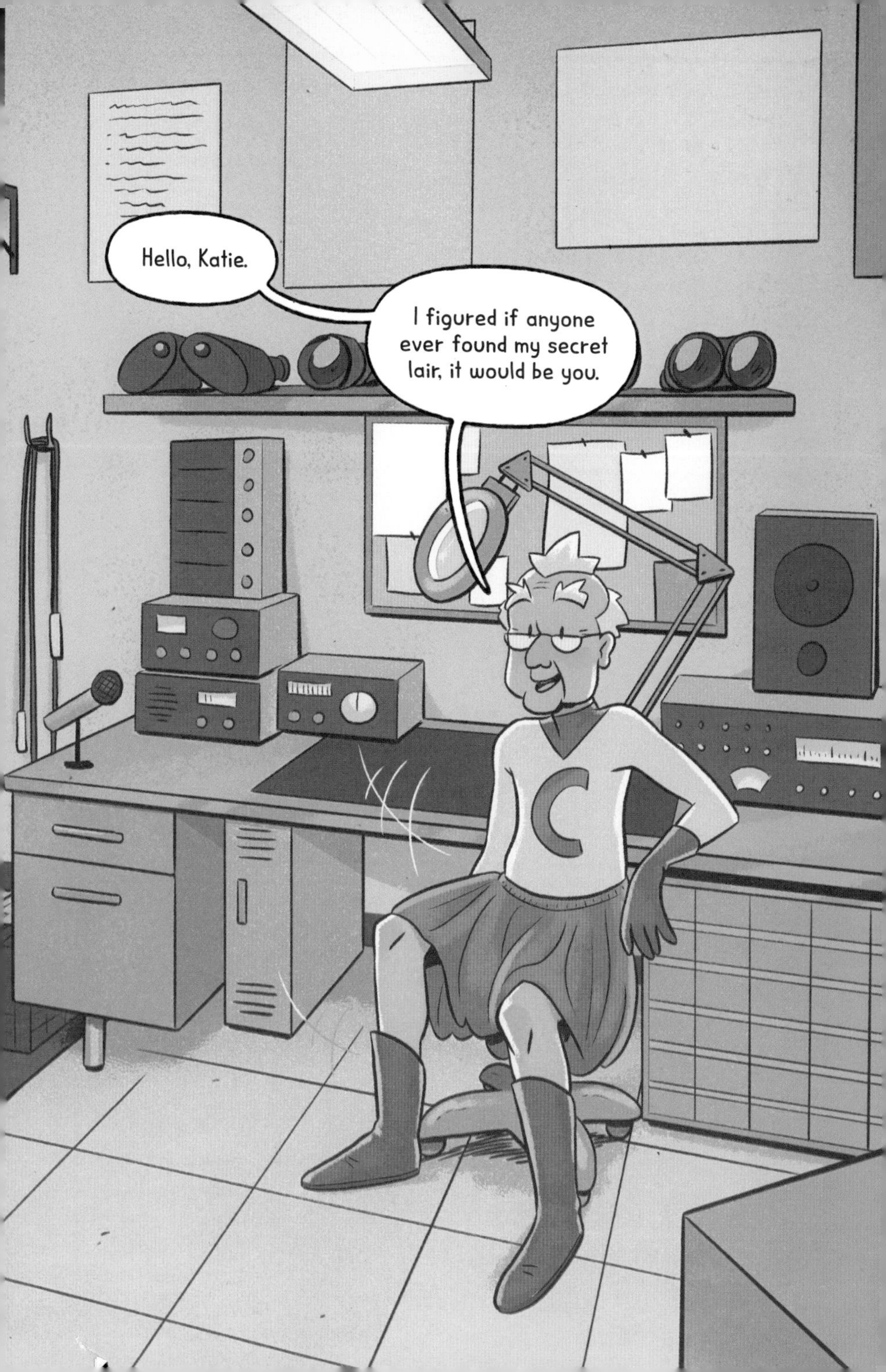
Hello, Katie.
I figured if anyone ever found my secret lair, it would be you.

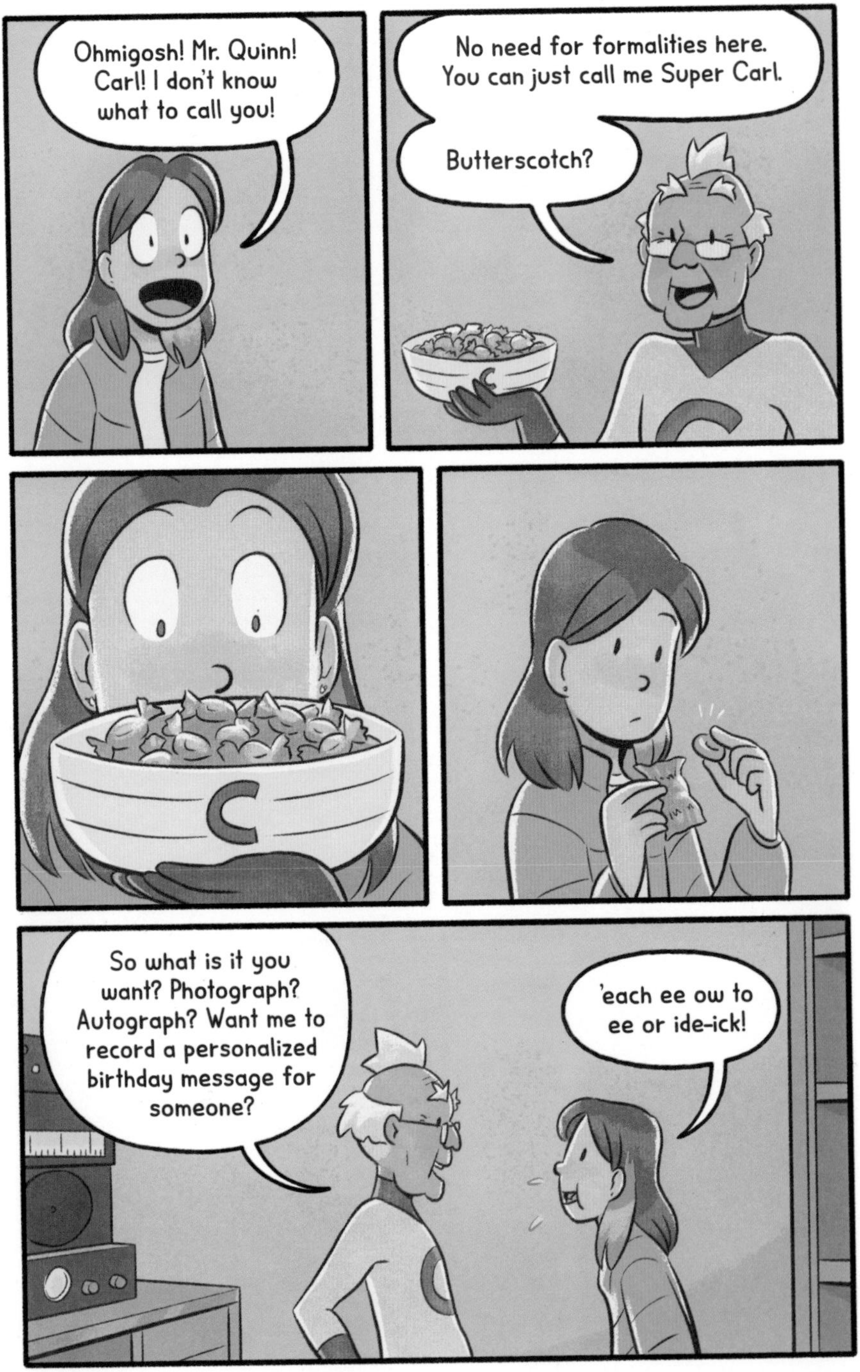
Ohmigosh! Mr. Quinn! Carl! I don't know what to call you!
No need for formalities here. You can just call me Super Carl.
Butterscotch?
So what is it you want? Photograph? Autograph? Want me to record a personalized birthday message for someone?
'each ee ow to ee or ide-ick!

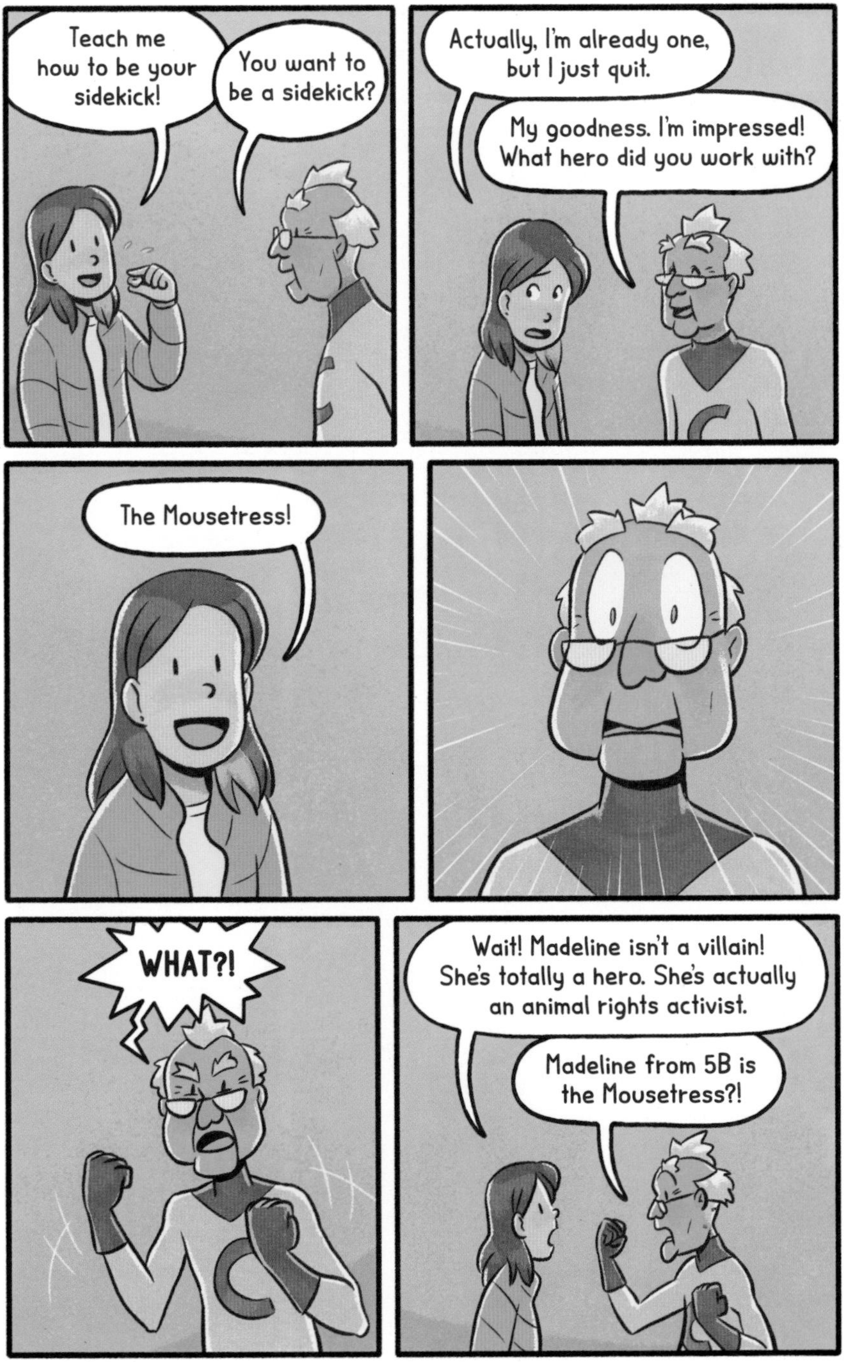
Teach me how to be your sidekick!
You want to be a sidekick?
Actually, I'm already one, but I just quit.
My goodness. I'm impressed! What hero did you work with?
The Mousetress!
WHAT?!
Wait! Madeline isn't a villain! She's totally a hero. She's actually an animal rights activist.
Madeline from 5B is the Mousetress?!

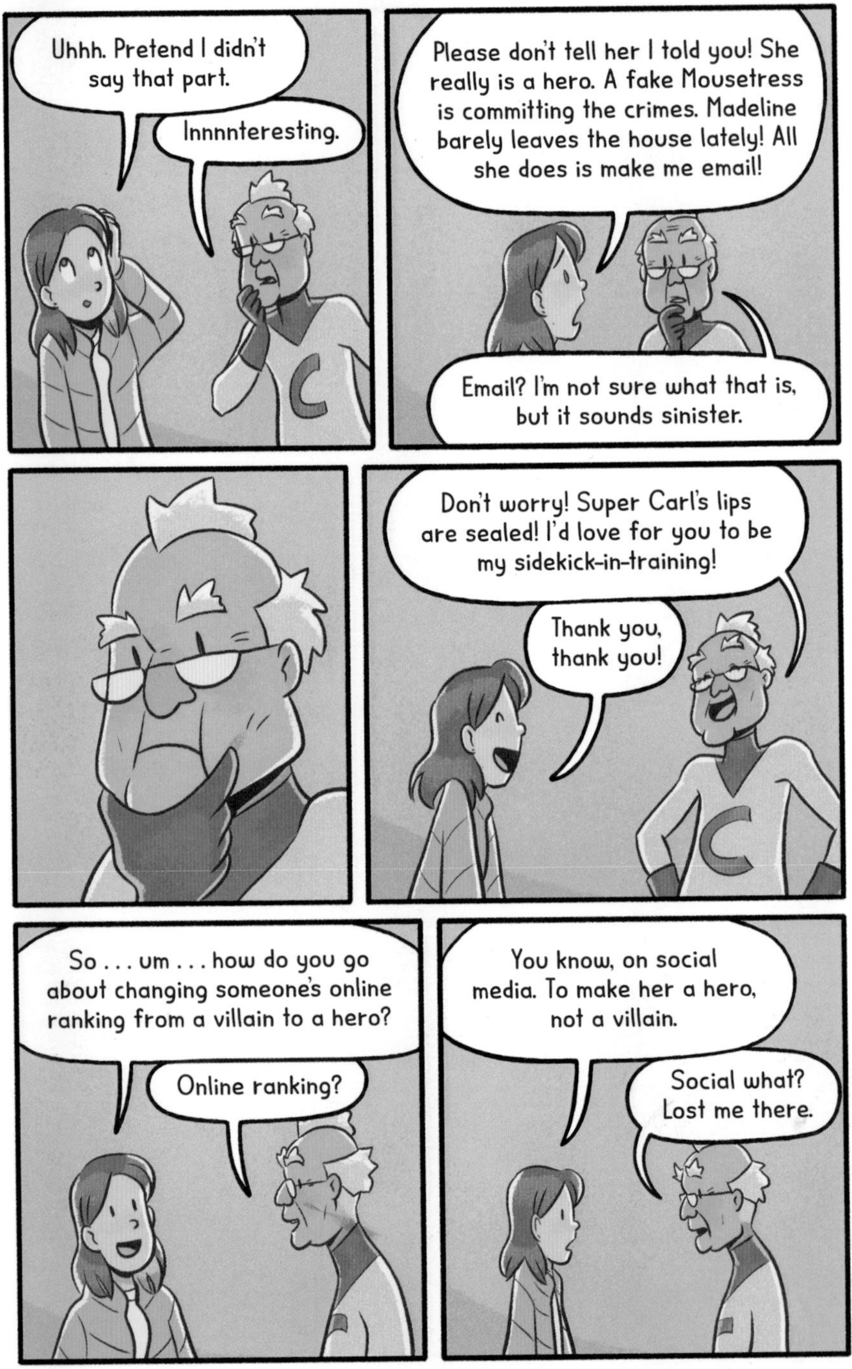

Uhhh. Pretend I didn't say that part.
Innnnteresting.
Please don't tell her I told you! She really is a hero. A fake Mousetress is committing the crimes. Madeline barely leaves the house lately! All she does is make me email!
Email? I'm not sure what that is, but it sounds sinister.
Don't worry! Super Carl's lips are sealed! I'd love for you to be my sidekick-in-training!
Thank you, thank you!
So . . . um . . . how do you go about changing someone's online ranking from a villain to a hero?
Online ranking?
You know, on social media. To make her a hero, not a villain.
Social what? Lost me there.

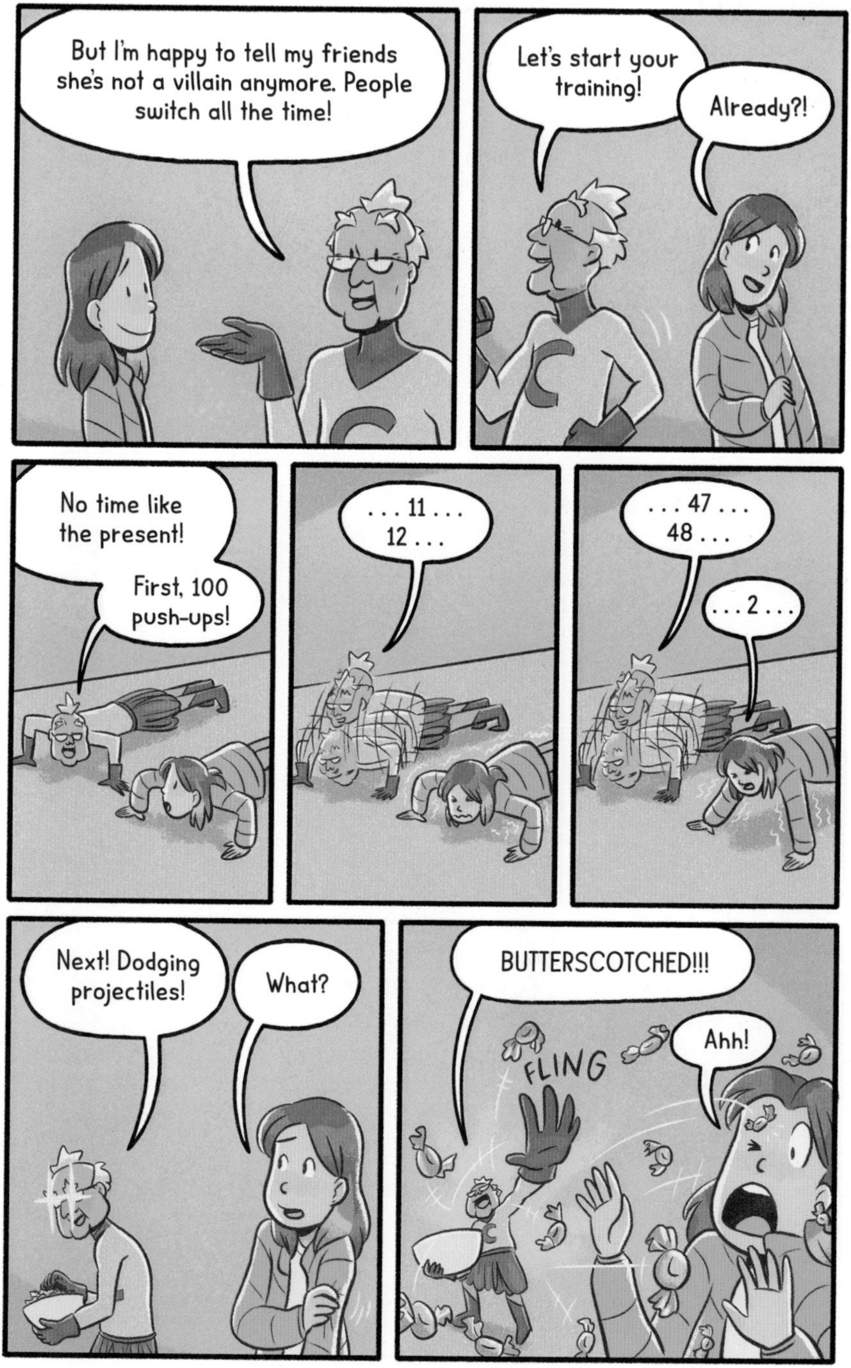
But I'm happy to tell my friends she's not a villain anymore. People switch all the time!
Let's start your training!
Already?!
No time like the present!
First, 100 push-ups!
. . . 11 . . .
12 . . .
. . . 47 . . .
48 . . .
. . . 2 . . .
Next! Dodging projectiles!
What?
BUTTERSCOTCHED!!!
FLING
Ahh!

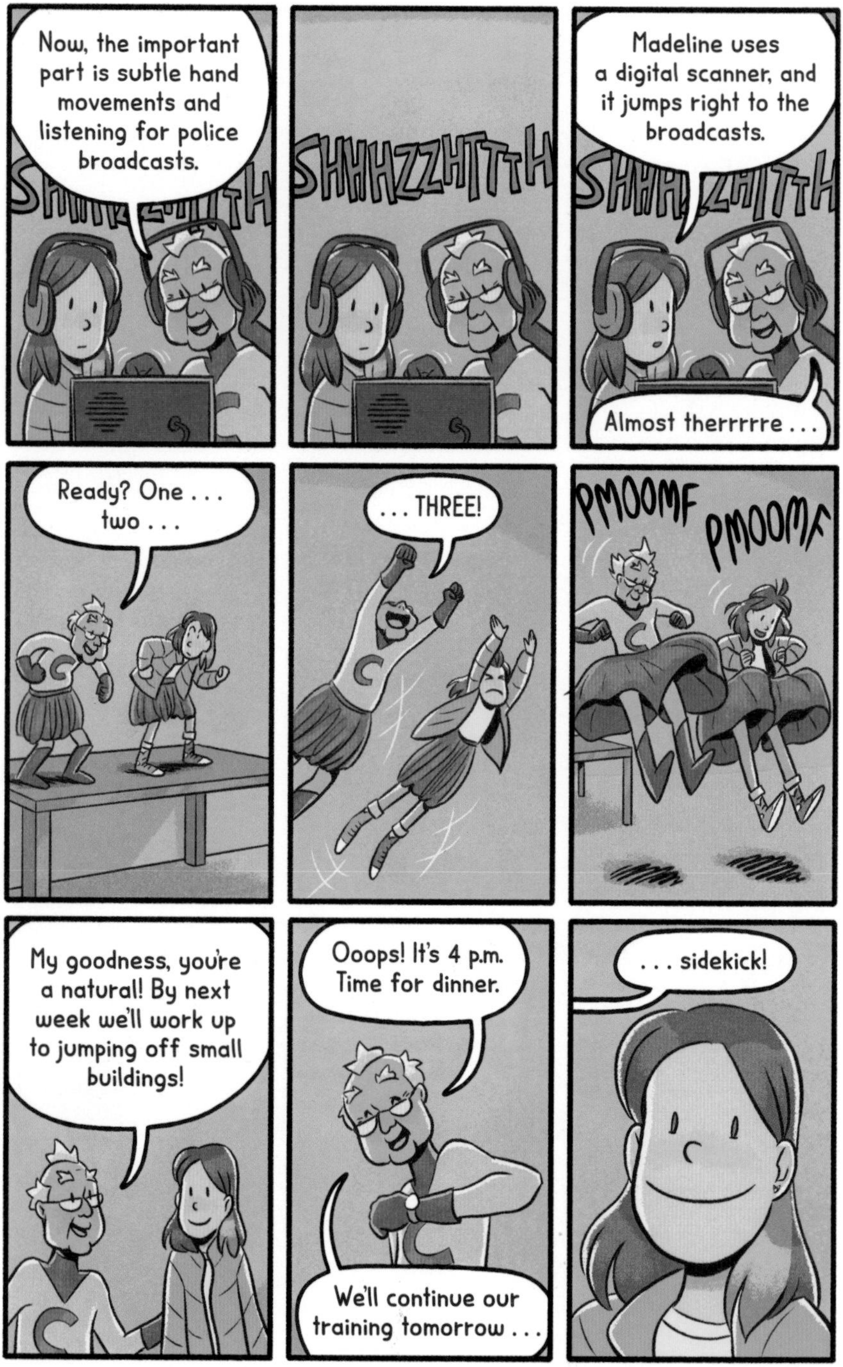
Now, the important part is subtle hand movements and listening for police broadcasts.
SHHHZZHTTTH
SHHHZZHTTTH
Madeline uses a digital scanner, and it jumps right to the broadcasts.
SHHHZZHTTTH
Almost therrrrre . . .
Ready? One . . . two . . .
. . . THREE!
PMOOMF
PMOOMF
My goodness, you're a natural! By next week we'll work up to jumping off small buildings!
Ooops! It's 4 p.m. Time for dinner.
We'll continue our training tomorrow . . .
. . . sidekick!

CHAPTER NINE

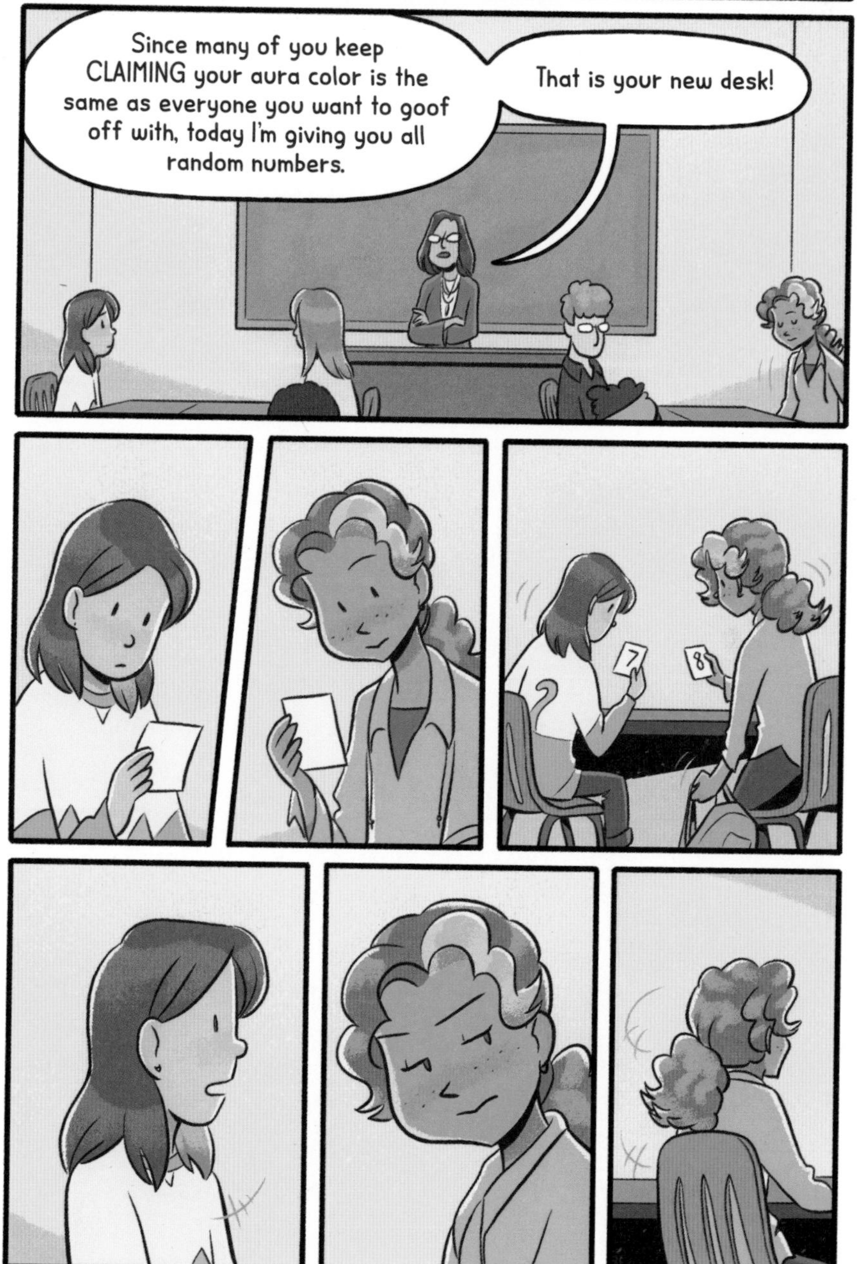

Since many of you keep CLAIMING your aura color is the same as everyone you want to goof off with, today I'm giving you all random numbers.
That is your new desk!
7
8

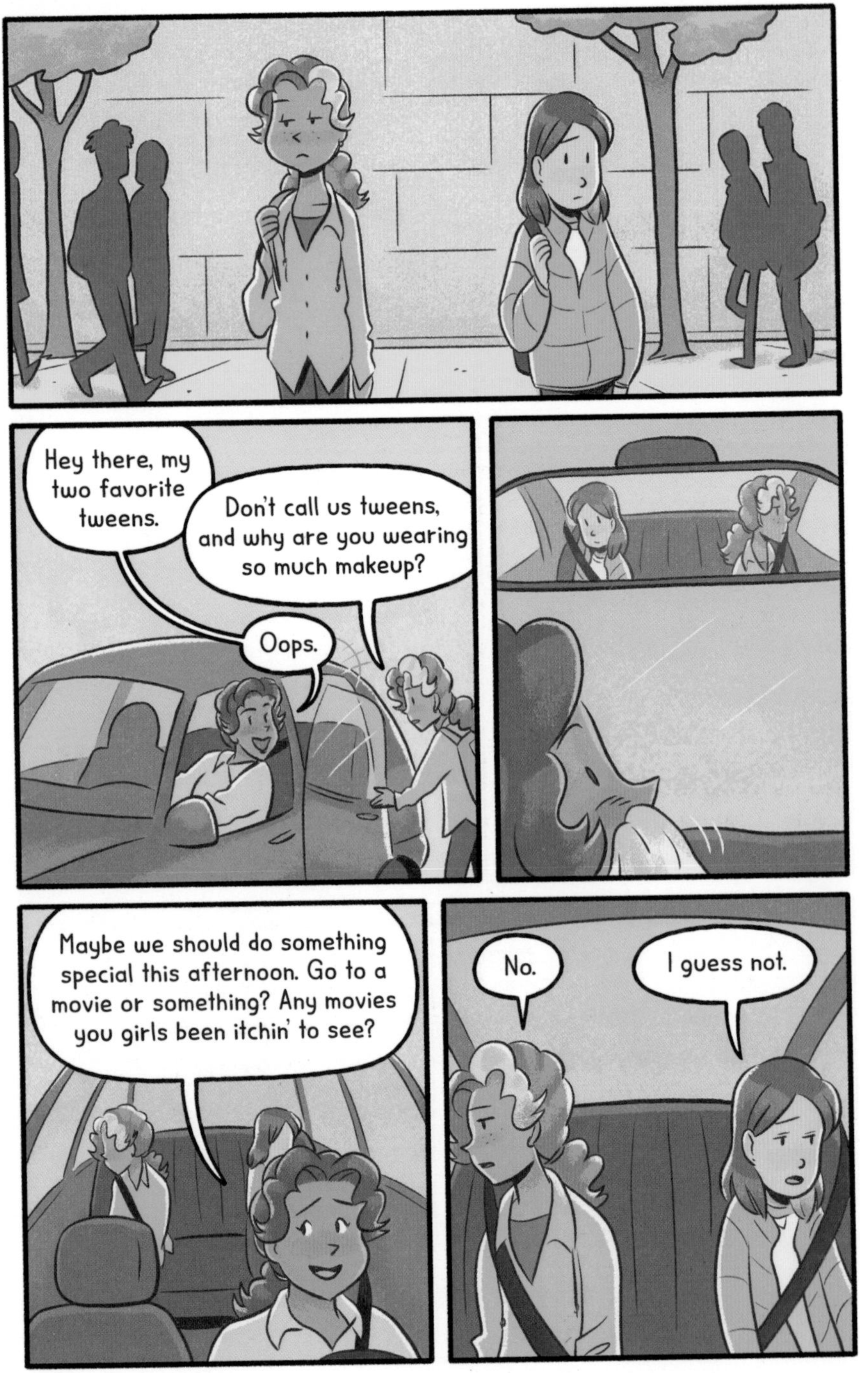
Hey there, my two favorite tweens.
Don't call us tweens, and why are you wearing so much makeup?
Oops.
Maybe we should do something special this afternoon. Go to a movie or something? Any movies you girls been itchin' to see?
No.
I guess not.

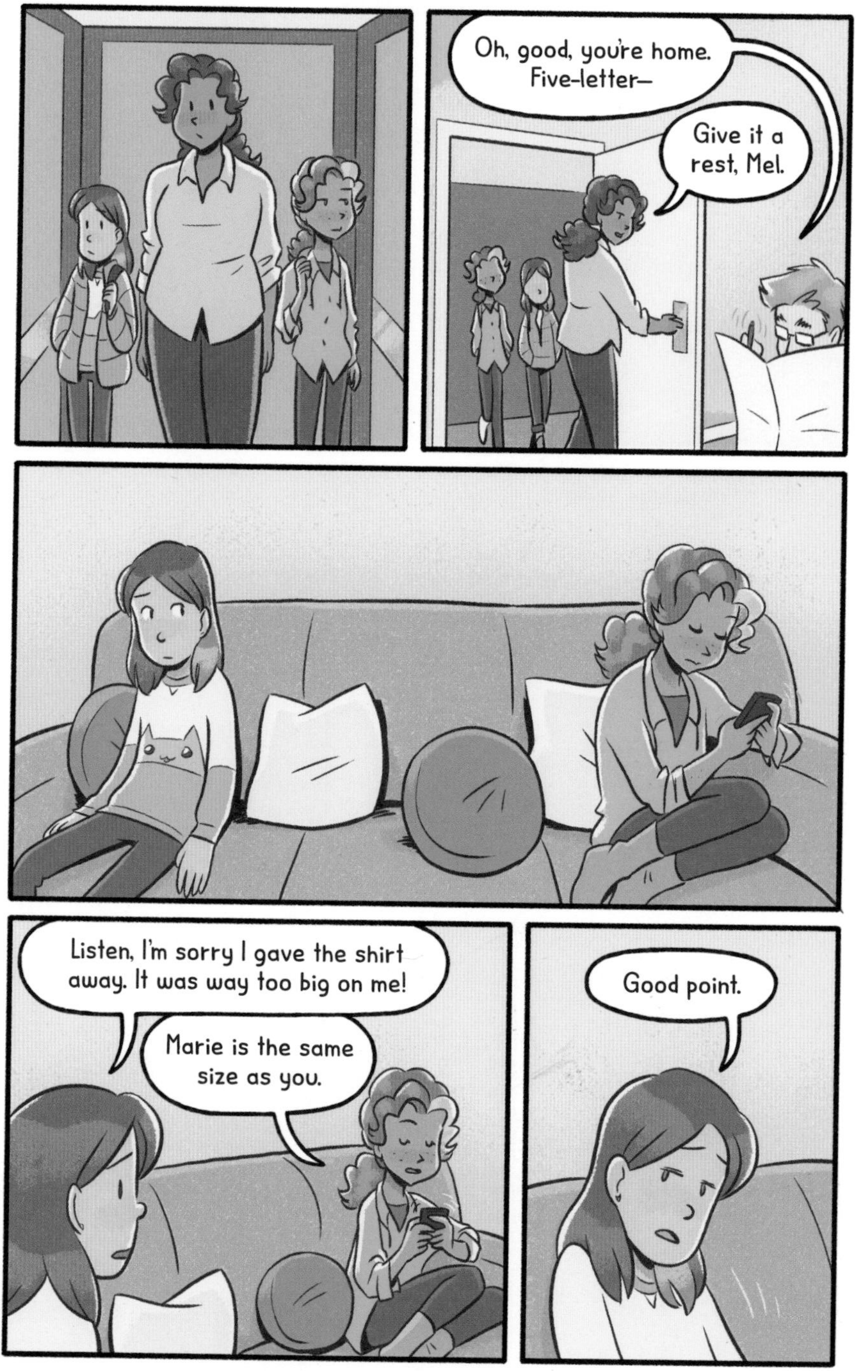
Oh, good, you're home. Five-letter—
Give it a rest, Mel.
Listen, I'm sorry I gave the shirt away. It was way too big on me!
Marie is the same size as you.
Good point.

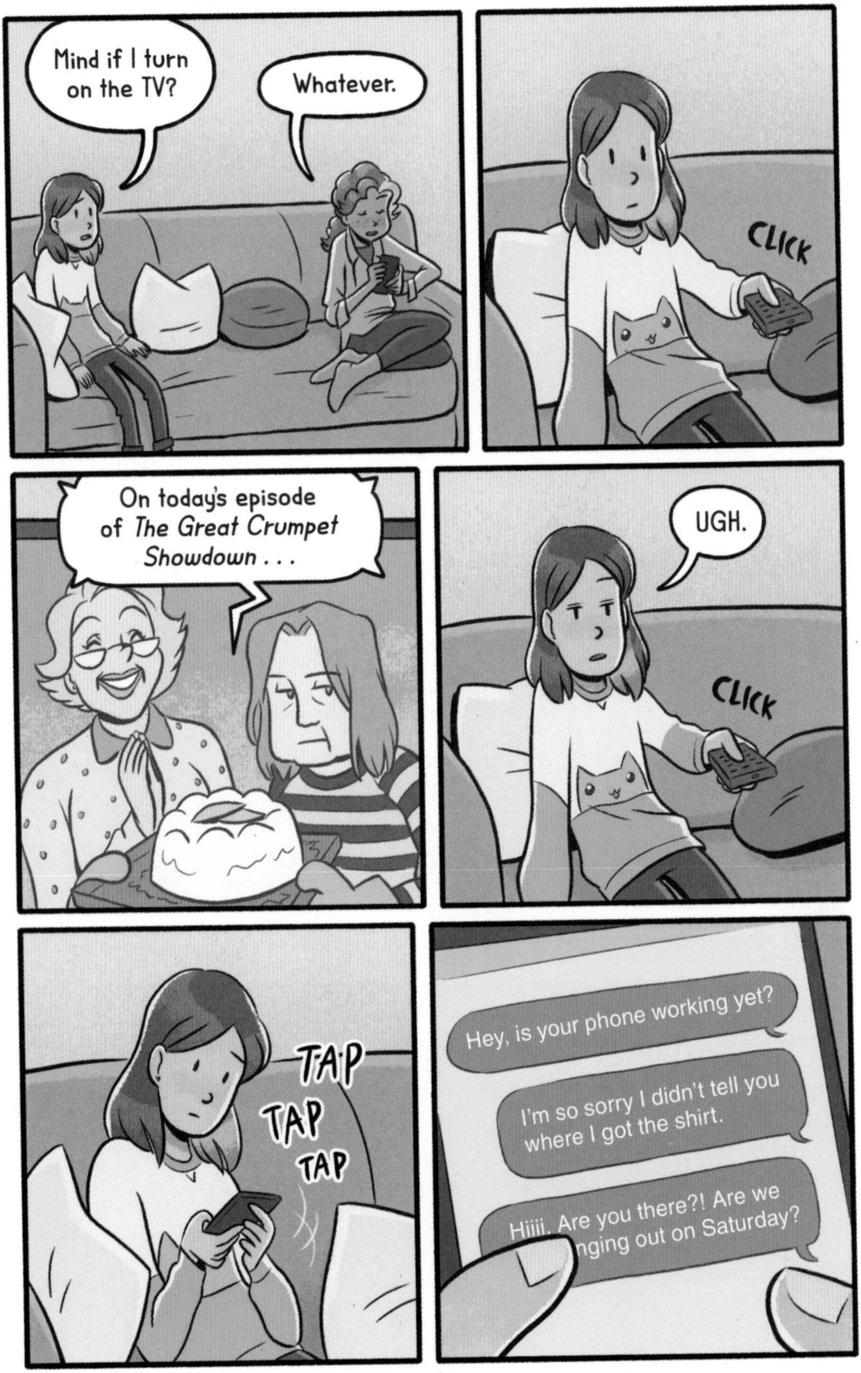
Mind if I turn on the TV?
Whatever.
CLICK
On today's episode of *The Great Crumpet Showdown* . . .
UGH.
CLICK
TAP
TAP
TAP
Hey, is your phone working yet?
I'm so sorry I didn't tell you where I got the shirt.
Hiiii. Are you there?! Are we
nging out on Saturday?

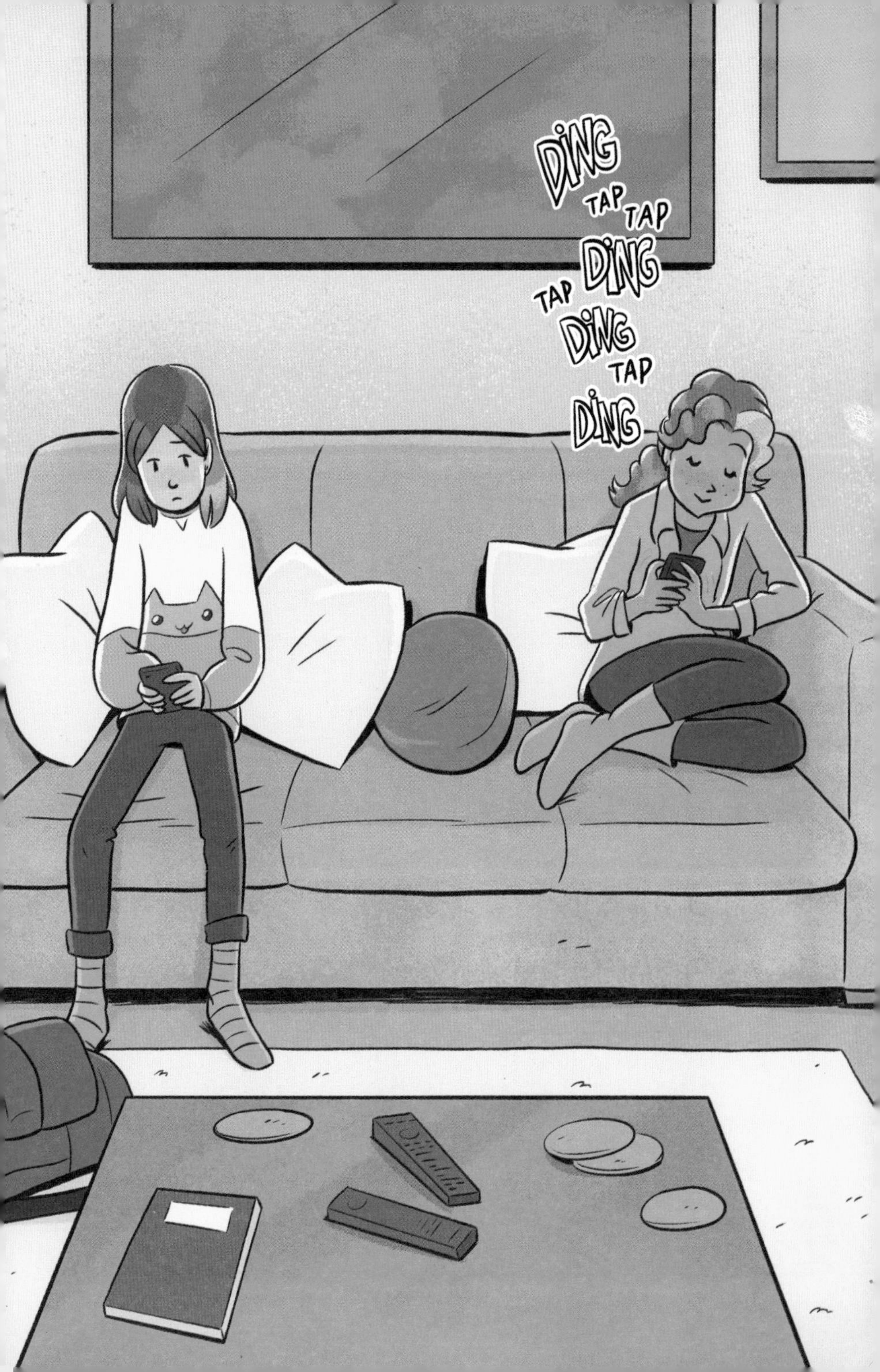
DING
TAP TAP
DING
TAP
DING
TAP
DING

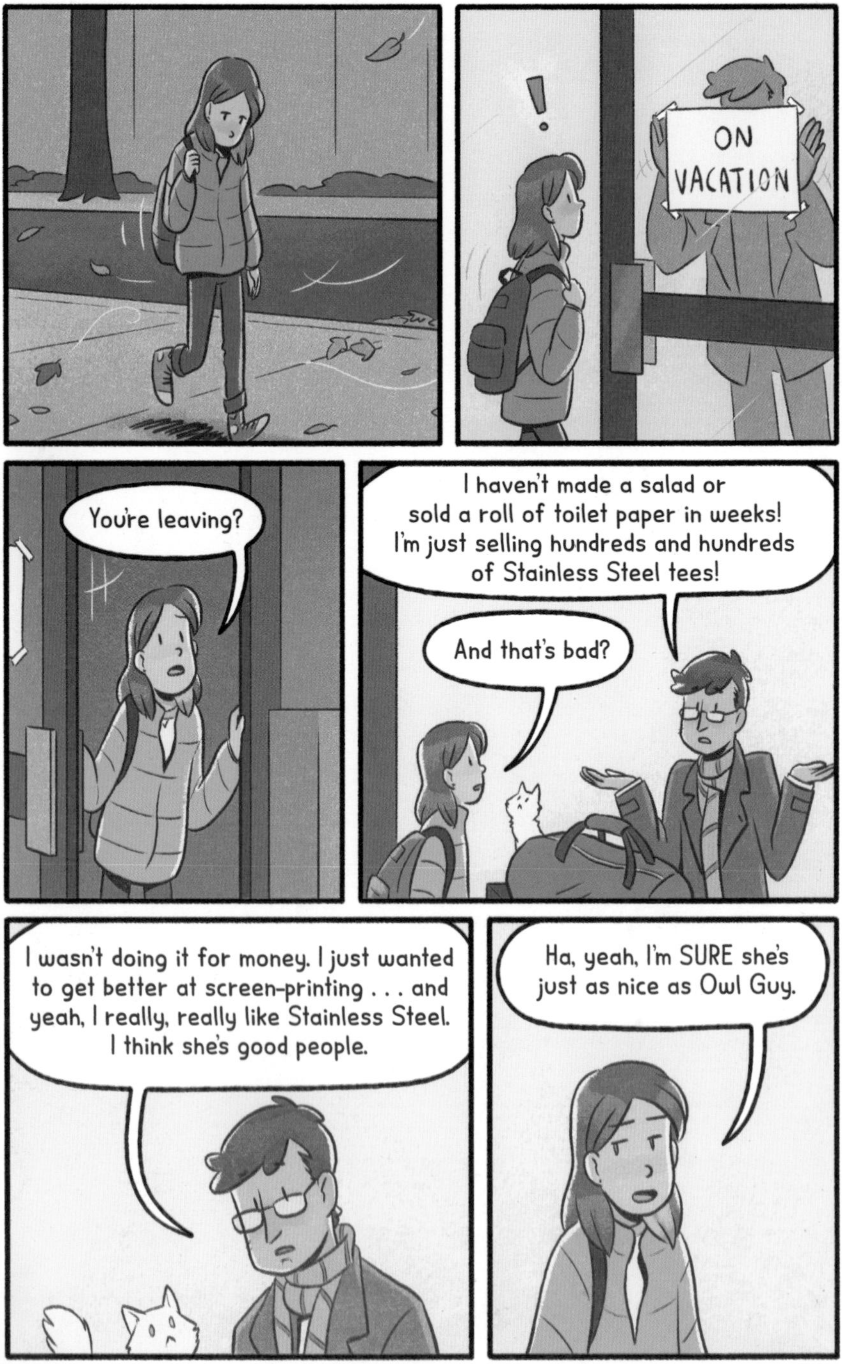
!
ON VACATION
You're leaving?
I haven't made a salad or sold a roll of toilet paper in weeks! I'm just selling hundreds and hundreds of Stainless Steel tees!
And that's bad?
I wasn't doing it for money. I just wanted to get better at screen-printing . . . and yeah, I really, really like Stainless Steel. I think she's good people.
Ha, yeah, I'm SURE she's just as nice as Owl Guy.

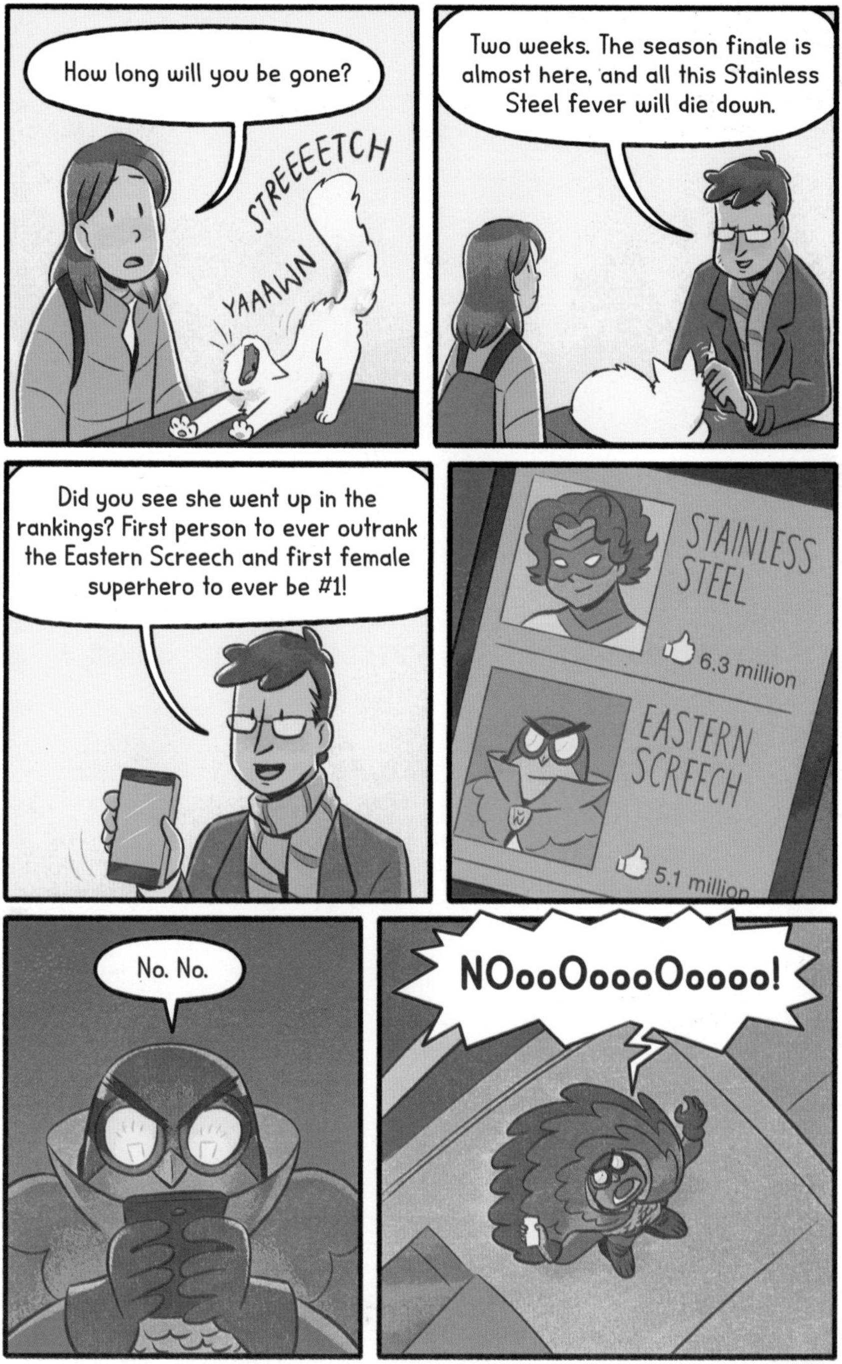
How long will you be gone?
STREEEETCH
YAAAWN
Two weeks. The season finale is almost here, and all this Stainless Steel fever will die down.
Did you see she went up in the rankings? First person to ever outrank the Eastern Screech and first female superhero to ever be #1!
STAINLESS STEEL
6.3 million
EASTERN SCREECH
5.1 million
No. No.
NOooOoooOoooo!

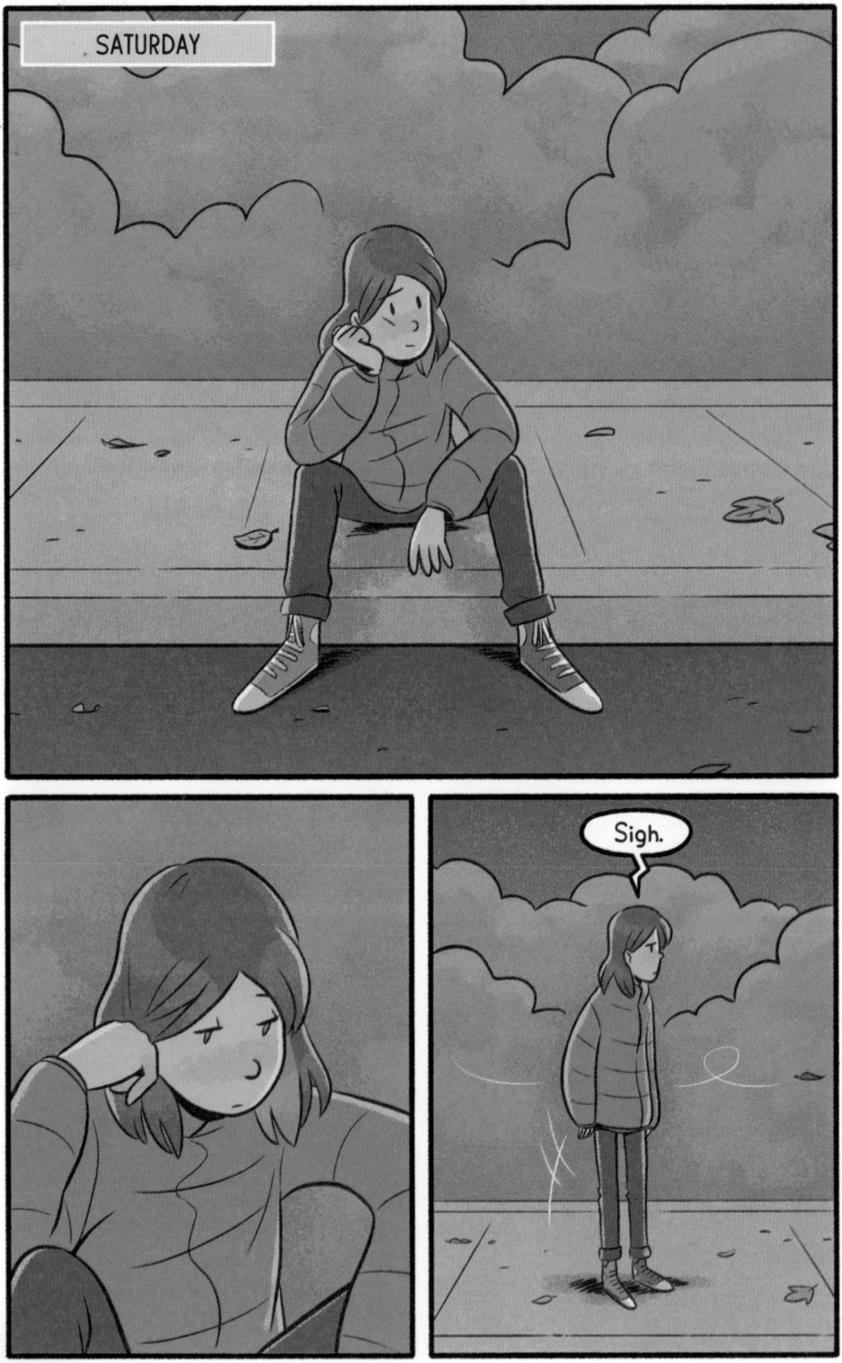
SATURDAY
Sigh.

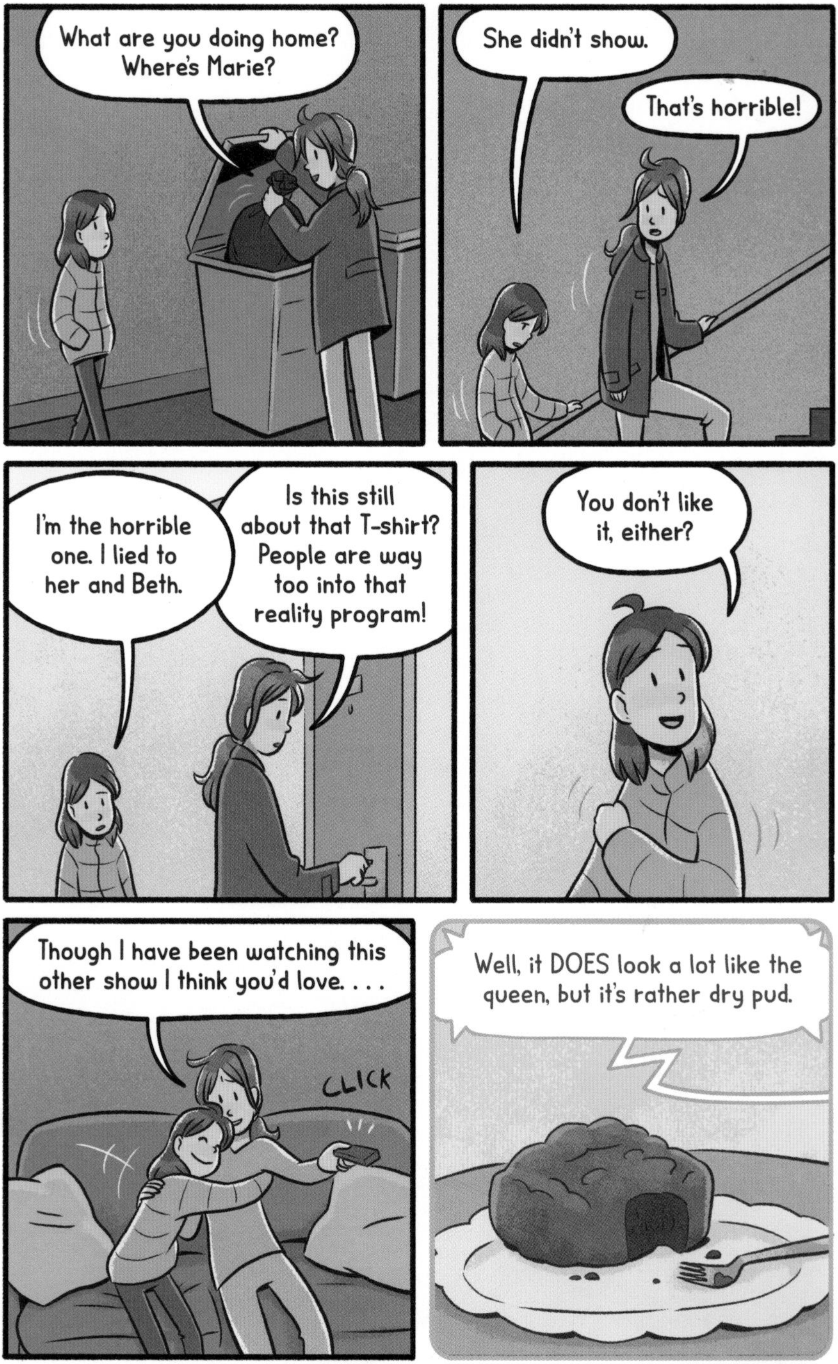
What are you doing home? Where's Marie?
She didn't show.
That's horrible!
I'm the horrible one. I lied to her and Beth.
Is this still about that T-shirt? People are way too into that reality program!
You don't like it, either?
Though I have been watching this other show I think you'd love. . . .
CLICK
Well, it DOES look a lot like the queen, but it's rather dry pud.

Move me down in the rankings. I gave you a shot on my show. You messed with the wrong bird guy.

Ready?

What are you doing, Stainless Steel? You're double-crossing me?

You're secretly a villain?!

I bet she's not THAT BAD a villain.

I'd double-cross Owl Guy if it meant not having to hang out with him.

We still love you, Stainless Steel!

Haha, that should do it.

WHAT? NOT FAIR!

STAINLESS STEEL
6.7 million

EASTERN SCREECH
5.3 million

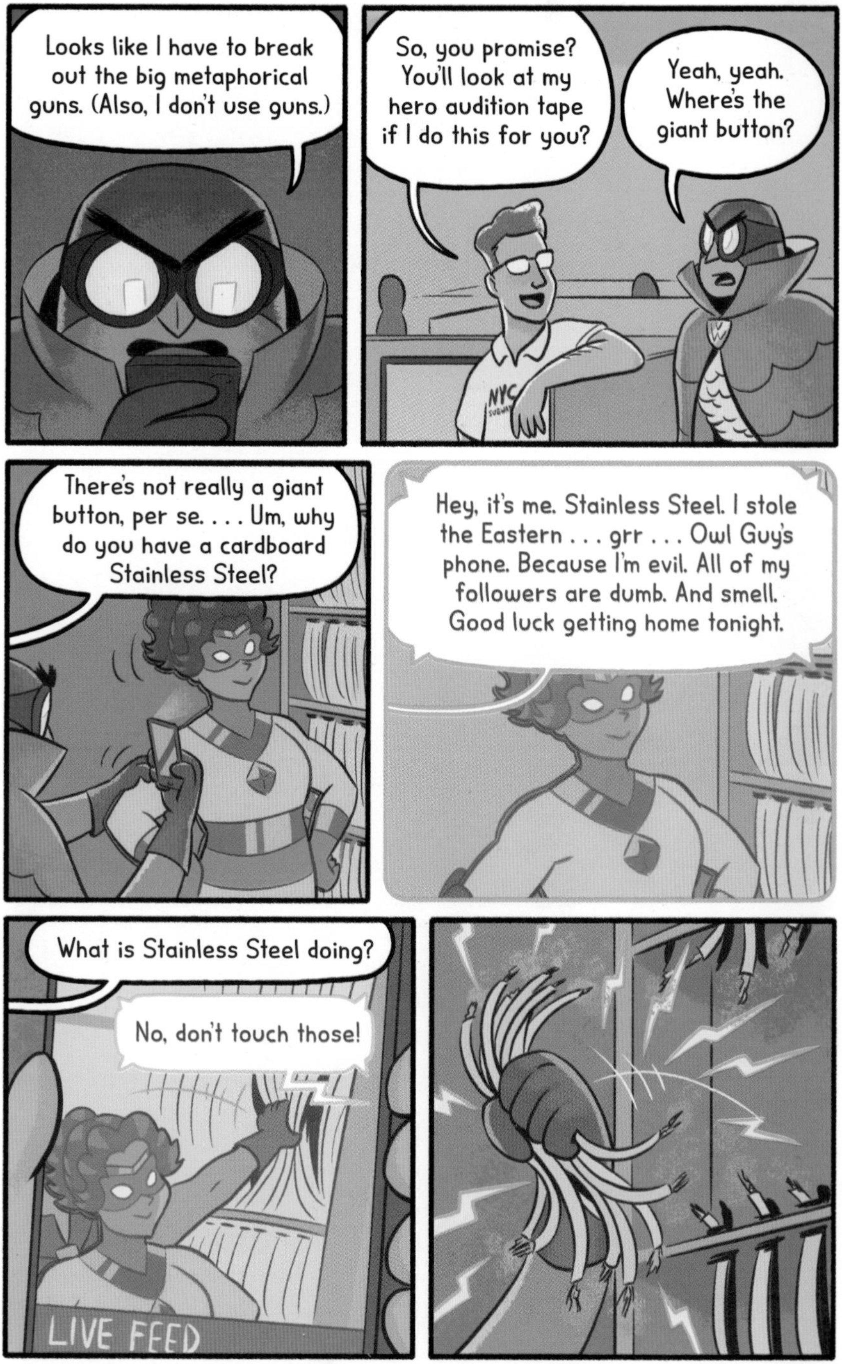
Looks like I have to break out the big metaphorical guns. (Also, I don't use guns.)
So, you promise? You'll look at my hero audition tape if I do this for you?
Yeah, yeah. Where's the giant button?
There's not really a giant button, per se. . . . Um, why do you have a cardboard Stainless Steel?
NYC SUBWAY
Hey, it's me. Stainless Steel. I stole the Eastern . . . grr . . . Owl Guy's phone. Because I'm evil. All of my followers are dumb. And smell. Good luck getting home tonight.
What is Stainless Steel doing?
No, don't touch those!
LIVE FEED

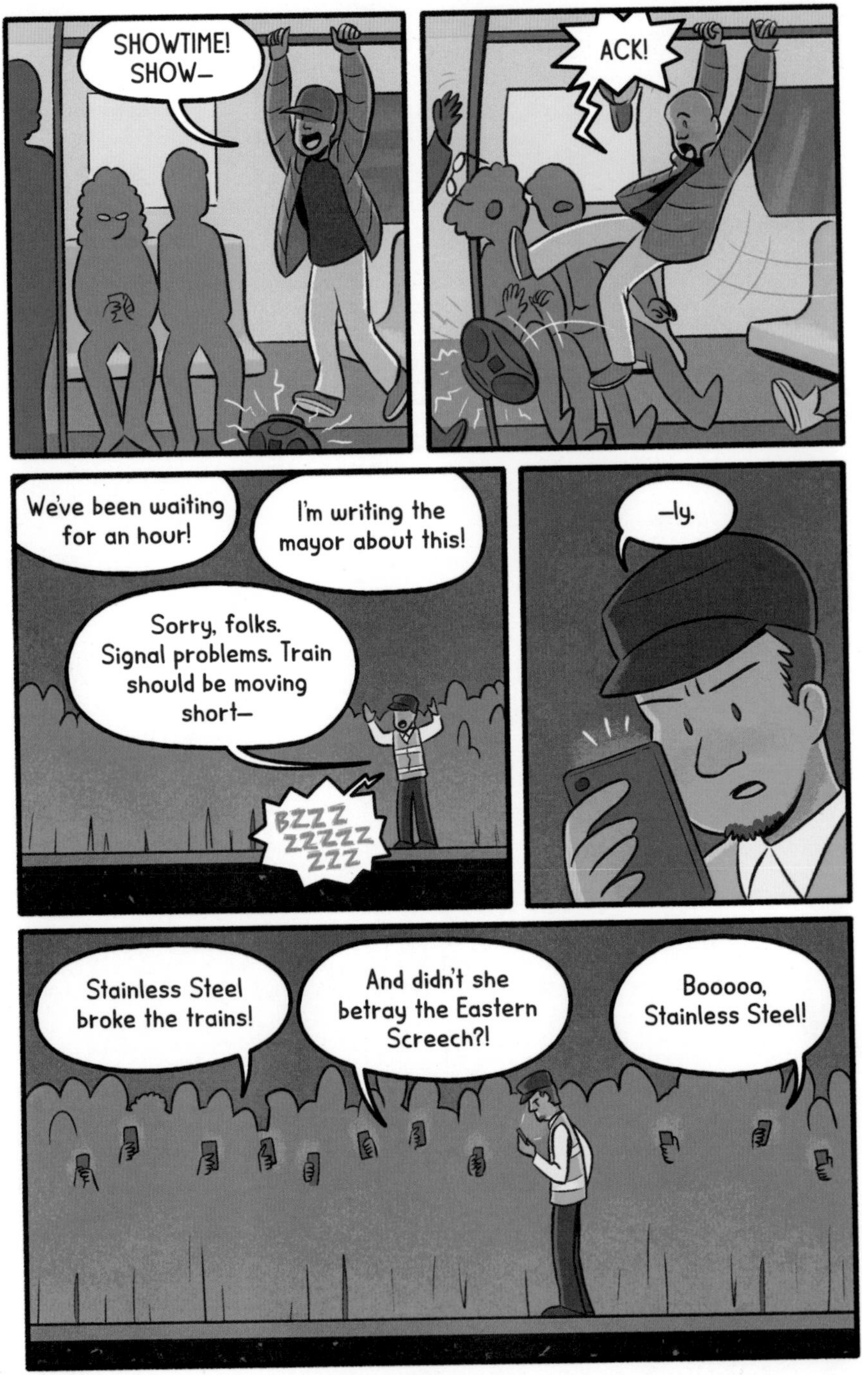
SHOWTIME! SHOW—
ACK!
We've been waiting for an hour!
I'm writing the mayor about this!
Sorry, folks. Signal problems. Train should be moving short—
BZZZ ZZZZZ ZZZ
—ly.
Stainless Steel broke the trains!
And didn't she betray the Eastern Screech?!
Booooo, Stainless Steel!

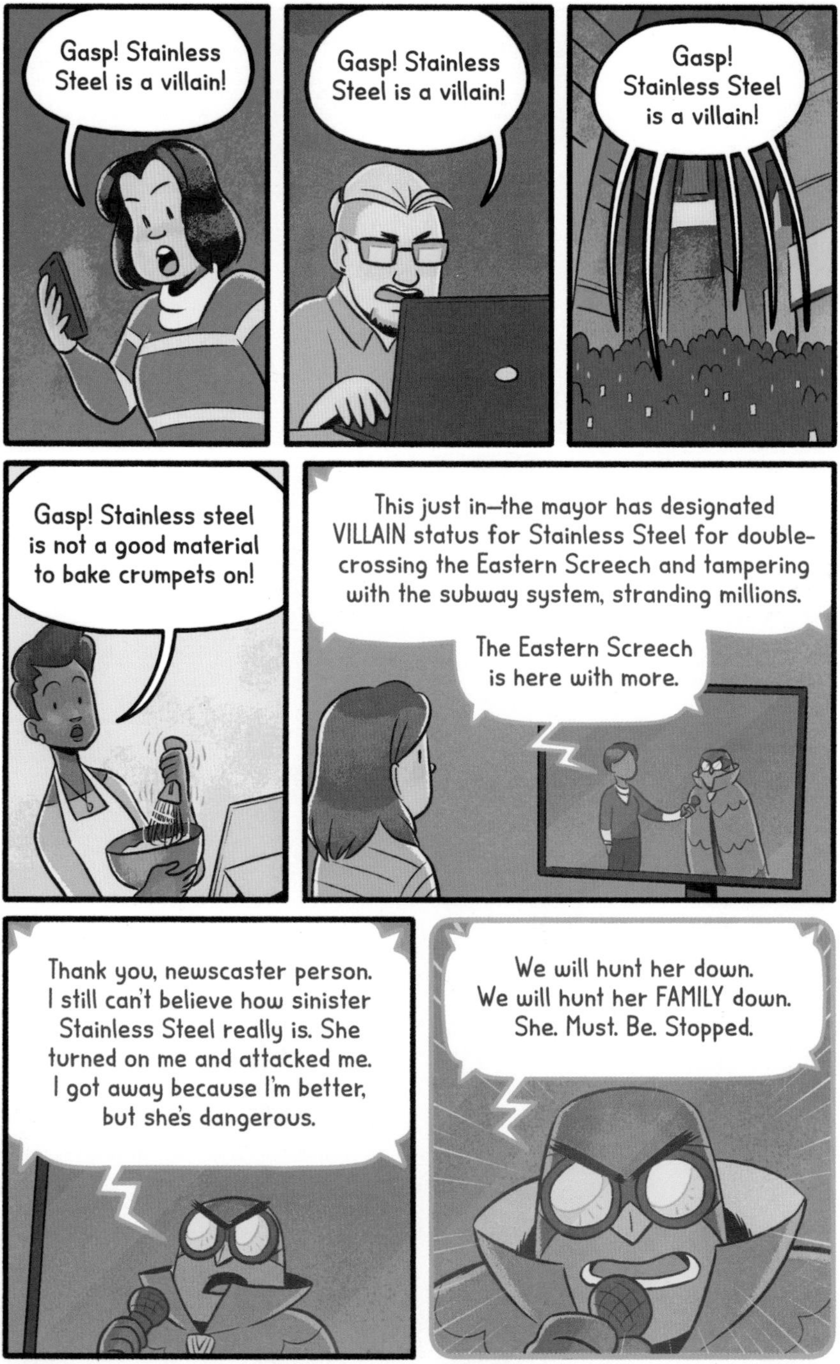
Gasp! Stainless Steel is a villain!
Gasp! Stainless Steel is a villain!
Gasp! Stainless Steel is a villain!
Gasp! Stainless steel is not a good material to bake crumpets on!
This just in—the mayor has designated VILLAIN status for Stainless Steel for double-crossing the Eastern Screech and tampering with the subway system, stranding millions.
The Eastern Screech is here with more.
Thank you, newscaster person. I still can't believe how sinister Stainless Steel really is. She turned on me and attacked me. I got away because I'm better, but she's dangerous.
We will hunt her down. We will hunt her FAMILY down. She. Must. Be. Stopped.

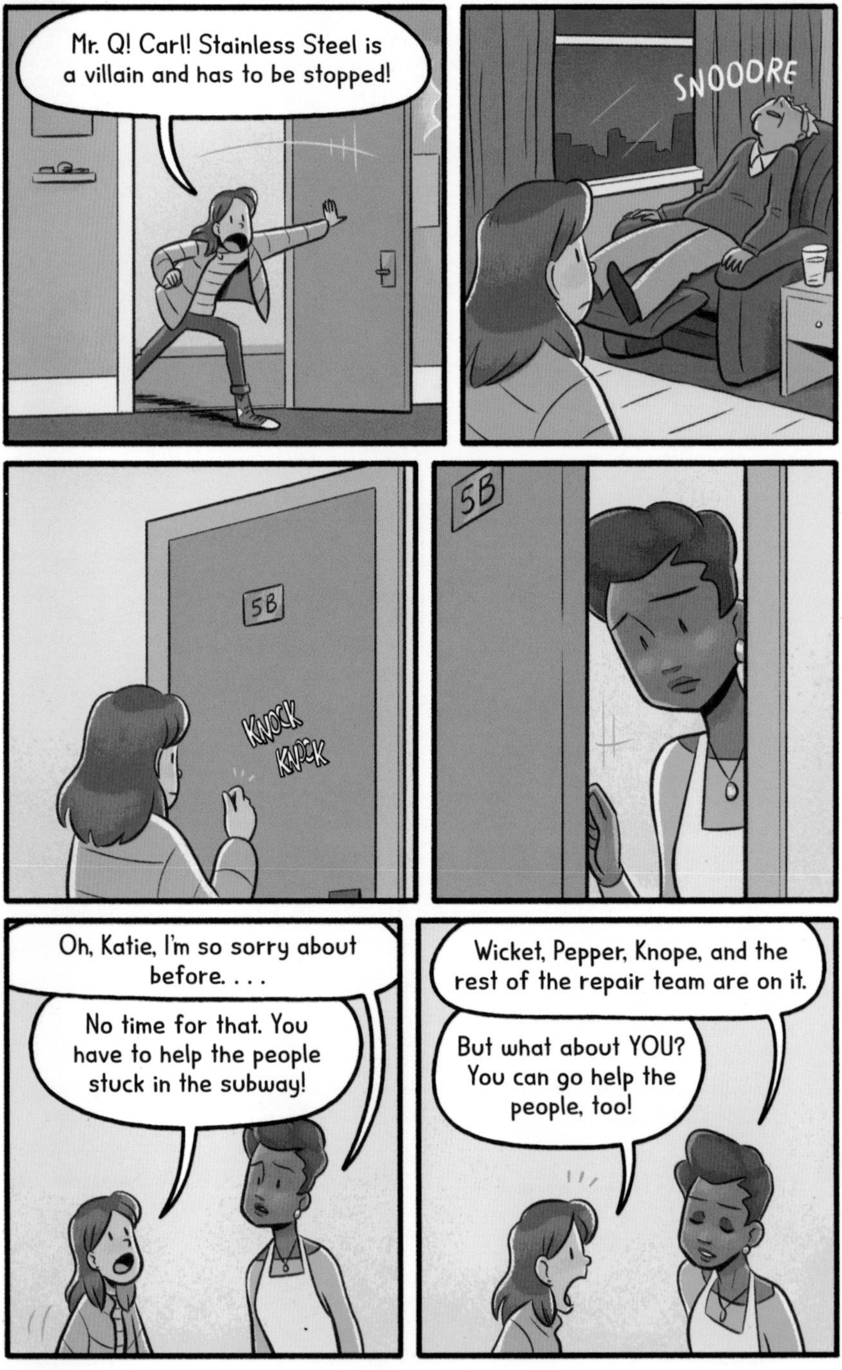

Mr. Q! Carl! Stainless Steel is a villain and has to be stopped!
SNOOORE
5B
5B
KNOCK
KNOCK
5B
Oh, Katie, I'm so sorry about before. . . .
No time for that. You have to help the people stuck in the subway!
Wicket, Pepper, Knope, and the rest of the repair team are on it.
But what about YOU? You can go help the people, too!

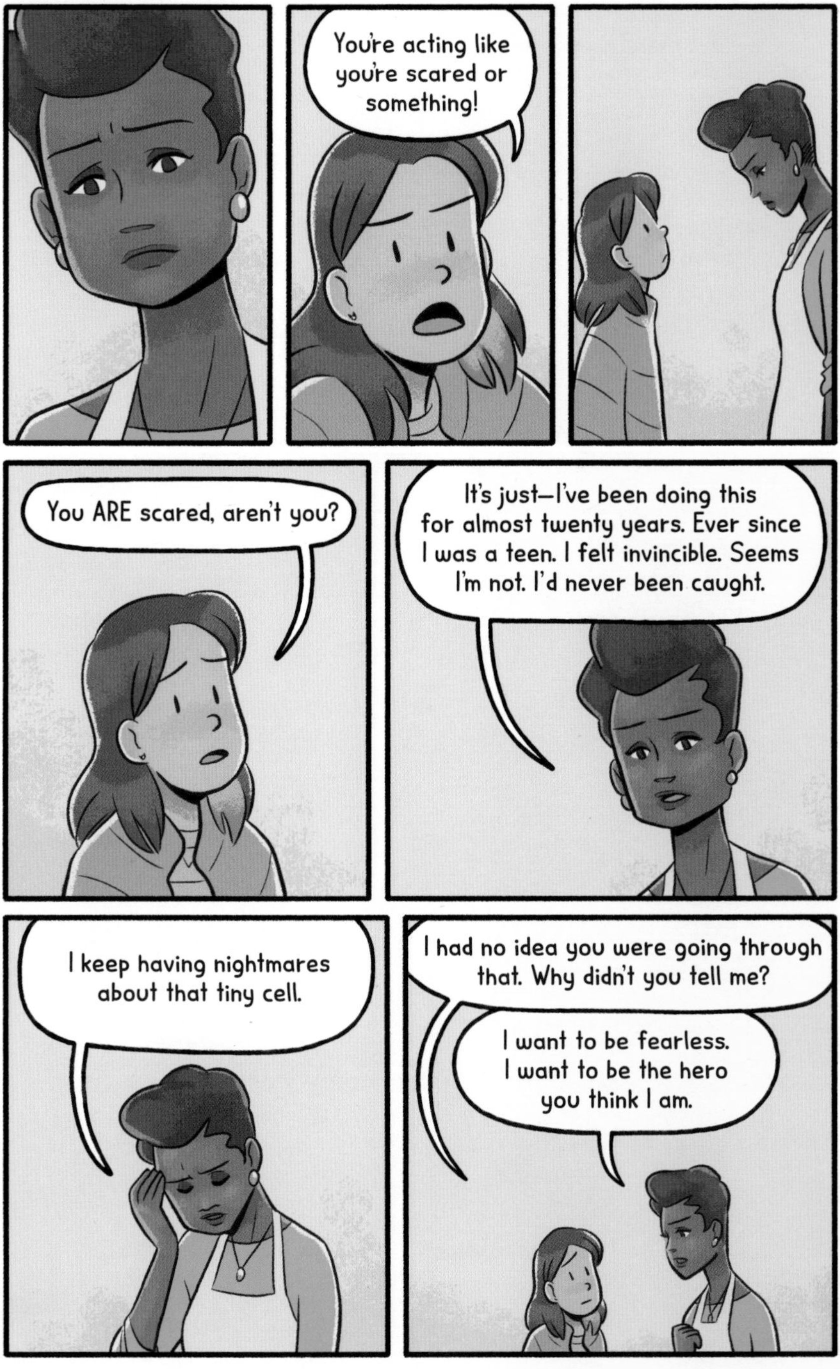
You're acting like you're scared or something!
You ARE scared, aren't you?
It's just—I've been doing this for almost twenty years. Ever since I was a teen. I felt invincible. Seems I'm not. I'd never been caught.
I keep having nightmares about that tiny cell.
I had no idea you were going through that. Why didn't you tell me?
I want to be fearless. I want to be the hero you think I am.

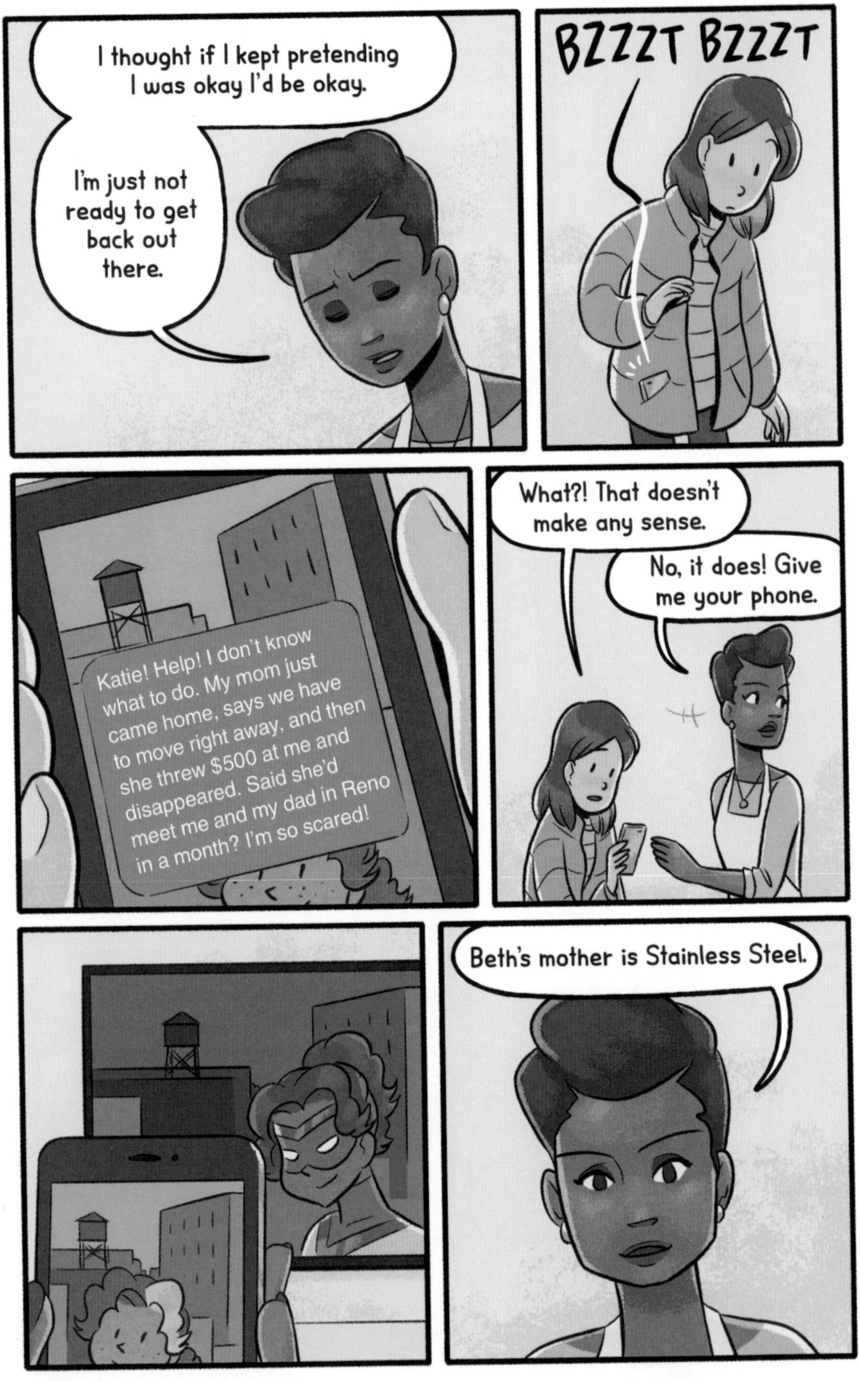
I thought if I kept pretending I was okay I'd be okay.
I'm just not ready to get back out there.
BZZZT BZZZT
Katie! Help! I don't know what to do. My mom just came home, says we have to move right away, and then she threw $500 at me and disappeared. Said she'd meet me and my dad in Reno in a month? I'm so scared!
What?! That doesn't make any sense.
No, it does! Give me your phone.
Beth's mother is Stainless Steel.

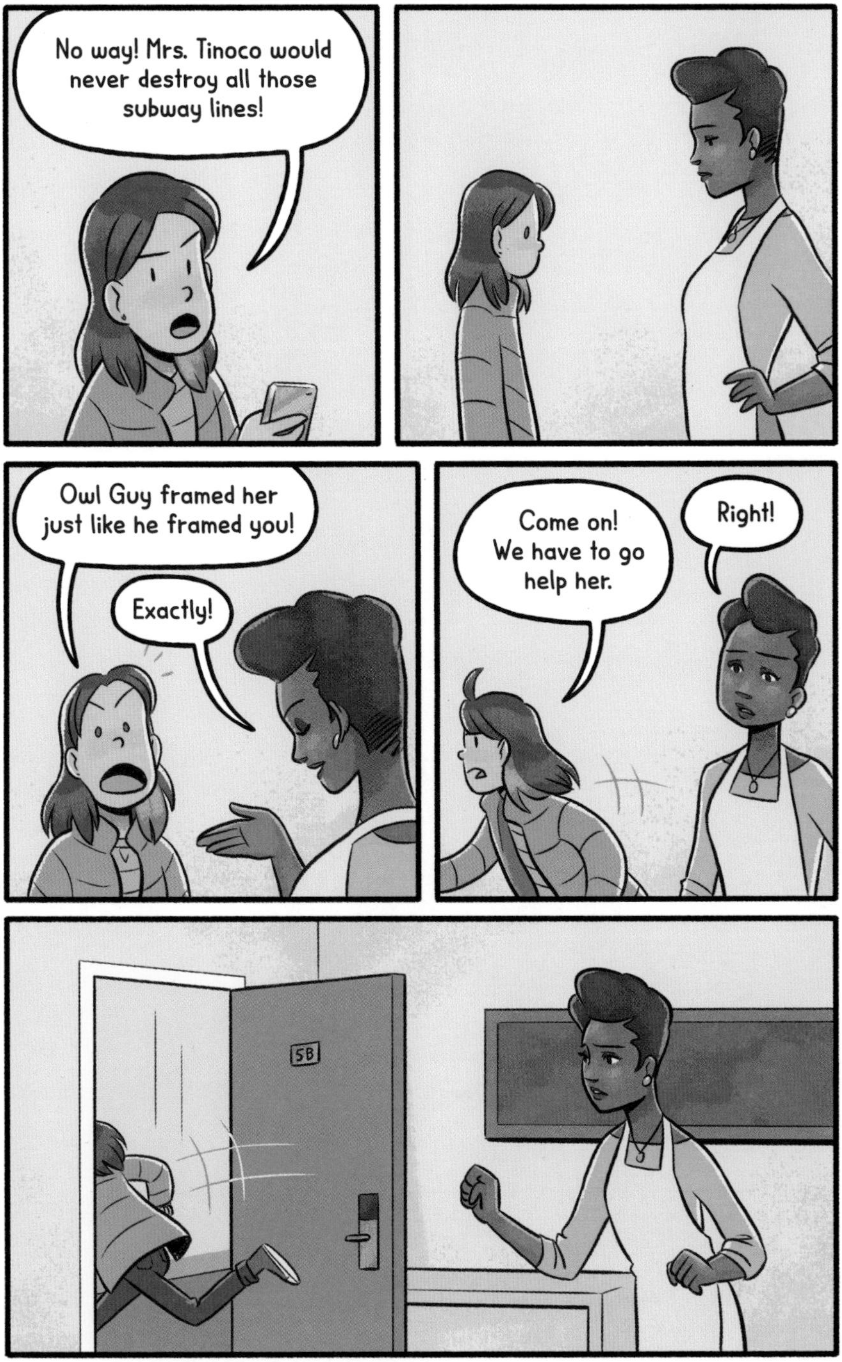
No way! Mrs. Tinoco would never destroy all those subway lines!
Owl Guy framed her just like he framed you!
Exactly!
Come on! We have to go help her.
Right!
5B

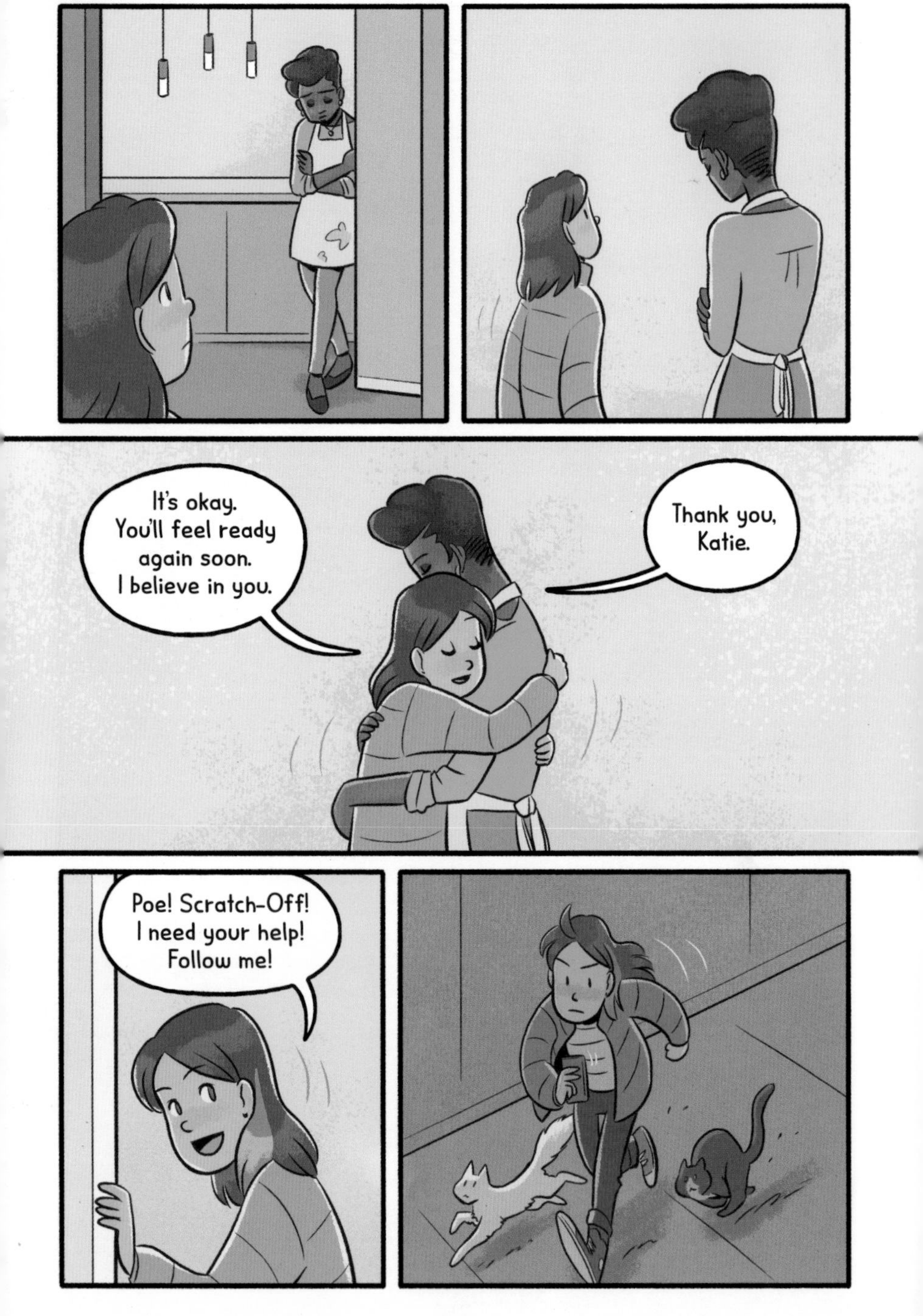
It's okay. You'll feel ready again soon. I believe in you.
Thank you, Katie.
Poe! Scratch-Off! I need your help! Follow me!

CHAPTER TEN

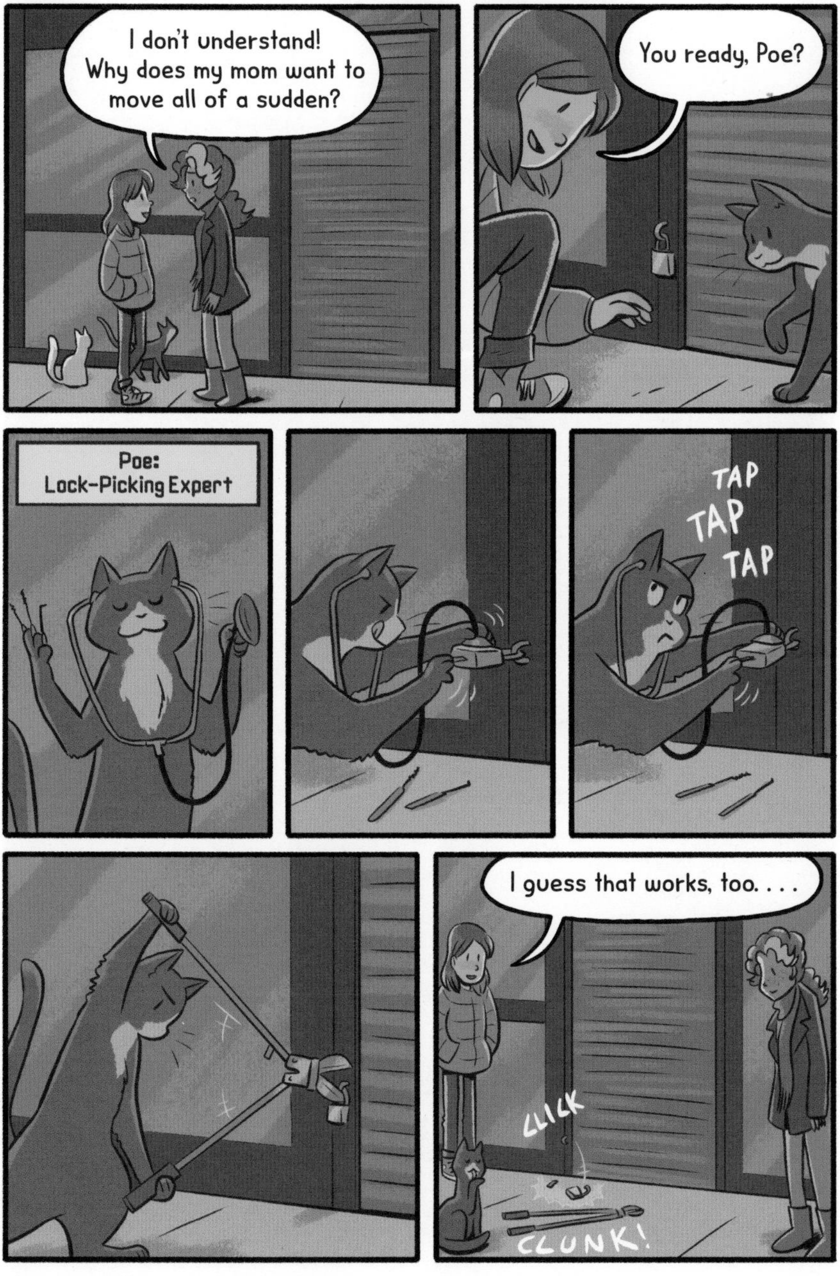
I don't understand! Why does my mom want to move all of a sudden?
You ready, Poe?
Poe: Lock-Picking Expert
TAP
TAP
TAP
I guess that works, too. . . .
CLICK
CLUNK!

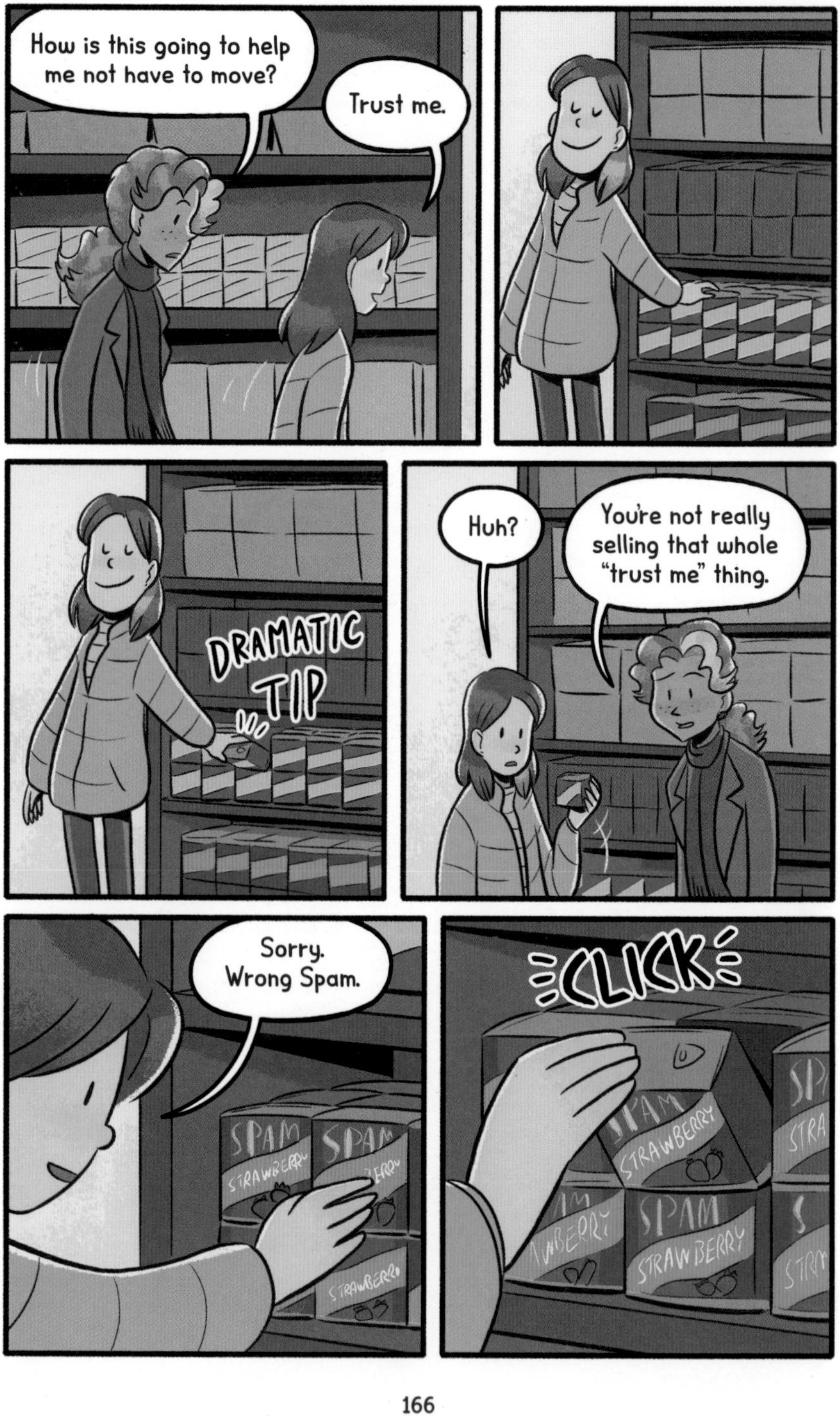
How is this going to help me not have to move?
Trust me.
DRAMATIC TIP
Huh?
You're not really selling that whole "trust me" thing.
Sorry. Wrong Spam.
SPAM
STRAWBERRY
CLICK
SPAM
STRAWBERRY

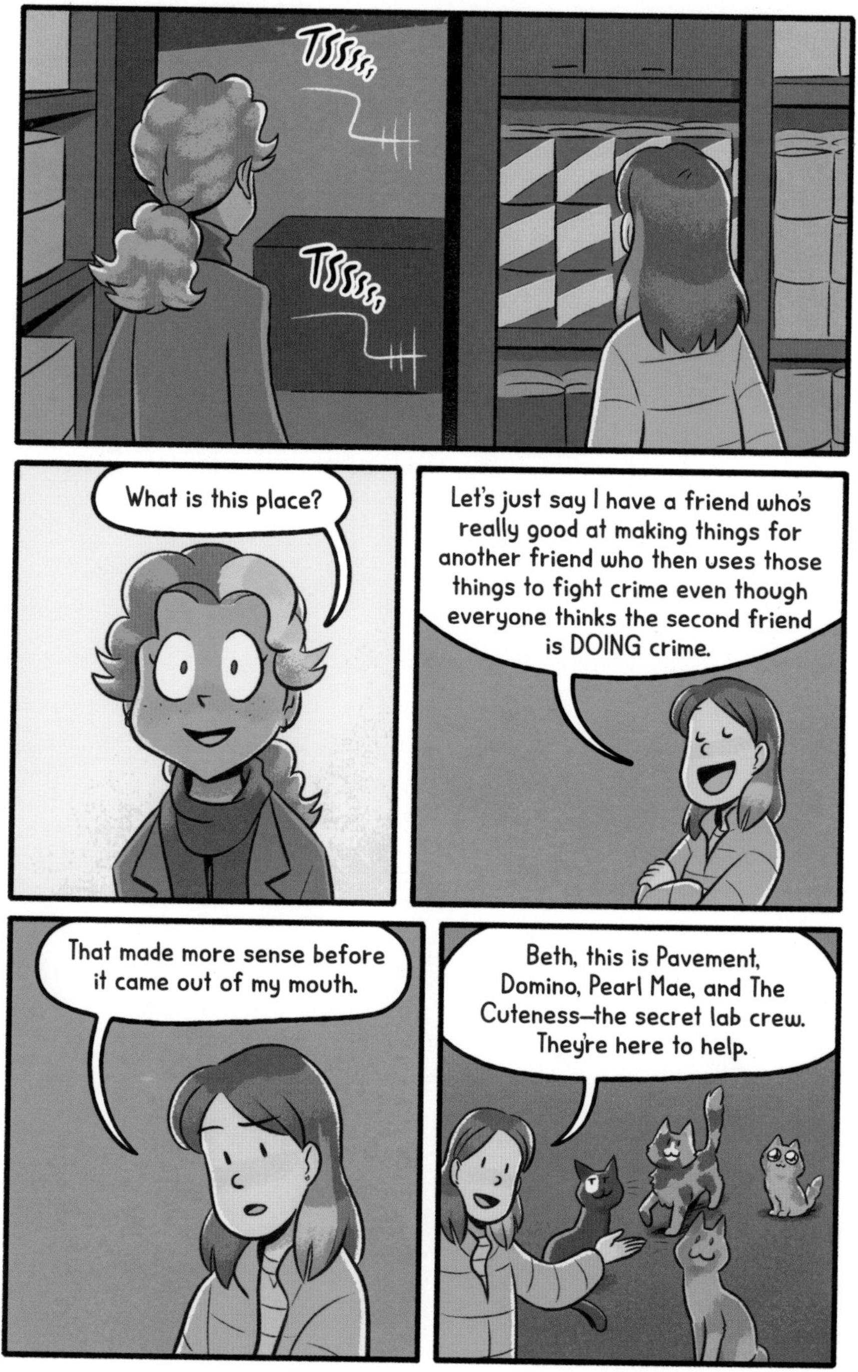
TSSSS
TSSSS
What is this place?
Let's just say I have a friend who's really good at making things for another friend who then uses those things to fight crime even though everyone thinks the second friend is DOING crime.
That made more sense before it came out of my mouth.
Beth, this is Pavement, Domino, Pearl Mae, and The Cuteness—the secret lab crew. They're here to help.

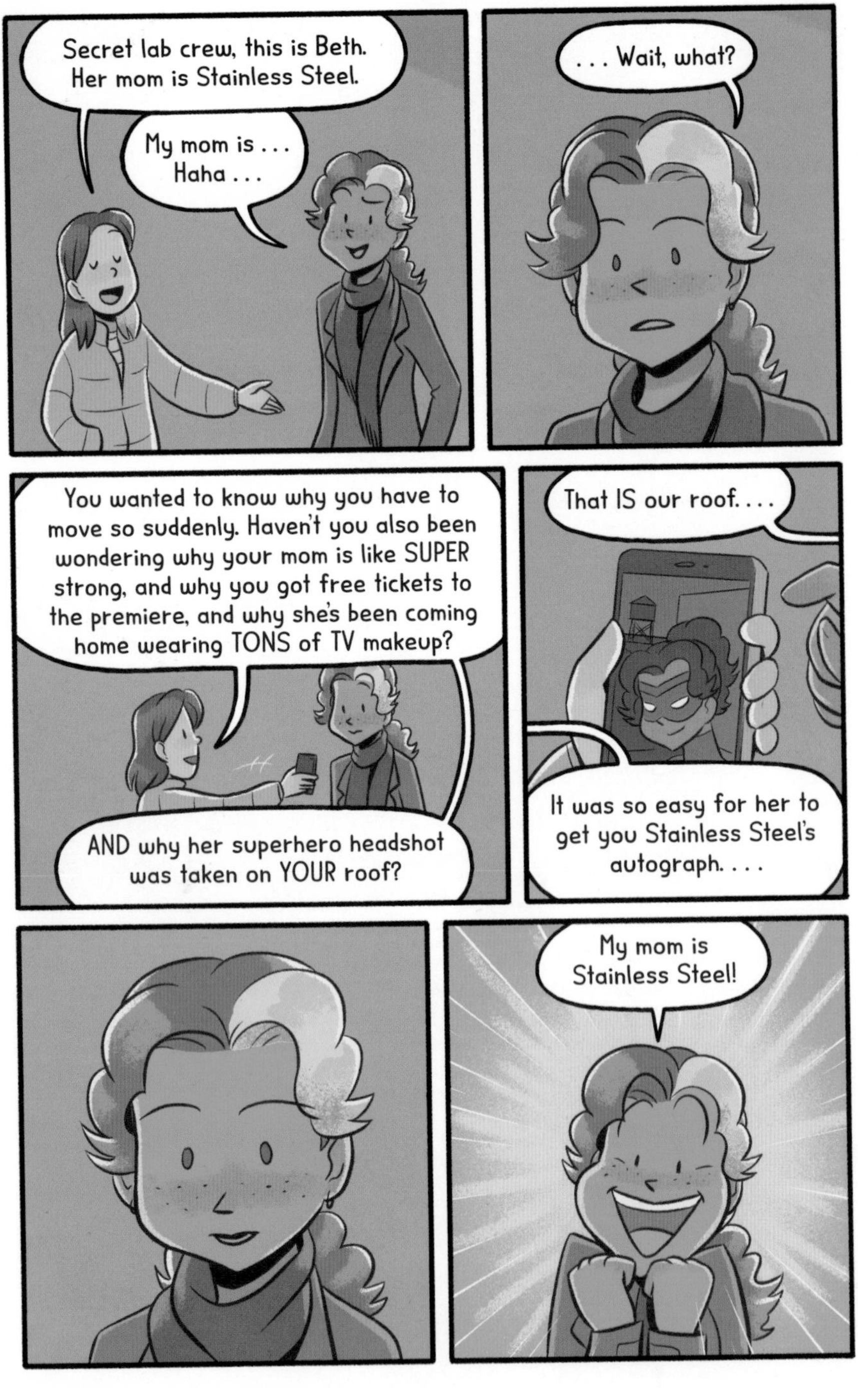
Secret lab crew, this is Beth. Her mom is Stainless Steel.
My mom is . . . Haha . . .
. . . Wait, what?
You wanted to know why you have to move so suddenly. Haven't you also been wondering why your mom is like SUPER strong, and why you got free tickets to the premiere, and why she's been coming home wearing TONS of TV makeup?
AND why her superhero headshot was taken on YOUR roof?
That IS our roof. . . .
It was so easy for her to get you Stainless Steel's autograph. . . .
My mom is Stainless Steel!

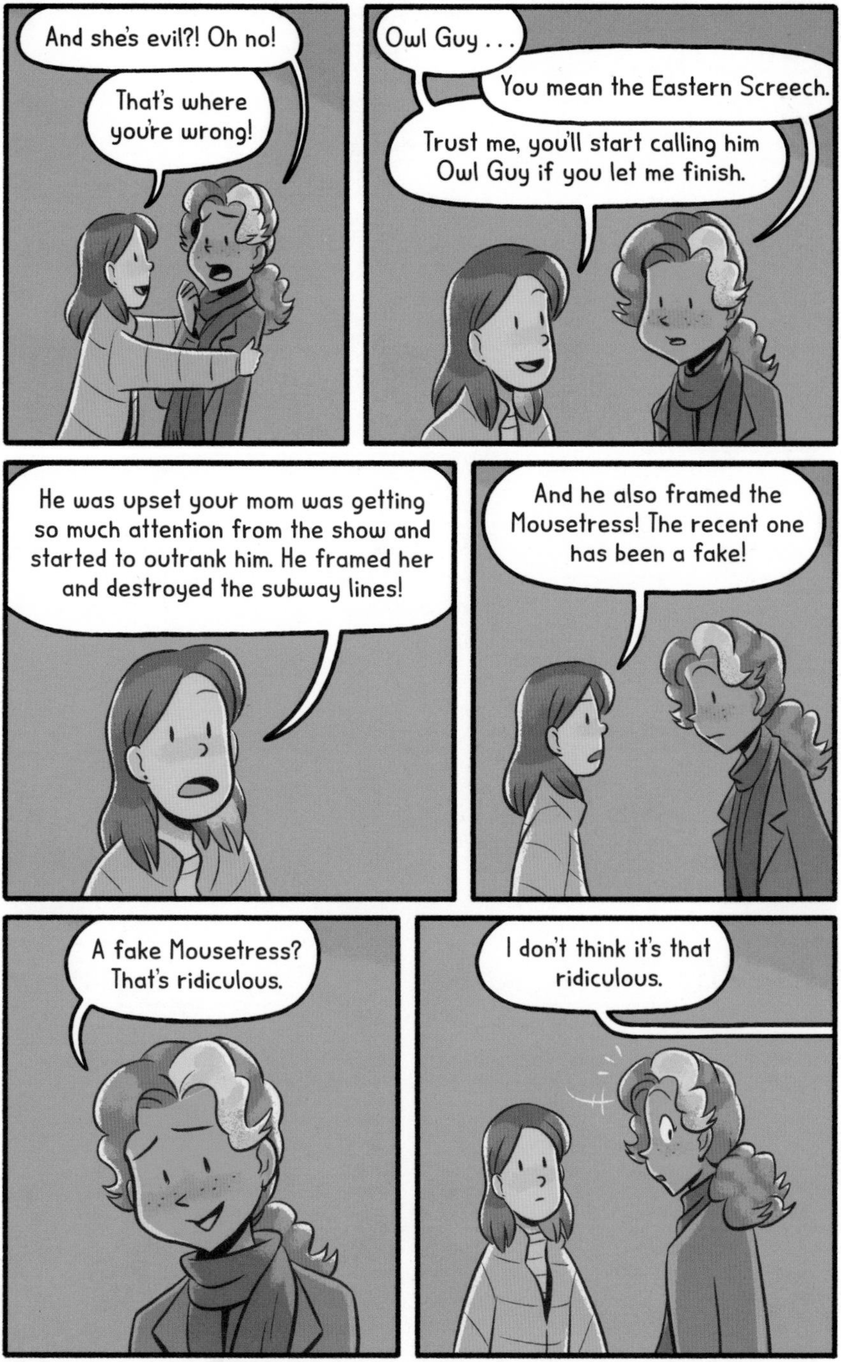

And she's evil?! Oh no!
That's where you're wrong!
Owl Guy . . .
You mean the Eastern Screech.
Trust me, you'll start calling him Owl Guy if you let me finish.
He was upset your mom was getting so much attention from the show and started to outrank him. He framed her and destroyed the subway lines!
And he also framed the Mousetress! The recent one has been a fake!
A fake Mousetress? That's ridiculous.
I don't think it's that ridiculous.

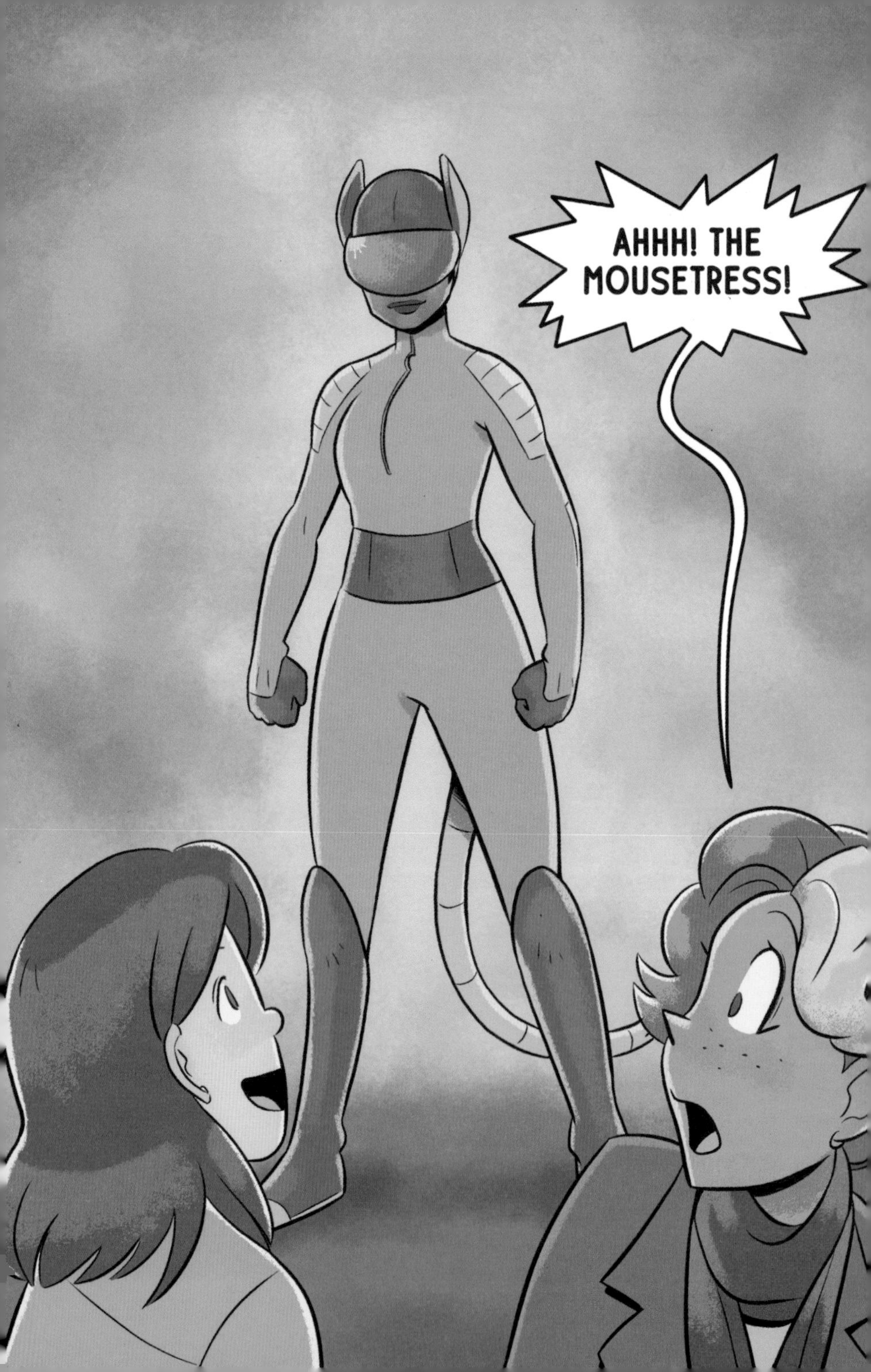
AHHH! THE MOUSETRESS!

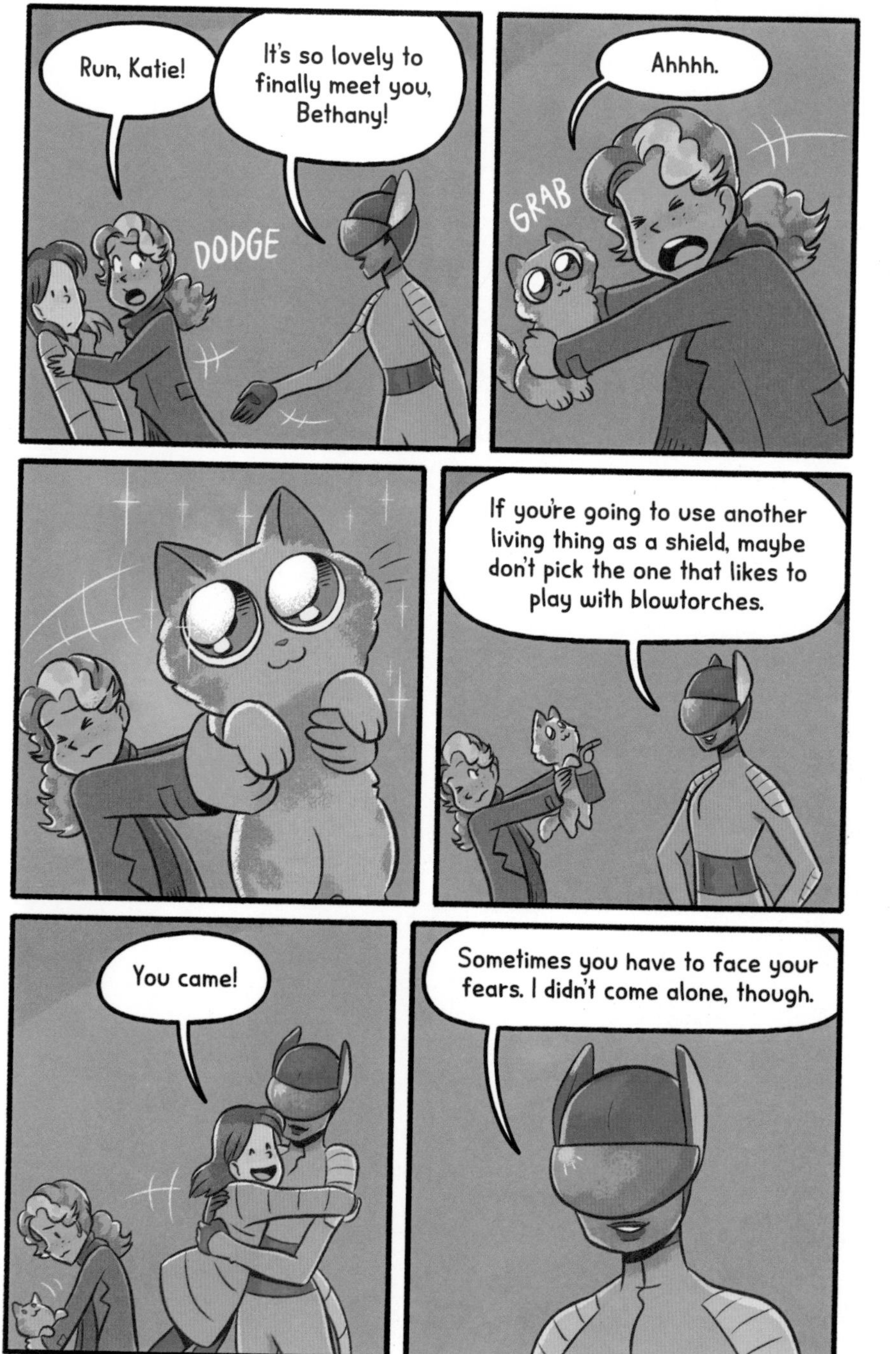
Run, Katie!
It's so lovely to finally meet you, Bethany!
DODGE
Ahhhh.
GRAB
If you're going to use another living thing as a shield, maybe don't pick the one that likes to play with blowtorches.
You came!
Sometimes you have to face your fears. I didn't come alone, though.

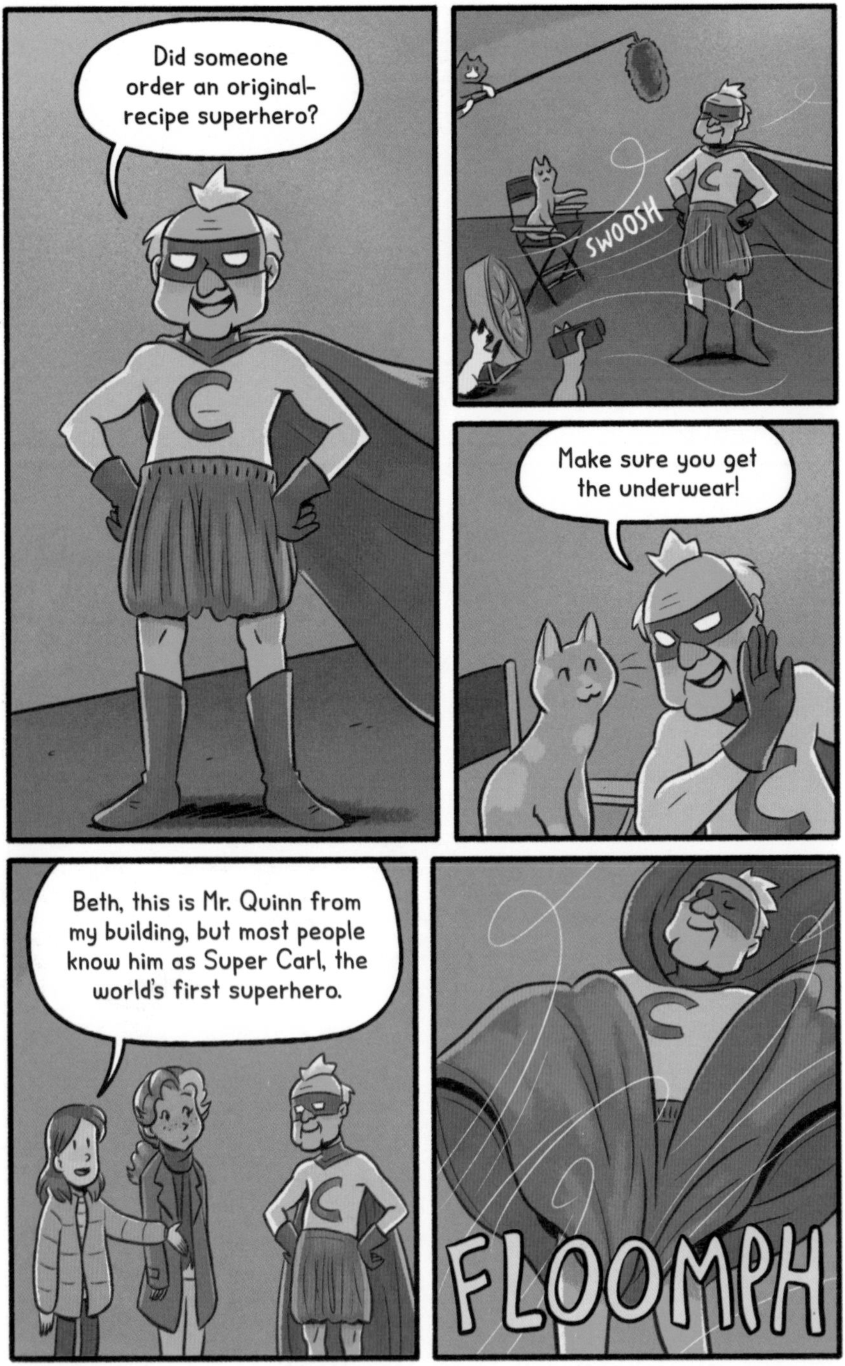
Did someone order an original-recipe superhero?
SWOOSH
Make sure you get the underwear!
Beth, this is Mr. Quinn from my building, but most people know him as Super Carl, the world's first superhero.
FLOOMPH

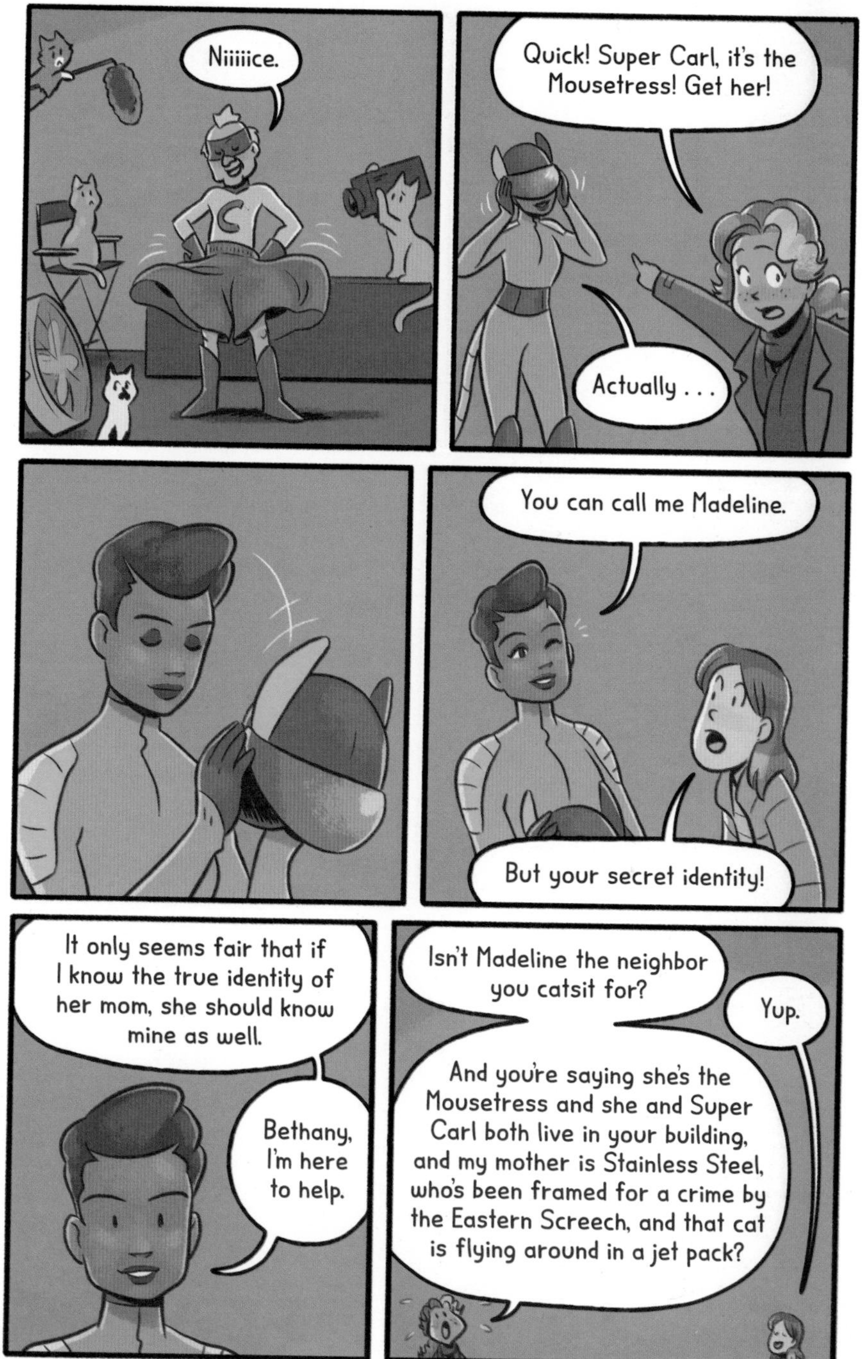

Niiiiice.
Quick! Super Carl, it's the Mousetress! Get her!
Actually . . .
You can call me Madeline.
But your secret identity!
It only seems fair that if I know the true identity of her mom, she should know mine as well.
Bethany, I'm here to help.
Isn't Madeline the neighbor you catsit for?
Yup.
And you're saying she's the Mousetress and she and Super Carl both live in your building, and my mother is Stainless Steel, who's been framed for a crime by the Eastern Screech, and that cat is flying around in a jet pack?

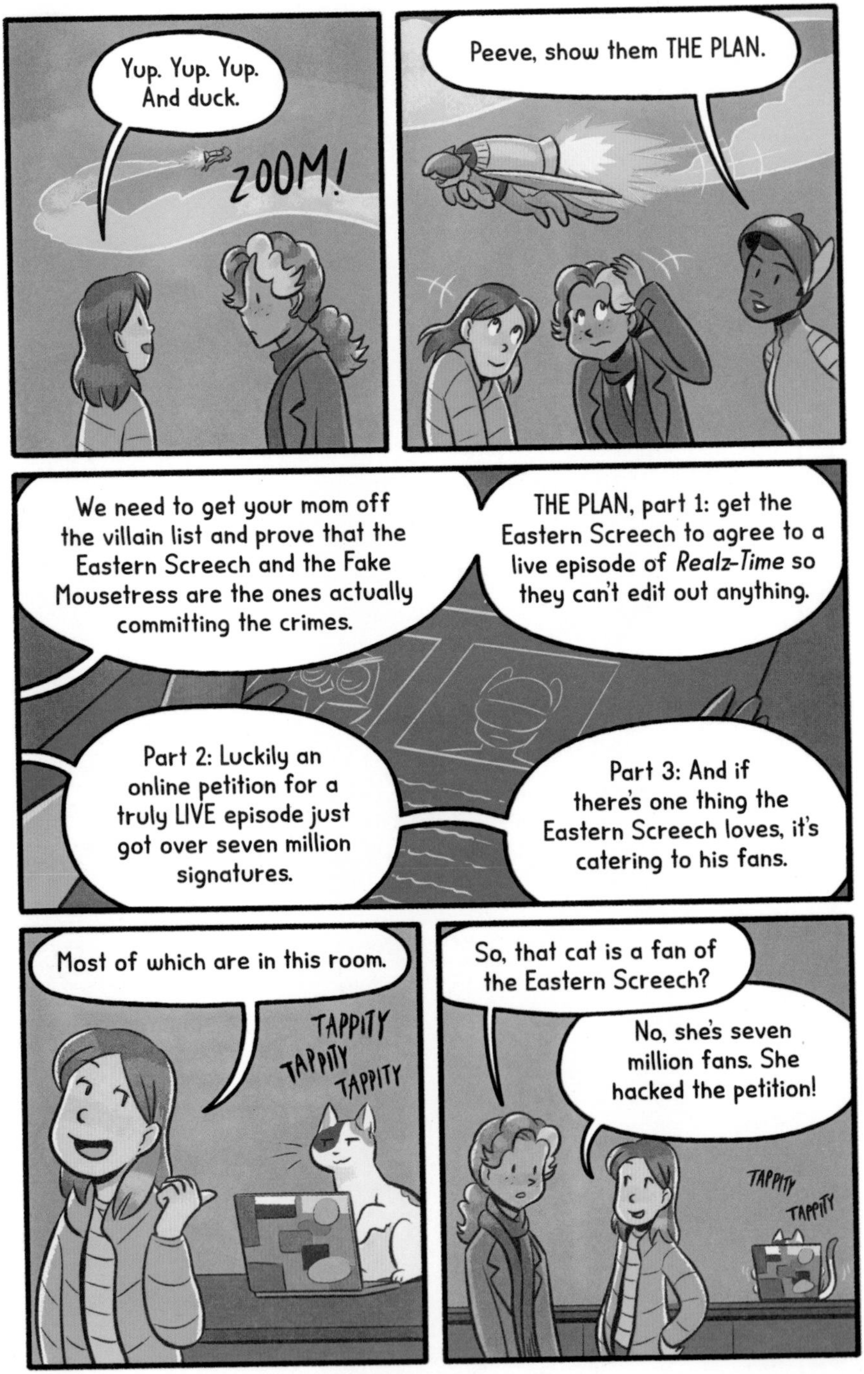
Yup. Yup. Yup. And duck.
ZOOM!
Peeve, show them THE PLAN.
We need to get your mom off the villain list and prove that the Eastern Screech and the Fake Mousetress are the ones actually committing the crimes.
THE PLAN, part 1: get the Eastern Screech to agree to a live episode of *Realz-Time* so they can't edit out anything.
Part 2: Luckily an online petition for a truly LIVE episode just got over seven million signatures.
Part 3: And if there's one thing the Eastern Screech loves, it's catering to his fans.
Most of which are in this room.
TAPPITY TAPPITY TAPPITY
So, that cat is a fan of the Eastern Screech?
No, she's seven million fans. She hacked the petition!
TAPPITY TAPPITY

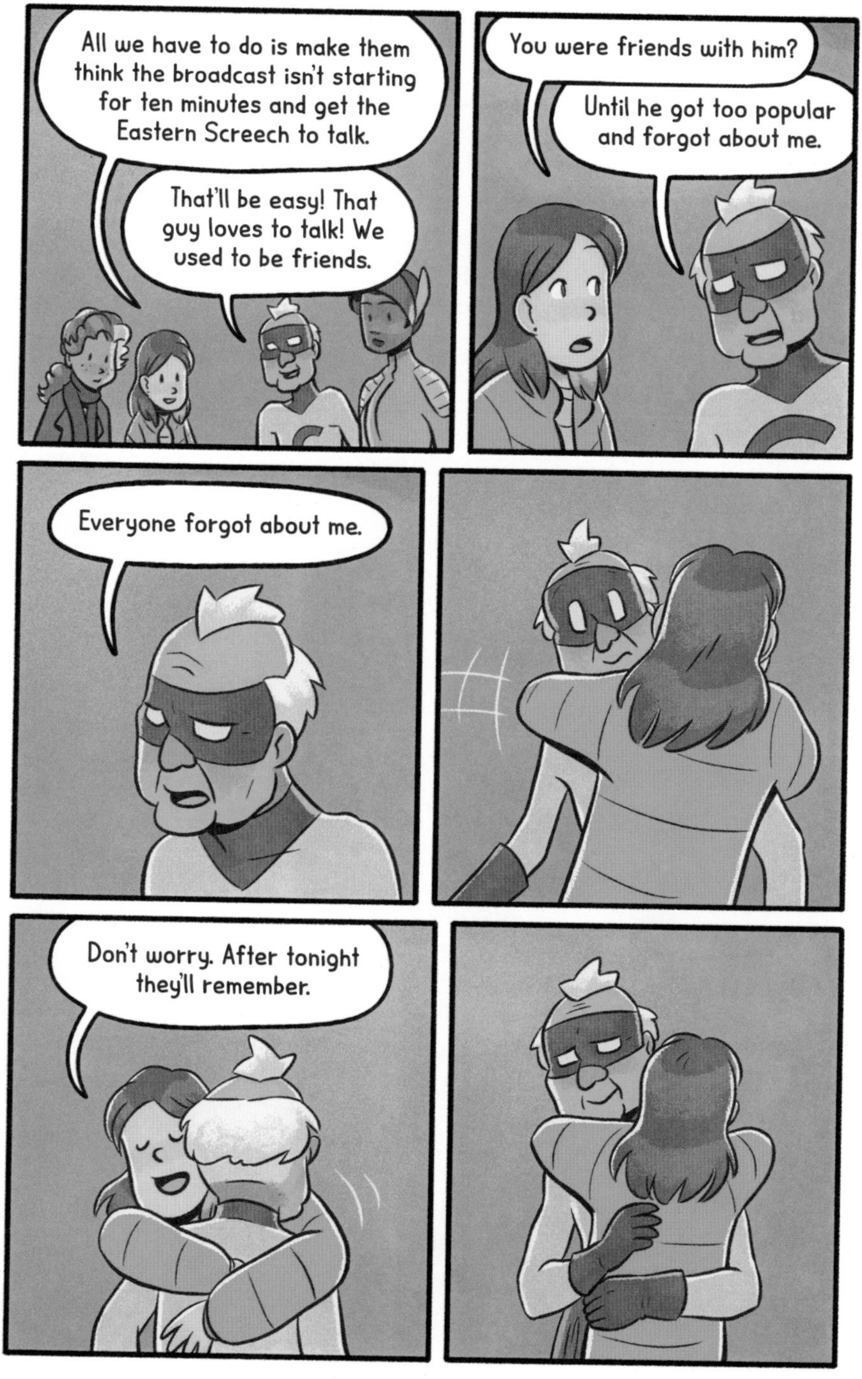
All we have to do is make them think the broadcast isn't starting for ten minutes and get the Eastern Screech to talk.
That'll be easy! That guy loves to talk! We used to be friends.
You were friends with him?
Until he got too popular and forgot about me.
Everyone forgot about me.
Don't worry. After tonight they'll remember.

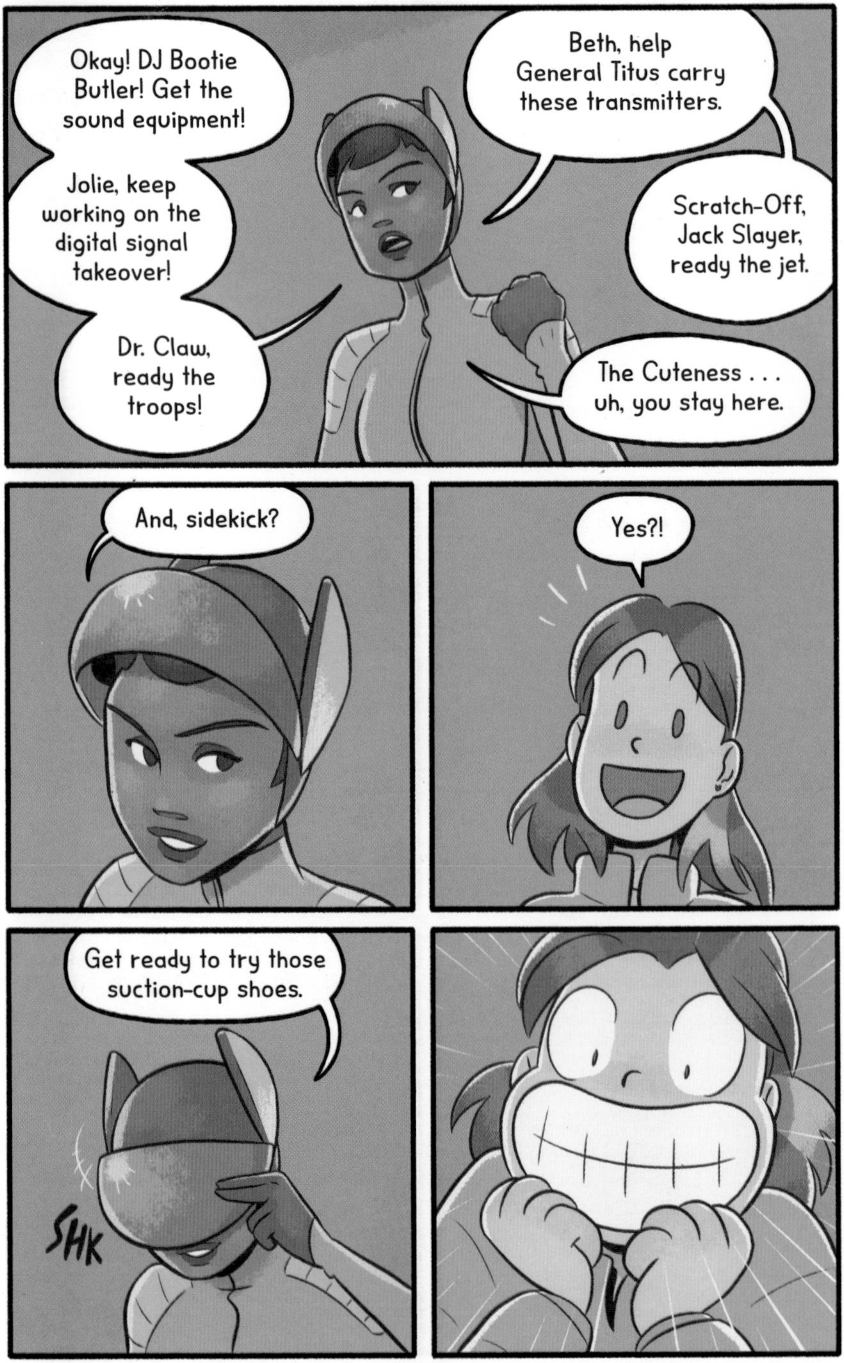
Okay! DJ Bootie Butler! Get the sound equipment!
Jolie, keep working on the digital signal takeover!
Dr. Claw, ready the troops!
Beth, help General Titus carry these transmitters.
Scratch-Off, Jack Slayer, ready the jet.
The Cuteness . . . uh, you stay here.
And, sidekick?
Yes?!
Get ready to try those suction-cup shoes.
SHK

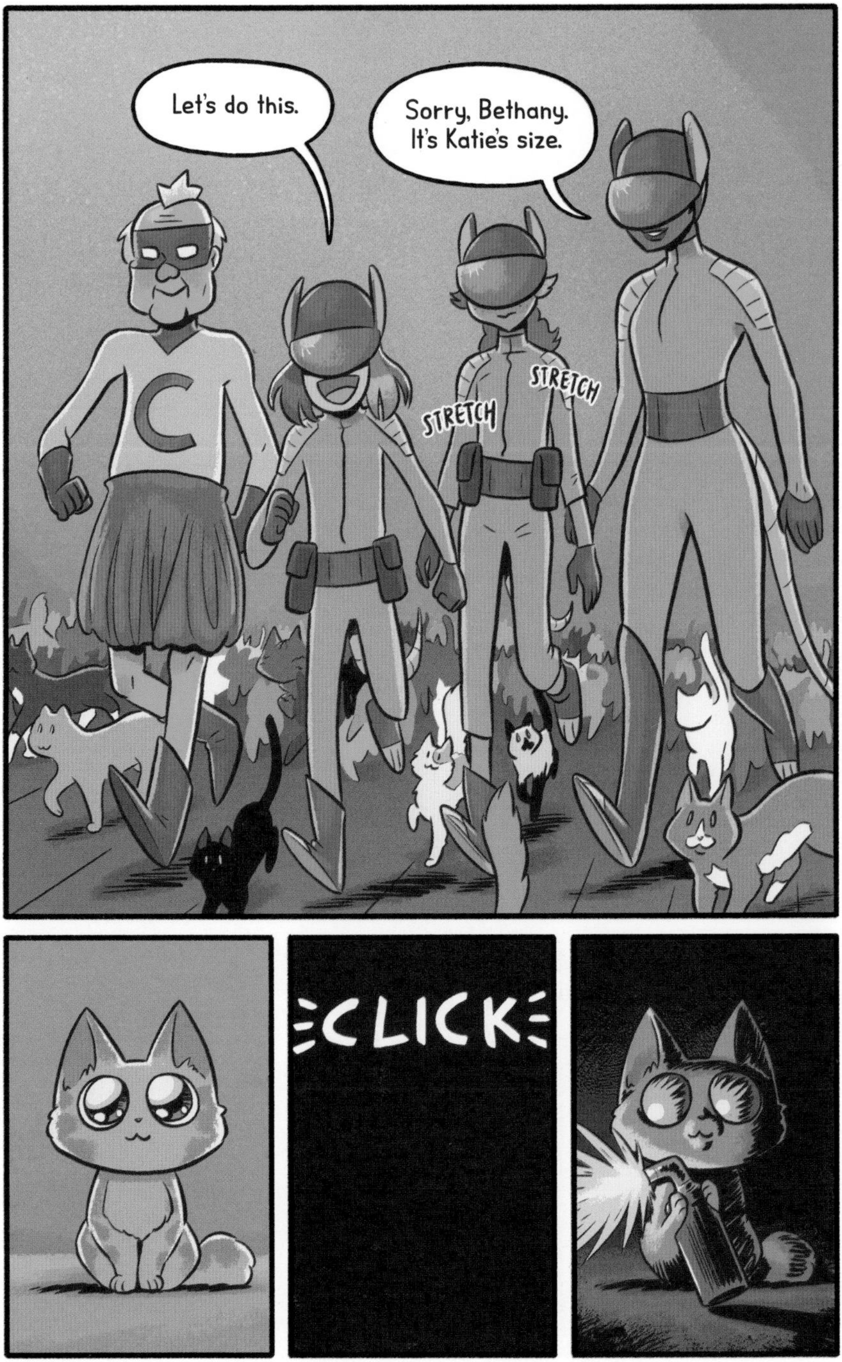
Let's do this.
Sorry, Bethany. It's Katie's size.
STRETCH
STRETCH
CLICK

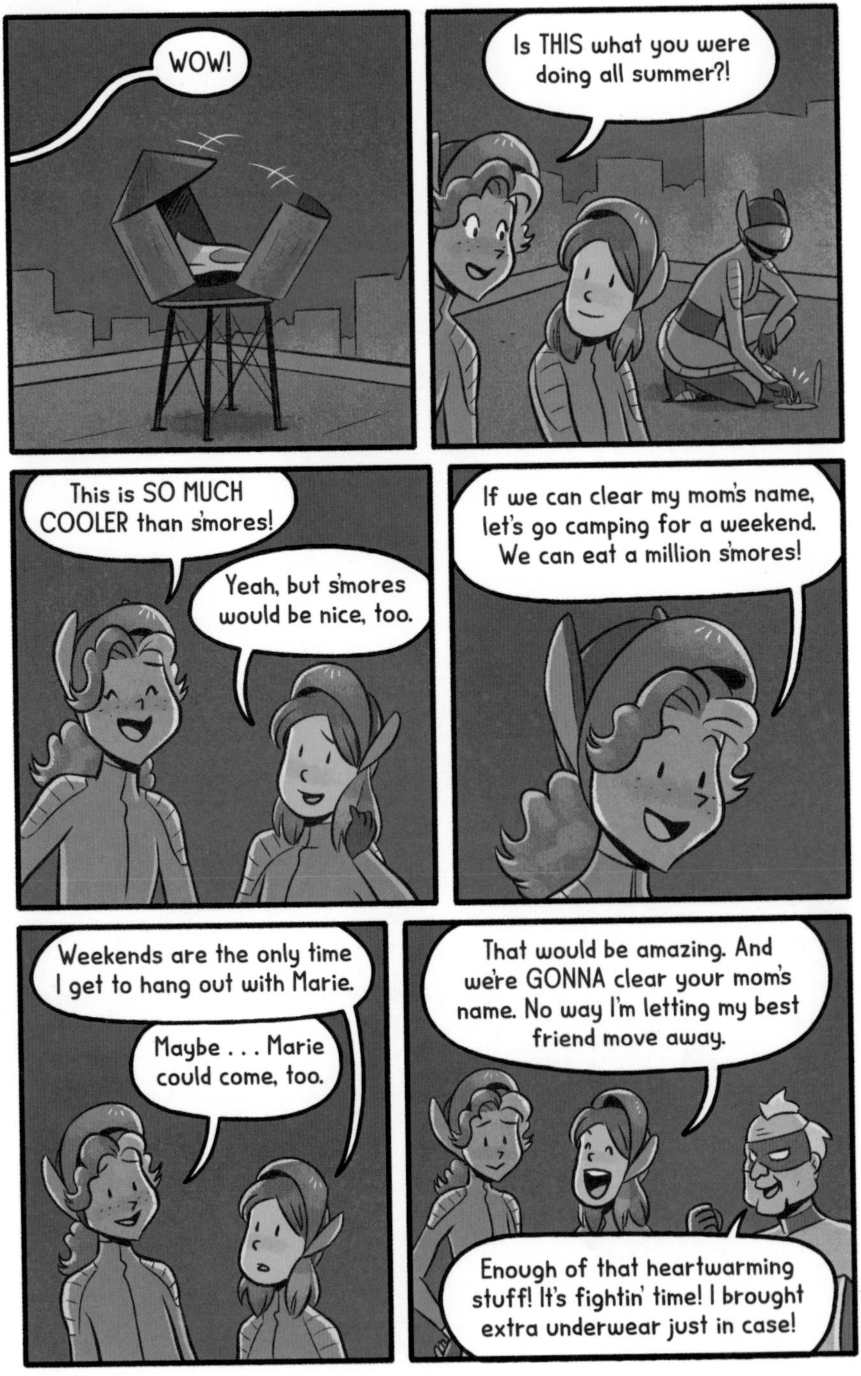
WOW!
Is THIS what you were doing all summer?!
This is SO MUCH COOLER than s'mores!
Yeah, but s'mores would be nice, too.
If we can clear my mom's name, let's go camping for a weekend. We can eat a million s'mores!
Weekends are the only time I get to hang out with Marie.
Maybe . . . Marie could come, too.
That would be amazing. And we're GONNA clear your mom's name. No way I'm letting my best friend move away.
Enough of that heartwarming stuff! It's fightin' time! I brought extra underwear just in case!

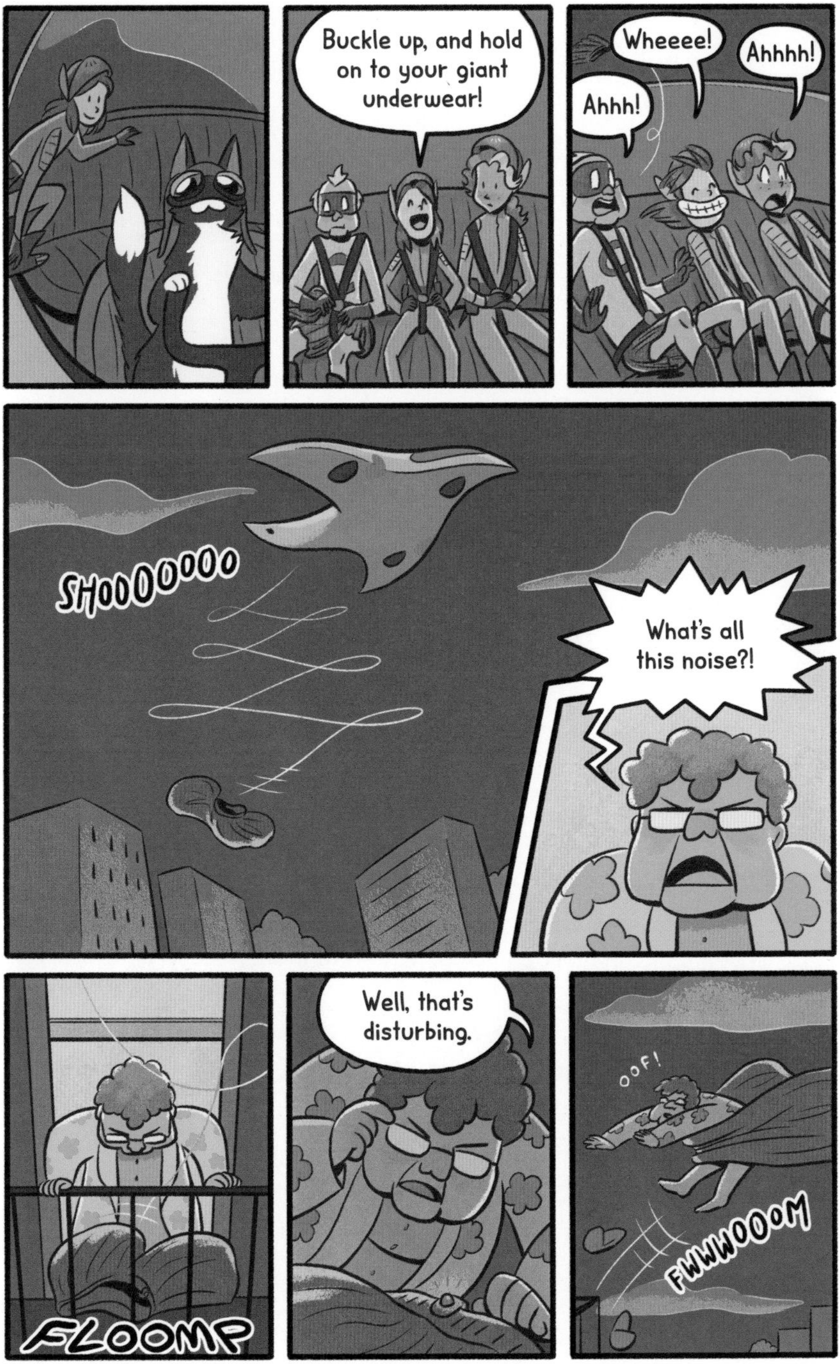
Buckle up, and hold on to your giant underwear!
Wheeee!
Ahhhh!
Ahhh!
SHOOOOOOO
What's all this noise?!
FLOOMP
Well, that's disturbing.
OOF!
FWWWOOOM

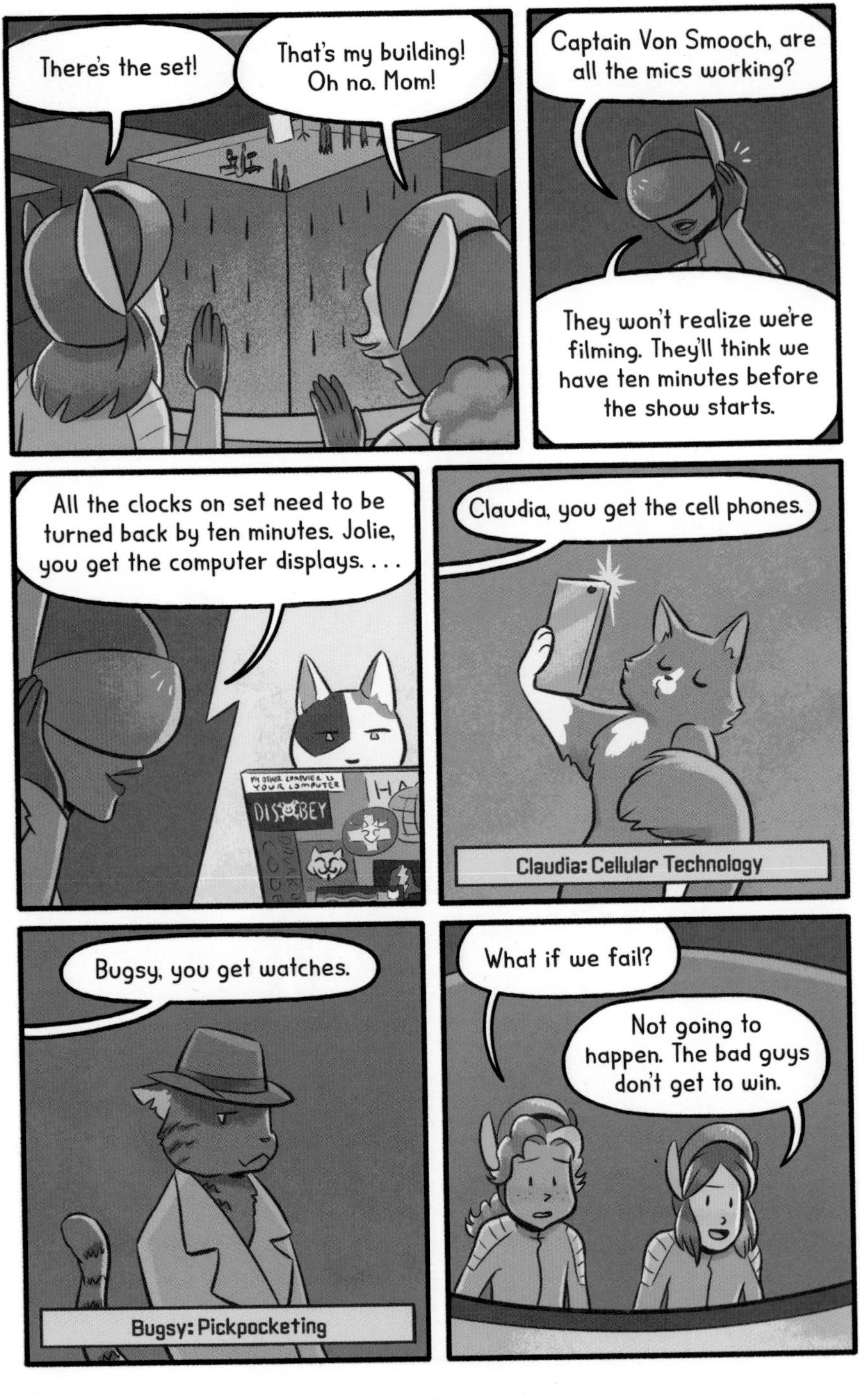
There's the set!
That's my building! Oh no. Mom!
Captain Von Smooch, are all the mics working?
They won't realize we're filming. They'll think we have ten minutes before the show starts.
All the clocks on set need to be turned back by ten minutes. Jolie, you get the computer displays. . . .
Claudia, you get the cell phones.
Claudia: Cellular Technology
Bugsy, you get watches.
Bugsy: Pickpocketing
What if we fail?
Not going to happen. The bad guys don't get to win.

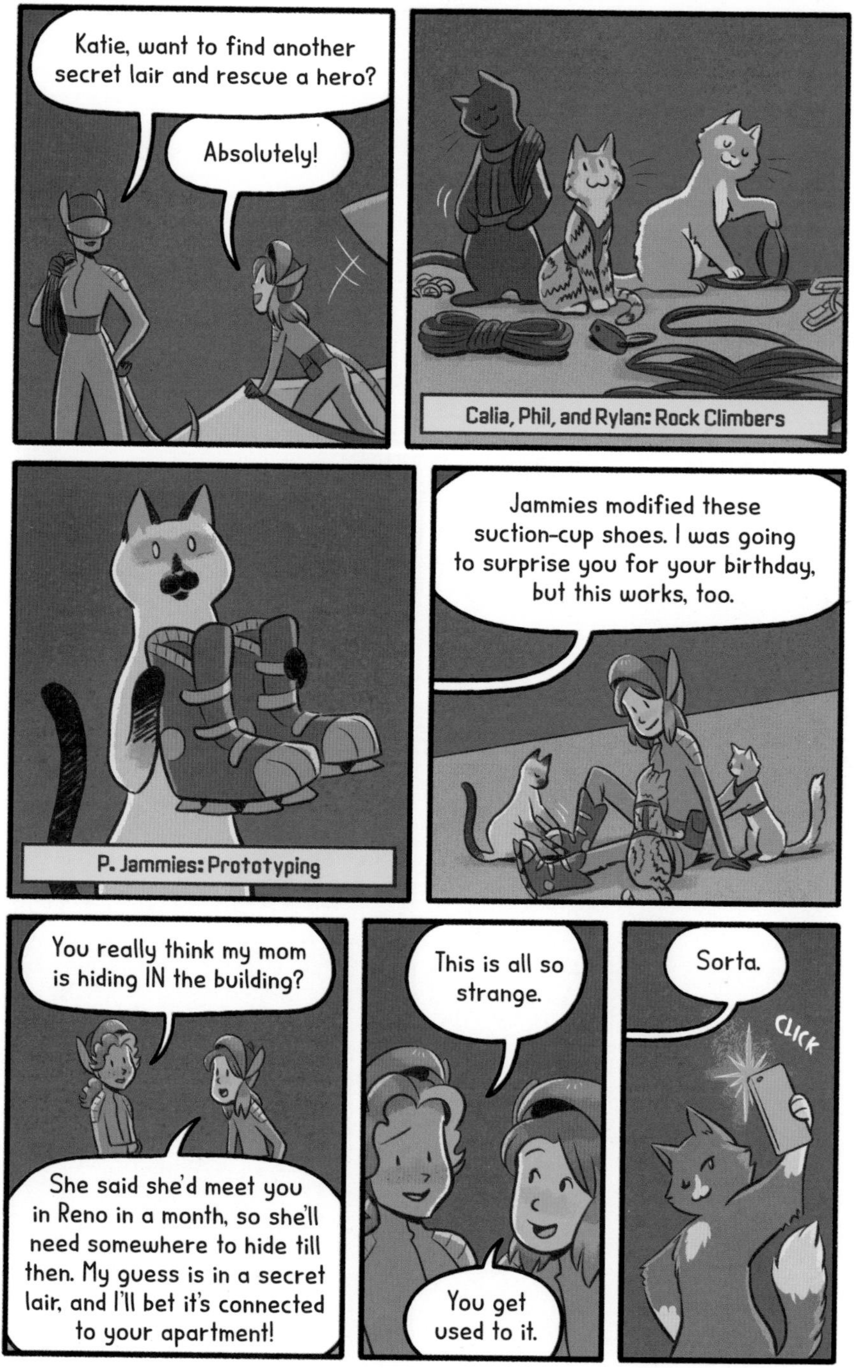
Katie, want to find another secret lair and rescue a hero?
Absolutely!
Calia, Phil, and Rylan: Rock Climbers
P. Jammies: Prototyping
Jammies modified these suction-cup shoes. I was going to surprise you for your birthday, but this works, too.
You really think my mom is hiding IN the building?
She said she'd meet you in Reno in a month, so she'll need somewhere to hide till then. My guess is in a secret lair, and I'll bet it's connected to your apartment!
This is all so strange.
You get used to it.
Sorta.
CLICK

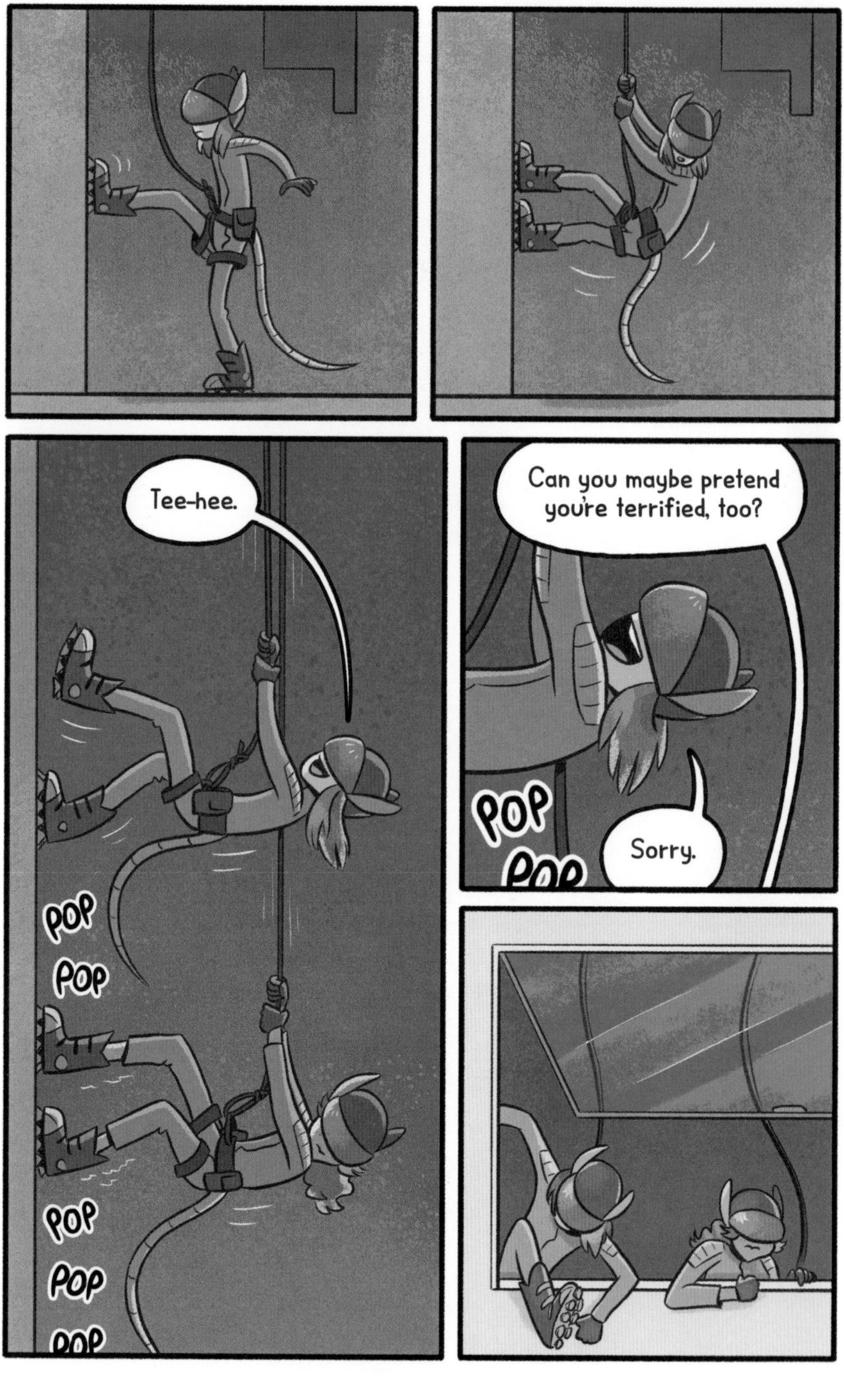
Tee-hee.
POP
POP
POP
POP
POP
Can you maybe pretend you're terrified, too?
POP
POP
Sorry.

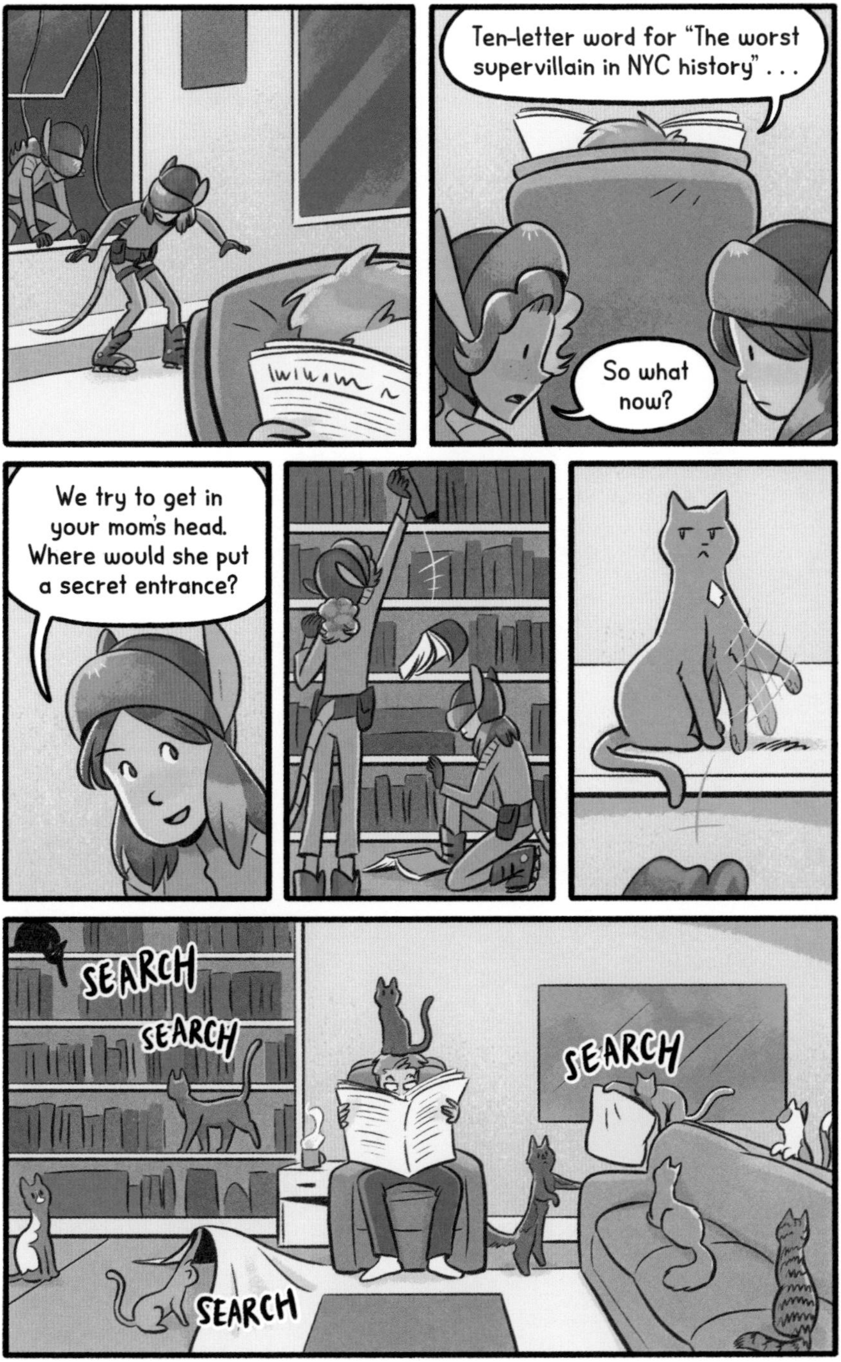

Ten-letter word for "The worst supervillain in NYC history" . . .
So what now?
We try to get in your mom's head. Where would she put a secret entrance?
SEARCH
SEARCH
SEARCH
SEARCH

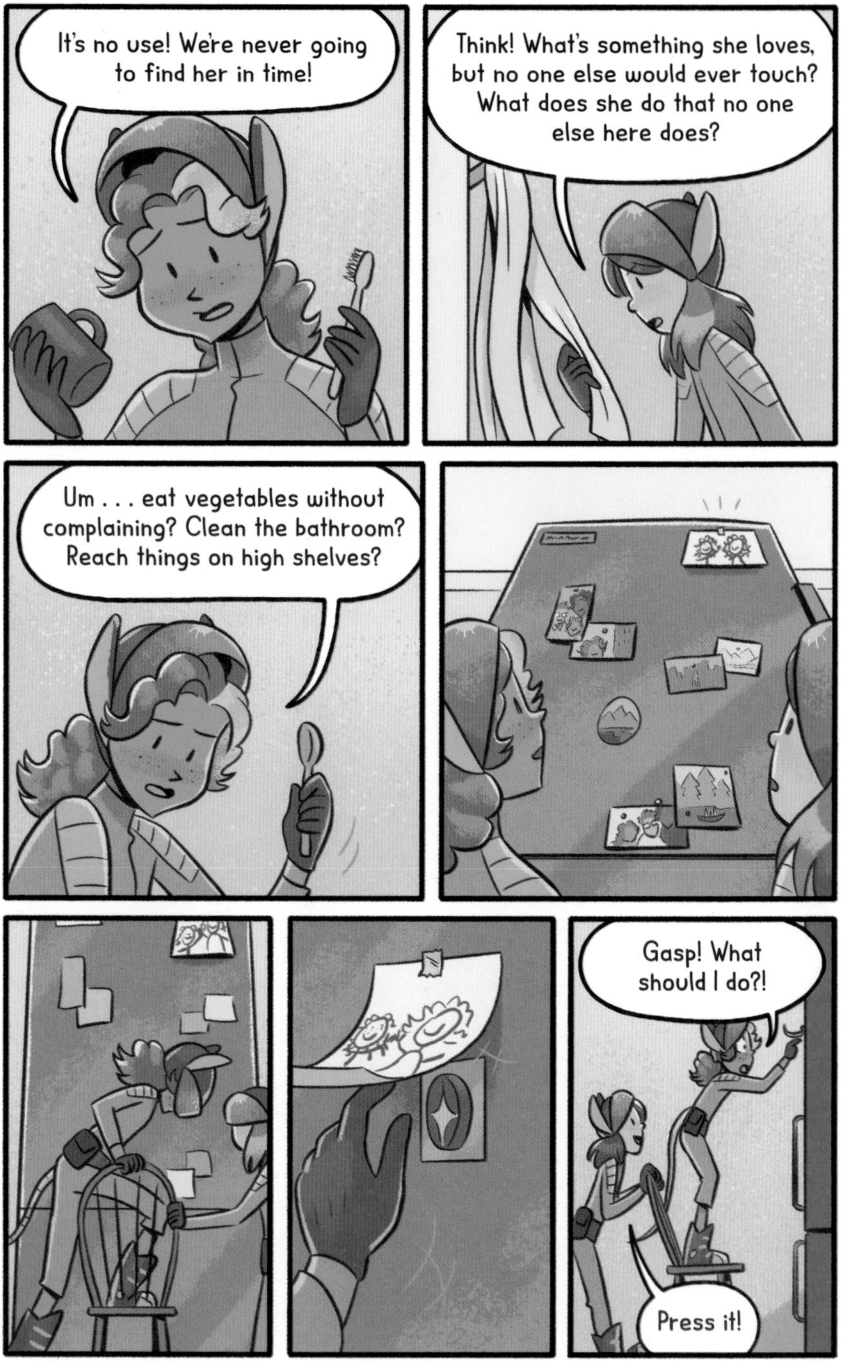
It's no use! We're never going to find her in time!
Think! What's something she loves, but no one else would ever touch? What does she do that no one else here does?
Um . . . eat vegetables without complaining? Clean the bathroom? Reach things on high shelves?
Gasp! What should I do?!
Press it!

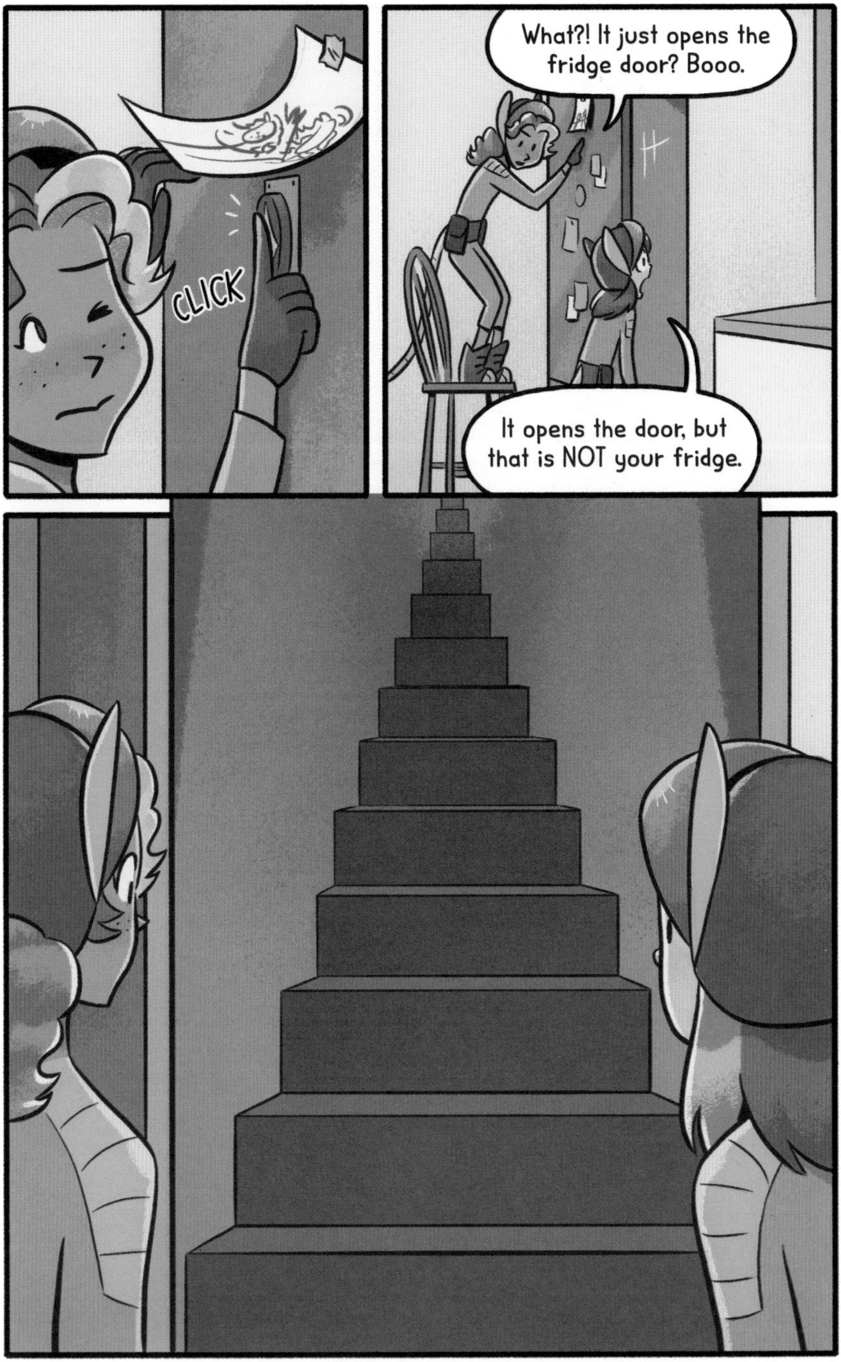
CLICK
What?! It just opens the fridge door? Booo.
It opens the door, but that is NOT your fridge.

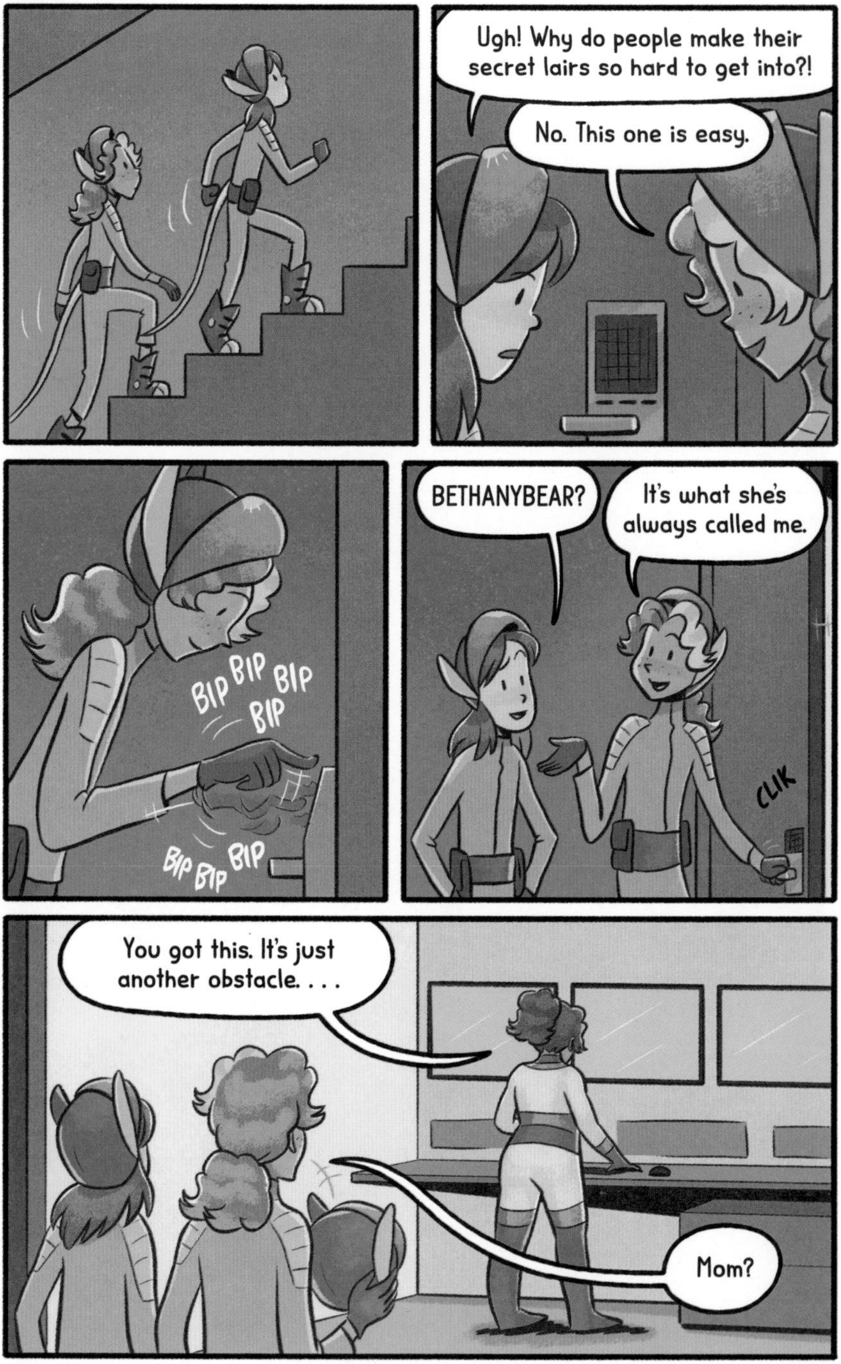
Ugh! Why do people make their secret lairs so hard to get into?!
No. This one is easy.
BIP BIP BIP BIP
BIP BIP BIP
BETHANYBEAR?
It's what she's always called me.
CLIK
You got this. It's just another obstacle. . . .
Mom?

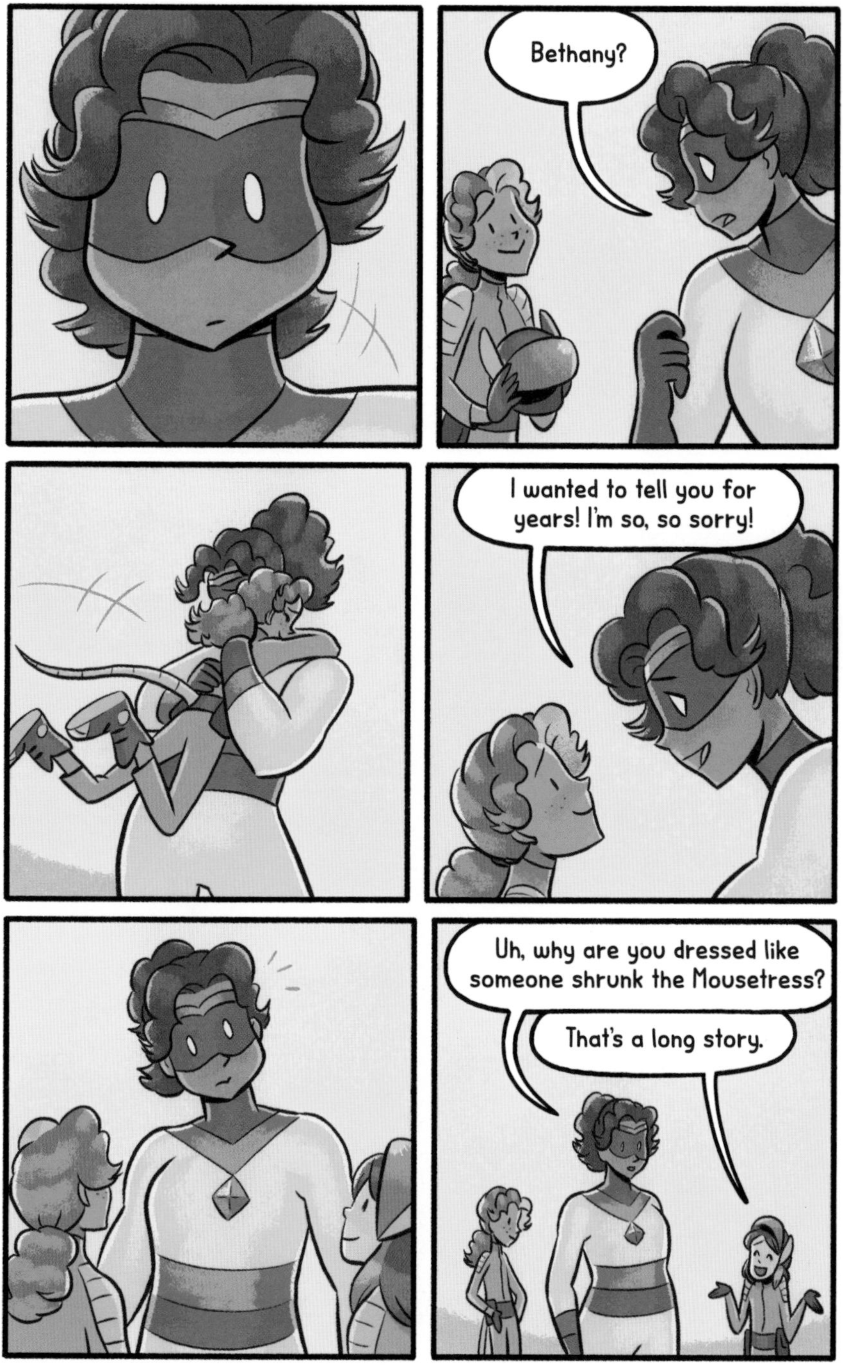
Bethany?
I wanted to tell you for years! I'm so, so sorry!
Uh, why are you dressed like someone shrunk the Mousetress?
That's a long story.

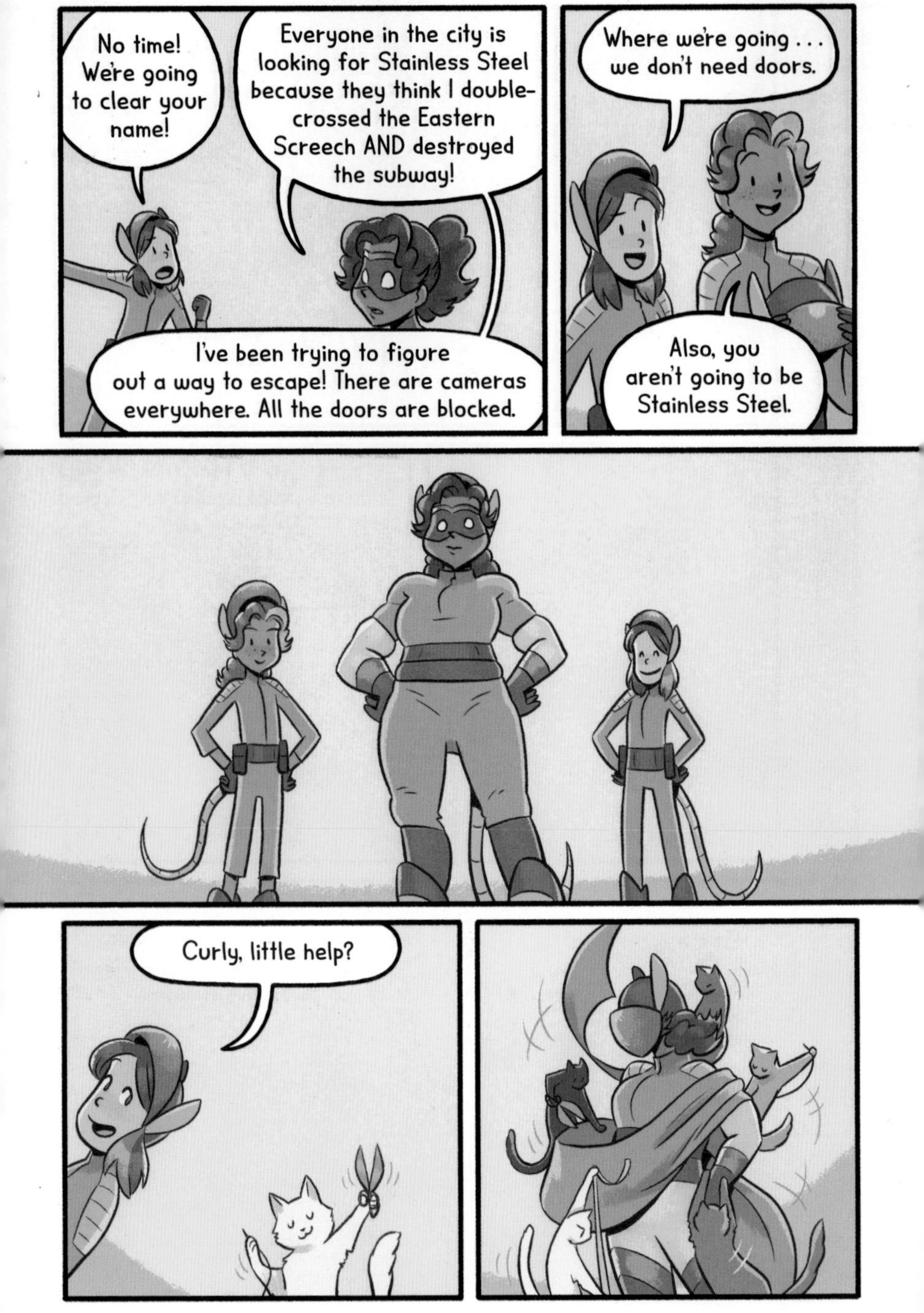
No time! We're going to clear your name!
Everyone in the city is looking for Stainless Steel because they think I double-crossed the Eastern Screech AND destroyed the subway!
I've been trying to figure out a way to escape! There are cameras everywhere. All the doors are blocked.
Where we're going . . . we don't need doors.
Also, you aren't going to be Stainless Steel.
Curly, little help?

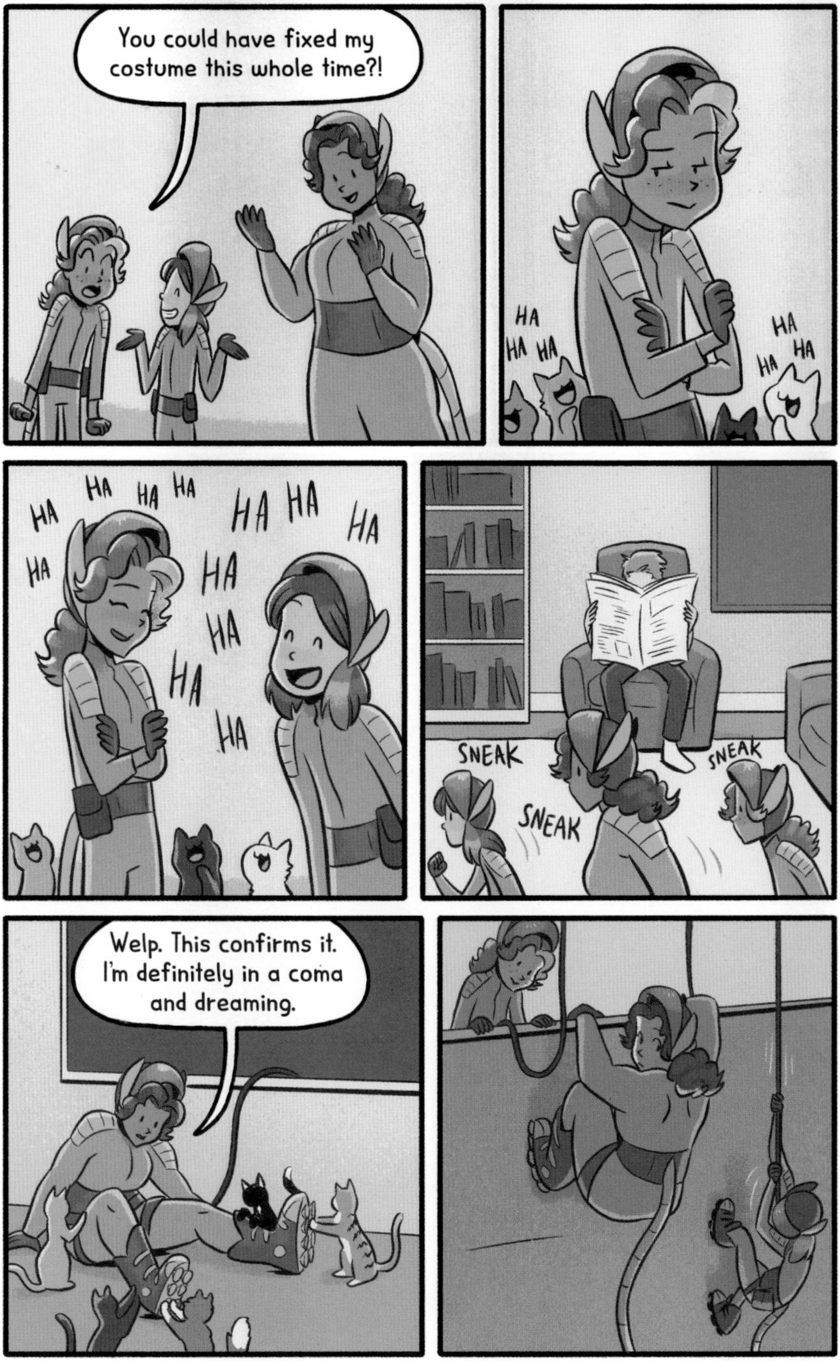
You could have fixed my costume this whole time?!
HA
HA HA
HA
HA HA
HA
HA HA HA
HA HA
HA
HA
HA
HA
HA
HA
HA
HA
SNEAK
SNEAK
SNEAK
Welp. This confirms it. I'm definitely in a coma and dreaming.

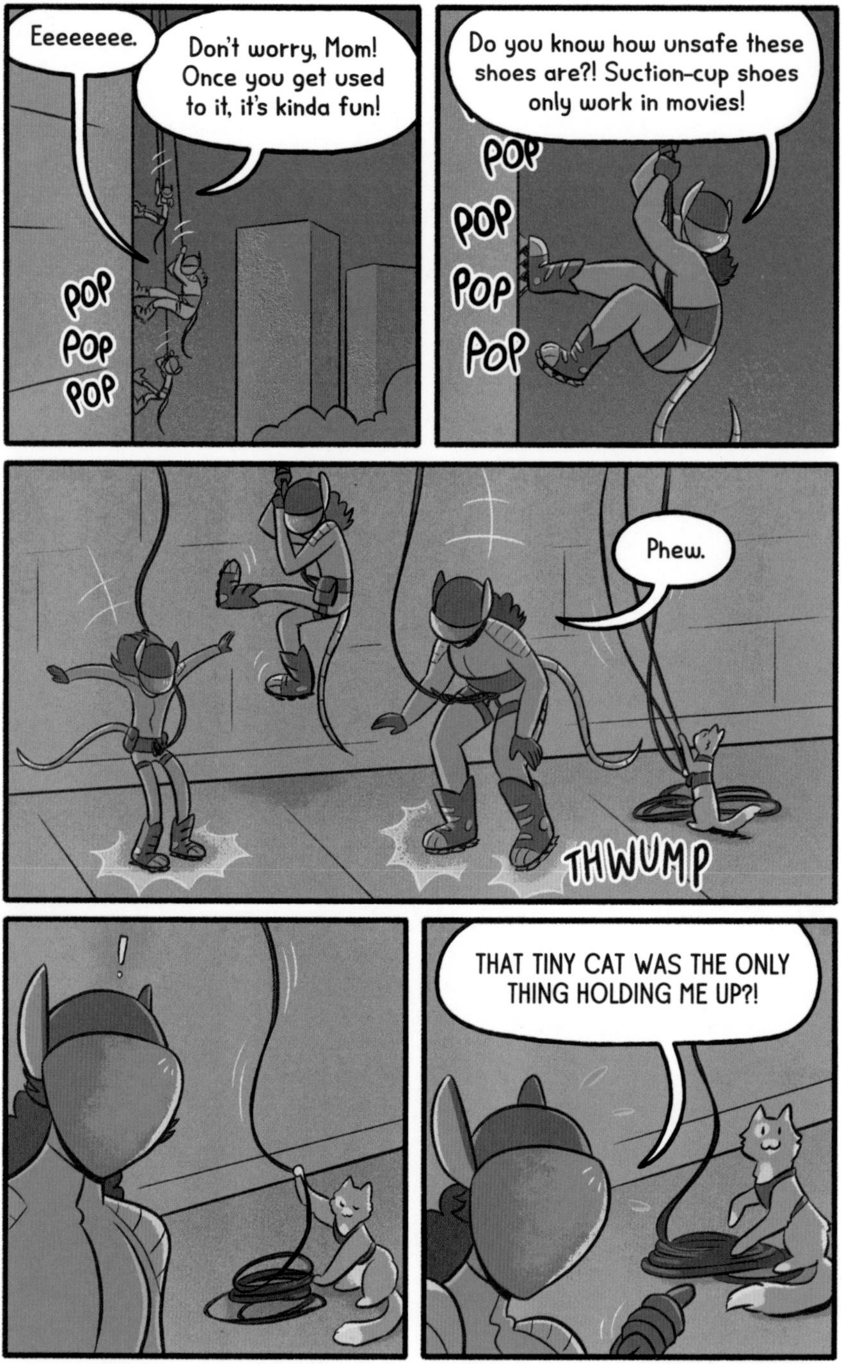
Eeeeeeee.
Don't worry, Mom! Once you get used to it, it's kinda fun!
POP
POP
POP
Do you know how unsafe these shoes are?! Suction-cup shoes only work in movies!
POP
POP
POP
POP
Phew.
THWUMP
!
THAT TINY CAT WAS THE ONLY THING HOLDING ME UP?!

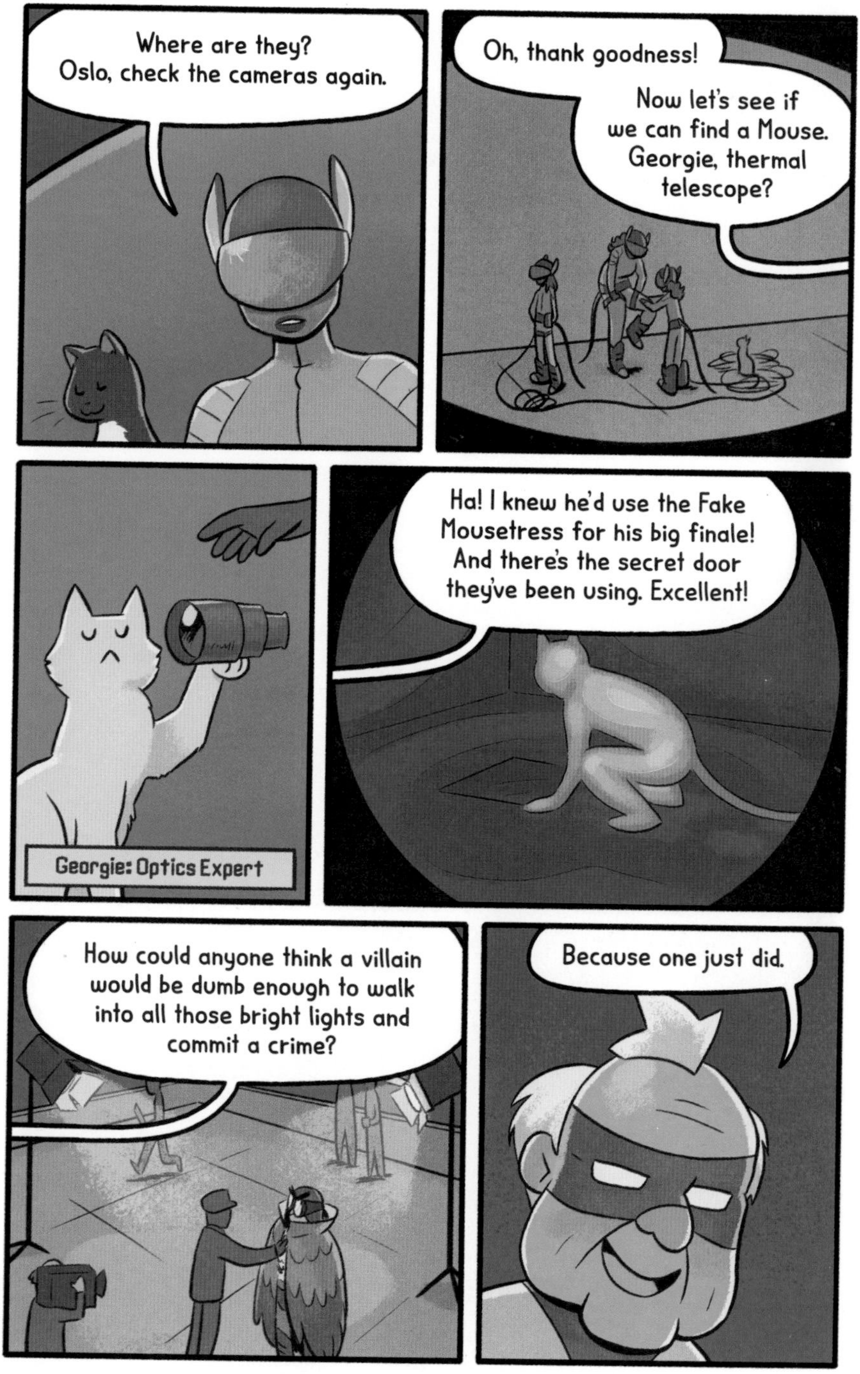
Where are they? Oslo, check the cameras again.
Oh, thank goodness!
Now let's see if we can find a Mouse. Georgie, thermal telescope?
Georgie: Optics Expert
Ha! I knew he'd use the Fake Mousetress for his big finale! And there's the secret door they've been using. Excellent!
How could anyone think a villain would be dumb enough to walk into all those bright lights and commit a crime?
Because one just did.

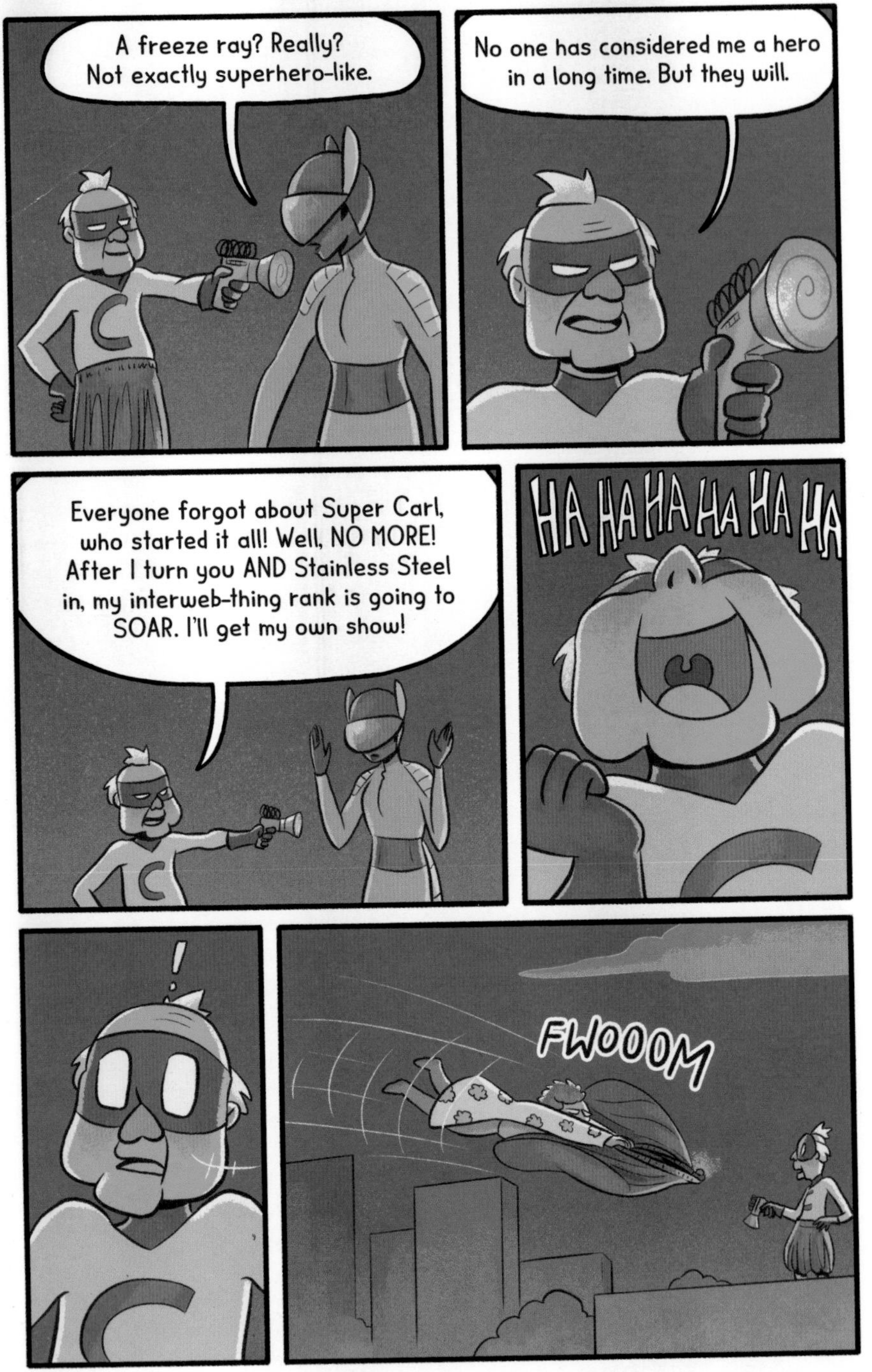
A freeze ray? Really? Not exactly superhero-like.
No one has considered me a hero in a long time. But they will.
Everyone forgot about Super Carl, who started it all! Well, NO MORE! After I turn you AND Stainless Steel in, my interweb-thing rank is going to SOAR. I'll get my own show!
HA HA HA HA HA HA
!
FWOOOM

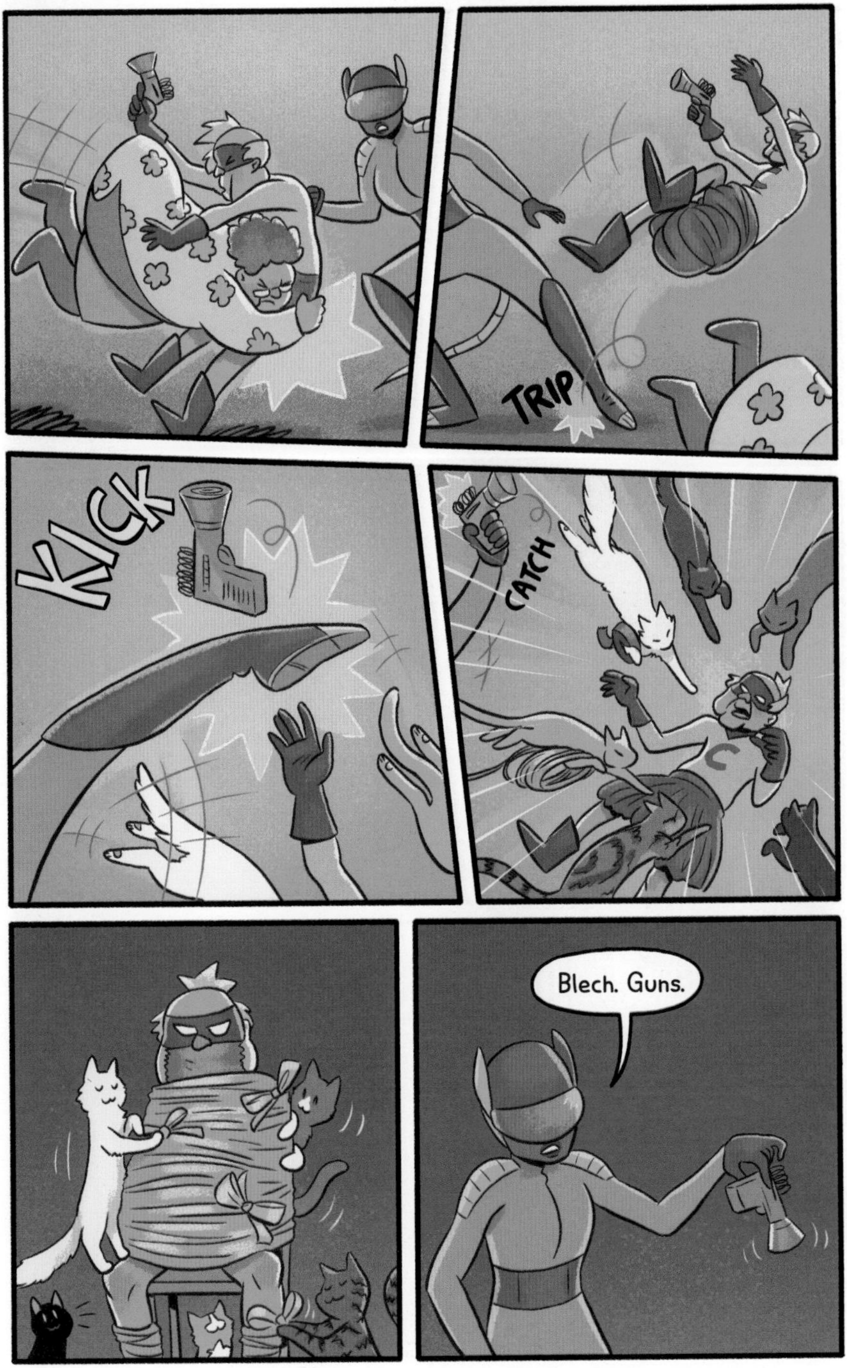
TRIP
KICK
CATCH
Blech. Guns.

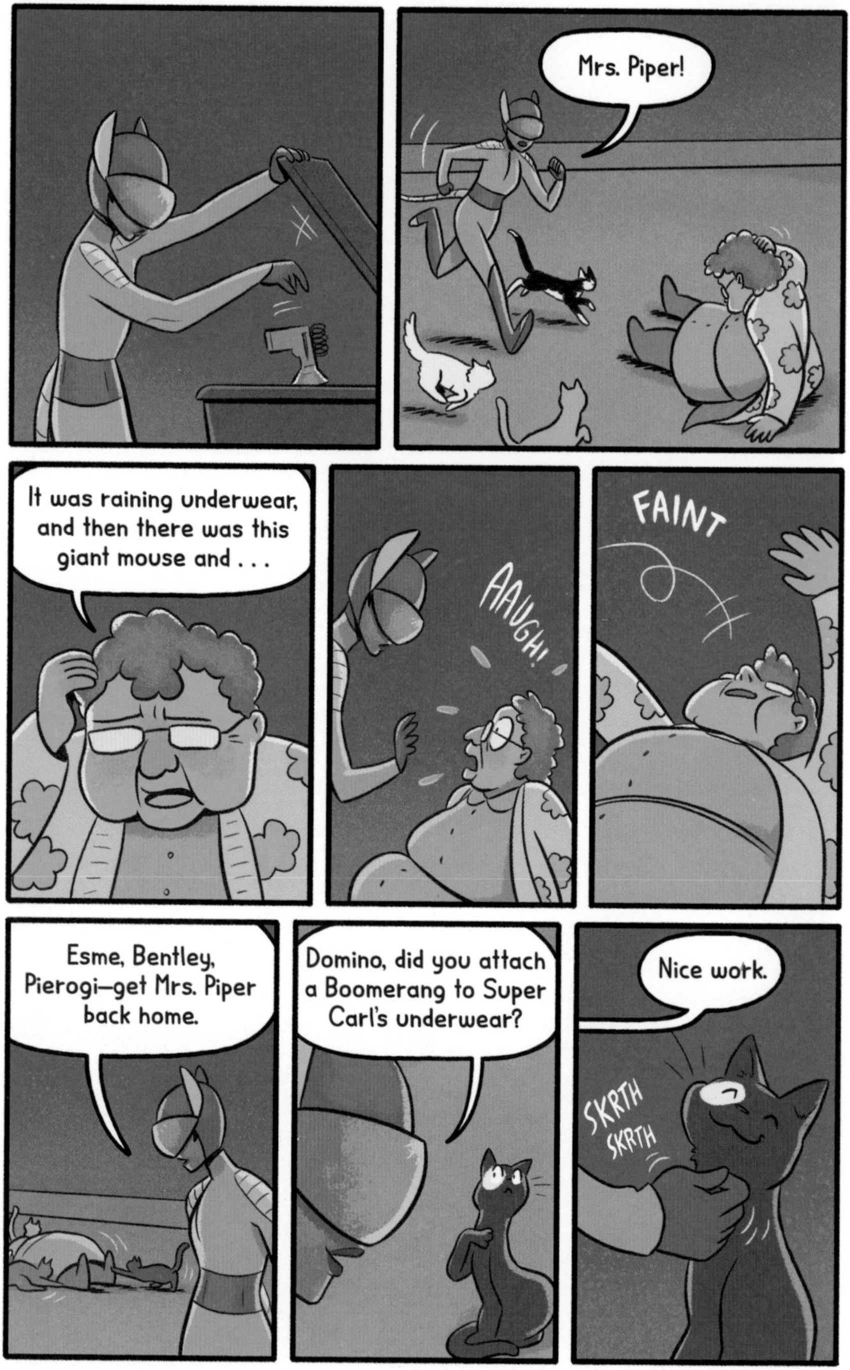
Mrs. Piper!
It was raining underwear, and then there was this giant mouse and . . .
AAUGH!
FAINT
Esme, Bentley, Pierogi—get Mrs. Piper back home.
Domino, did you attach a Boomerang to Super Carl's underwear?
Nice work.
SKRTH
SKRTH

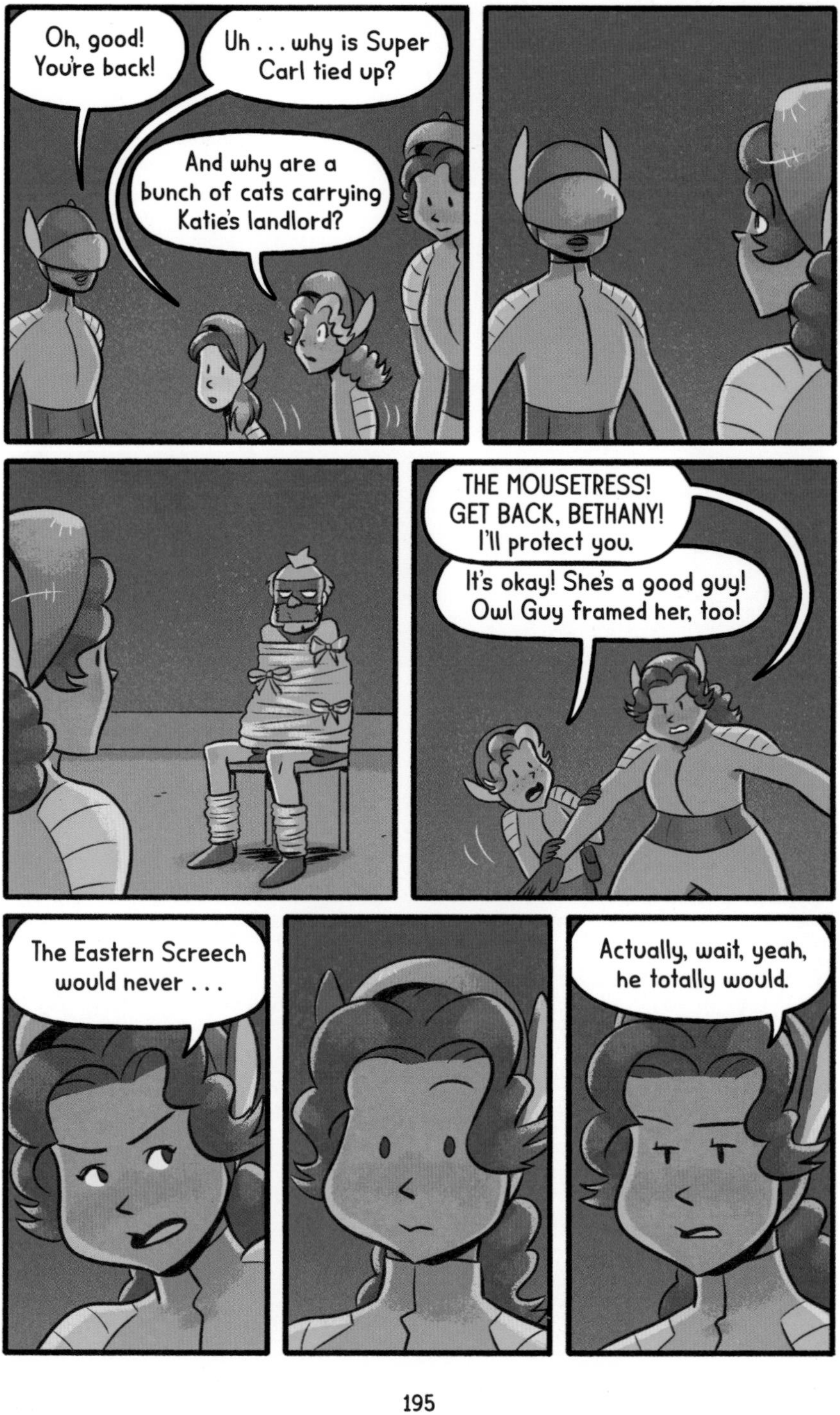
Oh, good! You're back!
Uh . . . why is Super Carl tied up?
And why are a bunch of cats carrying Katie's landlord?
THE MOUSETRESS! GET BACK, BETHANY! I'll protect you.
It's okay! She's a good guy! Owl Guy framed her, too!
The Eastern Screech would never . . .
Actually, wait, yeah, he totally would.

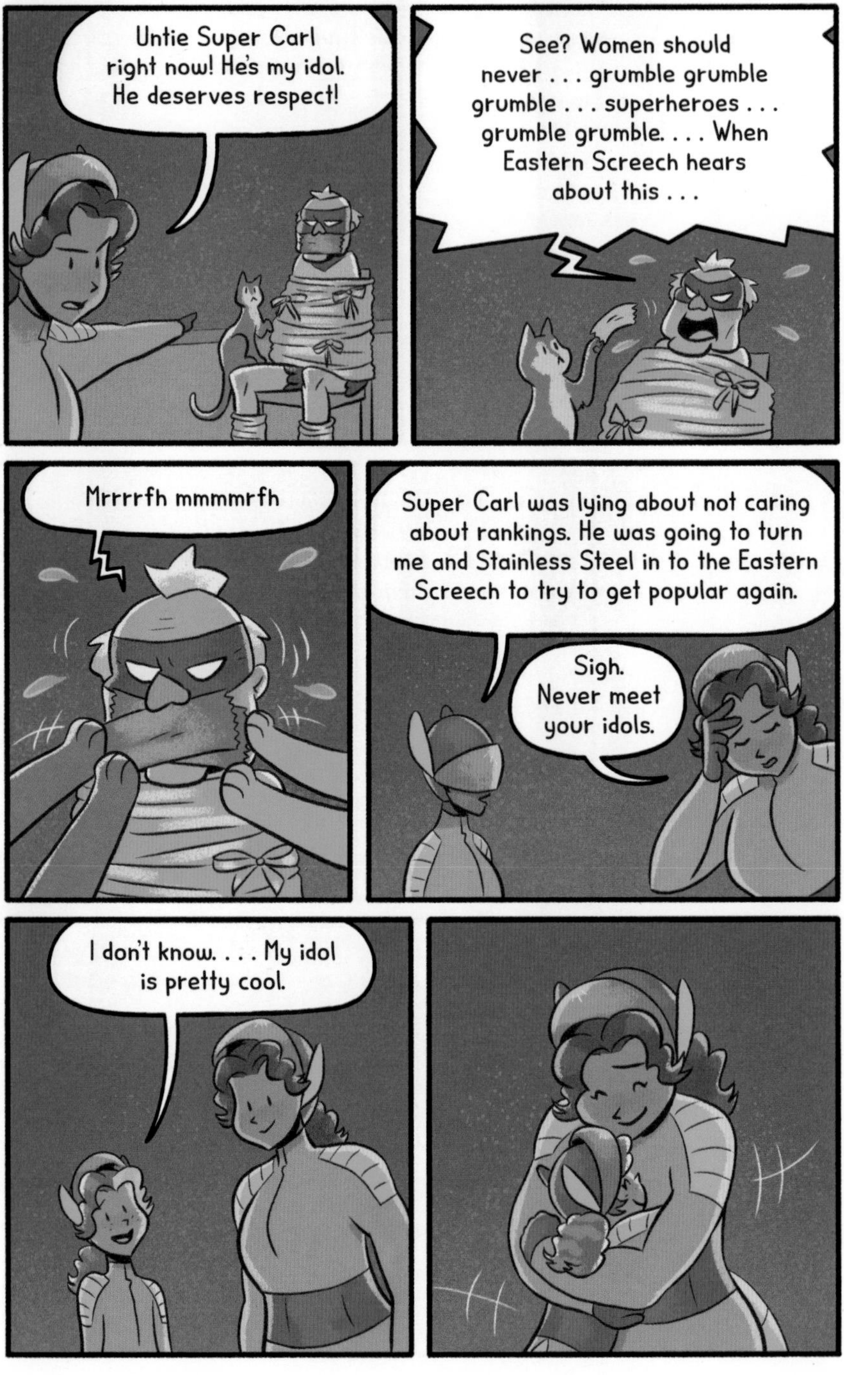
Untie Super Carl right now! He's my idol. He deserves respect!
See? Women should never . . . grumble grumble grumble . . . superheroes . . . grumble grumble. . . . When Eastern Screech hears about this . . .
Mrrrrfh mmmmrfh
Super Carl was lying about not caring about rankings. He was going to turn me and Stainless Steel in to the Eastern Screech to try to get popular again.
Sigh. Never meet your idols.
I don't know. . . . My idol is pretty cool.

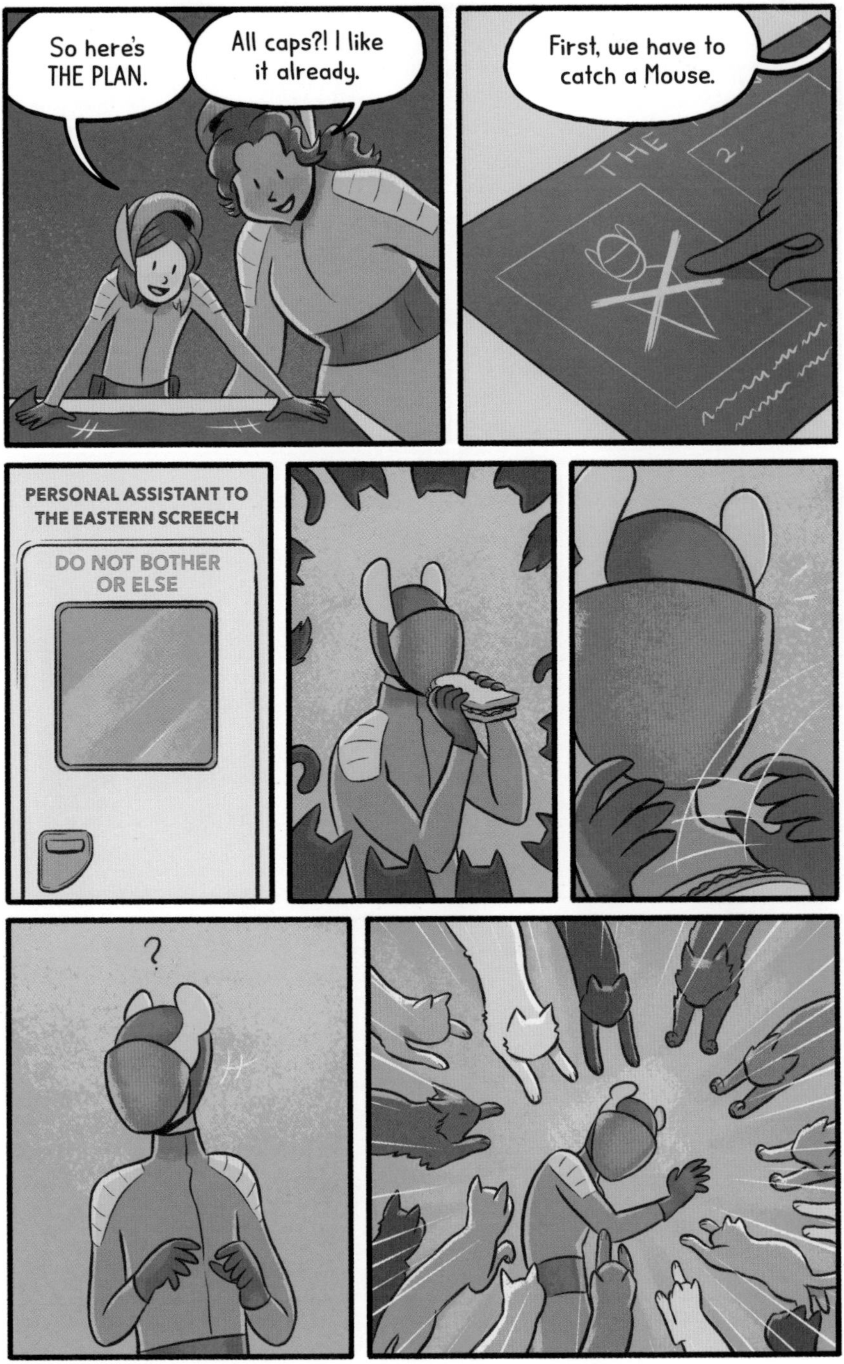

So here's THE PLAN.
All caps?! I like it already.
First, we have to catch a Mouse.
PERSONAL ASSISTANT TO THE EASTERN SCREECH
DO NOT BOTHER OR ELSE
?

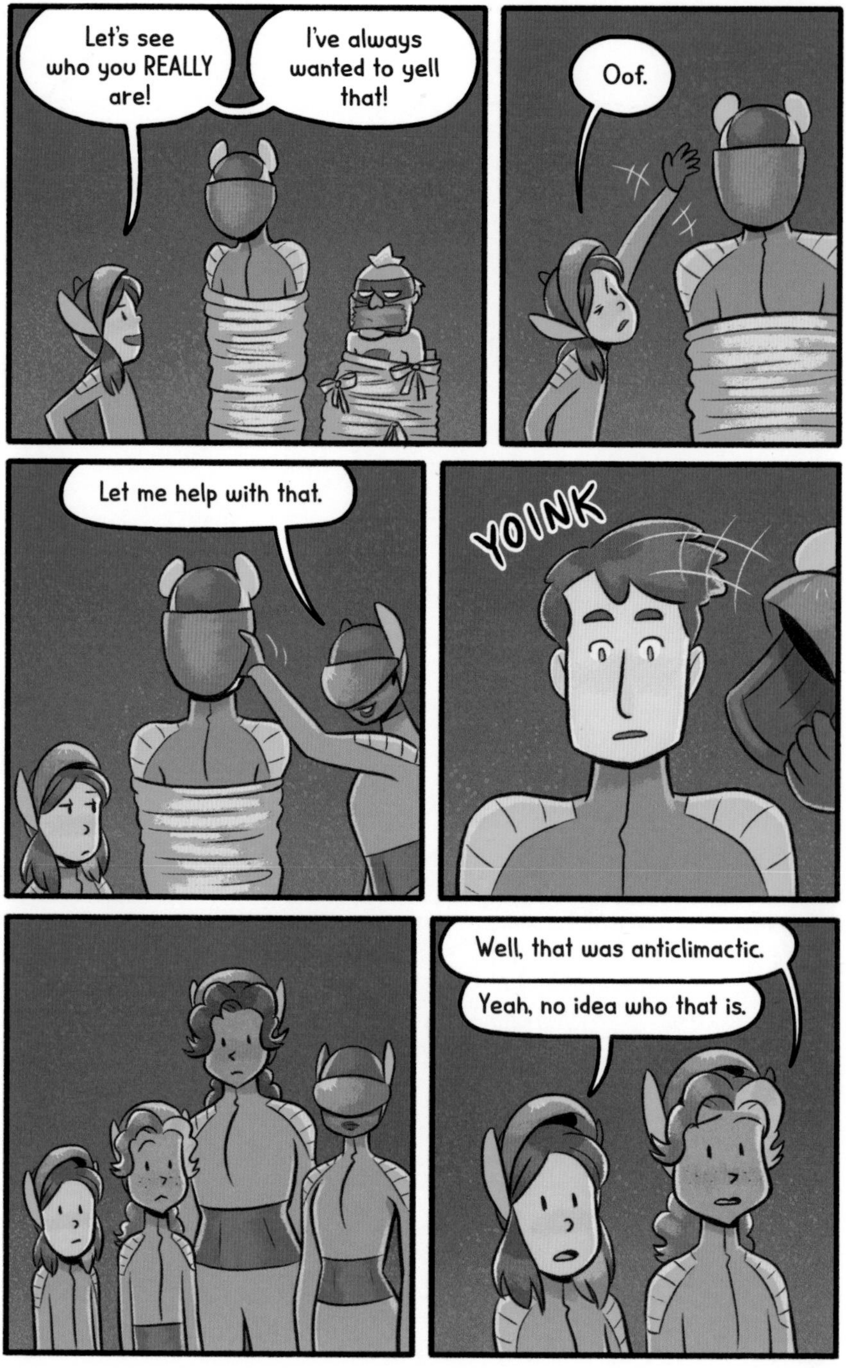
Let's see who you REALLY are!
I've always wanted to yell that!
Oof.
Let me help with that.
YOINK
Well, that was anticlimactic.
Yeah, no idea who that is.

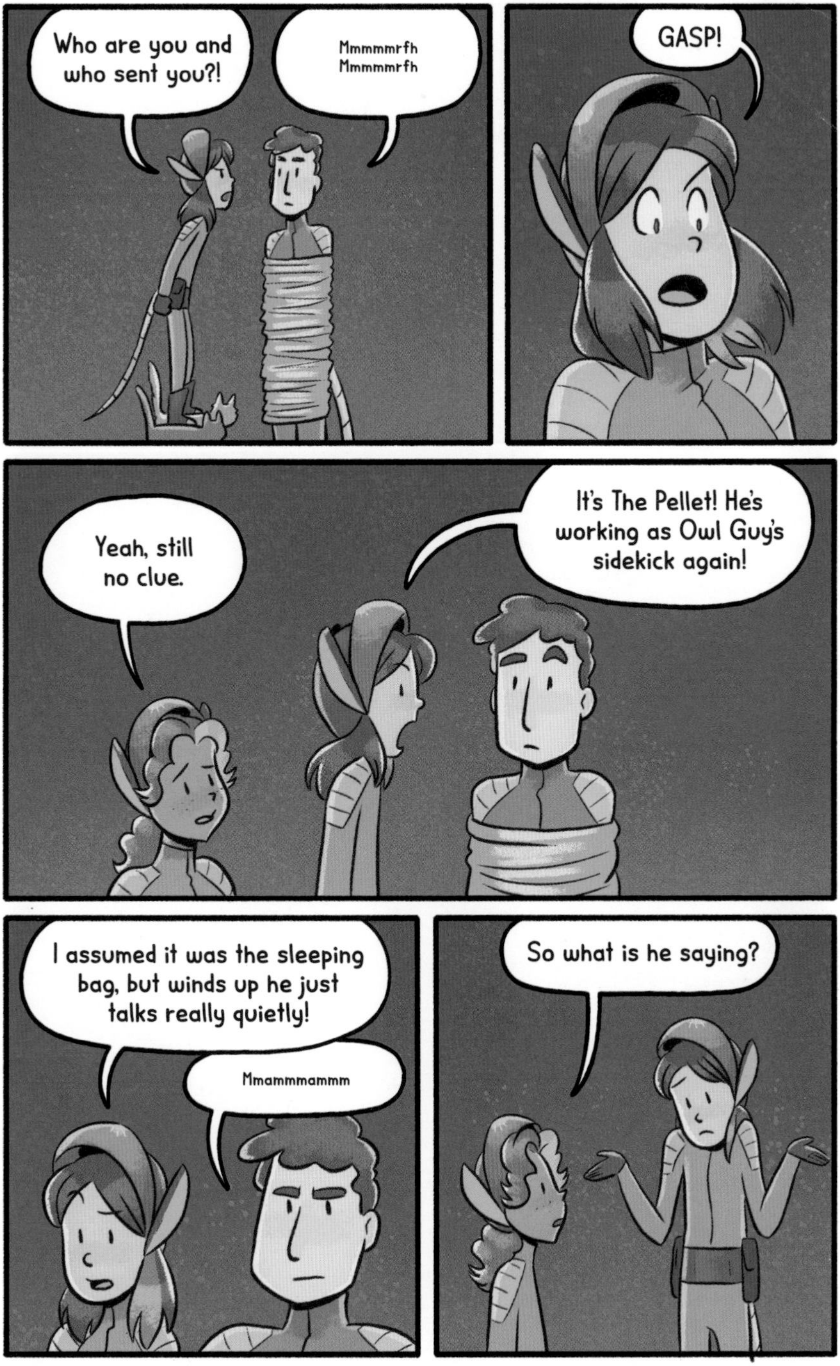
Who are you and who sent you?!
Mmmmmrfh Mmmmmrfh
GASP!
Yeah, still no clue.
It's The Pellet! He's working as Owl Guy's sidekick again!
I assumed it was the sleeping bag, but winds up he just talks really quietly!
Mmammmammm
So what is he saying?

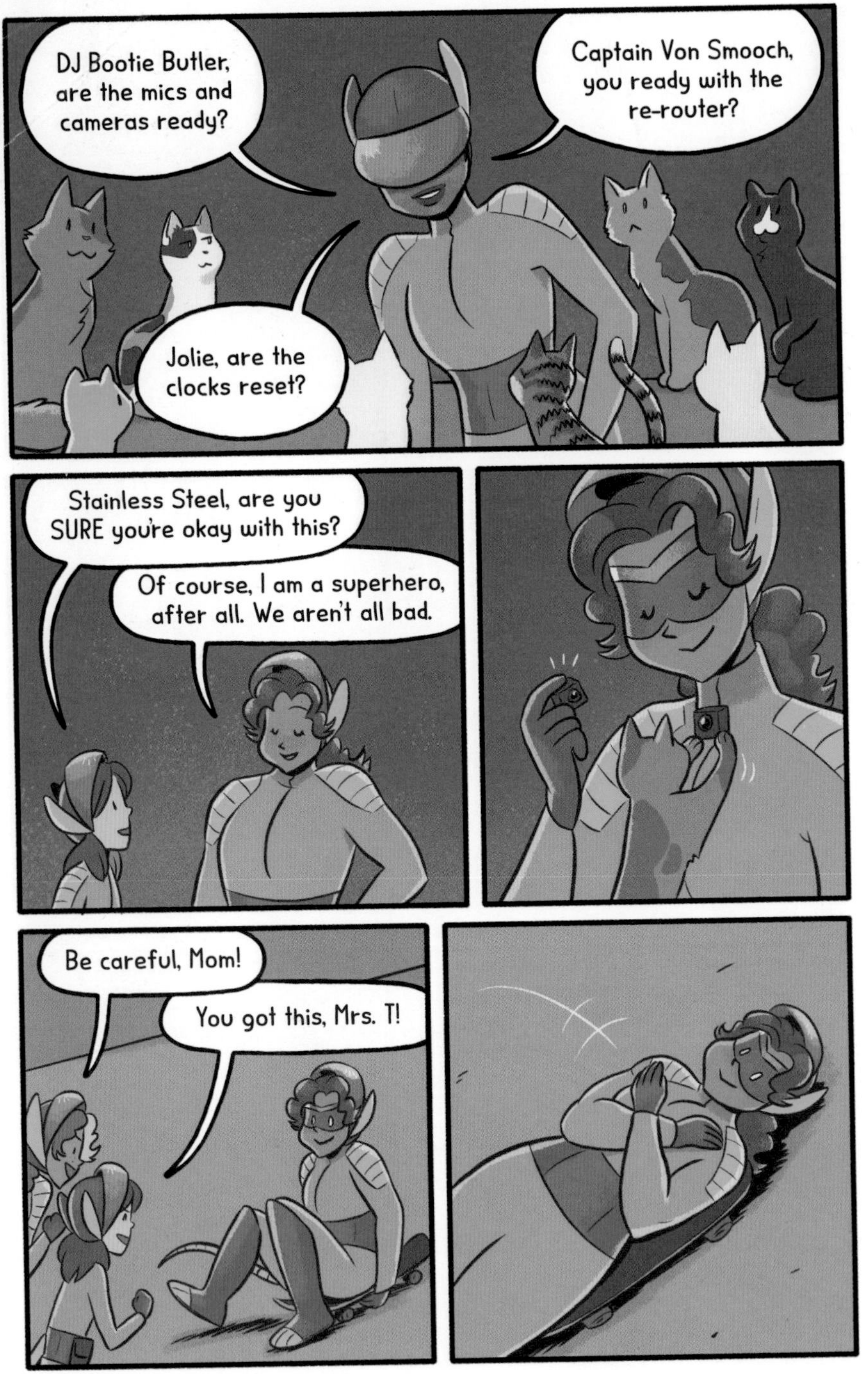
DJ Bootie Butler, are the mics and cameras ready?
Captain Von Smooch, you ready with the re-router?
Jolie, are the clocks reset?
Stainless Steel, are you SURE you're okay with this?
Of course, I am a superhero, after all. We aren't all bad.
Be careful, Mom!
You got this, Mrs. T!

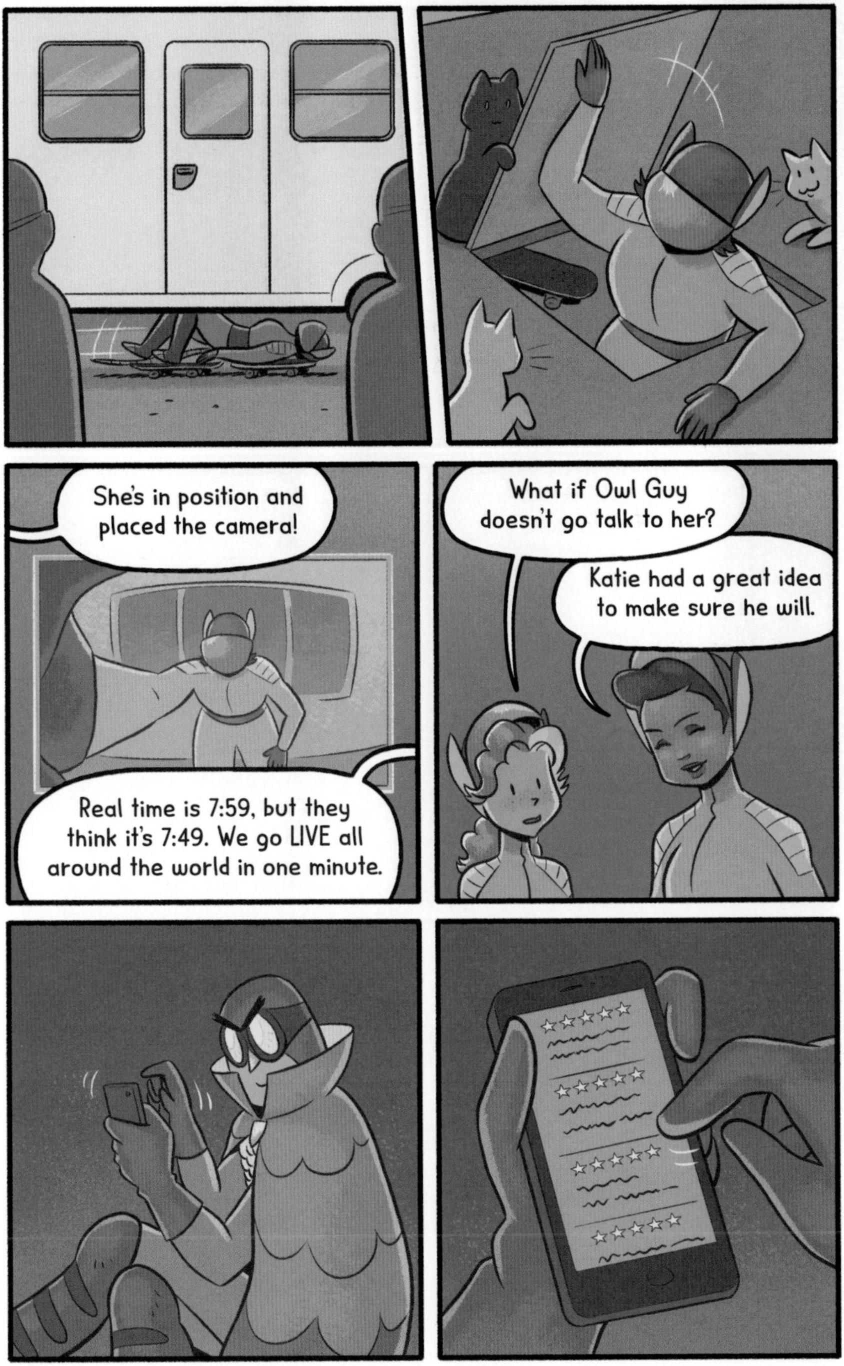
She's in position and placed the camera!
Real time is 7:59, but they think it's 7:49. We go LIVE all around the world in one minute.
What if Owl Guy doesn't go talk to her?
Katie had a great idea to make sure he will.

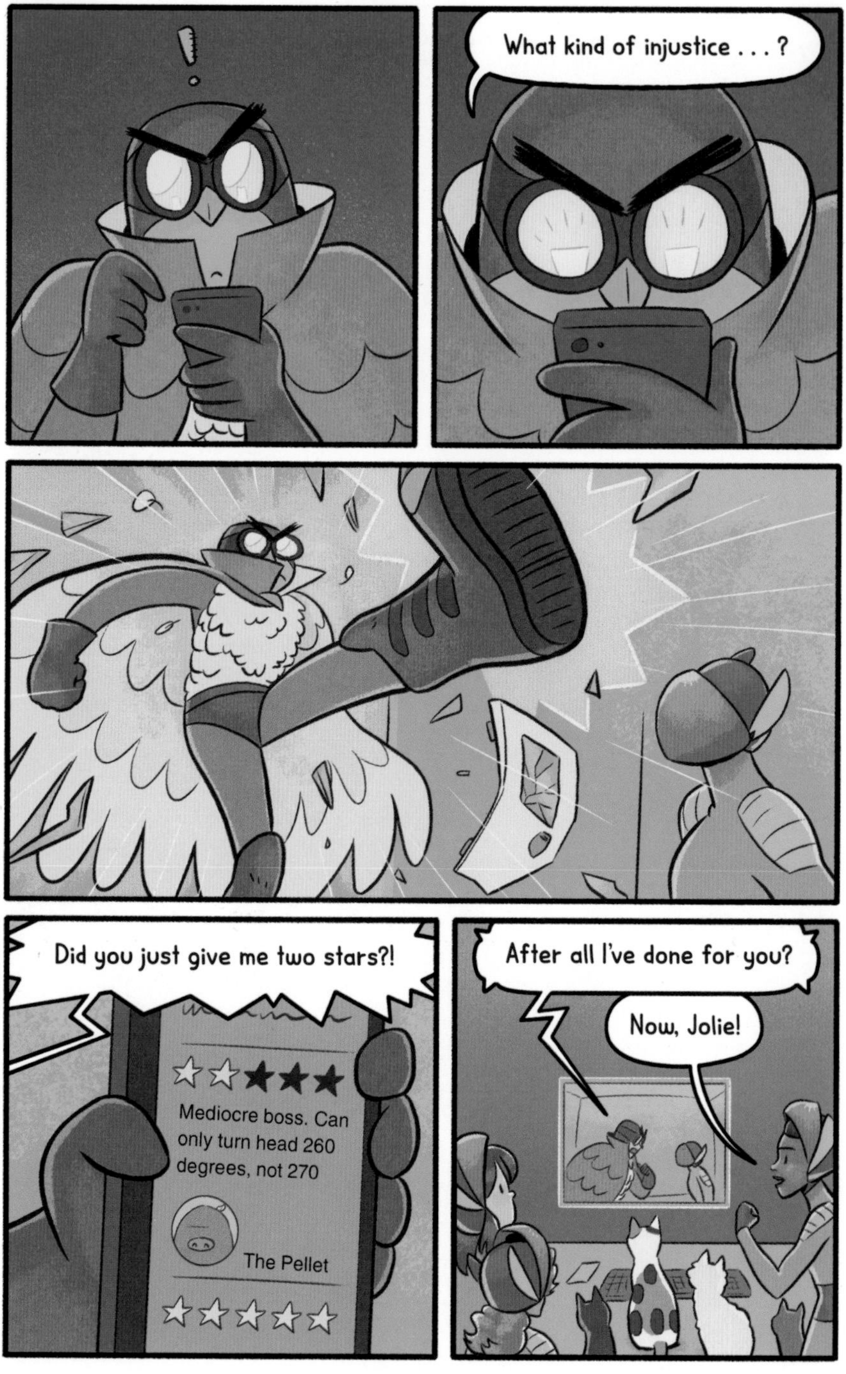
!
What kind of injustice . . . ?
Did you just give me two stars?!
Mediocre boss. Can only turn head 260 degrees, not 270
The Pellet
After all I've done for you?
Now, Jolie!

Oooh, it's starting!

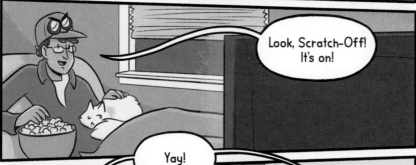
Look, Scratch-Off! It's on!

Yay!

These pizza rolls are too hot.

I'm lactose intolerant, but going to eat them anyway, because life is suffering.

Weird. The Mousetress looks taller.

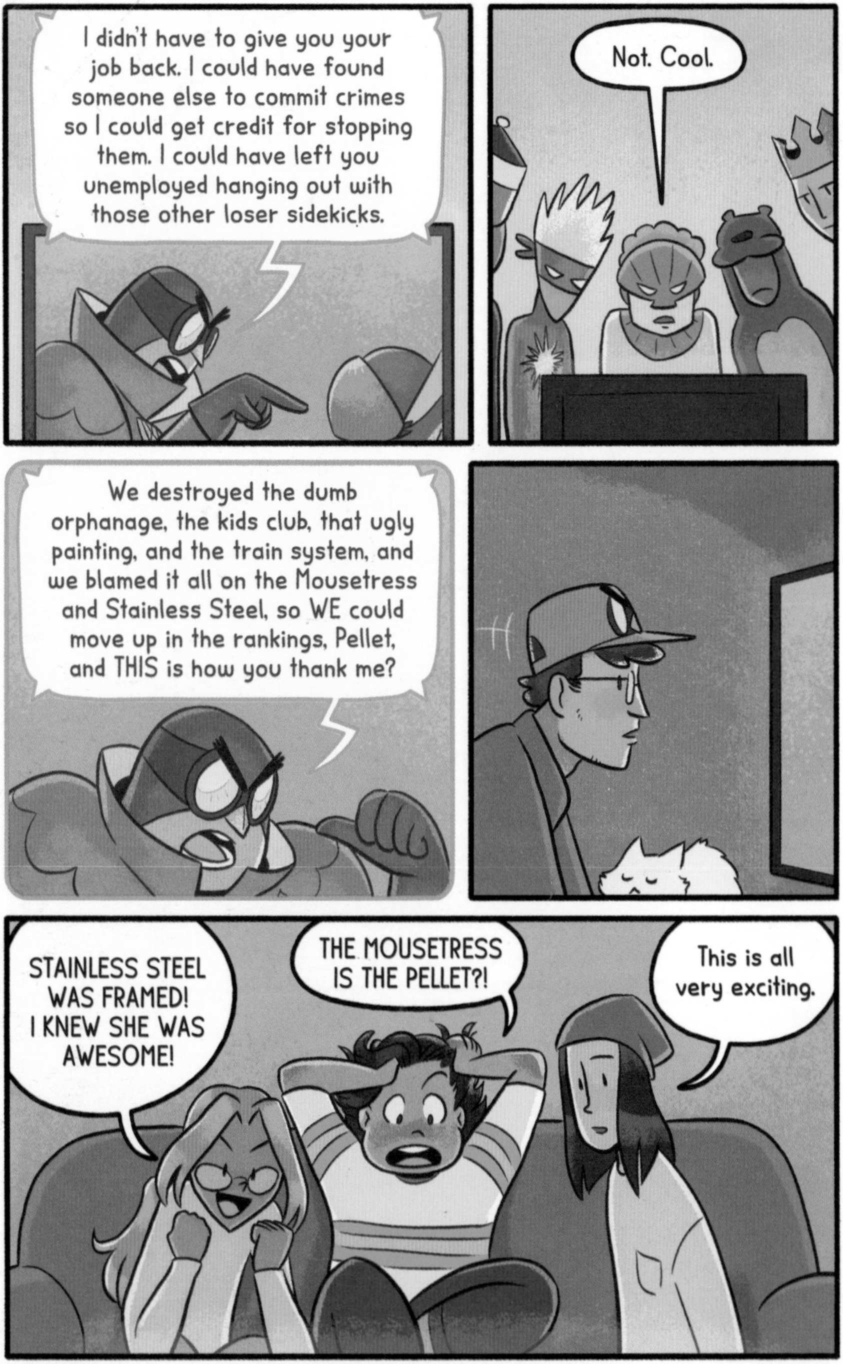
I didn't have to give you your job back. I could have found someone else to commit crimes so I could get credit for stopping them. I could have left you unemployed hanging out with those other loser sidekicks.
Not. Cool.
We destroyed the dumb orphanage, the kids club, that ugly painting, and the train system, and we blamed it all on the Mousetress and Stainless Steel, so WE could move up in the rankings, Pellet, and THIS is how you thank me?
STAINLESS STEEL WAS FRAMED! I KNEW SHE WAS AWESOME!
THE MOUSETRESS IS THE PELLET?!
This is all very exciting.

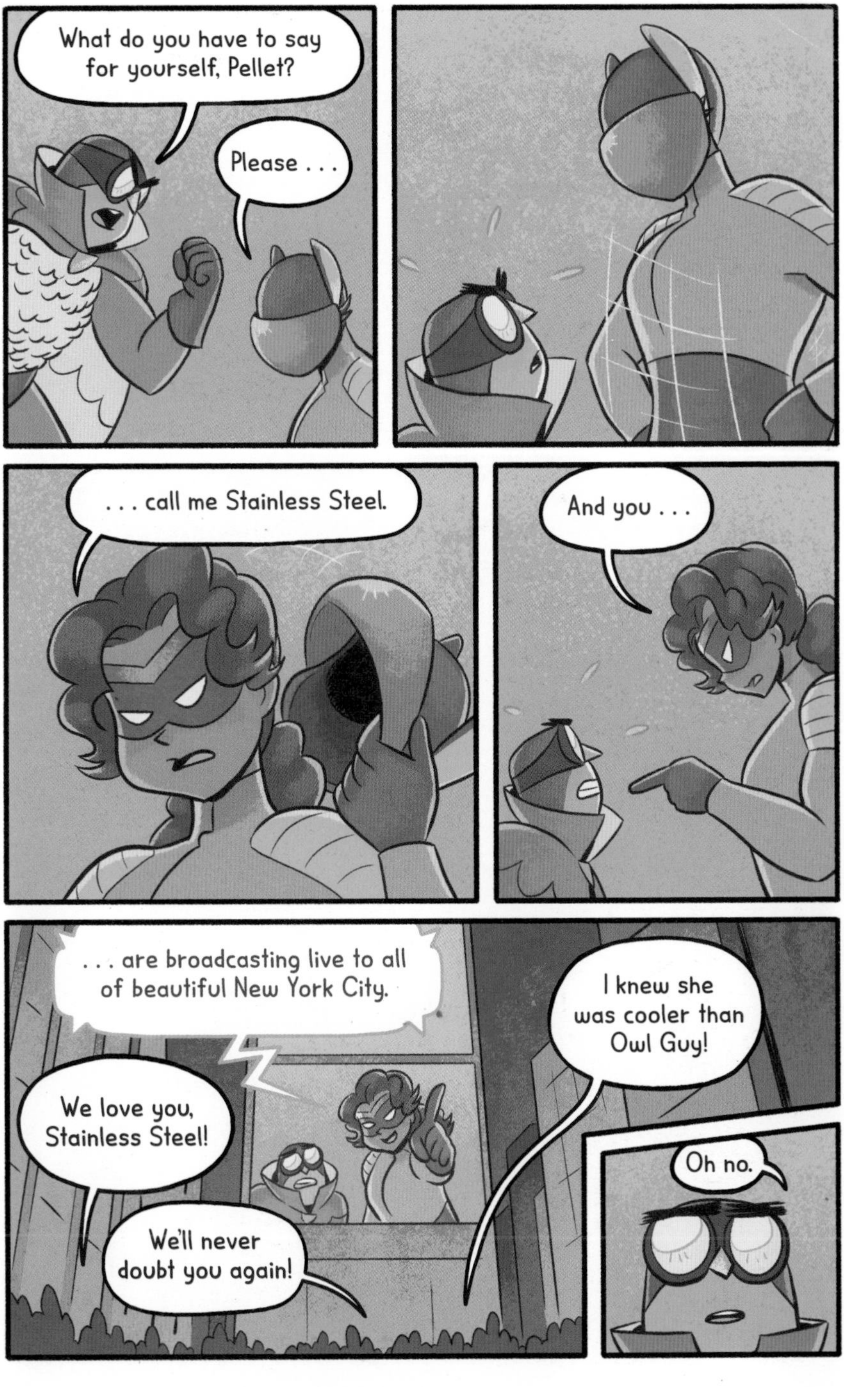
What do you have to say for yourself, Pellet?
Please . . .
. . . call me Stainless Steel.
And you . . .
. . . are broadcasting live to all of beautiful New York City.
We love you, Stainless Steel!
We'll never doubt you again!
I knew she was cooler than Owl Guy!
Oh no.

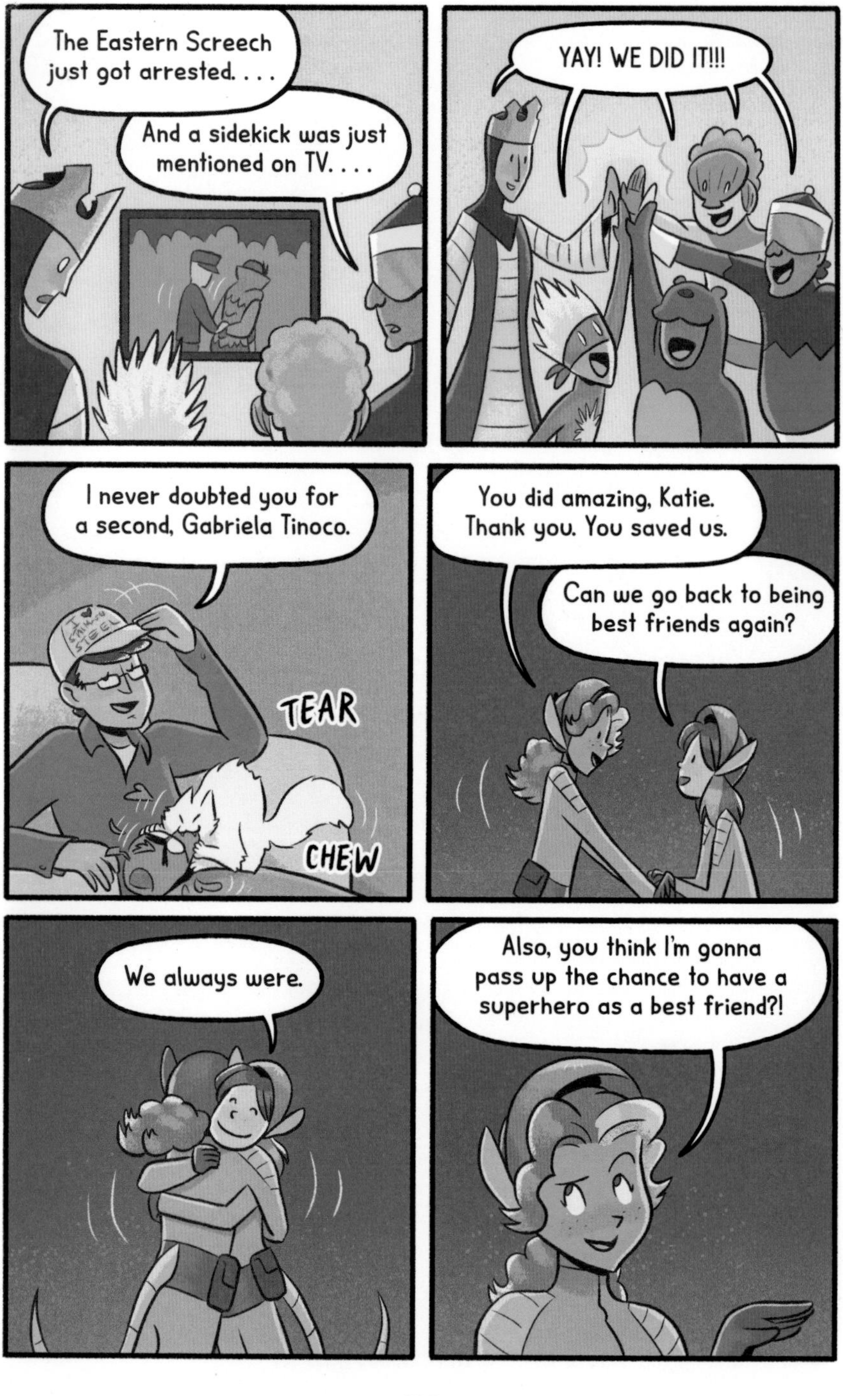
The Eastern Screech just got arrested. . . .
And a sidekick was just mentioned on TV. . . .
YAY! WE DID IT!!!
I never doubted you for a second, Gabriela Tinoco.
TEAR
CHEW
You did amazing, Katie. Thank you. You saved us.
Can we go back to being best friends again?
We always were.
Also, you think I'm gonna pass up the chance to have a superhero as a best friend?!

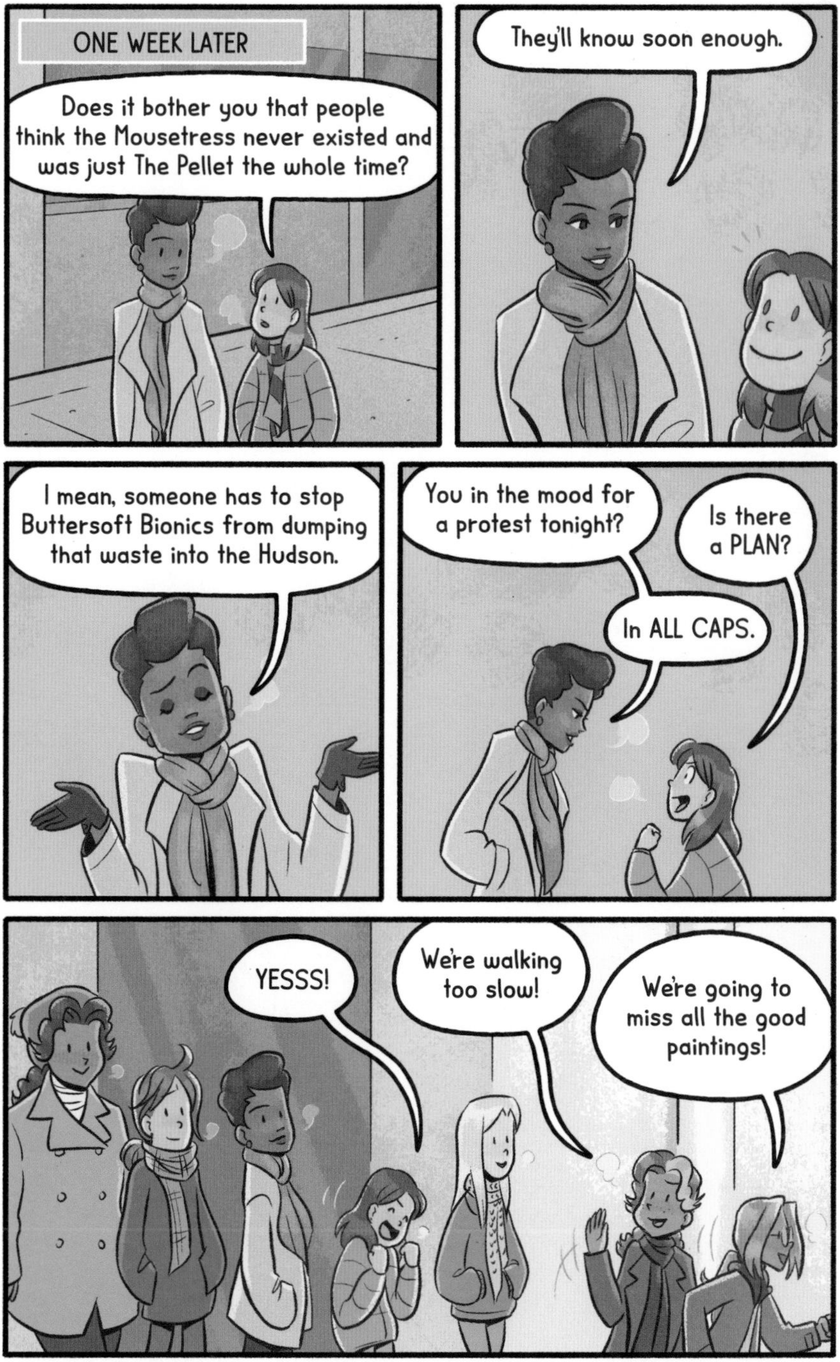
ONE WEEK LATER
Does it bother you that people think the Mousetress never existed and was just The Pellet the whole time?
They'll know soon enough.
I mean, someone has to stop Buttersoft Bionics from dumping that waste into the Hudson.
You in the mood for a protest tonight?
Is there a PLAN?
In ALL CAPS.
YESSS!
We're walking too slow!
We're going to miss all the good paintings!

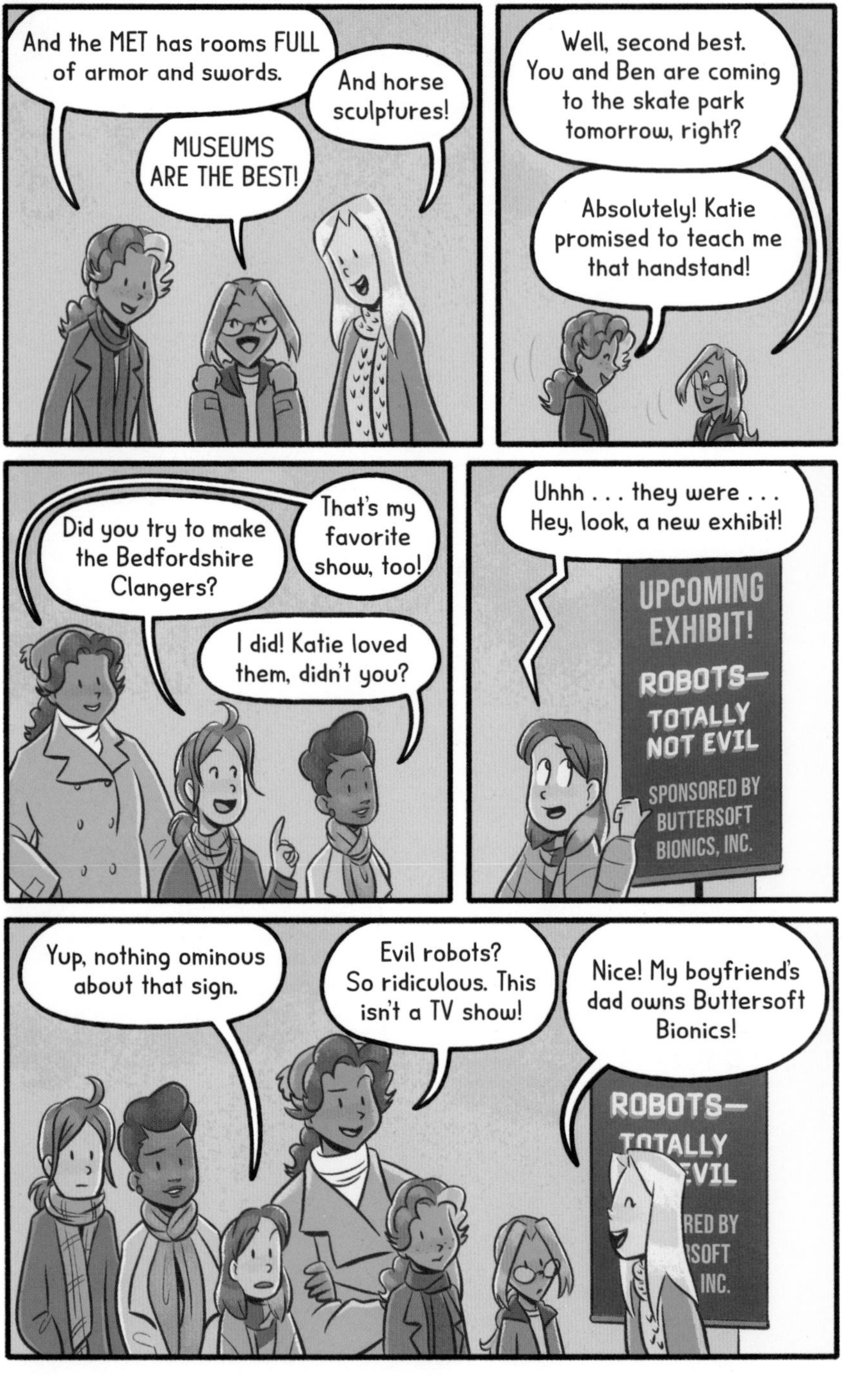
And the MET has rooms FULL of armor and swords.
MUSEUMS ARE THE BEST!
And horse sculptures!
Well, second best. You and Ben are coming to the skate park tomorrow, right?
Absolutely! Katie promised to teach me that handstand!
Did you try to make the Bedfordshire Clangers?
That's my favorite show, too!
I did! Katie loved them, didn't you?
Uhhh . . . they were . . . Hey, look, a new exhibit!
UPCOMING EXHIBIT!
ROBOTS—
TOTALLY NOT EVIL
SPONSORED BY BUTTERSOFT BIONICS, INC.
Yup, nothing ominous about that sign.
Evil robots? So ridiculous. This isn't a TV show!
Nice! My boyfriend's dad owns Buttersoft Bionics!

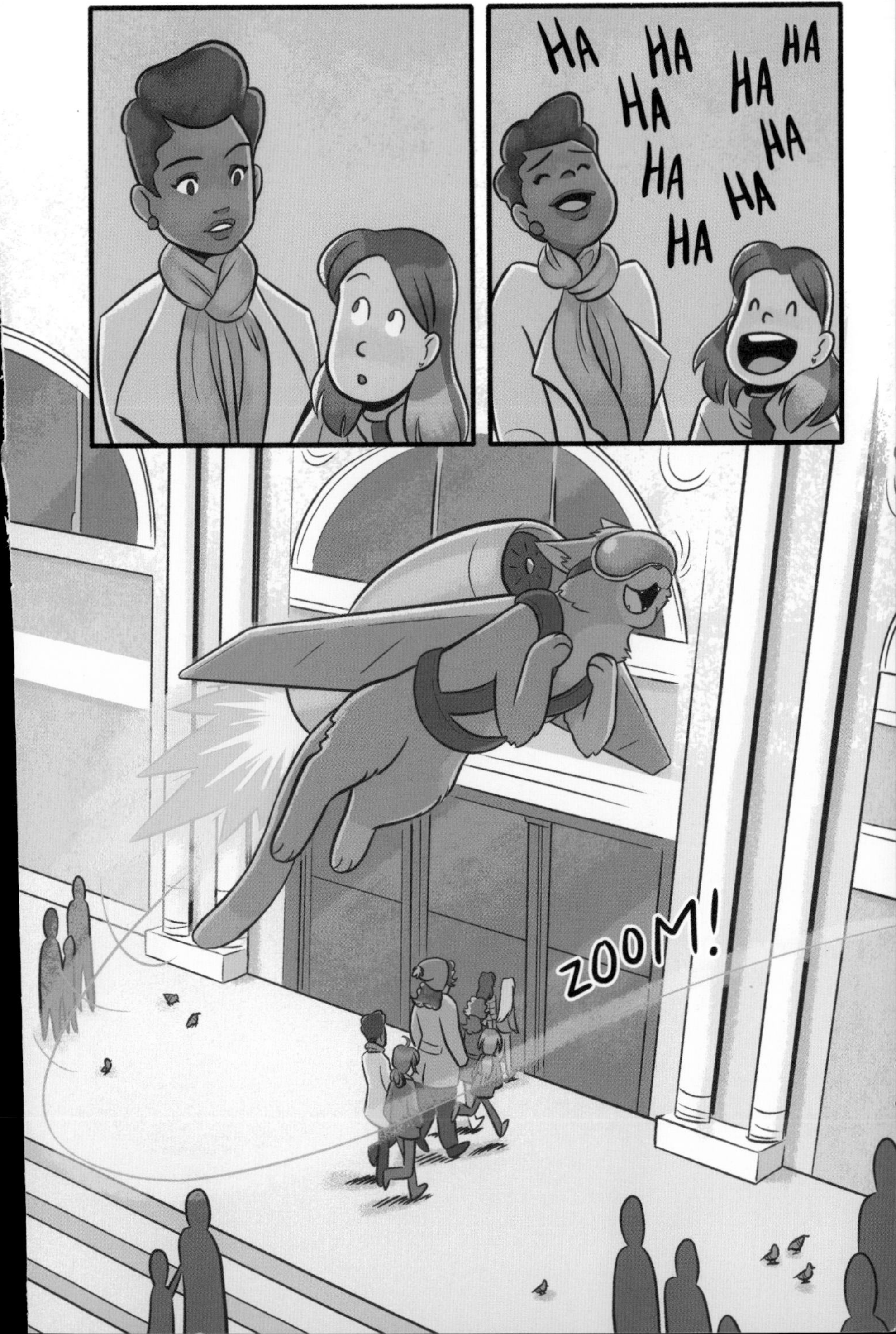
HA HA HA
HA HA
HA HA
HA HA
HA
ZOOM!

Don't miss the next
Katie the Catsitter!
Coming in 2023!

TOP 10 HERO RANKINGS

SPONSORED BY KELMOUNT CAPE WAX

"If it isn't Kelmount, it isn't . . . Kelmount? (We need a better slogan.)"

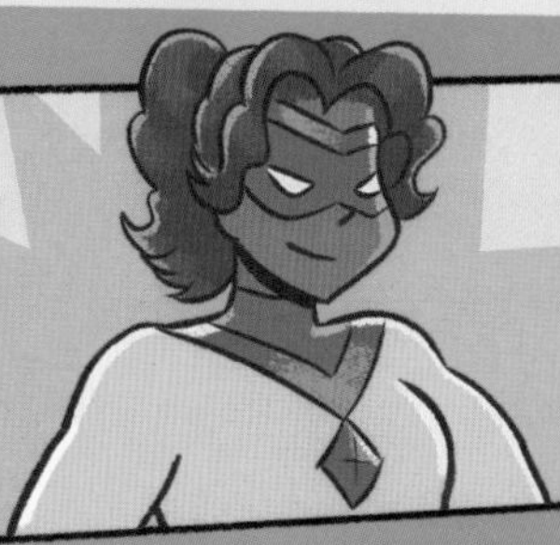

1. STAINLESS STEEL

★★★★★

"Both of my daughters want to be Stainless Steel when they grow up, and I can't blame them. I think I do, too!"

2. THE ANVILATOR

★★★★★

"The best hero in the city, hands down! (Anvil hands, that is. So rad!) Has a kinda weird sidekick, though, who asked if he could finish my sandwich."

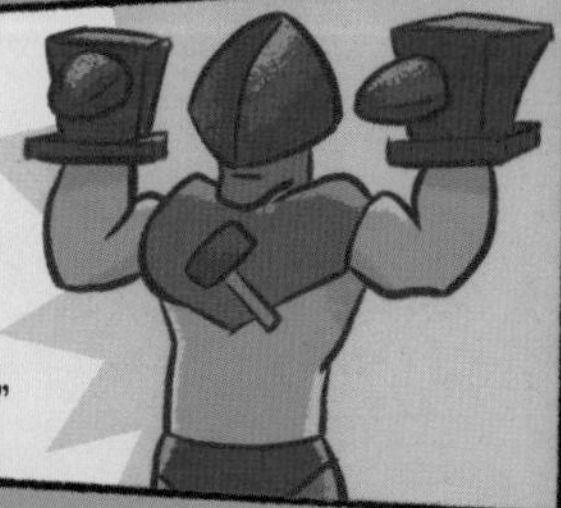

★★★★½

"Wait, it's 'Angle'? Not 'Angel'? Well, that explains the lack of wings and excessive protractor use."

3. JUSTICE ANGLE

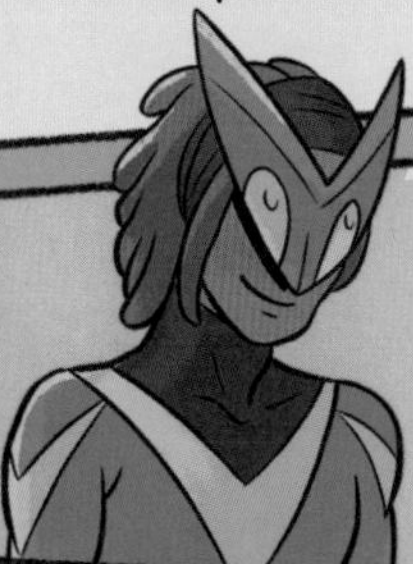

4. VERDE VENCEDOR (OR GREEN VICTOR)

★★★★½

"Dude! His outfit is like Perrrrrrfect green-screen green. Has anyone told him this? Please don't, because I'm having so much fun in Photoshop."

5. SLOTH-MAN

★★★★★

"I got mugged on Saturday, and he showed up to help on Wednesday. I guess I should be mad, but he's SO CUTE."

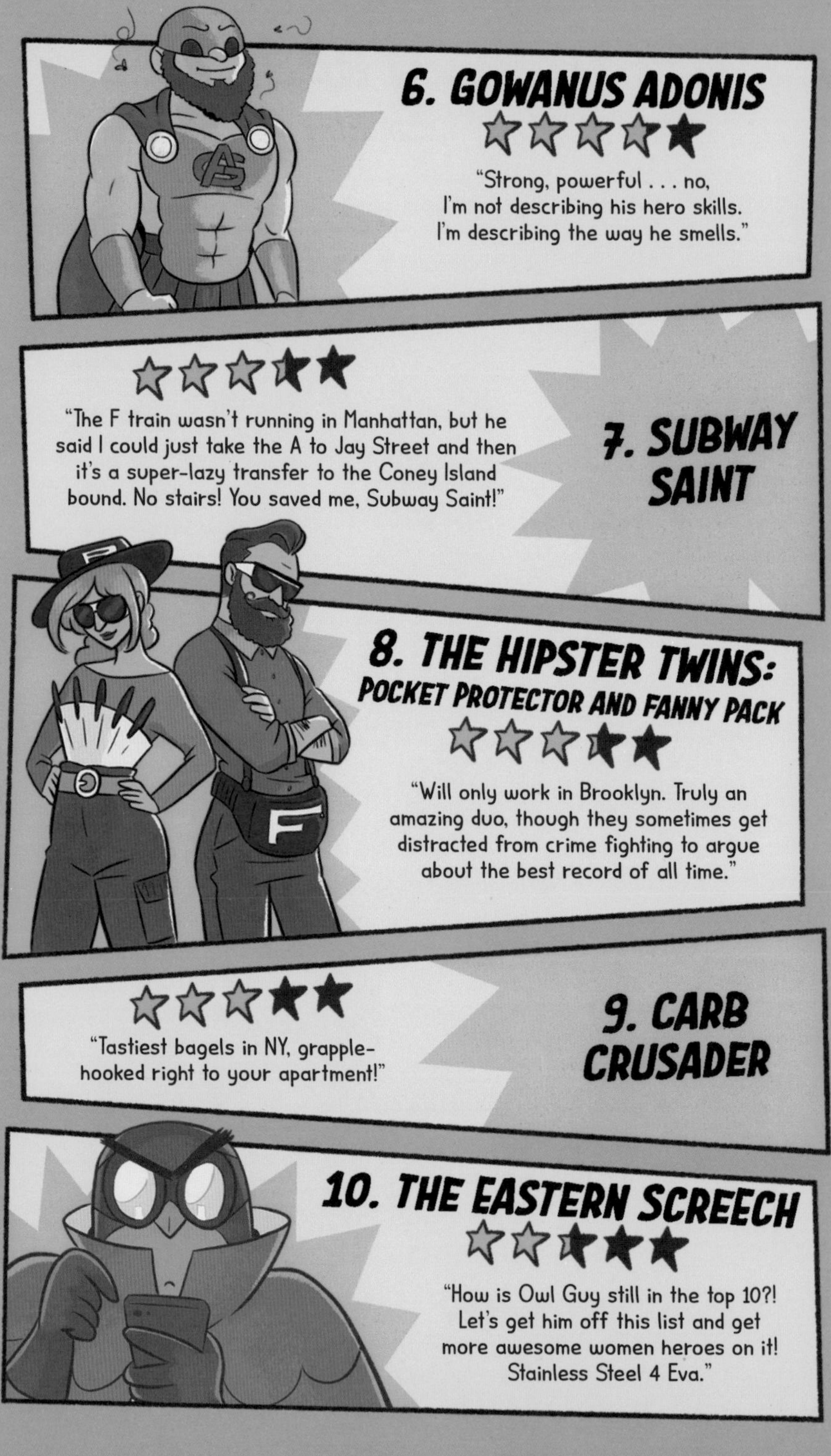
6. GOWANUS ADONIS
"Strong, powerful . . . no,
I'm not describing his hero skills.
I'm describing the way he smells."
7. SUBWAY SAINT
"The F train wasn't running in Manhattan, but he said I could just take the A to Jay Street and then it's a super-lazy transfer to the Coney Island bound. No stairs! You saved me, Subway Saint!"
8. THE HIPSTER TWINS: POCKET PROTECTOR AND FANNY PACK
"Will only work in Brooklyn. Truly an amazing duo, though they sometimes get distracted from crime fighting to argue about the best record of all time."
9. CARB CRUSADER
"Tastiest bagels in NY, grapple-hooked right to your apartment!"
10. THE EASTERN SCREECH
"How is Owl Guy still in the top 10?! Let's get him off this list and get more awesome women heroes on it! Stainless Steel 4 Eva."